Winter Warmers

Winter stories to warm your heart—
even on the coldest days.

About the authors:

Lynn Russell is a mother who works full-time, but she still manages to find time to write. She often makes up stories on trips, and while driving through the foothills of Montana, she decided to set a story in that beautiful part of the world. *Montana Christmas* is that story. It's also Lynn's first published novel.

Marie DeWitt lives in Minnesota with her husband, three sons aged eleven, twelve and fourteen, two dogs and three cats—a busy household, she says. She's a school teacher who's always wanted to write; her husband's a minister who's also a computer director. He encourages Marie's writing, taught her about computers—and even bought her a printer when *Daniel's Deception* was finished! Not surprisingly, this story is dedicated to him...

Isolde Evans lives in Utah and is very familiar with the ski resort and mountains depicted in *Snow Angel*. In fact, Isolde modelled the heroine's home after a house she lived in! Keeping to the theme of writing about familiar things—Isolde, like her heroine, once taught people how to ski. She is now a full-time writer, and *Snow Angel* is her first published novel.

Danielle Kelly had never intended to become a writer, but her love of books—and romance—eventually led to a writing career. Now she can't imagine doing anything else. She met her own real-life hero when she was sixteen and married him a few years later. They live in Rialto, California, with their two energetic young daughters, Danielle and Kellie.

Winter Warmers

MONTANA CHRISTMAS
Lynn Russell

DANIEL'S DECEPTION
Marie DeWitt

SNOW ANGEL
Isolde Evans

THE FAMILY MAN
Danielle Kelly

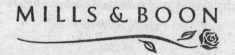

MILLS & BOON

MILLS & BOON and the Rose Device are trademarks of the publisher.
Harlequin Mills & Boon Limited,
Eton House, 18-24 Paradise Road, Richmond, Surrey, TW9 1SR

MONTANA CHRISTMAS—
Special thanks and acknowledgement to Donna L. Scofield
DANIEL'S DECEPTION—
Special thanks and acknowledgement to Marie DeWitt
SNOW ANGEL—
Special thanks and acknowledgement to Isolde Carlsen
THE FAMILY MAN—
Special thanks and acknowledgement to Janelle R. Denison

WINTER WARMERS © *Harlequin Enterprises B.V., 1996*

MONTANA CHRISTMAS © *Harlequin Enterprises B.V., 1993*
DANIEL'S DECEPTION © *Harlequin Enterprises B.V., 1993*
SNOW ANGEL © *Harlequin Enterprises B.V., 1993*
THE FAMILY MAN © *Harlequin Enterprises B.V., 1993*

ISBN 0 263 79635 3

67-9603

Printed in Great Britain by
BPC Paperbacks Ltd

MONTANA CHRISTMAS
Lynn Russell

In memory of my son Matthew

One

Jeanne twisted to look over her shoulder, trying to see her back in the dresser mirror. She sighed. It had been so long since she'd even cared what her back looked like, as long as it was covered with a white uniform or a warm flannel pajama top. What if her idea of "classic casual" was this Hank person's idea of "depressed dowdy"?

Emily, her three-year-old daughter, patted Jeanne's leg reassuringly. "You look pretty, Mommy."

Jeanne smiled down at her. "Thanks, honey." She turned to face the mirror, looped her dark brown hair loosely behind her ears, then whispered frantically, "No, no, no!" Hands moist with nervousness, she pulled the barrette out and fluffed the hair with her fingertips. Her dark brown eyes sparkled with what she hoped Hank would think was fun and enthusiasm; she knew, however, the sparkle was sheer panic.

It was almost funny. The only difference between this blind date and that horrible one in high school was that this time there was no zit on her nose. *Or was there?* Phew! Just a shadow, thank heavens, because creamy skin was one of the few things about her appearance she felt satisfied with. Well, she'd never claimed to be a raving beauty, and Hank *had* seen her picture.

She stepped back from the mirror to get as full a reflection as possible. Was her tummy popping out just a bit? She inhaled deeply, turned sideways and checked the mirror. No, just her imagination. The gray flared skirt she'd finished hemming only an hour ago had flattering princess lines, and she was pleased to see that the new pink sweater added a becoming flush to her cheeks. Good thing. She'd bought it yesterday at Nordstrom's for more money than her monthly utilities bill; it had damned well better make her look good!

Jeanne stood in the archway between miniscule kitchen and tiny living room. Clean, comfortable-looking, a bit shabby—but he shouldn't expect more. Hank Gustafson knew she was a single parent, making it on her own with a little girl. Just as she knew he was a single parent, struggling to provide a home for his daughter and two sons and run a 2,000-acre ranch at the same time.

Other than both being alone, the only thing Jeanne Fremont and Hank Gustafson had in common was a woman named Paula—Hank's sister and Jeanne's new best friend—who had talked them into this meeting, certain that they would be able to make each other's life complete. The eternally optimistic matchmaker.

The buzzer from the lobby rang while Jeanne was filling the coffeepot. Her hand jerked and she spilled the paper liner full of dry coffee into the sink. The caller was Hank. She spoke into the intercom in a voice more breathless than she would have liked, then quickly spooned more coffee into the basket and still had time to open the door at the first rap, leaving the knocker's knuckles suspended in midair.

"Uh...hi!" Jeanne said softly, hoping he wouldn't notice the rapid pulse beating in her throat. Aware she was staring, she pulled her gaze away and held out her hand for a handshake. But Hank was already shrugging out of his jacket, and he laid it across her extended arm. She turned to hang his coat in the closet, breathe deeply and quiet her nerves.

Paula had described her brother's humor and kindness, his devotion to his children and the stubborn tenacity with which he clung to the family homestead, but she hadn't said a word about how handsome he was. And the snapshots she'd seen hadn't revealed how his sun-bleached hair smoothed back from a tanned forehead, nor how his deep blue eyes emphasized the planes of his craggy face. The age-whitened jeans and soft corduroy jacket came as no surprise, although she was a bit amazed that a Montana rancher shared the fashion sense of Tom Cruise. But she definitely wasn't prepared for the way her heart sped up when she tipped her head back to look up into his face, or for the surprising way his warm smile seemed to light up the whole room. Good Lord, she thought, so the three kids had driven his wife crazy and the ranch was isolated and she yearned for fun and excitement, but how on earth could she have run off and left him?

Emily broke the awkward silence. Tugging at her mother's skirt, she exclaimed wonderingly, "Mommy, look, he's wearing cowboy boots!"

Hank looked down at his toes as if surprised. "I'll be darned!" he said. "So *that's* what was making so much noise out on the sidewalk!" He bent down to

Emily's level. "I'm sorry, ma'am. Next time I'll wear my Sunday best."

Emily gave him a serious, brown-eyed gaze. "That's okay. I like cowboy boots."

Bringing coffee and cookies from the kitchen, Jeanne was glad she'd insisted on this private first meeting, even though, right now, it seemed somewhat stilted and awkward. Paula had wanted a big family dinner at her place: Hank and his three kids, Jeanne and Emily, and of course Paula and Al and their two. It would be so much more relaxed and casual, she had urged. But Jeanne had stood fast. She'd see how Emily liked him and how she herself liked him, and take it from there. So calm, cool and collected she had been back then, arranging this meeting. Who would have dreamed that his grin would turn her to jelly?

Jeanne offered the plate of cookies to him. "What do you take in your coffee?" she asked. "Careful, Em, that milk glass is pretty full."

"Just black." He took a bite. "Great cookie."

"Chocolate never fails." The instant the words were out Jeanne wished them back. Which was worse? she thought. Sounded as if she was trying to be Little Miss Homemaker or doing a study on the cookie preferences of the blind date. She hoped that writhing on the inside didn't show on the outside.

Hank chewed a moment, eyes following Jeanne as she poured herself a cup and sat down. "This has got to be the most awkward first date in the world." His voice was rueful.

Jeanne took a cookie herself. "Still, maybe it's better. We don't have to mess around with 'What do you do?' and 'What do *you* do?' and 'What's your sign?'"

Hank chuckled and sipped his coffee. "I see you've done the singles bit."

"Actually, no." No feigned sophistication. That's what she'd decided when finally agreeing to go along with Paula's matchmaking. She knew that honesty had to be not just the best, but the *only* policy. "I haven't done the singles scene. I just read a lot."

He nodded. "Me, too. Up where I live, you either read a lot or go crazy. No, wait, strike that. I'm supposed to be selling you on the quiet country life." At her wary glance, he stopped. "No, we're not selling each other on anything. That's what we agreed. Complete honesty." He extended his hand to shake on it, and the moment his warm, work-hardened hand took hers, Jeanne knew, with a sinking heart, that what she was feeling was definitely not what she had planned. But she gave him a firm businesslike handshake, anyway, and sank back into her chair, hoping her hand didn't leave a charred imprint on her new skirt.

She still couldn't believe she had agreed to meet this perfect stranger—object, if all went well, matrimony. Up until three months ago she and Emily had managed just fine. She was accustomed to being alone. Her parents had died in a car accident when she was seven, and the aunt and uncle who'd raised her, although they had been scrupulously fair in handling her parents' insurance money, left no doubt they were only doing their duty. Jeanne had gone away to college with no regrets and no lingering goodbyes.

She had dated little during high school. Girls less attractive than she had steady boyfriends or played the field, but something in Jeanne's quiet reserve pinned a little Do Not Disturb sign on her slender shoulders.

At college she made a determined effort to drop the reserve, which met with some success. But it wasn't till near the end of her final year of nursing school that she fell head over heels in love with a med student who seemed to return the feeling. Jeanne threw her whole being into the relationship. When she told him she was pregnant, instead of responding with marriage plans as she'd expected, he said, "Are you sure I'm the father?" She was crushed and bitter.

Now Emily's voice brought her back to the present. "Where're his kids, Mommy?" The little girl sounded disappointed. "In the picture he had kids." She turned to Hank. "Did you leave your kids at home?" she asked reproachfully.

"No, they're at their aunt Paula's house. You know Paula, don't you?"

Emily nodded. "Can we go see them?"

"Maybe later, honey," Jeanne said.

"Can they go to the Children's Village with us?" Emily preferred to get arrangements nailed down; no dangling "maybes" for this child.

Hank's expression was serious as he turned to Emily. "Tell me what it's like, and maybe we can go tomorrow."

Emily launched into a detailed description of the Children's Village at Seattle Center. "Oh, it's wunnerful. It's got teensy houses and stores that kids can play in and pretend to be the grocery man or the library lady. It's got a big huge tower made out of Lego. Sometimes it's got science 'speriments or contests, like who can blow the biggest bubble..." The child's shyness vanished as she edged closer to Hank, caught up in her description.

Jeanne watched, amazed and relieved. Emily had always been a quiet child, and the hardship of the past three months had left her a bit wary of strangers, with a tendency to cling closely to her mother. Her quick response to Hank was reassuring. Jeanne let her chatter on for a few more minutes, then, when her travelogue began to wind down, seized the opportunity. "Time for bed, Em."

With Emily tucked in for the night, Hank's and Jeanne's conversation grew more serious. "When my sister first mentioned you," Hank began, "she said that although she hadn't known you before your accident, she'd learned from others that you'd been very self-reliant, very independent." His deep blue gaze was questioning. "That must have made being completely helpless like you were even harder."

Jeanne nodded, peering into her coffee cup. "It was horrible. When I came to, the last thing I could remember was pushing Emily toward the sidewalk. For all I knew the car had hit her, too. Even when they assured me she was okay, I was still crazy. Thank God your sister was a mother—it helped her understand how I felt. When she walked in carrying Emily I finally calmed down."

She smiled in remembrance and took a sip of coffee. Paula had been the social worker assigned to finding a temporary placement for Emily when the child and her unconscious mother were brought to the hospital. After Jeanne regained consciousness, Paula had helped Jeanne make arrangements with a friend to care for the little girl, and Emily was able to go back to the familiar day care that St. Vincent's Hospital offered its employees, staying with her mother's friend at night. It was a workable solution, but it made

Jeanne realize the awful vulnerability of Emily's situation. *She* could safeguard and protect Emily from the world, but if something happened to her, Emily would be completely alone.

Jeanne ran her finger around the rim of her cup distractedly. All the cards on the table—that was what she'd decided. "Did Paula tell you about Emily's father?"

"No. Probably didn't think it was any of my business."

Jeanne swallowed painfully. What if her next words sent him away? Or worse, made him think she was available for some free and easy fun?

"Well," she said, "if anything comes of our meeting, it is your business." She cleared her throat. "I haven't seen Emily's father since the day I told him I was pregnant. Evidently marriage didn't seem like a great idea to him." Strange how that still stung. Even though four years had dulled the original pain, knowing you'd meant less than nothing to someone you thought loved you was hard to face.

"Then he's a first-class jerk, and you're better off without him," Hank said bluntly. Then his face and voice softened. "But I know it's been hard for you. Paula told me that much."

Jeanne nodded. "I shudder to think how things might have been if Paula hadn't been assigned to me. When she took Emily and me home with her, she was definitely stepping outside her job description, but it meant I could be released weeks sooner—they hadn't been going to let me out till I was completely able to care for myself." She smiled, remembering Paula and the kindness of her studious husband and two children. Jeanne looked Hank full in the face. Might as well be perfectly frank. "Of course, it was during those weeks that she decided I was the perfect lost soul to fill your need."

"Lost soul? Ha! You've got too much going for you to be a lost soul." Hank stared into his almost empty cup. "How much did she tell you about the situation the kids and I are in?" Then he shook his head. "Never mind, don't answer that question. I'll tell you." He was silent for so long that Jeanne thought perhaps he'd changed his mind. Finally, "It wasn't so much that we were too young to get married, although that was part of it. We were in college. I was majoring in agribusiness so I could take over the home place. Cyndi was majoring in parties." He put his cup on the coffee table. "No, scratch that statement. I've got to be fair." He sat forward, gripping his hands together tightly between his knees. "It's kind of like your story, but with a different ending. She told me she was pregnant, and as far as I was concerned, marriage was the only answer. I knew she hated the ranch—one weekend there had been enough for me to see that. But I was crazy about her, and I figured she'd change. I guess...I guess I trapped her." His words came faster now, tripping over themselves.

"After Lisa was born, during that first year and a half on the ranch, Cyndi begged me to give it up and move to Helena, or better yet, Spokane. I should have listened to her. Instead, I got her pregnant again." He breathed deeply, striving for control. "That was bad enough. The third pregnancy was unbelievable. By that time we practically hated each other. But it happened."

He was silent for so long that Jeanne finally whispered, "How did it end?"

"She just left. I got one note from her, bubbling with excitement. She'd met up with some guy who was going to help her become a model. Over the next few months there were a couple of phone calls, when she'd either had too much to drink or was on drugs. After that, nothing. Then about a year ago her mother called me."

Jeanne snatched a quick glance to see if he was visibly upset, but except for clenched fists he wasn't, at least not outwardly.

"She said she was going to report Cyndi as a missing person, because she hadn't heard from her in a long time and she thought Cyndi had been taking a lot of chances."

"Like what?"

"Like drinking with strangers, and sleeping with strangers, and hitchhiking."

"Oh," Jeanne answered in a tiny voice, wishing she hadn't asked.

"I just figured Cyndi was enjoying life in the fast lane, but after the missing-persons report was filed, her mother learned she'd died in L.A. several months earlier."

"How did she die?"

"Drug overdose." Hank shook his shoulders, as if trying to rid himself of a physical burden.

"So then did your mother-in-law want to see more of the children, to sort of take Cyndi's place?"

"Nope. She'd never seen the baby, and she'd only seen the older two twice. She said, and I quote, 'It's less painful for me to just seal off the whole business as if it never happened.' And I guess she did just that. We haven't heard from her since."

"Oh, my." Jeanne was a little overwhelmed. Although Paula had told her the bare bones of the story, hearing it in Hank's tightly controlled voice brought the reality of it to her. "I'm so sorry."

Hank unclenched his fists, sat back and smoothed his hands on the thighs of his jeans. He drew a ragged breath and said, "Now, back to you. Paula's pretty intuitive, I'll admit that. She certainly knew I needed help. But you? I can't understand why you're worried about security and a family for Emily."

"What do you mean?" Jeanne sat up straighter.

"Well, even if Emily's father was a jerk and left you bitter, you're pretty enough to have found somebody else long ago. I'm amazed you're still alone."

Jeanne spoke with studied calm; this had been deeply thought through. "Most men aren't interested in a ready-made family. I don't want Emily ever to feel like she's in the way, like she's somebody's duty. I'd spend my whole life alone before I'd do that to her." Her eyes appraised him evenly. "Of course, that's why the whole bunch of us, your family and mine, are going to get well acquainted before we even think of carrying your sister's idea any further." The coolness of her voice belied the rush of delight at the very thought of Paula's goal.

After several weeks of getting to know Jeanne better than anyone ever had before, Paula had decided that she and her brother were made for each other. And now, after weeks of refusal, then doubtful consideration, then dubious halfway agreement, followed by weeks of exchanged letters, snapshots and phone calls, Paula's idea was being put to the test.

"Tell me about your children," Jeanne said, her voice warming. This was a safe subject; she could talk about the three youngsters without betraying the unexpected effect their father had on her. "I saw the pictures Paula has. They're cute kids."

Actually, it was when she saw Paula's pictures that she felt the first tug of interest in her new friend's harebrained idea. There was a wistfulness in the little girl's face, a protectiveness in the way she stood with an arm around the shoulder of each of her little brothers, that went straight to Jeanne's heart. "How old did you say they are?" she had asked Paula, noting the girl's too-short dress and too-long bangs, the jagged rip in one boy's jeans, the way a wide band of the tiniest boy's tummy was exposed between his short T-shirt and sagging pants.

"Lisa's six and a half—she's in the first grade. Timmy's five and Joey's four—they're a regular handful," Paula had responded. "I can understand their mother feeling she was in over her head, but how could anyone walk away and leave an eight-month-old baby? That's how old Joey was when she left." She shook her head. "Hank's managed on his own for over three years now. Oh, Ma helps when she can—she came and stayed with them when Cyndi first left, but her health is poor. She was forty when I was born, you know. She and Dad had long given up on having kids." Paula laughed. "Then Hank came along four years later." She flipped back a few pages in the album, to a picture of a couple, well past middle age, standing arm in arm with a pair of teenagers, a big two-storied farmhouse flanked by cottonwood trees in the background. "Daddy died not long after this picture was taken," she mused. "Ma managed as long as she could with the year-round hired man and his wife, and extra help during summer, but she was so relieved to turn the place over to Hank when he dropped out of college and brought Cyndi home. She'd been having heart problems for at least a year and hadn't even told us.''

Jeanne brought herself back to the present. Hank had reached into his shirt pocket and pulled out a packet of pictures. ''These are pretty recent,'' he said proudly. ''Here's one I took of Lisa on her first day of school.'' Jeanne studied the snapshot he held out to her. The little girl was wearing a big grin and a colorful gingham dress. Instead of being too short, this dress was woefully long, obviously purchased with enough room to grow into. Poor little kid, Jeanne thought. Her father obviously tried his best, but didn't quite succeed. Lisa looked like a child from the nineteenth century.

''Does Lisa like school?'' she asked.

Hank frowned. ''Not much,'' he admitted. ''In fact, she was thrilled when I withdrew her for a week for this trip.'' He glanced defensively at Jeanne. ''The teacher sent books,'' he said quickly, ''and Paula and I plan to help her with her reading.''

''Maybe I can help, too,'' Jeanne murmured. ''For years I'd wanted to be a teacher, then changed to nursing.'' What am I doing? she thought in amazement. I haven't even met these kids!

Two

She met them bright and early the next morning. Before going to bed the previous night, Emily had convinced her mother and Hank that a trip to the Children's Village at Seattle Center was a must, preceded by breakfast at the nearby pancake house where she and her mother ate whenever they made the trip. "Hey, maybe Paula and Al and the kids would like to come along, too," Hank suggested.

He brought his three children upstairs with him when they stopped at Jeanne's apartment to pick them up for the outing. Emily shyly disappeared behind her mother's denim-clad leg; Joey did the same with his father. Lisa and Timmy bravely stepped forward and offered their hands to Jeanne when Hank introduced them. "I'm very pleased to meet you, Mrs. Fremont," Lisa said, the phrase sounding as though her aunt Paula had finished the final rehearsal just moments before in the lobby downstairs. Timmy echoed the statement, a syllable behind his sister.

"Just call me Jeanne, like your cousins do," Jeanne murmured awkwardly. Even after four years of pretense, the "Mrs." still made her uncomfortable. She bent to their level and pulled Emily from behind her, and Hank did the same with Joey. Although the two youngest were quiet and shy for a while, Emily's experience at day care left her more outgoing with children of her own age than her mother had ever been, and by the time they arrived at the pancake house, all six kids were chattering nonstop. Paula's son and daughter, who shared friendship with both Emily and their younger cousins, were just enough older to see that all the kids felt welcome and included. As Jeanne cut Emily's pancakes into bite-size pieces and Hank did the same for Joey, Jeanne remembered the times she had envied large, happy family groups like theirs.

They had a wonderful day at the Children's Village. Although all the kids were tired and cranky by the time the outing was finished, the day still seemed to retain a certain glow. Paula's two children had good-humoredly helped shepherd the younger ones through the Center. Once during the afternoon Lisa had lagged, limping slightly, then willingly settled on a park bench while Jeanne sat beside her, searching in her bag for a bandage for the little girl's heel. "What pretty new shoes, Lisa," she said, "but they're rubbing your heel. You're going to have one heck of a blister by the time we're through."

"Daddy told me I should wear my tennis shoes, but I wanted to look nice," Lisa answered softly. "Daddy bought these new school shoes for me yesterday. My tennis shoes are old and yucky." Aha, Jeanne thought. Could we have here the reason Lisa doesn't like school? With her too-long or too-short dresses and yucky tennis shoes, have kids made fun of her?

"Are your old tennis shoes back in the van?" Jeanne asked, hoping they hadn't been thrown away at the shoe store.

"Yes, but I don't think Daddy will want to go back and get them, not after he told me and told me I'd be sorry if I wore these new shoes."

"Maybe you and I could go back together and get them," Jeanne suggested. And they did. Hank raised his eyebrows questioningly when Jeanne asked for the car keys, and she gave him an answering wink. Then she and Lisa walked slowly back to the van, Lisa carrying one shoe and sock and chattering a mile a minute about the ranch, her cat named Boo, their swaybacked old horse, Pat, the long bus ride to school. Suddenly she stopped.

"Am I talking too much?" the child asked, stricken. "Daddy told me this morning not to talk your ear off."

"You're certainly not talking my ear off!" Jeanne assured her, wishing she could give Hank Gustafson's ear a tweak for putting doubts in the mind of his daughter, who already had so little self-confidence. They continued in silence for a moment.

"Are you and my daddy going to get married?" Lisa asked suddenly.

"Uh...I don't know." Jeanne answered honestly. "How do you feel about that?"

"Well...we sure need a mom!" said Lisa, frank in the way only a child can be. Then, wistfully, "'specially when we're sick." She kicked a rock with her shod foot. "Everybody in my class has a mom. Some of 'em don't have dads, but *everybody* has a mom!" Jeanne was still thinking about this when the little girl asked her next question. "Do you have a curling iron?"

"Pardon?" Jeanne said, unable to quickly bridge the gap between "everybody has a mom" and "curling iron."

"Allison's mom uses the curling iron on Allison's hair every morning, and the teacher says, 'Oh, Allison, what beautiful curls you have!'"

Jeanne grabbed Lisa's hand and swung it in her own. "Yes, I have a curling iron, Lisa." She sneaked a look out of the corner of her eye at the child. "I kind of know how to cut hair, too. And I have a sewing machine—I love to sew stuff for little girls." A small smile was playing around the corners of Lisa's mouth. Jeanne swung their hands higher; Lisa did a little skip. "I'll bet we could make Allison turn green with envy," she said, "and shock the teacher's socks off!"

Lisa looked up at her, a twinkle in her eyes. "Do you know how to make cupcakes?"

"Sure, with fancy stuff on top, too."

"Allison says her mother's going to send clown cupcakes to school on her birthday." She kicked another rock. "Her birthday's just before Christmas."

"When's your birthday?"

"Couple weeks, right after Thanksgiving."

"Hmm. What's fancier than clowns?" mused Jeanne.

Lisa squeezed her hand, face glowing. "I *like* you, Jeanne!"

Three

The next day, Sunday, they went to the aquarium and had lunch at Ivor's Acres o' Clams. Jeanne had arranged to have Monday and Tuesday off work, although, thanks to her lost income because of the accident, she really couldn't afford to. But she did it, anyway, and they filled both days with fun.

On Monday they hit the Pike Street Market right after it opened, stopped at a muffin place for refueling, then tackled the walking tour of underground Old Seattle. They took the boat tour of Seattle harbor, treated themselves to gooey pizza for dinner, then collapsed into a row of seats for the latest Walt Disney movie. On Tuesday, it rained, but that didn't stop them. They had lunch in the Space Needle restaurant. After that, since the rain had let up a bit, they stood out on the deck in the gentle drizzle and the kids fed quarters into the telescope so they could watch the slowly revolving landscape.

"The children get along pretty well, don't they?" Hank observed, after Lisa had maturely stepped in when Timmy tried to elbow Emily away from the telescope before her turn was finished.

"Yeah," Jeanne murmured. Hank was holding the umbrella and had casually draped his other arm around Jeanne's shoulder. Just remembering to breathe was difficult; sparkling conversation was definitely out of the question. She rallied. "Of course, with four kids there'd always be a dull roar in the background."

"Oh, sure," he agreed. "And think of when they're teenagers—two prom dresses, two tuxes, four kids learning to drive."

Jeanne's head swam. They hadn't seriously discussed the future, although of course it was in the backs of their minds. After all, they had met for a purpose. Her shoulder was nestled under his arm; she could swear she felt his heart thudding away. Could she possibly hope that Hank's feelings for her were growing? How could she be such a dreamer? Although his presence turned her to mush, she was afraid that as far as he was concerned she was simply a practical solution to a problem—maybe a little more attractive solution than he had expected, but still just a solution.

So, she told herself, maybe ours won't be the great American love story. It'll have to do. And I'll learn to control my heartbeat, and I'll never be made a fool of by reaching out to someone who doesn't want me. Once burned, twice smart, or something like that. "That sounds so permanent," she said. "We haven't really talked about the future."

"Then we need to."

That evening they left all the kids with Paula and had dinner at a charming Italian restaurant. Over cocktails they discussed the obvious: the way their kids seemed to hit it off. Around bites of salad they explored the questionable: could she be happy isolated on a ranch for weeks at a time, sixteen miles from a store, thirty-five miles from the nearest one-horse town, sixty miles from Helena? And Spokane, the nearest *city*, was too far away even to talk about!

Jeanne skewered a bit of radicchio on her fork and swirled it in the vinaigrette dressing. "The isolation isn't a problem," she said. "I learned to entertain myself alone from the time I was a child." She grinned. "But, I don't really think I'll have to worry about entertaining myself with four kids and a house to take care of."

"And a husband," Hank added quietly, taking a sip of wine.

Jeanne hoped the warmth she felt in her cheeks wasn't visible. What did he mean? But she was getting better at presenting a calm front. "Well, yes, a husband," she conceded. "Are you a pipe-and-slippers guy?"

"Nah," Hank conceded, "although sometimes after a really hard day I need help pulling my boots off."

Luckily the arrival of their garlic shrimp interrupted that train of conversation.

"So, what do you say?" Hank's voice was still quiet, perhaps even tense. "Shall we join forces?"

"Goodness, I don't know if I can handle so much passion and romance," Jeanne replied lightly. "Fetch the smelling salts! Give me air!"

Hank grinned. "That *was* pretty bad, wasn't it? But it's hard to know how to do this. I mean, my sister brought us together for this purpose, but still, it's got to be more than a business deal." His hand covered hers on the snowy linen cloth. "Don't you think so?" he persisted. "Don't you think it's got to be more than just business? We're going to be raising four children together, after all.''

So that's how it is, Jeanne thought. Raising children together. Well, that's all I was counting on at the beginning. It's not his fault I seem to be falling for him. ''Yes,'' she said calmly. ''We'll need to be each other's best friends, not just business partners.'' She gently withdrew her hand and picked up her wineglass.

There was a heavy silence. ''I...I hope we'll be more than best friends,'' Hank said haltingly. ''After all, we're a healthy man and woman. I...I want us to be husband and wife in every sense.'' Her eyes widened and he said quickly, ''Oh, not right away, of course. I mean, not till you're...till we're ready. I'm not some high-school kid with raging hormones.''

A petty part of her was enjoying his discomfort, she realized. He blundered on. ''I mean...we'll just take it slow and easy, and we'll know when the time is right.''

''When the time is right—that sounds suspiciously like breeding a prize mare,'' Jeanne said lightly. Then at the confusion on his face, she added, ''Never mind, I know what you mean.''

Four

Able to get the three-day waiting period waived, they were married Thursday evening in Paula's living room by the minister of the church her family attended. A few of Jeanne's coworkers were there, as well as the staff she'd become acquainted with during her long hospital stay.

She wore a dress she'd purchased just that afternoon, pale aqua with full, flowing lines, and a pink rosebud corsage to grace its simplicity. Hank surprised her with a nosegay of the same pink rosebuds. "Just a corsage isn't enough," he told her, handing her the flowers. "A bride has to carry flowers."

Emily and Lisa wore pretty new dresses, and Timmy and Joey new corduroys and white shirts. Paula had pulled an incredible number of strings to get, on such short notice, a small wedding cake and even a photographer. He took a few pictures of just Jeanne and Hank and then, becoming more attuned to the atmosphere of the gathering, used the rest of the film for what turned out to be lovely candid shots of them surrounded by some or all of the children.

When the champagne was served, Paula's husband, Al, made just the right toast, simple and direct.

"To your future!" he said happily, and they all raised their glasses, even the six kids, whose festive crystal flutes contained white grape juice.

They spent the night at Paula and Al's. Thoughtfully, Paula had put Jeanne's overnight things in the small room she'd occupied during her convalescence. Hank had the other spare room, and the kids' sleeping bags were spread out on the family-room floor.

Having spent a frantic two days in preparation, they were ready to leave for the ranch the next morning. The van was loaded—*really* loaded. Jeanne was taking all of her and Emily's clothing, all of the toys, the items in the apartment that were uniquely theirs—favorite quilts, pictures, kitchen utensils—and her sewing machine. And the maple rocking chair that belonged first to her grandmother, then to her mother. Jeanne could dimly remember being held by her mother and rocked in that chair. Luckily, practical Aunt Irene had insisted that it be saved when Jeanne's parents' possessions were sold.

Jeanne had turned over the remaining contents of the apartment to the couple across the hall, who had helped her with marketing and errands when Emily was born, and again when she came home from Paula's after the accident.

Also packed in the van were the contents of an exhausting all-day shopping expedition. After their decision Tuesday evening to marry, Hank had said as they drove to Paula's to pick up Emily, "Listen, I know this doesn't sound very romantic, but we need to go shopping tomorrow. Make a list. Write down every single thing you can think of we might need to run a house for several months—including Christmas. Everything. Then we'll go through it and I'll tell you what's already there and what isn't, and we'll go shopping."

Jeanne gasped. "You mean I won't even be able to get to town before Christmas?"

Hank hastily reassured her. "Oh, we'll plan on a trip to Spokane before Christmas. But you can't always count on the weather. If a big whopper of a storm hits, we could get snowed in."

"Hmm," Jeanne murmured, "that sounds like fun. Kind of like *Little House on the Prairie.*"

Hank breathed a sigh of relief, then chuckled. "Fun? You must be crazy. But I'm glad the idea isn't sending you running."

So the van was crammed with bulky parcels shrouded in black garbage bags—the result of an adults-only trip to a discount toy store. And clothing for all the kids, with more for Lisa than the rest. "Spandex pants?" Hank said in confusion. "And ten pairs of tights, two of each color? And hot-pink snowboots?"

As Lisa eyed her father anxiously, Jeanne said, "Trust me, Hank, I know what I'm doing."

"Yeah, trust her, Daddy, she knows what she's doing," Lisa echoed.

Jeanne sent Hank away at the door to the fabric store, then hurriedly skimmed through the pattern book and yardage racks. When he came back to pick her up, she said nervously, "It won't always be this expensive, Hank, it's just that getting started—"

"No problem!" he interrupted, patting her cheek. "I notice you've bought nothing for yourself, not even a romance novel. You're doing for the kids what they've really never had anyone do before—being a mother to them."

Mildly intoxicated from the praise and the pat on the cheek, Jeanne groped for a response. "Hmm, I forgot romance novels," she said. "How far from the ranch is the nearest library?"

"Quite a ways," Hank answered seriously, "but when I was a kid Ma made arrangements for books to come by mail from the library in Helena." Then, remembering, "But we're going to stock up on groceries there, too, and they have racks of paperbacks."

At last the van pulled out of Paula and Al's driveway and headed out to the highway that led to Spokane, Helena and points east. Fortunately the van assured all four children of window seats, so most of the trip was accomplished without too much bickering. Lisa was the only child old enough to play license-plate bingo, but even Emily, the youngest, could count animals, so they worked their way through cows, then horses and even ducks, until at last all four of them fell asleep.

That night at the motel Hank asked for a room with two king-size beds. He and the boys shared one bed, Jeanne and the girls the other. He tactfully had his face turned to the wall, feigning sleep, when Jeanne came out of the bathroom in her flannel pajamas. The same scenario was repeated Saturday night.

Just before noon on Sunday, they pulled into Hank's mother's driveway in Helena, and the restless children piled out of the van. Her new mother-in-law won Jeanne's heart immediately by pulling little Emily into the circle of grandchildren. The fact that her daughter had no grandma had always troubled Jeanne. Now it appeared that Emily had one.

Their visit was short. Mrs. Gustafson kept the four children while Jeanne and Hank visited the supermarket, miraculously managing to find room in the van for the groceries. Hank's mother kissed them all goodbye before they set out for the last leg of their journey. As she hugged Jeanne, she whispered, "Since you don't have a mother of your own, maybe someday you'll feel comfortable calling me Ma, like Al, Hank and Paula do." Then she kissed Jeanne. "I'm so glad Hank has someone to love. He's been very lonely."

Jeanne kissed Ma Gustafson's withered cheek with a whispered thank you. Someone to love? Doesn't she know this is a business deal? Jeanne wondered with a twinge of sadness.

The sadness faded in the excitement of nearing her new home. "Only sixty miles more," Hank called out to the kids.

"Sixty miles? I thought we were almost there!" Timmy moaned. But the miles flew by as they took turns telling Jeanne and Emily about the ranch. In Glendora, the last small town before home, Lisa asked her father to drive past her school so Jeanne could see it, and she smiled with satisfaction as Jeanne made appropriately impressed noises. Soon they were slowing for the curving drive up into the Rocky Mountain foothills, with the children pointing out landmarks on the way: the three big side-by-side grain elevators that marked the end of what they called the Flat, the forestry department's water tower, a lightning-blasted pine, curious little shelters alongside the gravel road, with narrow lanes leading into the hillside behind them.

"Those are where kids wait for the school bus," Lisa explained importantly. Jeanne shuddered, picturing lonely Lisa, with frostbitten hands and cheeks, huddled inside a shelter waiting for a broken-down school bus that never arrived. As if reading her mind, Lisa reassured her. "Daddy drives me down in the Jeep and waits with me till the bus comes."

Finally they approached a mailbox and shelter that, according to the three Gustafson children's excited shouts, was theirs. Hank stopped and emptied the mailbox, opened the gate and drove through, then returned and pulled it shut behind them. Climbing back into the van, he glanced nervously at Jeanne, already fearing her reaction. "Not much farther," he said.

At last the moment came. They topped the final rise and the house stood ahead of them. Jeanne suddenly found herself with tears in her eyes. She turned to Hank impulsively. "Those old trees...that tire swing...that long veranda with a swing... Oh, Hank, all the time I was growing up I wanted to live in a house like that...in a *home* like that! Look, there's even smoke coming from the chimney!"

Hank watched her, a wide smile on his face. "Yep, I called Ben and asked them to be sure the place was warm and tidy." Seeing Jeanne's confusion, he added, "Ben's the hired man. His wife, Nora, has helped out when I was in over my head."

"Like when we all had strep throats," Lisa filled in.

With a little crunch of gravel Hank pulled up under the now leafless grape arbor at the back of the house. "We're home!" he called out unnecessarily. "Everybody grab something to carry in!"

By the time darkness fell the van was emptied, and the children had conducted a tour of the house for Jeanne and Emily, as well as checked on the well-being of their dog, cat and horse. Nora brought over a pot of chicken and dumplings and was heartily thanked for how tidy and inviting the house was. Finally the children were all bathed and in pajamas. Timmy and Joey, too tired to protest going to bed, climbed under the patchwork quilts in their room. Lisa started into her room, then stopped, a big smile on her face. "Now I have a sister to share my room! I don't have to sleep by myself anymore. C'mon, Emily, which side do you want?"

Emily hesitated for a moment, obviously overwhelmed by so many changes in such a short time. "Maybe she should sleep with her mama for a little while, Lisa," her father said, "till she gets used to being in a new place."

Well, thought Jeanne, *you don't have to hit me over the head with a two-by-four. I get the picture.* A little relieved to postpone the awkwardness of climbing into bed with a man who was still a relative stranger, she nevertheless felt rejected, as though he had leapt at the chance to decide the time wasn't right. Sweetly she said, "How very thoughtful, Hank," and extended her hand to Emily. "Come on to bed with Mommy, Em."

Their little room was cold. Jeanne investigated and found that the heat register was closed. She opened it, then got both herself and her daughter ready for bed. She climbed under the covers with Emily, gasping at the touch of the icy sheets.

Jeanne thought of Hank in the big bedroom down the hall. Was he thinking of *her?* she wondered sleepily. Or was he just feeling relieved that now he wouldn't have to carry the whole load alone? During the ride from Helena to the ranch she had daydreamed about a storybook happily-ever-after life, where they trooped out like the Waltons to cut their own Christmas tree, and decorated it together. She had pictured the two of them filling stockings by lamplight after all the children were asleep, then climbing the stairs arm in arm to their bedroom.

What was it Aunt Irene had said when she felt Jeanne was getting a bit "uppity," as she put it? Ah, yes. "Just be satisfied with what you have, young lady. There are princesses and there are plain folks, and don't you forget you're plain folks!" Jeanne drifted off to sleep reminding herself to be thankful for what she had, instead of dreaming of what she wanted.

Five

Jeanne awoke confused and disoriented. The room was completely dark, and for a moment she couldn't remember where she was. In a hospital bed, or in Paula's spare room? When she again heard the muffled clanking sound that had awakened her, she threw back the covers and leapt out of bed. Good Lord, it can't be later than two or three in the morning! she thought, but a glance at the illuminated face of the bedside clock showed that it was, in fact, five. Leaving Emily asleep, she hurried to the head of the stairs and looked down.

There was Hank, fully dressed, building a fire in the big iron kitchen range. She felt a moment of panic as she thought of trying to cook on the monster, then remembered the electric stove on the far wall of the kitchen. "We lose our electricity quite often during big storms, so when the folks modernized the kitchen this stayed," Hank had explained. "The fireplace in the living room has a heatilator, and between the two of them the whole downstairs stays pretty warm even without the oil furnace in the cellar."

Jeanne rushed into the upstairs bathroom, splashed her face with icy water, brushed her teeth, pulled her hair back into a ponytail and dressed quickly in jeans and a flannel shirt, then hurried downstairs. Hank was slipping into a denim, sheepskin-lined jacket. "What time does Lisa's schoolbus come by?" Jeanne asked, filling the percolator with water and reaching for the canister of coffee. "And I was thinking, do you suppose since she's missed several days of school, we should drive her today and talk to the teacher for a minute? Let her know her parents are involved and cooperative, even if she has been absent for a week?"

"Hmm, never occurred to me," Hank replied slowly, looking up at the clock on the wall. "It's only twenty after five...maybe..." He snapped his fingers. "No, I can't go. I told Ben last night we'd take the truck into Hawk Valley and haul back that damned busted baler, get it under cover before it snows, so we can work on it."

"Before it snows? Already? It's only November." Jeanne stared at him, a scoop of coffee poised above the percolator.

Hank smiled. "Honey, this isn't Seattle. We often have snow way before Thanksgiving."

Jeanne shook her head, grinning, savoring the "honey." She said, "Well, give me time. I'm just a...a...tenderleg."

Hank gave a snort of laughter. "Tenderleg! I think you mean 'tenderfoot,' Jeanne!"

"Oh, hush! It's rude to laugh at a tenderleg." Then she turned serious. "I can take Lisa down. It's at least three hours before school starts." She slid the coffee onto the burner and headed for the refrigerator. Returning with a slab of bacon and a carton of eggs, she asked, "How far away is this Hawk Valley place? Do you come back in for lunch or should I pack you one?''

Hank sank into a chair by the table, rolled his eyes toward the ceiling and laughed. ''I've died and gone to heaven!'' Then he looked at her and said, ''We should be back by lunchtime, but it'd be great if you made some sandwiches out of that ham Ma sent home with us, and a big thermos of coffee. That way, if it takes longer than we think, we're prepared.'' He got up and headed for the door. ''Could you make a couple extra for Ben? Nora's been sending both of us our lunch for over three years now. I'll go tell her she doesn't need to today.'' He plopped his hat on and started out the door, then stuck his head back in. ''I want to tell you...uh...you look damned pretty there!''

''Does this extra appeal come from the bacon in my left hand or the eggs in my right?'' Jeanne asked innocently. ''What's that old saying, 'The way to a man's heart is through his stomach'?''

Hank groaned. ''I knew it wouldn't come out right. What I meant is you look cute in a ponytail and a flannel shirt—like you're just headed for a 4-H cattle judging or something. Not many women look perky and cute at five in the morning.''

Jeanne waved toward the door. ''Oh, go on. You're forgiven. And thank you.''

When Hank returned a few minutes later with two big jugs of milk, the sizzle of frying bacon and hash browns greeted him. Six half-made sandwiches were lined up on the counter, and the big thermos was filled with hot water, tempering. Jeanne pointed at the milk with her knife. ''Where'd that come from?''

Hank turned to put the jugs in the refrigerator, answering over his shoulder, "I provide the cows and hay, Ben does the milking, Nora runs the separator, and we all share the milk—and butter and cream." Jeanne nodded, impressed. Maybe farmers don't get rich, but they don't go hungry, she thought. If Emily ever moves into Lisa's room and I move into the master bedroom, maybe we should turn that little nook I slept in last night into an exercise room to take care of all that butter and cream!

Jeanne ate breakfast with Hank, then swung into action as his truck pulled out. Soon all the kids were fed and dressed and ready to go. Lisa had picked out one of the new dresses and matching tights, and Jeanne used the curling iron on the shining hair she had trimmed for the little girl before she'd gone to bed last night. The three younger children looked up, suitably impressed. Emily's eyes were wide. "You're pretty, Lisa," she said admiringly.

"C'mon, kids, time to hit the road," Jeanne called, but as they struggled into jackets, a knock sounded on the kitchen door and Nora stuck her head in.

"Your hubby said you're driving Lisa to school this mornin'," Nora said. "Why not leave the others with me?" Jeanne, with an inward smile at the comfortable, old-fashioned term "hubby," accepted gladly, then followed Lisa out to the Blazer. She grabbed a shiny new lunch box off the counter as they left, and in the car she placed it on Lisa's lap.

"My own lunchbox!" Lisa crowed. "How'd you know I hated school lunch?"

"Because you told me about ninety-five times," Jeanne answered dryly. Lisa opened the box and examined the contents with little exclamations of pleasure.

"Teeny ham sandwiches with the crusts cut off!" she said happily. "Carrot and celery sticks, and what's in this little plastic thing? Ooh, ranch dressing to dip them in! And cookies! And fruit cocktail!" She closed the lid reverently. "Jeanne, this lunch is even better than the ones Allison's mother makes for her. Thank you a million zillion times!"

"You're welcome a million zillion times," Jeanne answered. "Now flip open that book and see how many pages you can read to me on the way to school." During the long drive from Seattle, Jeanne had realized that if Lisa was having problems in school, they weren't because of a lack of intelligence. The little girl was a quick learner, and they had very soon worked their way through the primer reader and simple math workbook the teacher had sent along. Jeanne strongly hoped that as soon as Lisa's new, cared-for appearance was noticed by the other children, she would begin to feel good about herself, and enjoy school.

Although she knew that as a daily event the thirty-some mile drive through the foothills to Glendora would be a chore, today it was a special treat. The firs and pines farther up the hillsides were smudges of deep green, the aspens lining the road had shed their leaves, making a deep golden carpet beneath the trees. The sky was like a huge overturned blue bowl. Whenever she could safely remove her attention from the gravel road, Jeanne gazed at the panorama surrounding her. It was no wonder people called this Big Sky Country. It made you realize there had to be a God.

Once at school, Lisa led Jeanne to her classroom and up to the teacher's desk. "Miss Clark, this is my new mother," she announced proudly.

"How wonderful to meet you!" Miss Clark said, holding her hand out to Jeanne. "It's so nice to have you back, Lisa—and I see you have a lovely new hairdo."

Lisa beamed. "My mother did it."

Jeanne chatted with the teacher for a moment about Lisa's progress through the books she had taken on the trip, then bent and gave Lisa a hug. "I'll meet the bus this afternoon, honey," she said.

Six

The days fell into a hectic sort of pattern. Jeanne mentally ate all the wicked, envious words she'd ever said about stay-at-home moms. It was no picnic. Still, except for the wistful wish that her husband was something more than a friend and business partner, she was happier than she could ever remember being. The college romance with Emily's father hadn't been happiness, she realized now, but just wild infatuation. A sort of puppy love. She felt as though this was where she belonged, where she was meant to be.

She was kept busy cooking and cleaning, of course, but found time to settle on the couch with the kids for stories. Tim, at five, should have been in kindergarten, but because of the long bus ride his father had decided to keep him home. Jeanne hoped that with activities she could enable him to keep pace with the other children when he started first grade next year. She was glad for the television satellite dish Hank had installed on the hillside above the house several years earlier. "Sesame Street" wasn't kindergarten, but it would help.

Tim was also a very handy extra pair of legs and hands, and Jeanne was able to tie in counting, letter recognition and vocabulary with many of his tasks. "Please bring me five potatoes from the pantry, Tim," she would say, holding up five fingers, or, flinging open the cupboard door, "See if you can find three things here that start with the 'buh' sound, Timmy, like 'buh-acon' or..."

"Bacon's in the refrigerator," Tim would answer sensibly.

"But look for other things," Jeanne would insist, and soon Tim would spot the can of baked beans, or the picture of biscuits on the box of baking mix.

Hank came in for lunch during one of these letter games, as Tim called them. He looked at Jeanne quizzically. She turned the heat off under the clam chowder and explained, "It's a phonetic letter-recognition activity."

"It is?" Timmy asked in surprise, looking over his shoulder from the utility stool where he was perched. "I thought it was a game."

"Oh, it *is* a game," Jeanne assured him. "Hey, if you're looking for 'puh,' you shouldn't've missed that red-and-black can right in front of your nose."

"Puh-pepper!" the little boy crowed. "Hi, Daddy! I'm looking for 'puhs.'"

Hank hung his hat on the hook by the back door. "You're awfully smart, as well as puh-pretty," he said to Jeanne, as he headed for the utility sink in the corner.

She set aside the "puh-pretty" to think about later. "Oh, I've read my share of yuppie women's magazines," she answered, setting out the soup bowls. "Tim's going to be able to give those city slickers a run for their money when he starts school, aren't you?"

She ruffled the little boy's blond hair, reaching past him for crackers.

Tim lost all interest in finding "puhs." Excitedly, he asked, "Do we run for money at school? How much money? I'm a pretty good runner!"

Jeanne and Hank both chuckled, and Hank slipped his arm around her waist in a little hug before stepping to the door to call Joey and Emily for lunch. Jeanne quickly grabbed the pitcher of orange juice from the refrigerator, wondering if the rivets in her jeans waistband were going to leave scorch marks.

Since Nora had turned over a basically clean house to her, Jeanne was soon able to start sewing during the children's afternoon nap. A small room just off the kitchen, piled full of boxes, empty suitcases and strange odds and ends, intrigued her. She asked Hank about it after lunch one day, and he stood in the doorway with her. "Back in the good old days, when every farm wife had at least one hired girl, this was where she slept," he explained, "close to the kitchen, so she could get the fire built and the kitchen warmed up every morning before anybody else got up."

"Sheesh!" Jeanne exclaimed. "Servants in America?"

"Well, sure," Hank continued seriously. "There'd be a little pile of rags there in the corner for her to sleep on, and a little table over there where she could eat her bread crusts...or was it gruel... Oof!" Jeanne had elbowed him lightly in the ribs, and he gripped the doorjamb, grimacing and moaning till her face showed a tiny bit of alarm, then laughing. "And what do you have in mind for this room?"

"Since you ask," Jeanne began, "here's what I'd like to do." She took a few steps into the room, pulling him with her. "First I'd get rid of all this stuff, then I'd paint the walls yellow or cream. I'd bring down the braided rug from the empty back bedroom upstairs, and make some bright checked curtains." She looked over her shoulder to see if he was paying attention. He was. "Then I'd put my sewing machine there by the window, and on that back wall I'd make shelves out of planks and bricks and have the kids bring all their toys down and keep them here." She was gesturing excitedly now, and he seemed to enjoy just watching her. "Then I'd bring that daybed down from the attic and make a cover for it to match the curtains, and a bunch of puffy pillows, and that's where kids could rest when they're sick." She turned to him, and he quickly smoothed his hand over his grin.

"You've been in the attic?" he asked.

"Well, sure," she said, a bit defensively. "If I'm going to make this the most comfortable home I can, then I have to know the potential." She looked at him sternly. "You're laughing at me!"

He pulled her into his arms and rested his cheek on her soft brown hair. "I'm not laughing at you, honey. I just get a kick out of seeing you get so fired up. I've never heard anybody talk so fast!"

Her arms were shyly reaching up of their own accord to encircle his neck when Tim burst into the room behind his father. "I just saw Ben already starting out to the field with the wire and stuff!" he said importantly.

Jeanne reluctantly stepped out of Hank's arms. He put on his jacket and hat and headed out. Watching him plod through the barren square where she had already planned a kitchen garden for next spring,

Jeanne wondered, certainly not for the first time, what her husband actually felt and thought.

While her feelings for him grew every day, he seemed good-naturedly unaffected. When his hand accidentally touched hers passing dishes at the table, she felt the touch to her very core, while he reminded Timmy not to chew with his mouth open. The night they met in the upstairs hallway, both headed for the bathroom from their individual bedrooms, she was immediately conscious of her breasts free from a bra, touching the flannel of her plaid nightgown. He bowed, gestured to the bathroom doorway and said with a grin, "Ladies first."

He teased her, said nice things to her and playfully put his arms around her, but what did those things really mean? He did those same things with all the children, and even the old dog, Jake. Oh, great! she thought. Isn't that just wonderful for the ego? Maybe he'll get me a flea collar for Christmas!

Seven

As Jeanne stood at the kitchen window watching Hank stride across the stubbled field, remembering the feel of his arms holding her close, she was brought back to earth by a hand tugging at her shirttail. "I don't feel so good, Jeanne," a small voice said.

"Oh, Joey, you don't look so good, either," she said, laying the back of her hand across his forehead. "You're pale, and I think you have a fever. Are you going to...." Yep, he was definitely going to. She grabbed him up and raced to the bathroom.

"I *hate* frowin' up," Joey complained later, as she buttoned him into a pair of fresh pajamas, "and my head hurts!"

By late afternoon Joey still hadn't managed to keep any liquid down, and Jeanne was sponging his forehead, arms and legs with alcohol and cool water. "Tim, would you run over to Nora's and ask her if she could drive down to meet Lisa's bus?" she asked. "Hurry, honey. Or if she'd rather stay here with Joey, I'll drive down, tell her."

When Hank came in that evening, beans were simmering on the stove, instead of the usual meat-and-potatoes dinner. Jeanne had been able to snatch a few minutes to get them started while Joey slept fitfully. Now he was awake again, lethargically resting his head on her breast while she rocked him.

Hank leaned over the pair and laid his cold hand on Joey's hot forehead. "I'm sick, Daddy," the little boy said.

"You sure are, fella." Hank shrugged out of his coat. "Just let me go wash up and I'll take him for a while," he told Jeanne.

"No!" Joey cried fretfully. "Not you, Daddy. Jeanne rocks better."

"You're gonna hurt Daddy's feelings, Joey," his big sister said reproachfully.

"No, that doesn't hurt my feelings, Lisa," Hank assured her. "Joey's no dummy. Of course Jeanne rocks better." He went to the kitchen to wash up and see what he could do to finish dinner. Watching his retreating back, Jeanne was almost grateful that for a few days, at least, she wouldn't keep halfway expecting some action from him that would move their marriage out of neutral, and then be disappointed when nothing occurred. At least she knew where she was and what was expected of her: taking care of sick children.

By the time Joey was able to keep down gelatin and ginger ale, Tim was feeling sick. Just like clockwork, Emily went down next. Then, surprising even himself, Hank. Followed by Lisa. Hank was just beginning to feel halfway human again when Jeanne paled and ran for the bathroom.

All in all, it was not a time that memories are made of. The marginally well ones helped each other as long as possible. Ben took over all the ranch chores, and Nora came by several times a day with soup and aspirin, hurrying out again as quickly as possible. On what felt like the ninth or tenth or seventieth day, Jeanne raised her head from the living-room couch where she lay, counted the children listlessly watching cartoons on TV, took a sip of flat soda, and lowered her head to the pillow again. "Do you suppose this is what it was like during the Black Plague, whole families...uh...sick at the same time?" she asked nobody in particular. Actually, "whole families *dying* at the same time" had been more like it, she knew, but she didn't want to scare the kids.

"Probably," came a disembodied voice from behind the couch. Hank was there, napping on the floor, covered with a quilt. "Shall I go see if Nora's painted a big black *X* on the door?"

"Nah, never mind," Jeanne answered. "Who cares?"

"Bet you wish you were back in Seattle."

"Flu's flu, no matter where you are. At least here there's plenty of company when you're sick. Do you have the box of tissues back there?"

Hank pulled himself up and handed it to her. Leaning down, he brushed a wisp of hair off her forehead. Her nose was red-tipped, her lips were chapped, and dark shadows ringed her eyes. He frowned fiercely.

Jeanne gazed up at him, reading in his expression that she looked a real sight. "Well, you're no Prince Charming yourself right now!" she snapped, then turned on her side, face to the back of the couch.

"I didn't say a word!" Hank said, amazed.

"Well, you thought it!"

He chuckled. "Does this mean the honeymoon's over—reading my mind and bawling me out for what I'm thinking?"

"Hah! What honeymoon?"

He pulled the afghan up over her shoulders and let his fingers linger a moment on her cheek, then crossed to the fireplace to put another log in. He brushed the bark dust from his hands and headed for the back porch.

"Don't get chilled when you're just getting over the flu," Jeanne called as she heard the back door open.

"No, I won't. Just getting more wood." He brought an armload, laid it gently in the wood box in case any of the kids were sleeping and brushed off his chest. He lifted Jeanne's feet, laid them on his lap and tucked the afghan under them carefully.

She opened her eyes and gazed at him for a moment. "What day is it?"

"I don't know. Let's see . . ." He stared into space, obviously trying to find an event to hang a date on. "Uh, I think it's Wednesday. Why? You going someplace?"

"No, just trying to figure out how many days of school Lisa has missed."

"Heard on TV that Glendora schools have been closed for a couple of days. Fifty-percent absenteeism. Guess we're not the only sick family."

"Good. I mean, not good, somebody else is sick, but good, Lisa won't be far behind the rest of the class." Then she fell asleep.

Eight

In a few days they were all in various stages of recovery. Jeanne noticed that Hank's fingers seemed to linger on hers longer than necessary in the usual "Please pass the carrots" transaction, and that he sometimes kissed her cheek as he left for his outside work.

Defiantly she pushed Aunt Irene's "princesses and plainfolks" rule into the far recesses of her mind and allowed herself to dream again.

On a gray afternoon she stood at the sink gazing out the window at the empty landscape, peeling Winesaps for applesauce, toying with a wonderful fantasy. It had Hank stealing into her tiny bedroom in the middle of the night when the children were sleeping, picking her up and carrying her down the hall to the master bedroom, the frothy pink lace of her satin nightgown spilling over his strong arms. Just as the knowledge that she didn't even own a satin nightgown brought the daydream to a standstill, the Jeep pulled up and Ben beckoned to her urgently.

Instead of carrying Jeanne down the hall to the bedroom, Hank was carried into the house on a makeshift stretcher by Ben, Nora and Jeanne, had his

ankle temporarily splinted by Jeanne, then rode down
the mountain to the doctor's office in the back seat of
Ben's big old '72 Buick. He was not a jolly passenger.

"How could I be so stupid?" he muttered, clench-
ing his teeth when Ben hit a bump. "Stepping in a gopher hole! Damn!"

Jeanne turned around to soothe him from the front
passenger seat. "It could've been worse, Hank. Just
think, if you'd been riding Molly and she'd stepped in
it, she'd probably have a broken leg and you'd have
Lord knows what broken!"

Ben said seriously, "You listen to your wife, man.
She's right." He snickered. "'Course, Molly's too
smart to step in a gopher hole!"

"I heard that, buddy!" Hank said through gritted
teeth. "Lucky for you I've got to be nice to you no
matter what you say, because I doubt I'll be out riding any fences for a week or two."

"A week or two?" Jeanne said to Ben in a stage
whisper. "More like a month or two, at least."

She was right. Hank had broken three bones in his
ankle. The doctor kept him in Glendora's little six-bed
emergency clinic overnight just to be safe, and the next
day Ben and Jeanne drove back down to bring him
home. He hobbled to the car with a cast and crutches,
and with instructions to stay off his feet for a month.

"Well, look on the bright side," Jeanne said calmly.
"At least you don't have to punch a time clock, and
you won't get your wages docked for being off work."

Hank grabbed his knee to pull his leg in, threw his
crutches on the floor and heaved a big gusty sigh.
"May the good Lord protect me from a Pollyanna!"
he snarled.

Jeanne slammed his door and climbed in the front seat. "Well, pardon *me!*" she snapped, and slammed her own car door.

"I'm sorry, Jeanne. Just don't be...don't be so damned cheerful, if you can help it," Hank apologized lamely.

Jeanne sniffed.

Ben started the car. "Now I don't want to interfere, but remember this old boat is more 'n twenty years old. Another coupla slams like that and she might just fall into a pile of rust and bolts!"

Jeanne turned her head for a quick peek at Hank, and they both started to laugh. "No more slams," Hank guaranteed.

Even though Ben was doing all the ranch work, Hank's day, and thus Jeanne's, still began early. The two men had coffee in the kitchen while they went over Ben's plans for the day. Ben could have managed fine without the consultation, and Jeanne appreciated his thoughtfulness in letting Hank feel he was still running the ranch.

The first few days after she had arrived from Seattle, Jeanne had moaned when the alarm went off each morning, but soon her body accepted the new schedule; the changing shifts of her hospital nursing job had prepared her for a quick adjustment. Now that Hank was confined to the house, the quiet time before the children awoke was very pleasant. They were getting to know one another in a depth that would have taken much longer with Hank spending his days out on the ranch. Sometimes they had a peaceful breakfast together; sometimes one or more of the children joined them.

Often Emily became aware of her mother's absence in bed and padded down the stairs. Jeanne sensed that her daughter loved being around Hank. She had often regretted Emily's not knowing a father's affection, so seeing the bond growing between her daughter and Hank was deeply satisfying.

One evening when Emily took an "ouchie" to her stepfather instead of her mother, Jeanne was moved almost to tears at the sight of the little girl sitting on Hank's lap, trustingly holding her palm up to him so he could search for the splinter. He found it, and Jeanne brought the tweezers and alcohol. "This might hurt a little, honey," Hank warned. "Are you tough?"

Emily nodded seriously. "I'm very tough." She clenched her teeth, then gave a big sigh of relief when the sliver came out. Hank hugged her, and she sat quietly on his lap for a few minutes before joining Tim and Joey and the Lego village they were building, sure that it was only a matter of time before they eclipsed the structure they had seen at Seattle Center. Hank reached for his newspaper, and his eyes met Jeanne's. The smile she gave him was tender.

One afternoon when Tim, Joey and Emily were napping, Hank called Jeanne into the den, where he did the record-keeping for the ranch. She entered with two mugs of coffee and handed him one. He got right to the point. "Jeanne, I'd like to adopt Emily, if you agree."

"Why...yes. I'm glad you want to do that. I...I've worried about Emily's future ever since the accident."

"Being a ward of the court or having foster parents would *legally* take care of Em's future, Jeanne. But how do you feel about having me be her *father?*"

Jeanne looked at him soberly for a moment. "I don't think anyone could be a better father, Hank," she said softly, meaning it with all her heart. He worked hard for the children and made time for them even when he was tired. He treated all four of them with equal attention and affection. Someday she would tell him so, but for now she just said, "You're a great dad."

"Good. I'll call the lawyer who handles the ranch business and have him find out how we go about it." Reaching for the phone, he paused for a sip of coffee. "Seems like I read somewhere that you have to put a legal notice in the newspaper a certain number of times, giving the natural parent a chance to respond." He took another sip. "Good coffee."

"Wait," Jeanne said quickly. "Before you call, what about the other kids?"

He looked at her, puzzled. "What about them?"

"What if something happened to you? Would their mother's parents take them?"

"I . . . I don't know," Hank said. "Cyndi's parents were divorced long ago. Her father hasn't even seen the kids. And you already know about how her mother wrote them out of the picture when Cyndi disappeared." He sat silently for a long moment, gazing into his cup. "I hadn't thought about that. Didn't think anything would ever happen to me, I guess."

"Probably never thought you'd step in a gopher hole and break your ankle in three places, either."

Hank stared out the window at the frosty gray stubble in the nearest field. "In my will, Paula and Al would have custody of the kids." He swiveled back to face her. "Three kids are a big responsibility."

"What if I adopted them? I think they're beginning to think of me as their mother." Jeanne sipped her coffee thoughtfully. "I love them, Hank. Even if something happened to you—*especially* if something happened to you—I'd still want to be their mother."

"Yes. I'd want you to be. Let me see what we have to do."

"But it has to be their choice. Lisa's old enough to remember her mother, and Tim remembers a little, too. I only want to do this if it's what they want."

"All right, we'll talk about it tonight at bedtime." Hank grinned. "That'll be a switch. Instead of reading a fairy tale about a wicked stepmother who sends the children out to get lost in the woods, we'll talk about a sweet stepmother who wants to adopt them. In the meantime, I'll call and find out about the legalities." He swallowed the last of his coffee and reached for the phone again.

Jeanne stood up. "Let me know what he says. I've got to get back to work. I'm almost ready to start on some Christmas projects." As she leaned over Hank to pick up his mug, he caught her hand, pulled it to his mouth and pressed a soft kiss into her warm palm.

She felt electrified. He released her hand, and almost of their own volition, Jeanne's fingertips drifted to his forehead, where the sun-lightened hair waved crisply back. Before she had a chance to think about the wisdom of wanting more than she already had, she bent down and pressed a butterfly kiss right there. Then she turned in confusion, grabbed the mug and hurried from the room. What was happening to her? Was the disciplined woman who was learning all about ranching and mothering and running a household turning into a bowl of jelly?

The murmur of Hank's voice on the telephone followed her down the hall. In the kitchen, she put their cups in the dishwasher and, lost in thought, was gazing out at the gray sky meeting the gray fields when he limped into the room on his crutches. "Sam says it'll be quick and simple for you to adopt the kids," Hank said, leaning against the counter and propping his crutch alongside. "Since their mother is dead, we don't even have to put a notice in the newspaper, giving the natural parent a chance to respond. It'll take a little longer for me to adopt Emily."

"For the advertising in the paper?"

"Yeah. But Sam said he didn't anticipate any problems under the circumstances. We'll have the notice in the paper, and Sam will take care of the paperwork. I told him to draw up a new will, too, including all these changes. Then we'll make a trip to Helena to wrap everything up." He limped to the refrigerator and peered inside. "Are these apples still crisp?"

"I think so. I had one yesterday and it was okay." She moved to the open refrigerator. "Not the Delicious, though. They're past their prime. Try one of the Granny Smiths."

Hank took an apple, found the salt shaker in the cupboard, retrieved his crutch and started back to the den. "You know where I am if you need me," he said around a mouthful of apple.

Jeanne watched her husband limp down the hallway. So they would all be a family, as she'd dreamed. But did Hank's moment of tenderness allow her to include in that fantasy family a husband and wife who loved each other?

Nine

Hank's mother called regularly once a week just to "stay in touch." Jeanne was pleasantly surprised that from the very beginning, Mrs. Gustafson had never immediately asked to talk to her son, but chatted with Jeanne until Jeanne herself broke off the conversation to get Hank.

Mrs. Gustafson had invited them to spend Thanksgiving at her home in Helena, and everyone, for their different reasons, was looking forward to the trip.

Tim, Joey and Lisa couldn't wait to visit Grandma. The two boys had filled Emily's head with so many exciting details about their grandmother and her house that Jeanne, overhearing some of the conversations and learning the rest from Emily, could hardly keep a straight face as she relayed them to Hank during breakfast one morning.

"Em must have had jet lag when we stopped in Helena on the way up here, Hank. She doesn't remember too much about your mom's place," she reported, refilling their coffee cups. "She can hardly wait to visit again. From the boys' details, she's expecting a situation sort of like Mary Poppins in charge of a giant toy store."

Hank chuckled. "She'll have fun. Ma and her friend Eunice always hit the yard sales to make sure they've got a good supply of grandkid entertainment."

Lisa's anticipation was for a different reason. One morning as Jeanne was using the curling iron to put a couple of waves on either side of the child's face, Lisa asked, "Jeanne, can I take all the new school clothes you made me to show to Grandma?"

"You're going to have a pretty full suitcase for a four-day visit, honey," Jeanne answered. "Wouldn't you rather just tell her about them?"

"Oh, she'd like to see them, I know," Lisa said to her stepmother's reflection in the mirror. "Before you came, whenever we visited her, she always took us downtown to buy some clothes, even when she didn't feel good." She stretched her lips to inspect the new gap where the first baby tooth had recently come out. "I think Grandma's gonna be glad we have a mom now."

Jeanne unplugged the curling iron and fluffed the waves with her fingers. "There! You're gorgeous!"

Lisa hadn't moved, but still spoke to the reflection in the mirror. "When am I s'posed to call you Mom?" she asked.

"Well, anytime you want to," Jeanne answered. "We started working on adoption after we talked to all of you about your dad adopting Emily and me adopting you and the boys. I just don't want to rush you, though, and make you think you *have* to call me Mom."

"It's not 'cause I *have* to. It's 'cause I want to... Mom."

Jeanne thought for a moment her heart would burst. Then she wondered if Emily would be jealous when she heard the other children calling her Mom. Her doubts were settled a few minutes later when all the children piled into the Blazer to take Lisa down the hill to the bus stop and wait with her there.

"Em," said Lisa conversationally, "would you like to be my sister?"

"I already *am* your sister."

"Not really," Lisa said, with the authoritative wisdom that the three-year age difference allowed her. "We're really just stepsisters till we're adopted, but if I give you my dad and you give me your mom, *then* we're sisters."

"Okay." Seemed like a reasonable deal to Emily—and to the little boys, who had listened to the exchange and were quite secure in the knowledge that their big sister knew everything in the world there was to know. So Jeanne had become "Mom" to Lisa, Tim and Joey, although Joey often called her Mommy, as Emily did, especially when he was tired. Lisa, Jeanne knew, could hardly wait for her grandma to know that Jeanne really *was* their new mom.

For his part, Hank had declared he looked forward to the visit so that he and Jeanne could have a little time away from the kids. He knew he'd be able to count on his mother to watch them while he and Jeanne went out to dinner and a movie.

As for Jeanne, she *needed* that trip to Helena. She needed to be a little removed from the four walls that held together six people who were a family, and yet, in one important regard—the parents' physical intimacy—were not.

On this frosty November morning Jeanne sat idly at her sewing machine, watching through the newly-curtained window as Hank hobbled toward the barn on his crutches. She had always thought marriages of convenience were a thing of the past. Now she was living one. Often, after an evening of reading, watching television or playing Scrabble with Hank, Jeanne longed to simply walk into his room with him and climb into bed. Each time, though, she remembered the distant stare he sometimes had, as though he were a million miles away—with someone else. For her own pride and self-respect, she wouldn't make the first move. As he'd said back in Seattle, they were both healthy adults and they'd know when the time was right. Except it was beginning to seem it never would be.

Well, it *was* a marriage of convenience, and she'd best keep that in mind, she reminded herself, and not build some fragile fairy-tale romance that only existed in her mind and then be devastated when it came crashing down around her.

She sat a moment longer looking out the window, watching Hank's breath puff out in little clouds in the cold air. Then she sighed and slid the cornflower-blue corduroy under the needle. It was to be a warm robe for Hank, the exact color of his eyes.

The trip to Helena would be fun. She had called her Seattle bank, where Hank had insisted she leave her savings, and requested a draft be sent to her, so she could do some Christmas shopping to round out what they had bought before they left the city. She hadn't known Hank's children then, so she had purchased generic toys, but now she wanted to buy special things for each child. And she'd like to get herself a few nice things. Maybe a silky nightgown in the dark rose she knew flattered her, and a soft, fluffy robe in the same color. She could put them on after tucking in the kids, and Hank would see her sitting there, firelight glowing on her cheeks, and he'd come over and sit down by her, pull her into his arms, and the robe would slip off one shoulder, revealing the silky gown and her creamy skin...

A pipedream! But she still looked forward to the Thanksgiving trip. Hank's mother would no doubt put them in the same bedroom. Probably nothing would happen. The house was small, the walls thin. And Hank's cast would have put a crimp even into love-making between two people with the ease of years between them, with the old-shoe comfort that allowed them the ability to laugh at awkwardness, to improvise. But at least she'd be able to feel his nearness in the night, and pretend he loved her.

At last the day before Thanksgiving arrived. With the suitcases loaded into the van, Hank and Jeanne and the three younger children were waiting in the parking lot when Lisa got out of school. Jeanne drove, and Hank copiloted by body language and sharp little intakes of breath until finally, in exasperation, she gave him a meaningful glare.

"I know how to drive, Hank," she explained a few minutes later, feeling guilty for the glare. She'd seen her aunt use it effectively on Uncle Bert many times, but for the past few miles she'd been remembering that Aunt Ireñe and Uncle Bert had rarely seemed even friendly to each other. She wondered if the glare had anything to do with it.

"I know you do, Jeanne," Hank answered. He reached over to pat her knee. "It's just that I'm about as bad a passenger as I am a patient."

"Well, surprise, surprise, as Gomer Pyle used to say. For some strange reason I already knew that!"

Darkness was falling as they drove into Ma Gustafson's driveway, and the yellow lamplight of her windows welcomed them. Kids exploded out of the van, with Tim and Joey pulling Emily between them, eager to show her the sights. Ma hurried out, and she and Jeanne helped Hank down on his crutches.

When she entered the house, Jeanne stopped for a moment and took a deep breath. Hank looked at her, a question in his eyes. She laughed shakily. "It's just...when I was a kid and daydreamed about having a family like everyone else, this was what Thanksgiving was like." She shook her head. "I'm sorry. It sounds corny, I know. But the smells—" she sniffed appreciatively the combination of faint wood smoke that had drifted in with them, spicy potpourri from the brass dish on the hall table and freshly baked mince and pumpkin pies "—and the kids running in, all excited, and Grandma..."

Hank reached out and pulled her into a quick hug. Then he simply stood there, holding her close.

Is he pitying me? Jeanne wondered. Am I just Emily with a splinter, or Joey with a stubbed toe? She didn't move from the shelter of his arms, though, until Tim, Joey and Emily, hand in hand, raced pell-mell down the hall toward them, dropping hands at the last minute to swerve to either side. Hank and Jeanne stepped apart, but Jeanne knew the closeness of that embrace would warm her for a long time—perhaps, she hoped, even till the next time she felt like a wife of convenience.

The four days seemed to fill all their expectations. Grandma Gustafson was true to Tim and Joey's extravagant advance billing. Her latest yard-sale treasures were stored in the guest-room closet: a tulle-and-net prom dress, sequin-spattered evening gown, a couple of veiled and feathered hats, even an old tux and top hat. She admired Lisa's new wardrobe, read stories to them all, and better still, she listened while Lisa demonstrated her own new recently acquired reading skill.

On Friday, Hank stayed with the kids while Ma and Jeanne went shopping. Jeanne finished her Christmas buying and found all the supplies needed to finish the projects already started. They had a long, leisurely lunch, with no mother-in-law advice or questions.

That night, Ma watched the children while Hank and Jeanne went out to dinner and a movie. In the theater, his arm made a slow but purposeful descent to encircle Jeanne's shoulders, and he pulled her close enough that the warm exhalations of his breath stirred the hair along her temple.

And best of all, they shared the guest-room bed. It was awkward. Oh, yes, it was awkward. It was also worth every shy, uncomfortable minute. They began each night staidly back-to-back, facing opposite walls. When morning came, staidness had departed. The first morning Jeanne awoke still facing her wall, but in his sleep Hank had pulled her close and her back was cradled against his warm chest. The next two mornings the roles were reversed. She was nestled tightly against *his* back. And the last morning, they awoke in each other's arms.

Jeanne had been slowly surfacing into wakefulness, so deliciously comfortable that her body resisted morning. Her internal alarm, accustomed to going off at five o'clock, told her it was much later than that, and the lightness of the room confirmed the feeling. She stirred and was jolted awake by the firmness of Hank's body against hers, by his arm resting over her hip. At her movement, his arm tightened and pulled her closer, though he still slept. Bittersweet emotion flooded through Jeanne as she realized how happy awakening in Hank's arms every morning for the rest of her life would make her. Oh, if only... if only they could have met and loved and then married. If only he loved her, instead of just requiring her services as a housekeeper and her body for his physical needs. If she couldn't have more from him than a certain appreciation and the matter-of-fact sex she knew would be a part of her life soon, then she'd be much better off if she didn't love him. Love. The word lingered bitterly. Yes, she did love him, and she wished she didn't. She wished his touch didn't make her catch her breath and melt inside. She had experienced one-sided love before and felt its pain. She had sworn it would never happen again, and look at her now.

She felt Hank's body stir against her. His hand left her hip and lifted her chin. Their lips met. *If I can't have what I want, then I'll take what I can get,* Jeanne thought, and then stopped thinking, lost in the kiss.

The bedroom door was flung open. "Daddy, Daddy, it's snowing!" Joey shouted, running to the bed. Then, conversationally, "Were you kissin'?"

"Can we build a snowman, Dad?" Now Tim was in the room, too. "Mom, Grandma told me she's makin' Dutch babies for breakfast. Do I hafta eat 'em? Dutch babies!" he ended in horror.

Hank moaned softly. "First thing when we get home, I'm putting a lock on the bedroom door," he whispered to Jeanne as she threw back her side of the patchwork quilt and leapt out of bed, giving him a small, uncertain smile as she did so.

"First breakfast, then a snowman." She grabbed her robe and moved Tim and Joey briskly ahead of her. "Tim, you'll love Dutch babies," she assured him. "You like applesauce and puffy pancakes, don't you?"

Hank listened as their voices moved away down the hall. "Well, yeah," Tim responded slowly. "But if it's just pancakes 'n' applesauce, why's it called Dutch babies? That's gross."

"I don't know," Jeanne answered. "Maybe little Dutch babies love it. Or maybe a Dutch baby spilled his applesauce on his daddy's pancake one morning, and his daddy took one taste of it, and said . . ."

The kitchen was full of laughter and the mouth-watering aroma of frying bacon. Jeanne slid a puffy pancake onto Hank's plate and he sniffed appreciatively. "Hank, do you think if we stopped in Glendora the doctor would put the lighter cast on?" She stepped to the stove and pulled the pan off the burner, having seen that Ma was tired and needed a break. "He told us to come back around the first of December, and this is pretty close to it."

Hank spread warm applesauce on half his pancake and poured syrup on the other half. "Maybe he would," he said. "It's Sunday, but he's usually around the clinic in the afternoon."

"Well, then, you kids had better hurry with your snowman," Ma reminded them. "You'll want to be in Glendora no later than three-thirty or four at the latest."

Ten

As she negotiated the steep lane and parked by the back door, Jeanne felt a thrill of homecoming. She marveled that after less than two months, the weather-beaten old farmhouse in its stand of cottonwood and oak seemed to hold out welcoming arms to her.

Jeanne heated the homemade turkey noodle soup Ma had sent home with them and made grilled cheese sandwiches, while Hank, with his lighter cast and one crutch, started a fire in the kitchen range and then supervised the two bath sessions. Tim and Joey were out of their shared tub and into pajamas in jig time. When Lisa called that she and Emily were ready to get out, Hank went in for the ritual inspection of necks and ears, although it really wasn't necessary. Lisa, in the big-sister role she so enjoyed, always made sure that Emily bathed properly.

A few minutes later, they were all seated around the kitchen table eating while the sticks of pine in the stove snapped crisply. Emily intently chased a plump homemade noodle up the side of her bowl, finally maneuvering it into her spoon. Then she looked up brightly and announced, "Me and Lisa are going to tell Christmas secrets in our room."

"Oh, are you and Lisa going to share a room now?" Jeanne asked.

"Yep," Emily answered. "Daddy said we could."

Jeanne's eyes met Hank's over the children's heads. He smiled a bit self-consciously and nodded. So, he'd had a talk with the girls when he'd gone to supervise their bathing. And he'd apparently been successful. She suddenly felt a rapid little pulse in her throat that she hadn't noticed before, and was aware of warmth creeping up her cheeks. She hoped Hank didn't see it.

While she tucked the kids in for the night, he put the dishes into the dishwasher and lit the kindling already arranged in the living-room fireplace. When she emerged after settling the noise level in the boys' room, the mellow sound of Phil Collins drifted up the stairs from the stereo. Jeanne hesitated a moment, then took a quick shower and slipped into her flannel pajamas. Now that she finally had the silky rose nightgown, she hesitated to wear it. It would look so...so *calculated,* as though she expected a big romantic event, she thought ruefully. And while she might hunger for a tender, emotional beginning that worked toward a passionate finish, it was not what she expected. Still...oh, what the heck! She could at least wear the robe!

She picked up the book from her nightstand and started downstairs, feeling the music swirl around her and into her senses.

Hank stood at the fireplace, back to the stairs and poker in hand. He turned and grinned at her as she sat down on the couch. "Sounded there for a while like the boys got a second wind."

"And a third and a fourth," Jeanne replied. "I think the idea of Christmas secrets being told in the next room drove them crazy." She pulled a cushion under her elbow. "They evidently figured if they couldn't beat the girls at telling Christmas secrets, they could win with sheer volume." Jeanne shivered slightly. The new pink robe might look great, but it wasn't much for warmth.

Hank leaned his crutch against the couch and lowered himself beside her. Putting his arm around her, he drew her near. "Cold?" he asked. "Takes this old place a long time to heat up after the thermostat has been turned down for a few days."

I think romance, he thinks thermostat! Aunt Irene's words again rang in Jeanne's mind. "Be satisfied with what you've got."

His other arm came around her, too, and he pulled her closer, till her head was against his chest. She let it rest there, listening to the strong, steady thrum of his heart. "If it was cold enough to snow in Helena, then it was probably a lot colder than that up here," Jeanne said, finally thinking of a response to his thermostat comment.

Oh, Lord, I sound so stupid! she thought. What am I, Wendy the Weather Girl? I'm trying to be so calm about this...this next step in our arrangement. Maybe he'll never love me, but at least he'll never know that I love him. If I can't save my heart, at least I can save my pride.

Hank stirred. "Let's sit over there by the fire," he said, and stood slowly, his crutch in one hand, Jeanne's hand in the other. He sank into the big leather platform rocker by the fire, and pulled Jeanne down onto his lap. Holding her close, he began to rock.

Jeanne nestled closer. She couldn't help it. The fire was crackling, the wind that had come up whined around the corners of the house, the grandfather clock ticked, soft music from the stereo enveloped them. Hank's arms were strong and gentle at the same time, and she felt more completely safe and cared for than she could ever remember. Hold on to this, she told herself. If this is as good as it's going to get, if this is what I have, instead of romance and passion, okay. This will be good enough. She closed her eyes and relaxed against him.

For a long time they just fitted against each other, quietly rocking in the big chair. Hank's breathing and his hard body against Jeanne revealed his arousal. Although Jeanne knew it signified nothing except that he had been lonely and hungry for a woman's touch for a long time, she was grateful that he left her this illusion of tenderness, that he didn't rush to satisfy his own needs.

Eventually Hank slipped his hand beneath her pajama top and began to slowly stroke her back, from the little knobs at the base of her neck to the elastic of her pajama bottoms, then up to softly massage her neck, around to the tender hollows behind and below each ear. Jeanne whispered something he apparently didn't catch. "What did you say?" he whispered back, leaning down so his ear was near her lips.

"I said, that if I were a cat I'd be purring," Jeanne murmured, opening her eyes and turning her face till their lips met. The kiss was as gentle as the caresses had been. His lips moved to the corners of her mouth, her cheeks, her temples, her closed eyelids, the wildly fluttering pulse at the base of her throat, then back to her mouth. Their lips parted sweetly, and the sound of

Hank's labored breathing joined the other nighttime noises. A tiny moan escaped Jeanne, and Hank struggled awkwardly to his feet.

"I'd like to carry you up to our bedroom," he murmured unsteadily, "but I can't." Instead, he slipped his arm around her waist and they slowly climbed the stairs, stopping often while their lips and bodies met. Once in their room, Hank quietly closed the door behind them.

Afterward, Jeanne could never remember who led whom to the bed and who threw back the quilt. Perhaps it was a joint effort. Undressing certainly was. He opened her pajama top and kissed her taut breasts until her whole body quivered, then slid the elastic waistband of the bottom down over her hips. She unbuttoned his flannel shirt, and while he shrugged it off his shoulders, she struggled with the buckle of his belt and the stubborn metal fasteners of his jeans. He fell back on the bed as she maneuvered the denim over his cast, then pulled her down beside him. In the privacy of their own little haven, it was difficult to know if the sighing moans were the wind whispering around the eaves, or Hank... or Jeanne.

He held her in the circle of his arms until he fell asleep. She lay there in his embrace for a long time before sleep finally took her. She remembered his voice saying, "Oh, Jeanne, Jeanne." But he'd never said, "Oh, Jeanne, Jeanne, I love you."

Eleven

Jeanne stood at the sink, gazing out the kitchen window as she smoothed lotion on her hands. She sighed. The gray of the sky met the brownish-gray of harvested fields and sleeping earth, matching her mood.

This was stupid, she told herself angrily. I should be taking advantage of nap time to work on Christmas projects I can't do while the kids are around. Resolutely she went to her cozy sewing room just off the kitchen and pulled down a box from the top of the storage shelves. Then she stood aimlessly again, rubbing the soft, Santa-printed outing flannel with her fingertips. Two uninterrupted hours would finish the girls' nighties and the boys' pajamas, but she just couldn't seem to get with it today.

She tried a mental pep talk, a variation of the one she'd been giving herself for the past three weeks: You should be grateful, instead of whining. You have a beautiful old house to live in, the kind you always wanted. You have a husband who is good to you and your daughter. His children have accepted you as their mother. Think of how bad it could be. You took a real chance, marrying someone you didn't know and letting him bring you way out in the boonies. He could've been a Bluebeard . . . or the the home could have been like the one you grew up in, with nothing more than cool tolerance between husband and wife. Instead, there's laughter and affection. He's gentle and sweet, and considerate of you.

Her hands moved to gather up the partially finished garments, while her mind wandered. And there's warmth. Oh, yes. Sometimes, lots of warmth. Under that patchwork quilt there's warmth that blazes up like a flash fire, until sometimes I could almost think he loves me. But that's not love—it's lust. He needs me . . . needs my body, anyway. And I need his just as much.

She carried the cloth to the sewing machine, sat down and began pinning eyelet ruffling to the neck of a nightie. So why can't I just accept what I *do* have? Why can't I just enjoy the pleasure his passion gives me and forget about love? But passion isn't enough. Instead of just a little sip, I want the whole glass. I want him to love me with his heart and soul. The way I do him. But he doesn't and probably never will. So I won't let him know how I really feel. After all, we're not giddy teenagers. We're two mature adults making the best of a marriage of convenience.

As if her concentrated thoughts had created him, through the window she saw Hank limping slowly toward the house, and the giddy teenager instantly evicted the mature adult. Angry at being betrayed by her own body, she violently pressed the sewing-machine pedal. By the time the back door opened, the steady whir of her machine filled the room. Hank moved stealthily behind her chair and put his cold hand on her neck. She gave a little yelp.

"I could use some coffee. How about you?" he said. "Hey, that's pretty snazzy. You're almost finished."

"Almost," Jeanne replied. "Yeah, coffee sounds good. I'll go start a pot."

"No, I'll fix it. You need to make hay while the sun shines. Or the kids sleep. Carry on."

As the coffeepot clinked and the water ran, Jeanne's Pollyanna side took over. *See? See how sweet he is to you?* Then her cynical side spoke up. *Oh, sure. A loaf of bread, a jug of coffee, and thou.* Once again her foot pressed the pedal.

Soon Hank was back with two steaming cups. Carefully placing Jeanne's on the chest beside her, he lowered himself into the maple rocker with a low "Ah-h-h."

"You're not staying off that leg enough."

"No, the leg's fine. It's just that I haven't been on a horse for about six weeks, and my body's reminding me how long it's been."

The whirring of the machine stopped. Jeanne stared at her husband in disbelief. "You were on a horse with that leg? You're crazy!"

"Nah, no big deal. I rode Smoke, the only one lazy enough to stand still while I climb up hay bales and fling my bum leg over his back." He took a sip of coffee. "The truck's great, so's the Blazer, but some places you can only get to with a horse."

Jeanne shook her head in dismay, trying to rid herself of a vision of the horse taking a few steps forward while Hank was "flinging his bum leg over." It was a frightening picture. "Sounds to me like a good way to have two bum legs, instead of just one," she commented dryly.

"No, I'm careful," Hank said cheerfully, then tried to change the subject. "There's a pretty little stand of fir just beyond that ridge you can see from the kitchen window. Got a few Scotch pine and spruce, too. I rode over to check on Christmas trees."

"Wow, cutting our own tree!" Jeanne exclaimed. "Just like a Christmas story! Do we have decorations?"

"Yup, boxes of 'em, up in the attic," Hank assured her. "Since Ma moved to Helena, she has a little pink tree with silver ornaments. Said she'd always wanted one like that." He chuckled. "Pa probably rolls over in his grave every December. He was a great one for tradition. Always had the tree picked out a year or two ahead, a big one. His favorite ornament, a blue glass bird, always had to go in the same place." He was silent for a moment, and when he spoke again his voice was fond. "Pa knew how to celebrate Christmas," he said simply.

"I wish I could have known him."

"I wish you could have, too. Pa would have loved you." He stood stiffly. "Well, I'm rested up. You want to come pick out the tree, or do you trust me?"

"When spring comes I'm going to learn how to ride," Jeanne said firmly, "but for now, you'd better pick one out without me." She glanced at him with a little grin. "Who are we kidding? You've already got it picked out."

Hank nodded sheepishly and headed for the door.

"But take Ben with you!" Jeanne called after him.

"Yes, Mother dear," Hank answered dutifully, already out of the room.

"I'm not your mother," Jeanne growled at the sewing machine.

"And I'm awfully glad you're not!" Hank stuck his head back inside, grinning so lecherously Jeanne couldn't help laughing, even as she threw a package of bias tape at him.

Late that evening, staring almost reverently at the pine he'd cut, Jeanne knew she had never seen such a beautiful tree. It was huge, bushy and fresh, nothing like the city trees she had known. The old glass balls caught the firelight's glow and reflected varied colors from the strings of lights. The children and Hank had trimmed the lower branches, and Jeanne, on a stepladder, had done the higher reaches, putting the angel in place on top. After the kids were in bed, she and Hank, exhausted, sat in the darkened living room and admired the tree before going up to bed themselves.

The rooms upstairs were chilly, and Jeanne made the rounds, pulling up covers, tucking arms and legs back under the blankets. In the boys' room Tim, as usual, had barely disarranged the bedding before falling asleep while Joey's bed, also as usual, looked as though a tornado had blown through. Joey muttered something, moving restlessly, and Jeanne bent to kiss his cheek and say softly, "It's okay, Joey. Nighty-night."

When she joined Hank in their bedroom, he seemed to know how truly tired she was. Once under the covers, he hugged her, kissed her good-night and then cuddled her back against his chest, spoon-fashion.

As she drifted off to sleep, Jeanne's Pollyanna half thought, *See, it isn't just sex.* And her cynical half replied, *No, it isn't just sex—it's a very cold bedroom.*

Twelve

Jeanne rubbed the fogged window of the Blazer with her jacket sleeve, clearing a view of the road. The defroster was on full force, but it couldn't keep up with the breaths of three chattering children. The kids were getting bored waiting for Lisa's bus, but it couldn't be helped.

Jeanne had sensed almost from that first morning when she helped Lisa get ready for school that, although she tried to hide it, the child was edgy about the bus trip home. When, much later, Jeanne mentioned it to Hank, he told her about the time he and Ben were out in the fields longer than expected, and by the time Nora realized she'd better pile the kids in the old Buick and go down the lane, Lisa's bus had already dropped her off and she was walking home alone.

"But she didn't raise a fuss," Hank had said. "She was just really quiet and kind of pinched-face about it."

"Well, it evidently frightened her," Jeanne had responded at the time, "so I'll just be sure to always be there on time, and she'll finally forget to worry about it." So now, no matter if she was wrist-deep in cookie dough or two inches from the end of a seam, when it was time to meet Lisa's bus, she gathered up the kids and hopped into the Blazer.

At last, Lisa's bus arrived. Climbing into the Blazer, Lisa exclaimed before the door closed behind her, "Oh, boy! Christmas vacation!" Then, peering suspiciously at the three children on the back seat, "Did you guys do fun stuff today while I was gone?"

Jeanne answered for them. "Gosh, no! They cleaned the hearths, and beat the rugs and scrubbed the toilets and chopped firewood and..."

"Okay, you're kidding! Daddy doesn't let us use the ax!"

"Oh, all right, I'm kidding," Jeanne confessed. "We made cookies, but I saved some of the dough so you could make some, too." Missing out on the Christmas preparations that took place while she was at school upset Lisa terribly.

"Good. I'm glad you saved some dough for me." Then, in her six-year-old fashion, she was off in another direction. "Don't look in my lunch box. There's a secret there. I'll carry it in the house so you won't see it. The buses came before we even finished eating lunch today." Then she darted back to the original subject—making cookies. "Can I make cookies as soon as we get home?"

Jeanne pulled up by the back door. "Yup. The kids haven't had naps yet, so while they sleep you can make your cookies and I'll finish some sewing." She unlocked the rear of the vehicle and the two boys scrambled out, followed more slowly by a sleepy Emily.

"In the sewing room?" Lisa asked, her voice disappointed.

"No, it's hand-sewing, so I can bring it into the kitchen."

"Good. It wouldn't be much fun by myself."

Tim suddenly got the gist of the conversation. "I'm not sleepy," he said quickly, "not even a little bit!"

"Me, too!" echoed Joey.

Emily clamped off a yawn to add her own, "Me, too."

"Well, that's too bad," Jeanne said sympathetically, "because that means you'll miss the popcorn and movies tonight. If you don't take a nap you can't stay up late."

Tim's small freckled face grew serious as he tried to calculate how he could avoid a nap and still stay up late. "What movies?" he finally asked.

"All those Christmas specials that came on school nights right after Thanksgiving, usually past your bedtime," Jeanne replied. "Daddy taped them all, and tonight we're going to have popcorn and watch as many as we want to—'Rudolph,' 'Frosty,' 'The Night Before Christmas,' and the Walt Disney Christmas special, and—"

"I guess I'll take a nap," Tim decided, and was echoed by his two loyal followers.

"Good choice!" Jeanne complimented him. "Off with the boots and coats, kids." Within thirty minutes the three younger children were down for naps.

Lisa was finishing her leftover lunch. "When is Grandma coming up? I forgot."

"Either tomorrow or Sunday, Christmas Eve," Jeanne replied, "if the weather stays good."

"Well, I hope she can come," Lisa said after a last bite of cheese sandwich. "She would be sad to be alone at Christmas."

"Very sad," Jeanne agreed, "but if the weather stays like it is now, one of us will be able to drive down and bring her back." She looked out the kitchen window doubtfully. The sky had been threatening snow all week, but maybe it would hold off for a little while longer.

The day brightened for her as she saw Hank coming in from the machine shed by the barn. He was walking much, much better these days—still a limp, but not nearly as severe as it had been. He only used a crutch on stairs or when he was extremely tired.

"Here comes your dad, Lisa. Why don't you get him a couple of those one-armed gingerbread men to go with his coffee? Joey and Emily had trouble getting their cookies into the oven without broken arms or legs, but they'll taste just as good."

By the time Hank had washed up and sat down at the kitchen table, Jeanne was able to cover her little rush of emotion by doing a good imitation of a sturdy, practical farm wife. "How's them thar oxen doin', Pa?"

"Purty good, purty good," Hank replied between swallows of gingerbread man. "Ole Belle's kinder stove up in her off hind leg, but Bessie's pullin' hard enough to make up fer it."

Lisa stared at her father. "You're being silly again," she said finally, reaching for the raisins to button up her gingerbread men's coats. "I thought grown-ups weren't supposed to be silly."

Hank winked at Jeanne. Jeanne grinned back, picked up her notepad and began listing the items that weren't life or death, but would certainly come in handy if someone made a trip to town to pick up Ma.

That evening, after Jeanne had removed all traces of the children's baking cookies from the kitchen, everyone gathered around the big table for a light supper. After baths, as they watched the Christmas specials and ate popcorn, the wind came up and began to sigh around the eaves with a lonely, mournful sound. By bedtime the sighs had grown to shrieks, and a pervading cold was creeping across the floors of the old rooms.

As Hank pulled Jeanne across the cold sheets into the warm haven of his arms, she thought for a moment that now she knew why so many of the country wives of older generations greeted each spring pregnant.

Thirteen

Jeanne had fallen asleep in Hank's arms and after what felt like only a few minutes was awakened by noise from downstairs, loud enough to be heard over the howling wind. Hank's side of the bed was empty and very cold. Getting up and jamming her arms into the sleeves of her robe, she hurried down to see Hank limping in with an armful of wood.

"It's wicked out there, a regular blizzard," he said, dumping the wood by the stove. "You'd best keep a fire going all day—that oil guzzler down in the cellar won't keep up with this cold." He stood rubbing his hands together over the warmth of the wood range. "Ben and I are riding up to the high pasture. Got a few early-bred heifers ready to calve mixed in with the rest of the herd up there. Should've brought them down earlier, but this damned leg slowed us down. We can't afford to lose 'em." He headed out for more wood.

"What do I send with you?" Jeanne called after him. "Will you be back for lunch?"

Hank turned at the door. "Just whatever you can throw together in a hurry," he answered, "and no, we won't be back for lunch. We've got an old log shack up there, what's left of a cabin—more like a three-sided lean-to. We'll try to get the heifers in there out of the weather."

Jeanne sliced ham into an iron skillet and while it sizzled on low heat she ran up and dressed in jeans and flannel shirt. By the time Hank had stacked several armloads of wood on the porch, scrambled eggs were firming in the pan and she was putting thick slabs of ham and cheese between pieces of bread.

Hank came in from the back porch with two dusty kerosene lanterns. "I'll put these in the pantry," he said, "and if the electricity goes, set one in the kitchen window and one in the side living-room window so we can see them coming in." He filled his plate and slid into a chair at the table. "I didn't intend to wake you up. It's a long time till morning yet, and you were sleeping so nicely."

"Which must mean I wasn't drooling on the pillow or sleeping with my mouth open," Jeanne commented dryly. "Your intentions were okay, but I would have been really ticked off if I'd woken up to find you'd ridden off into a blizzard!"

Just then Ben came in the back door, accompanied by a gust of cold air and blowing snow. Hank motioned him to the table. "Pull up a chair, Ben. My wife cooked enough for an army!"

Ben sniffed the warm aroma of fried ham and didn't argue. "Lemme go tell Nora not to bother. Keep it hot!" he called over his shoulder as he left for his bungalow.

Hank shook a dollup of catsup on his eggs. "Could you put together some supplies in case we get stuck up there?" he said casually.

Jeanne stared at him. "Stuck up there? For...for how long?"

Hank took a big swig of coffee. "Oh, enough for a couple days, just to be safe." Seeing her widened eyes, he quickly added, "Probably won't happen, but best to be ready. Just grab stuff we could heat over a campfire. There's an old coffeepot and iron skillet in the lean-to. The stuff needs to fit in the saddlebags— bacon, coffee, bread, canned hash and chili, all that kind of thing."

The two men ate quickly, then zipped themselves into their heavy down parkas and gloves. Ben went out, and Hank pulled Jeanne into his arms for a hard, quick kiss. Then he stepped from the warm kitchen into the blowing snow on the porch. "Candles and kerosene lamps are in the pantry, remember," he called over his shoulder. "Take care!"

Take care, Jeanne thought bleakly. "You take care!" she shouted from the doorway, but her voice was lost in the shrieking wind. She went upstairs to make sure the children were sleeping warmly, and found them cuddled snugly together under their blankets and patchwork quilts. She thought about going back to bed, but she was too edgy for sleep, so she turned on the electric heater in the sewing room and finished up the doll clothes for Lisa and Emily.

Fourteen

Although Jeanne hadn't thought it possible, the storm increased in fury. As night finally became morning, daylight only added to her anxiety, when she realized that visibility was less than two feet. Although she could see nothing beyond the wall of blowing snow, her eyes went often to the kitchen window facing the high pasture, where she knew Hank was headed.

It felt like afternoon when the kids finally came downstairs, but the clock said it was only twenty after eight. Blown snow was plastered against the windows, and the combination of howling wind and white windows unnerved the kids, Jeanne could tell. The two younger children looked ready to cry, and Jeanne was especially touched by Tim's and Lisa's attempts to appear unaffected.

"How about teddy-bear pancakes for breakfast?" she asked, hoping to take their minds off the storm.

"Teddy-bear pancakes?" Tim said, ever the cautious one. "I never had them before. Have you, Lisa?"

"No," his sister answered, "but I bet they're good." As Jeanne had hoped, they all gathered around with fears temporarily forgotten as she ladled circles of batter for the bear's head and ears, and gave him chocolate chips for eyes and nose.

The electricity went off just as the ears of the last teddy bear were being eaten. The noise of the storm had been somewhat muted by the distant murmur of television cartoons from the living room and soft carols from the radio on the kitchen counter. In their absence, the sounds of the storm seemed even more menacing than before. "I wish Daddy was here," Lisa said in a small voice.

Oh, honey, so do I! thought Jeanne. Aloud she said, "Come help me get the candles and lamps, kids."

The sound of someone at the back door brought Jeanne a momentary rush of relief, but it was only Nora. She came in, snow crusting her jacket and her stocking cap, which was pulled down over her ears. "I thought you might be afraid," she said, rubbing her hands over the heat of the wood range, "and I wanted to be sure you didn't go outside without using the rope."

"The rope?" Jeanne asked. "What rope?"

"The rope hanging by the back door," Nora answered. "A person could get turned around out there, lose their sense of direction and not be able to get back to the house. There's a rope by your back door and ours, and one out at the barn, too."

Jeanne shivered as she hurried to the sink to fill the coffeepot. No water came from the faucet. "The pump works on electricity," Nora said calmly, turning to get a large soup kettle from the pantry. "You'll have to start a pan of snow melting." Opening the back door, Jeanne saw they wouldn't have to leave the safety of the porch to scoop up snow; the wind had drifted it against the back steps and onto the wooden flooring.

"Nora, what about the men?" Jeanne shouted above the roar of the storm.

Nora closed the door behind them before she answered. "They're holed up in the lean-to with a fire going," she reassured the younger woman. "They know the weather, and the horses know how to get home." But to Jeanne, the words seemed to lack conviction.

Nora stayed only long enough to see that Jeanne and the children were able to manage alone, then pulled on her jacket, stocking cap and boots again. Jeanne urged her to stay, but the older woman shook her head.

"Got to keep the fire going, or we'll have frozen pipes," she explained, "and I turned off the lantern when I left—never safe to leave candles or lamps burning when you're not around to tend 'em." She pulled on her mittens and stopped with her hand on the doorknob. "I've got to get back and light it. They'd see our window sooner than they'd see yours on the way back. It's closer."

The house was cooling rapidly, and Jeanne realized the furnace wasn't working. *Well, of course, you idiot. Even an oil furnace would have an electric motor.* She hurried to add wood to the fire that was almost out in the living-room fireplace.

The day wore on slowly, a continuous round of stoking fires while trying to proceed with the usual tasks of the day so the children wouldn't be frightened. Darkness came early, a gradual dimming of the luminescent whiteness at the windows, and Jeanne had to face the fact that she and the children would probably spend the night alone. She knew the stack of wood on the porch would never last the night, so, instructing the children that Lisa was in charge and they were not to touch the candles or lamps, she pulled on Hank's old work coat and boots, and stepped quickly out the back door.

The wind hit her like a physical blow, and she grabbed in panic for the rope tied to a large hook by the door. It trailed off into the snow, and she pulled steadily until the ice-crusted end was in her hands, then after a moment of indecision, tied it around her waist. With a desperation fueled by wind and fear, she plunged in the direction of the woodshed, filled her arms with logs and plodded back to dump them on the porch. She made trip after trip until she was sure there was enough to last the night, then untied the rope and gratefully stumbled into the warmth of the kitchen.

For a few moments she could do nothing but beat her numb, mittened hands together, but finally stinging needles of pain told her that circulation was returning.

Jeanne heated soup on the wood range for their supper, and by eight o'clock the children were all settled on the living-room floor. Jeanne had carried quilts and blankets from their beds; without the furnace the upstairs was far too cold. She closed off the living room to hold the heat in, hoping that enough warmth from the kitchen stove would creep up the stairs to keep the bathroom pipes from freezing. She sat with the children, reading the old familiar Christmas stories and making up new ones till they finally fell asleep.

Then she brought her paperback mystery from the bedroom, made herself coffee on the wood range and sat with it at the kitchen table. She didn't feel sleepy yet, but didn't want to take a chance on nodding off in the warm comfort of the living-room couch. She had to stay awake, she told herself, to keep the fires stoked. And most importantly, in the kitchen she would be more likely to hear outside noises. What if Hank managed to get close enough that a call for help could be heard over the storm, she thought, and she was sleeping and didn't hear him?

Each time her eyelids began to droop, Jeanne roused herself and made a tour of the house—stoked the fires, pulled the quilts up around the shoulders of the sleeping children—then returned to the kitchen. In the lonely small hours of the morning she made more coffee and sat with it, the paperback facedown on the table. Added to the shrieking of the wind were the small, comfortable inside noises—the fire snapping, the quiet hiss of bubbles rising to the surface of the pot on the stove, the old house creaking as it cooled, the ticking of the grandfather clock in the living room. She hurried in to wind it as she had seen Hank do, relieved that it hadn't started to lose time yet. Then she returned to the kitchen and sat warming her shaking fingers around her coffee cup.

Why am I being so silly? she asked herself. Hank and Ben know what they're doing. They're holed up in that shack, perfectly safe. They're dressed warmly and have food and shelter.

Then the frightened child deep inside took over. What if they weren't able to make it to the shack? What if they couldn't find it and they're riding in circles out there in the blizzard? What if the horse stepped in a hole and broke a leg?

She saw a bleak future without Hank stretching out before her. Oh, yes, they had started all the proper legal steps to protect her and the children if something should happen to Hank. But what would *she* do without him? They'd been so calm and sensible in arranging their marriage, and then somewhere along the way she had fallen in love. Pushing aside the coffee cup, she rested her face on her folded arms and cried quietly.

A small hand stroked her hair, and Lisa pleaded, "Don't be scared. It's only the wind."

Jeanne wiped her face with a flannel-clad forearm. "I know. I guess I'm just…just a sissy. What are you doing up? Did you get cold?"

"No, I think I got too hot. Em was squinched up on one side of me and Joey on the other side. I'm all sweaty—feel my neck." Then, with one of her usual conversational swings, she asked, "What time is it?"

Jeanne looked at her watch. "It's almost three in the morning—Christmas Eve morning."

"I guess Grandma won't be coming, will she?"

"Nope. And we won't be going anyplace, either."

Lisa sighed. "Well, I just want Daddy to get back, that's all. Only us is really all we need to have Christmas."

"You're right," Jeanne agreed, "only us." She shivered. "I'm glad you're awake. I need to go for more wood, and you can be in charge of the lamps."

Fifteen

Plunging through the snow with the rope around her waist, it seemed to Jeanne that the wind was a little less fierce than it had been on her previous trip. In a momentary lull she held her breath while she listened for shouts or the sound of horses. Then the wind renewed its fury, as though trying to make up for the few seconds lost.

Back inside, Jeanne had cocoa with Lisa and then tucked the little girl back under her quilts and blankets. "Stay here till I go to sleep, okay?" Lisa asked.

"Sure," Jeanne answered, sinking gratefully onto the soft couch for just a few minutes.

She woke with a start, uncertain which had awakened her, the cold or the silence. The wind had stopped. She dashed to the kitchen and laid kindling over the embers in the big iron stove, then blew the fire to life. Back in the living room, the children awakened as she stirred the coals in the fireplace. "Stay under the covers till it gets a little warmer," she instructed.

"Is Daddy home yet?" Tim asked.

"No, honey, not yet, but I bet he'll be here soon. The storm is over."

"Is it Christmas yet?" Emily's voice was still sleepy.

Jeanne looked at the grandfather clock. "It's Christmas Eve morning. As soon as it warms up a bit, we're going to put away these blankets and get dressed, and then we're going to make a big pot of vegetable soup to thaw out your daddy when he comes home. Then we're going to finish getting ready for Christmas."

She kept them busy, for her own comfort, as well as theirs. The turkey was thawing in the nonfunctioning refrigerator, and the children crumbled bread for stuffing and pinged frozen cranberries into the pan. They crimped piecrust around the edges and carried cans and jars from the pantry.

Nora came over to check on them midmorning. She accepted a cup of tea from Jeanne and looked around the busy kitchen with a grin. "Well, shoot, I don't have to worry about you folks. You're managing just fine!"

After the brief visit, Jeanne followed Nora to the door where the kids wouldn't hear. "Shouldn't the men be home by now, Nora?" she asked.

Nora gazed out at the white expanse. "No need to worry yet," she said quietly. "The horses'll have to break a trail all the way. It'll be a long trip." She pulled the stocking cap down over her ears. "I'm hopin' they'll get here by dark." She set off for her own house, carefully stepping in the holes she'd made on her trip over.

The sun came out briefly during the day and, combined with the heat from inside, melted the snow that had stuck to the windows. "Look!" Tim cried, "the fences are covered!" Jeanne looked out at the white world with dismay. How could horses struggle home through snow so deep? No fences to guide them, landmarks covered with snow... She turned away from the window.

As the early dusk began to fall, Jeanne refilled the kerosene lamps and set them in the windows. What was she to do? She'd been brave for the children, but her stock of courage was just about used up. Another cold, lonely night to get through, and then it would be Christmas—and no Hank. At what point, she wondered, do Nora or I try to go for help? She lifted the chimney of the lamp and struck a match. As she carefully replaced the glass she heard noise on the back porch. Afraid to get her hopes up this time, she stood motionless until the door swung open.

Hank stumbled in.

She was across the kitchen in a few bounds, in his arms, patting his cold face with her fingertips to prove that he was really, truly there, crying, laughing and talking all at once. "You scared me to death!" she gasped, tears streaking her cheeks. "Don't you ever do that again! Are you all right? How's your ankle? Are you—"

Hank silenced her with his lips. When the long kiss ended, Jeanne rested her head against his chest, the strong thud of his heart comforting her. The four children clamored around them, filling the air with questions.

From city-kid Emily: "Did you save the cow babies, Daddy?"

From Lisa, Tim and Joey: "Did you sleep in the shed? Did the horses drink snow?

From all of them, a chorus of "Daddy, Daddy, tomorrow's Christmas!"

I don't care who says what first anymore, Jeanne thought. To hell with pride. "Oh, Hank, I—"

He interrupted her. "Jeanne, Jeanne—" the words were caresses "—I hadn't told you how much I love you. I kept thinking, what if something happens and I never get to tell her I love her?" His chilled fingers awkwardly brushed the tears from her cheeks and then framed her face as he kissed her again, a kiss so deep she felt herself falling into it.

"Oh," she whispered, "oh, I love you, too—so much!"

At that moment, Jeanne realized she'd become a princess, after all.

DANIEL'S DECEPTION
Marie DeWitt

To El,
My resident computer expert
and best friend

One

Daniel O. Simmons stopped tapping the keyboard just long enough to give his black-framed glasses a little shove back into place.

It had been a long day, a grueling day. To the average businessman, it was the kind of day that can't end soon enough. The kind of day that calls for a good brandy to put it all in perspective.

But to Daniel, this day was the stuff of dreams. Because Daniel absolutely *loved* his work. As Information Systems manager—or resident computer expert—for an insurance company, he'd been putting in twelve-hour days for the past month.

And as if that wasn't enough, he spent his "free" time creating computer programs.

It was a secret to many that Dan had been born with a silver spoon in his mouth and had not discovered computers until the age of thirty. He'd taken to them like a cowboy takes to the local saloon girl after months of celibacy. Now, at the age of thirty-five, Dan was one of the most respected computer directors in the state. Though employed by a small company, he was often called in to troubleshoot for other firms in the area.

Dan gave his glasses another firm push, then returned his fingers to the keyboard. Just a few more minutes, and he'd be through. Much as he'd enjoyed his day with all its challenges, he was looking forward to going home; tonight, he was going to finish his first computer game. He hoped to sell it to an international toy company.

He smiled with genuine satisfaction. A new computer game was about to be born—one that had been nurtured under his watchful eye. Life couldn't get any better than that.

The shrill ring of the phone interrupted his work. He raked his hand through his sandy hair and grabbed the receiver.

"Dan Simmons."

"Dan? This is Becky."

"Hello." Dan cradled the receiver on his shoulder as he exited his own computer program. "Problems?"

Becky cleared her throat. "Well, yes."

"What is it?" he asked, stifling a sigh. Problems in the secretarial department were nothing new. The secretaries ran into computer problems more often than stock car drivers dented their vehicles. "What is it?" He repeated the clipped question, revealing his impatience at being disturbed.

"Uh, could you come down here for a minute?" Becky asked nervously.

Dan groaned inwardly as he glanced at the clock. For once, he didn't want to stay late. There were only fifteen minutes left of the workday. However, he could probably take care of their problems in that time. Then again, he might not be able to. They were notorious for jamming up the works. If it was anyone else, Dan would wait until tomorrow. But he admired Becky's efficiency and knew that if she was calling him at this time of day, it must be important.

"I'll be right there." He replaced the receiver and shut down his own terminal. He began the trek to the second floor and to the secretarial pool—the remedial room, as he privately called it.

As he entered the spacious room, he surveyed the scene. Fourteen terminals sat back-to-back in two rows. Fourteen terminals—which usually meant a *hundred* and fourteen problems. No, a *thousand* and fourteen. No, *ten thousand* and...

Becky motioned to Dan to join her at the very last computer. Her signal was unnecessary, he thought. She stood out from the others. In a room filled with young women, every latest fashion statement was made. But not by Becky. Ever since Dan had known her, she had ignored the fashion trends, preferring sedate business suits or conservative dresses. Navy blue seemed to be her color.

Today was no different. As he walked over to her, he noted her straight, below-the-knee navy skirt with matching jacket. She had unbuttoned the jacket, revealing a tailored white shirt with a crisp collar. Despite her staid, almost old-fashioned appearance, the rest of the women respected her because she had the fastest typing speed this side of the Mississippi. They were right; he'd seen her in action.

Dan didn't care how she looked. He never noticed a woman's appearance. Well, maybe that wasn't quite true. He noticed women all right; appreciated them as much as the next guy. Their hair, their eyes, their legs—especially their legs... But he didn't have the time or the energy to spend on getting to *know* a woman. There was just too much to do. While most young, single men spent their Saturday evenings out on the town, Dan was usually holed up in his apartment researching the latest computer technology or working on his game. He was busy enjoying his newfound freedom and anonymity, and that included freedom from countless social obligations. The fewer people who knew his background, the better.

He made his way toward Becky, glancing at her shapely legs—what he could see of them. One thing about Becky: she had legs that wouldn't quit. He'd sure like to discover the feel of them for himself.... Dan was perturbed by the direction of his thoughts. He didn't have the time or interest to pursue a relationship, he reminded himself. Not at this point in his life, anyway.

Becky smiled as he approached. She had a lovely smile that seemed to light up the already bright room. Some of the secretaries considered Becky a tough supervisor, but Dan didn't agree. In his experience with her, Becky had always seemed reasonable. She was a woman highly committed to her job and to the company. It was evident in everything she did. Her call tonight was a good example. She preferred to deal with a situation immediately. He liked that.

Dan admired the way her long blond hair was neatly held in place by side combs. When she turned, he noticed how it fell in waves down to the middle of her back. He also noticed, as though for the first time, how dainty she looked. Old-fashioned word, dainty. It suited her.

Six feet tall himself, Dan towered over her. Suddenly he itched to touch those small pink-nailed hands; he wanted to feel her skin to see if it was as smooth as it looked. The pearl shirt buttons caught his attention and he followed them—up, up—to the collar that was buttoned primly at her slender neck.

What would it be like to gently unfasten those buttons, kissing her neck, touching her with soft kisses as he made his way lower and lower? His dark brown eyes darkened as they met her cornflower-blue ones. The contact shocked him back to reality. What was the matter with him? Soon, all too soon, his pilgrimage would be over, and he'd be forced to return to California. And he couldn't subject a woman like Becky to his life-style there. She was the type of woman who probably wanted to live in peace and serenity, with a white picket fence, two kids and a dog. A normal, ordinary life. And that was something he could never give her; he could never give it to anyone.

Dan experienced the old familiar twinge of disappointment. As the only heir to the Simmons Corporation, there'd been expectations placed upon him. In fact, with the death of his father a few years ago, the expectations had become an albatross, choking every bit of life from him until he couldn't stand it. So he'd taken off and wound up in Minneapolis, Minnesota, in a normal job with a normal routine. Keeping his identity a secret was wonderful. For the first time in his life, people knew him for the person he was, for his values, his beliefs, his skills, and not as an appendage of an extremely wealthy family. He wanted it to remain this way for as long as possible. For that reason, he knew he had to avoid personal entanglements. And *especially* with a woman like Becky who obviously valued privacy. He knew very well that a romance was out of the question. Now, if his body would only cooperate! Becky was, to put it simply, one good-looker.

She licked her lips nervously when her eyes met Dan's. He was so handsome! Ever since he'd come to work here, she'd noticed him. As he gazed at her, Becky found her mouth going dry. Lord, he was tall! For a man who spent his days at a desk, he certainly had a good build. Even his two-piece, well-pressed brown suit couldn't hide his physique. He always dressed impeccably. Today he wore an off-white shirt with a brown-striped tie. His wavy hair was brushed perfectly into place, the ends of his hair just touching the top of his collar.

He was leaning over her desk, frowning, as he studied her computer screen. He smelled clean and masculine, with a hint of some woodsy after-shave. His long fingers tapped on her keyboard, and the action drew her attention to his gold watch and the onyx ring on his right hand. No, he wasn't married; she knew that. The whole company knew that! She wasn't the only woman who'd been swept away by his good looks.

However, Becky was the only woman who knew this man was out of her league. She sighed. For one thing, he was thirty-five, which made him ten years older than her. And there was something about him. Something hard to define, hard to pin down... And if that wasn't enough to stop her fantasies, all she had to do was remember her disastrous past and her mother's warnings.

Dan Simmons had his pick of women. He'd never even give her the time of day. And if he ever found out the truth, found out what had happened to her, she'd be lucky if he remembered she was alive.

He studied the display on the screen, then asked, "What's the problem?"

Becky forced a smile, dismissing her errant thoughts. "We, uh, can't seem to exit this program," she began as she pushed a lock of hair behind her ear.

Dan was quiet for a minute. "Did you follow my directions on that sheet I handed out?" Silence. She was staring at her feet. "Becky, did you hear what I said?"

"Yes," she replied faintly, gripping the back of her chair.

She licked her lips again. Dan saw the action and experienced a tightening in his stomach.

She raised her eyes to his. As supervisor, she'd called on him any number of times. But today was different somehow. *He* was different somehow.

She swallowed before she said again, softly, "Yes, I did, but I think I need you to explain a few things to me."

Dan leaned over and quickly pushed a couple of keys. Within seconds, the program was gone and the main menu displayed. "Sure," he said distractedly as he shut down the terminal.

Becky glanced at her watch. "Oh, I didn't mean right now. It's almost five. How about when you have a few moments in the next day or so?"

Dan watched her silently. For a woman a few years out of college, she handled herself very professionally. Although he was determined to ignore the attraction he felt for her, he'd made it his business to find out as much as he could. It had been easy—he'd just listened to gossip in the lunchroom.

Becky Thorpe, age twenty-five, lived alone in a small downtown apartment. She'd graduated summa cum laude with a degree in business and took this job three years ago. Dan could see that she performed her job flawlessly, but kept to herself except for Sarah Swan, who worked over in Accounting.

And from Sarah, he'd managed to learn—by way of casual questioning—that Becky was originally from Eaton, Minnesota, a small farming community north of the Twin Cities. She had only one living relative—her mother, who still lived in the farmhouse that Becky grew up in.

So Dan had all the superficial information that he needed. But he realized he wanted more. Why was she such a loner? Why wasn't she married? Did she date? If so, who? Did she like classical music, soft rock or jazz? What was her favorite food? And why did she look as if she hid some inner sadness? All right, so he *was* interested in her. There. He'd admitted it. Maybe it was time to act. The computer game didn't seem so important tonight, after all. Besides, he rationalized, their relationship could be strictly platonic, couldn't it?

Nonchalantly he glanced at his watch. "It is five, isn't it?" He cupped his chin in his hand. "How about a hamburger across the street, while I tell you about the program?"

Dan watched as she considered his suggestion. Frowning, she bit the tip of her nail. Why was she so uncomfortable? He'd only suggested an informal, impromptu meal. What was she afraid of? Him? He didn't think so. Yet if he was a good judge of character—and he believed he was—he'd say she definitely seemed uneasy.

Dan didn't like the fact that he apparently made her nervous. He wanted her to relax with him; yes, dammit, he wanted to get to know her better. Irritably, he jammed his hand into his pants pocket.

Becky stared at him in disbelief. He was asking her to have supper with him? Okay, it was just a hamburger at the fast-food place across the street, but it had been a long time since any man had requested her company. Correction. It had been a long time since she'd *allowed* any man to request her company. It was just safer that way.

Until now. She thought about all the nights she ate alone. Suddenly she knew she wouldn't be able to bear another evening like that, not when she could be eating with a very exciting, attractive man. Even if it *was* work-related. One mistake in a person's life didn't mean she had to give up everything, did it? Besides, what harm was there in going out for a hamburger with the man? As long as she remembered that, things would be fine.

Becky's mind was made up. "Thank you. That sounds fine," she said resolutely. "Just let me grab my coat, all right?"

Dan nodded. "I'll meet you at the front entrance. I need to clean up my desk first."

"All right." Dan was treated to a smile. All of a sudden, he was filled with pleasure that he was the person who'd put that smile on her face. For a young woman, she sure didn't smile often. Maybe he could change that.

He hummed softly to himself as he returned to his office.

Becky was waiting for him when he arrived at the doorway. It was early October and the air was chilly, so she'd put on a dark blue coat that covered practically all of her. Where the hemline ended, her shoes peeked out. She clutched her navy shoulder bag as though it was a life jacket and she was about to board the *Titanic*. Dan wished he could put her at ease.

She watched him approach and tried not to stare. He was just a man, she reminded herself. Maybe if she said it often enough she would begin to believe it. Just a man? Dan Simmons embodied every aspect of masculinity she knew. Of course, this wasn't a true date. That knowledge gave her enough courage to continue with the evening. Because if it *was* a date, she'd have run as fast as she could in the opposite direction. Before anything else happened.

"Shall we?" Dan held the heavy glass door open for her, nodding her along.

"Thanks." She hadn't been reduced to one-word answers for a long time. Right now, though, one-word answers seemed all she could manage.

Crossing Second Avenue took hardly any time. In tense silence, they waited for the signal to change and walked toward the little restaurant. While traffic in downtown Minneapolis would be congested right now, here, in the suburb of Roseville, where the insurance company's offices were, things moved more slowly. Becky loved living in the Twin Cities. When she'd decided to relocate here, she had been delighted by all the concerts, plays and movies there were to see. By the museums, galleries and sports events she longed to attend. So far, she hadn't been to any of them.

Dan's hand rested lightly on the small of her back. His gesture gave her an unfamiliar sense of security. He was a real gentleman, she thought. How lucky for the woman in his life!

As they entered the small restaurant he commented, "Well, I suppose we should brace ourselves for the upcoming Minnesota winter." Becky knew she should respond with more small talk about the weather, the city, the job—anything. But she just couldn't. All she could do was murmur an agreement.

Dan located a booth by the window, then helped her slip her coat from her shoulders. His touch made her shiver.

"Cold?"

Becky shook her head. "Not really."

She slid into the booth and Dan leaned toward her. "What can I get for you?"

Reaching for her purse, she replied, "A hamburger and fries, I guess."

Dan's hand rested on hers. "Put your purse away. My treat."

"Oh, you don't have to—"

"I know," he interrupted. "I want to. All right?"

His smile was broad, reassuring, and it displayed two dimples she'd never noticed before. How she could have failed to notice *anything* about him was a mystery to her. It had been years since she'd been interested in a man. Six years ago, she'd vowed never to let a man get close to her again. And until now she'd succeeded. Until Dan.

She couldn't deny it any longer. He was handsome and kind, always willing to help. He had an easy manner and charm to spare. Everyone in the office wondered why he kept to himself. Maybe he was like her, she thought, just needing a little privacy. Whatever the reason, she understood. Sometimes it was just easier to be alone; that way, no one could hurt you.

His touch made her knees weaken, and she was glad she was sitting down. "All right," she quietly agreed.

His finger touched the tip of her nose. "Don't go away. I'll be right back."

Becky watched as he strolled confidently to the counter and placed their order, then paid for the meal, the waitress beaming happily all the while. No woman was immune!

Becky sighed and leaned back as she let the soft vinyl cushion her neck. She closed her eyes for a moment, feeling drained, exhausted. She'd kept herself busy with work, taking any overtime she could get—not only to avoid social pressures, but to make extra money. With her mother's arthritis worsening, Becky had to send more money to cover the needed medications.

Her father, a farmer, had died three years before, leaving no insurance money. Until his death, they hadn't known he'd not bothered to provide for his family. It hadn't been difficult to obtain health insurance for herself, but her mother was a different story. Her preexisting illnesses made her virtually uninsurable. So Becky was left with the outrageous medical bills that her mother's arthritis and asthma caused. She moved to the Twin Cities where her skills would be highly paid. Leaving her mother and the family farm hadn't been easy. She worried constantly about her mother living alone, but there was nothing she could do about it. Marge Thorpe had refused to move with her.

Becky didn't mind taking care of her mother financially. It was the least she could do. Her parents had always stood behind her, especially when her world had caved in. She owed them everything.

A few minutes later, Dan returned to the table and found her with her eyes closed. "Hey, are you falling asleep?" He grinned as Becky's eyes flew open and she sat up straighter.

She smoothed her hair unnecessarily. "Oh, sorry. I was just resting my eyes."

Dan placed the tray of food on the table before he slid into the seat opposite hers. "Staring at a computer screen all day is hard on the eyes."

"Mmm." Becky smiled as she took the hamburger from him. Then he handed her an order of fries, a large Coke and a cherry pie. "I don't think I'll be able to eat all this," she mumbled.

Dan had chosen the same meal for himself. He bit enthusiastically into a french fry. "I love these," he stated, before squirting a dollop of catsup on the plate. "Of course you'll be able to eat all this. It's been a long day, hasn't it?"

"That it has." Becky opened her cardboard box, revealing a double-decker hamburger smothered with tomatoes, lettuce and pickles. "It's been a long time since I've gone out for fast food."

He thought it must've been a while since Becky had done much of anything just for the fun of it, but he'd be a fool to say so. He watched as she took her first bite. But while the experience was obviously pleasant for her, it made him damned uncomfortable. The woman made eating a plain old hamburger a sensual experience. After all these years, he would have thought he was far too old for the kind of thoughts he was having. Why was it that in one short hour his self-imposed celibacy had suddenly become a burden? Sensual awareness of Becky Thorpe seemed to occupy his entire nervous system! True, he'd thought of her almost daily. Yet these had been only passing thoughts; brief fantasies he managed to keep under control. Until tonight. A man couldn't dream forever; desire had finally caught up with him.

Right now, she was swirling a fry in her own catsup, looking like she was enjoying every minute of it. When was the last time he'd seen anyone take such delight in simple things? Back home in California, life had been complex and fast-paced. Because of his father's success, Dan had had everything a boy could want—the latest dirt bike, the flashiest sports car, anything he asked for. Then he'd grown up and decided that life was more than the accumulation of material wealth. Life meant taking delight in small things, experiencing the moment, sharing with others. Tonight he was watching a woman eating a hamburger with obvious pleasure. It was wonderful.

"Looks like you're enjoying it," he commented, determined to keep things friendly and straightforward. If she knew how her actions inflamed him, she'd take off running.

She nodded, touching the side of her mouth with her napkin, and Dan silently cringed. Didn't she have any idea how *appealing* she was?

She shrugged. "I never seem to have a chance to eat out."

He'd often noticed her in the company lunchroom, eating her sandwich from a brown sack as she read a library book. Usually she sat alone; sometimes she was with her friend Sarah. He'd also noticed that she avoided all the company's social events.

"Then you're too busy," Dan ventured. "You need time to go out, have fun."

"It can't be helped."

Dan frowned, dipping another fry into catsup. "What can't be helped?"

"Oh, just work, that's all."

"You live alone, don't you?"

"That's right. How'd you know?"

Dan tried to appear nonchalant as he answered. "Oh, I just assumed it."

"How about you? You live by yourself? What about your family?"

Dan knew she had changed the focus of their conversation to him. For now, he'd go along with it. "I live alone, too," he replied. "In a town house on Snelling."

Becky listened as he mentioned one of the main streets in town.

He went on, "My mother lives in Los Angeles."

She shook her head. "That's so far away. What brings you out here?"

Dan sighed, finishing his hamburger before he answered. "Just wanted to try things alone for a while." While his statement ended the topic, she was sure there was more to Dan than he'd said. Men just didn't pop out of nowhere these days—especially sophisticated men who wore obviously hand-tailored, expensive suits.

The rest of the meal passed with the usual light conversation. Becky was surprised to find herself relaxing; she even contributed her share of banter. They found that they both enjoyed listening to jazz and soft rock, liked Italian food and thought the Minnesota Twins had a good chance to win the World Series.

Becky couldn't remember when she'd had more fun.

"I'm stuffed," she said at last, picking up the cardboard box that held her pie. "And I haven't even had a bite of this."

Dan was just finishing his dessert. He looked up and grinned. "Take it home, then. A midnight snack."

Becky laughed, dropping it into her purse. "You talked me into it."

"Good." Dan didn't know why he felt so inordinately pleased that she'd enjoyed the cheap meal. He just knew that he did.

"Come on." He was on his feet, offering his hand to help her slide out of the booth.

She placed her small hand in his large one. The touch seemed magnetic, and they stared at each other for just a minute. Becky was the first to look away, but Dan was the first to speak. Holding out her coat, he said, "I'll walk you to your car."

"I take the bus."

"You don't have a car?" Dan asked. How did she manage in a large city like this without a car?

Becky shook her head. "Never got around to getting one." She looked at his expression and laughed. "It's not that bad. The buses are convenient."

"Well, not tonight." Dan helped her put her coat on, his fingers resting longer than necessary on her shoulders. Slowly, and very gently, he put his hand under her hair, lifting it over the collar of her coat before his hands smoothed it back into place. Becky shivered. She was having a hard time remembering that he probably had several women at his beck and call.

"It's perfectly safe." She managed to find her voice.

"Uh-uh, not tonight. I'm driving you home," he insisted.

"You don't—"

"Yes, I do." His face softened as he looked at her. "Now, don't argue."

"But—"

He put his finger to her lips to silence her. Just his touch was enough to jolt her into silence. She'd better give up before anything else happened. So she simply nodded.

"That's better." He ushered her out of the restaurant. Walking quickly to the office parking lot, he helped her into his black, midsize, luxury car. Getting into the driver's seat, he reached over to fasten her seat belt. The closeness unnerved her, and she was glad the darkness hid her reaction. The car hummed softly to life, and with one flick of his finger, quiet instrumental music flooded the air. Becky reveled in the comfort. Except for a brief exchange about the best route to her apartment, they were silent.

When they arrived at her building, Dan parked the car and began to unfasten his seat belt. Becky's hand on his arm stopped him. "I'll say good night here."

Dan shook his head. "I'll see you to your door."

"No." She inwardly cringed as she realized how clipped her answer sounded. But she couldn't help it. In some vague yet certain way, she sensed that allowing him into her building meant allowing him into her life. She couldn't risk it. Even after all this time, what Michael had done to her still festered. Although something told her Dan was different, and she wanted to trust him, she just couldn't. Not yet.

"Please, let's say good night here."

"No, I insist on walking you to the door."

Becky shook her head. "I'll be fine. It's not that late."

Dan gave up. Whatever her reasons for ending the evening out here, he had to honor her request. She was a private person, and he didn't want to rush things. Intruding in her life too quickly would only make her run in the opposite direction.

Fear. Looking at her right now, as the streetlight cast a warm glow over her features, Dan saw fear in her eyes. But why? Who or what had put that fear there?

He raised his hand to her cheek, gently stroking the smoothness of her skin. "All right," he whispered. "But I'm going to kiss you."

Becky started to draw away, but Dan had placed his left arm around her, resting it on her back as he coaxed her to him. "Don't be afraid. I'd never hurt you." His last words were spoken in a whisper, the warmth of his breath fanning her face. His right hand sneaked under her hair, cradling her neck, tilting her head toward him. "All right?" She thought she saw a faint smile, but she wasn't sure. Everything blurred as he bent closer, closer, until their mouths touched....

The feeling was like nothing Becky had ever experienced. When he said he was going to kiss her, she'd wanted to run—and run fast. But she didn't. She had to find out if she could be kissed by a truly decent person without the panic and fear she remembered so well.

His kiss was gentle, tender, soft and sensuous all at once. And she felt herself responding, matching his kiss with her own, giving back the tenderness he was giving her.

He stopped much too soon. Yet he seemed unhurried as his hand stroked the back of her neck. "Good night," he murmured before his lips touched her forehead, her nose, her cheek in little kisses that rained delight. "Say good night, Becky," Dan teased.

Becky looked up, her arms braced on his for support. "Good night. And . . . thank you."

"My pleasure," Dan returned. "I always enjoy feeding hungry, gorgeous women."

She blushed at the compliment, letting him believe that the meal was exactly what she was thanking him for. It wasn't. She was thanking him for that kiss, which had opened the window to her heart, just a little. It had been so long.

She hurried out of the car and waved. Dan made sure she was safely inside the building before he drove off.

Later, in bed, she realized they hadn't even mentioned the computer program she was supposed to learn that night.

TWO

The next morning Becky awoke to the sound of a ringing telephone. Glancing at her alarm clock, she groaned. Almost time to get up. Sleepily she groped for the phone.

"Hello?"

"Good morning, darling," the soft voice replied.

"Mom." Becky sat up, smiling. "You sound good, Mom."

"Oh, I am, darling. You'll never guess what I've just done."

It wasn't unusual for Marge Thorpe to begin a new hobby or adventure. Her health problems slowed her down, but she kept trying new things. It was her mother's infectious zest for living that gave Becky the encouragement to go on after her disastrous love affair. If you could even call it a love affair.

"What are you trying now, Mom?" She cradled the receiver on her shoulder as she reached for her hairbrush.

"I pulled out that quilt we were working on last year. Do you remember it?"

"Sure I do," Becky returned. "It was that wedding-ring pattern. I'll never forget how hard we worked on that thing. It was way too ambitious a project for one week of vacation."

Marge chuckled. "We did work, didn't we? But I thought I'd finish it and enter it in the annual craft show. It's in a couple of weeks, you know."

"Already? I didn't realize how fast the time's going. Just don't work too hard, Mom, all right?" Becky was worried; her mother tended to overdo and then pay the price later. "Are you taking your medication faithfully?"

"Oh, Becky," her mother said, "you don't have to worry so much. Of course I'm taking the medicine, but I've never felt better."

"Good." Becky stood up. "I have to go, Mom. I need to get ready for work."

"It is that time, isn't it? I wouldn't have bothered you this morning, but I tried last night and you didn't answer."

"I was out, Mom."

"Obviously." Marge hesitated for a minute. "With your friend Sarah?"

"No, Mom, not Sarah."

"Darling, it wasn't a man, was it?"

Becky shut her eyes. She couldn't lie to her mother, but she knew what was coming. "Yes, it was."

"Oh, do be careful, Becky," her mother warned. "I don't want to see you hurt again."

"He won't hurt me, Mom."

"And how do you know that?"

Becky smiled, thinking about Dan. "He's nice. He's helped me at work so many times I feel I know him already."

Marge waited a minute, then said, "You haven't always been the best judge of character, dear. I don't mean to remind you, but..."

"I know, Mom. I really have to go. It's getting late."

"All right," Marge answered. "Be careful, you hear?"

"Yes, I will," Becky answered patiently. "I'll be looking forward to seeing that quilt."

"It'll be done soon," Marge predicted. "Perhaps you could come home for the craft show?"

Becky twisted the telephone cord. "I might just do that." She gave a small laugh. "Then I could check up on you."

Exasperated, her mother replied, "I'm not a child, Becky."

"Humor me, okay, Mom?"

"All right. I love you, Becky."

"Love you, too, Mom. G'Bye."

Becky hung up, then glanced at the time. She'd have to hurry. Punctuality was important to her; she'd never once been late for work.

"I'll see if I can restore the files." Dan finished speaking with the personnel manager just as his second line buzzed. Another call. He'd never finish if things were going to keep interrupting him. Thanks to his evening with Becky, his computer game—Daniel's Revenge—was still unfinished.

He thought for a minute, still holding the phone receiver against his ear. Not that last evening had been a washout. Far from it. Becky was delightful, in an unpretentious sort of way. He suspected that the clothes she wore were purposely selected to allow her to fade into the background. But it didn't work.

Dan smiled as he remembered how her suit clung to her petite frame, showing off her feminine curves. She was lovely, and he wanted to touch her, slowly and sweetly. He wanted to hold her.

And her taste. The little kiss last night had been wonderful. He felt his body respond accordingly as he imagined how it would be to make slow, tender love with her, to have her respond to him as a woman. He was curious to see just what was under those clothes. Would her lingerie be just as discreet and simple? Or outrageously feminine? Lace? Silk?

He cleared his throat and ran his finger under his collar. This was not the time to be daydreaming. He knew from company gossip that she hadn't dated anyone recently, but that didn't mean he was the right man for her. His life—his real life—was demanding, harried and public. Very public. In a few short months, he'd have to return to the family business in California. He found himself thinking about it often, dreading it. No, that wasn't the kind of life for a woman like Becky; he was more sure of that than ever. She valued her privacy too much. She hadn't even wanted him in her apartment building last night! So why was he suddenly thinking these crazy thoughts about big feather beds and white picket fences, about falling in love...and getting married? He hardly knew her! But he did know that she had nothing in common with who he really was.

She enjoyed the simple pleasures in life, like that hamburger last night. Once in California, Dan knew his meals were far more likely to be five-course lobster or steak dinners, eaten with business associates.

And then there was his mother. No, there were just too many obstacles.

He was struggling to keep his perspective. Their kiss last night had been just that—a warm, cozy kiss. Short and sweet. That was all it was for her. Just a kiss. And for him, too. Wasn't it?

He'd never allowed his mind to wander like this before. Determinedly he punched the button on his phone. ''Dan Simmons here.''

''It's me, darling,'' a pleasant voice crooned to him. Dan grimaced. He should have written sooner.

''Hello, Mother,'' he answered dutifully. ''How are you?''

''I'm just fine, Daniel. But I miss you. And I haven't heard from you in a while, so I thought I'd do the motherly thing and check up on my one and only child.''

''I'm sorry, Mom. I should have written or called.''

''As long as you're all right.''

Twisting a paper clip into a yet-to-be-defined shape, Dan listened to his mother. Audrey Simmons was one of a kind. Left alone when his dad died, she'd insisted that Dan continue with his own life and not worry about her. She'd encouraged him to leave California, to sow the proverbial wild oats. To experience a different kind of life—for a while. In time, he knew, she expected him back, running the company his father had worked long and hard to develop and make flourish. Both he and his mother wanted it to continue to flourish. They were beginning to branch out, marketing their gourmet coffees, teas and desserts in Europe and Canada. They didn't need him now, did they?

He began straightening the paper clip. "Mom, you worry too much. I'm fine. Uh, is everything going smoothly there?"

His mother chuckled before she replied. "Yes, of course. And a mother *is* entitled to worry." She paused briefly, then continued, "Daniel, I'd like to see you. We could have the jet at Minneapolis-St. Paul International in a few hours. How about it? There's a stockholders' party in—"

"No, Mother. Not now." Dan firmly interrupted his mother's plans. While he loved her dearly, and while he was willing, eventually, to assume company responsibilities, Dan didn't think he'd ever be able to live the highly social, highly visible life of a business tycoon.

As the only child of Audrey and Owen Simmons, it was taken for granted that he would step into his father's shoes, and become the company's CEO.

In a few years, he would, but right now he was enjoying his life in Minneapolis. He treasured his anonymity. For the past few years, he had succeeded in fooling the press. Absolutely no one had connected him with the Simmons empire, and he'd been free to continue his employment in the computer field unknown.

He stayed away from California, venturing there only at Christmas and on June twelfth, the day on which his baby sister had died twenty years earlier, of sudden infant death syndrome. Keeping to this strict schedule had been difficult, because he was aware how much his mother missed him. But for the first time in his life, Dan knew the freedom he'd always craved—the chance to do what he wanted, with no one's expectations to satisfy but his own. And he loved it.

"Mother, we've been through this before. The press follows you everywhere. They'll find out about me and that'll be the end of my life here. I don't mean to sound selfish, but I'm not ready to come back yet."

"Daniel Owen Simmons, what am I going to do with you?" His mother's voice rang out, clear and crisp.

"Mom, just be patient, please?" Dan leaned back in his chair, tossing the bent wire across his desk and into the trash.

"All right," Audrey replied, obviously resigned to the fact that she wouldn't be visiting him. "But this party is special. Frank Putnam is bringing his daughter, Alicia, and I wanted you to meet her. And what's the point of having a jet if you can't use it for your own purposes?"

Dan rolled his eyes and stifled a groan. "No, Mother. For Pete's sake, stay away from Minneapolis with that jet. I'd be forced to move on after that kind of publicity."

"Or move home."

"Not yet." Dan's voice was low. "I told you. I'll come back to Los Angeles when I'm ready."

"Daniel, really. Haven't you tired of Minneapolis by now? I want to see you."

"And see me married, I'm sure," Dan added.

Audrey chuckled. "Well, that too, of course. I'm not getting any younger dear, and I *would* like a grandchild or two."

Dan winced. This was the area in which he felt particularly guilty. He knew how desperately his mother wanted grandchildren. If she could have had more children of her own, he was certain he'd have several brothers or sisters. But it hadn't happened, and Audrey was content with Dan—as she'd assured him many times.

Dan wanted to fulfill his mother's wishes, all of them. But right now, he just couldn't. Especially not after last night...

It was practically through divine intervention that last night had gone so well. And he wanted more. He wanted to part those warm, welcoming lips of Becky's. He wanted to hold her, touch her, experience that softness he'd imagined so many times.

It would be wonderful to hear her laugh, to be able to chase that sadness from her face and replace it with joy.

But he had no right to hope for these things.

Because he couldn't tell Becky who he was, not now, when they'd only begun to know each other. Someone had already made her shy, fearful, afraid to trust. He didn't need to read her mind to know that she'd turn away from him the minute she learned he'd already deceived her.

Deceitful. Like it or not, that's what he was by not telling her the truth. He would tell her, though. Soon. Or so he promised himself.

He was not about to express his fears and doubts to his mother. On the one hand, he couldn't reject the very life his parents had worked so hard to give him. But he wasn't willing to give up his chance for a relationship with Becky, either.

"I'll see you soon, Mother."

"All right, Daniel," Audrey answered. "But I do miss you. I love you, you know."

Dan smiled. "I know, Mom. I'll talk to you later."

Before he pulled the phone away from his ear, his mother added, "Daniel?"

"Yes, Mom?"

"How much longer, do you think, before you come home for good?"

Dan sighed as he raked his fingers through his hair. "Probably in a few months, Mother."

"Good. I'll look forward to that. Goodbye, darling."

"'Bye, Mom." Dan hung up just as a wave of nausea flooded him. It was always like that. The thought of going home rattled him; he couldn't help it. It wasn't the work or the business decisions or even the social obligations; it was the public scrutiny. He no more wanted his private life scrutinized than he wanted root-canal work. But there was no use fighting it.

If only he could grab that brass ring before he left Minneapolis. Being a success in the business world wasn't enough. He'd finally found a woman who interested him, and he was determined to have some time with her.

After observing her these past months in the office, Dan knew that Becky was different from any woman he'd ever known. He'd watched her do little things for her coworkers. When one of them had a problem, Becky was there, cheering the person with a small plant or some freshly baked cookies. She'd been the one to decorate the office for Christmas. During her lunch hour, he'd noticed her reading, obviously absorbing every word.

It was plain to see that underneath her quiet exterior was a woman with a passion for living. And he wanted to be the one she smiled for, cared for. And he wanted to care for her. He'd worry about the complications later.

It was late in the afternoon when Becky found herself outside Dan's office. She traced the letters carved into the nameplate on the door: "Daniel O. Simmons, Manager, MIS." Such a common name. There must be thousands of people called Simmons. But there was only one as far as she was concerned. A most uncommon man.

A brief smile curved her lips as she thought of the night before. She'd always wanted to get to know him. For the first time since Michael, she really wanted a man to be interested in her. But with her limited experience, she suspected that was going to be difficult. She sighed. If only things had worked out differently for her... But none of that mattered now.

She knocked sharply.

"Come in." The voice was muffled, indistinct. Not sure she'd heard correctly, she knocked again.

"I said, come in!" The voice was clearer now, and Becky opened the door just in time to see Dan crawling out from under his desk. His six-foot frame looked comical emerging from the small space.

"Just fixing a loose connection to the terminal," he explained as he brushed off his dark blue slacks and jacket. The process pulled the fabric taut over some of his more intriguing body parts.

Becky's face turned rosy as she realized she'd been staring. One look at Dan and she knew he'd noticed. Well, it was too late. So she'd been looking, all right?

"Hi." Dan noticed how her black skirt outlined her shapely hips, then fell in soft folds. His eyes trailed upward as she walked toward him. She wore a lilac blouse underneath the black suit jacket. Her long blond hair was pulled back into a French braid with a few tendrils escaping. Small pearl earrings were her only jewelry. She looked lovely. He swallowed hard.

"Uh . . . did you need to see me, Becky?"

She glanced down at the manila folder in her hand. "About this."

"What about it?"

Becky gestured to a chair set against the wall. "May I?"

"Of course."

Settling herself in the blue upholstered chair, she placed the work in her lap, then folded her hands primly on top. Dan thought she looked like a schoolgirl ready for a lesson.

"May I see it?" he asked.

It was hard to keep her mind on business when he stood there, looking so handsome. "Oh—oh, yes, of course," she mumbled.

While Dan sorted through the papers, she noticed her surroundings. This was the first time she'd actually been inside his office. It was tastefully decorated in shades of blue and gray. From the carpeting to the draperies, everything was perfectly coordinated.

"I had a good time last night," Dan said casually.

"Me, too." Becky was at a loss for words. Why did that always happen around him? Were old memories always going to get in the way, making her uneasy around men? Around *him?* Since last night, Becky realized that she

wanted her past to be just that—her past. She had used it as
a shield long enough. She wanted to *feel* again, to know
what it was like to be held, to be wanted. Last night had just
intensified this need. Maybe Dan would understand about
Michael . . . and the baby . . . and everything.

"Becky, did you hear me?" Dan waved his hand across
her face to get her attention. "This is your proposal for the
new color monitors on your floor. It looks fine to me."

"Good."

Dan smiled as he realized he'd been right. There *was*
something between them. An attraction, a mutual interest.
He briefly studied the folder, then passed it back to her.
Their hands touched, and Becky was reminded of the kiss
last night. So short, but so wonderful. She'd never felt as
wonderful as she had last night.

It was happening again. Just being in the same room with
Dan, noticing how he looked at her, she felt desirable, even
beautiful.

He was obviously attracted to her, too, she thought. *And
that's all there is to it. Just attraction.*

"Where were you?" He met her eyes. "You seemed a
million miles away."

She shrugged. "A thousand maybe. Certainly not a million."

What could she say? That she'd been wondering how to
tell him about her sordid past? She gave her head a slight
shake. She couldn't risk it; it might ruin everything. She
liked Dan. But this was more than sexual attraction, she had
to admit. He was a genuinely nice person, one who really
seemed to care about other people. Now that she knew he
was interested in her and she was falling for him, common
sense and past mistakes told her to be very careful. She'd
believed she loved someone once, and all it had brought her
was heartache. Becky couldn't forget. She mustn't.

Now what? Dan asked himself. Forget the whole thing?
If he was smart, that was what he'd do. Stop it now before
they went too far. Before he cared too much, loved too much

and, ultimately, hurt too much. But he couldn't. Already his body was betraying him, his mind following close behind. Here was a woman he could be friends with and more, a woman he could fall in love with. Could he risk it? Should he? Lord help him, he wanted to. And he *would* find a way to chase the sadness from those round eyes of hers, dammit. He just prayed he didn't put more sadness there.

"I'm working on a new computer game," Dan said abruptly. "I'd, uh, like to get your reaction. If you're interested . . ."

Becky nodded, eyes shining.

"You would?"

"Sure. If you don't think it'll be too technical for me." Becky pushed a strand of hair behind her ear. Dan watched the movement, every part of his body stimulated by that small action. What would it feel like to run his own fingers through her hair?

"How about tonight?"

"Tonight?" She swallowed. "I—I don't know."

Dan watched her hesitancy and again saw that closed look in her eyes. There was a part of her she wasn't willing to share. "Why not?" he persisted. "In fact, I have the disk with me and I could show you after work."

"You mean here?"

"Sure. It's in my briefcase, in case I felt like working on it during lunch."

Becky laughed. "You certainly are dedicated to the project."

Dan chuckled. "Either that or obsessed with it." He arched an eyebrow. "How about it?"

"Sure."

"Good. Is around five-thirty all right?"

She glanced at her watch. "Perfect. It gives me enough time to tie up some loose ends at my desk."

"Do you like Chinese food?"

"I love it," she told him, "but I'm not too good with chopsticks."

Dan laughed. "Neither am I."

She enjoyed watching this man laugh. His laughter was full-bodied, uninhibited. Gone was the serious businessman; a playful, lighthearted man stood in his place. She was seeing a side of him that she'd never known existed.

She grinned. "Tonight, then."

He smiled back. "Strictly forks."

"See you then." She walked out of his office, unaware of the appealing sexiness of her walk. But Dan wasn't.

Three

"Now, if you press 'escape,' you can go back one screen to check your position before going on."

Becky was only half listening. The game seemed interesting enough, but she was too conscious of the man sitting next to her. Since he was engrossed in his technology, she had the freedom to study him. He was tall, lean and lanky, with just the right amount of muscle, she decided. He'd removed his suit jacket and rolled up the sleeves of his light blue shirt. With his tie gone and the top two shirt buttons opened, Becky was treated to a glimpse of the light brown hair that curled underneath. It was downright tempting. But what could she do about it? The sad fact was that Becky Thorpe hadn't a clue how to seduce a man—or even if she should. Her time with Michael had been brief, limited to one experience when he'd seduced her on a night she'd drunk too much wine.

But things were different this time. She was falling in love with the man. She hadn't expected it to happen, hadn't even been thinking about it. She'd seen him every day, worked closely with him when computer problems arose, and this attraction had just developed, taking on a life of its own. Sneaking up on her. She hadn't been able to stop it, even though she'd done her best to ignore it. And then the other night when they'd had dinner together, she knew it was too late. She was halfway in love with Dan Simmons, and heaven help her, she wanted more than a professional relationship with him. She wanted a personal relationship.

And that meant a physical relationship. Now, with a sudden, frightening urgency, she wanted to seduce this man. Tonight, and every night for the rest of their lives. She was ready to try. To be open, warm and willing. But how? Oh, she knew all the corny lines. She watched movies. "Where have you been all my life?" "Isn't it warm in here?" "Why don't I slip into something more comfortable?" She was sure the last one could only be used if they were in *her* apartment, but the others didn't seem likely to work, either. If they were drinking something—say a vintage wine— she could accidentally spill it on him. Even then, she'd risk dumping some in the computer, and any idiot knew that wouldn't gain her any bonus points. She sighed audibly.

"Becky?" Dan turned toward her. "Are you listening?"

"What?" Becky nervously bit her lip.

The intercom buzzed before he could answer. Dan leaned behind the terminal to shut the computer off. "Never mind. I think that's our food."

Becky stood and smoothed her long skirt, and while he left the office she walked over to the grouping of chairs in the far end of his office. Noticing the glass end table between the two chairs, she smiled. A plant would look nice there, perhaps a golden pothos. Then there was that blank wall above his desk. The perfect place for a wildlife scene. Pheasants, maybe.

Her eyes fell on the bookcase and she walked closer. When she'd first entered Dan's office, she'd noticed his collection of books, ranging from computers to the latest psychology. Now, as she made a more careful study, she frowned. If she wasn't mistaken, the top shelf held some very expensive-looking leather-bound volumes. Classics, possibly first editions. Where did a computer manager get that kind of money?

But that wasn't the only thing. Around the office, the gossip was that Dan played a good game of golf. After the company tournament, people had talked about his expensive equipment. Somehow, that didn't fit Becky's picture of the dedicated, hardworking man with no time for anything but computers. He'd managed to raise everyone's curiosity, Becky's included.

"The food's here," Dan announced as he came back in.

Ignoring the questions crowding her mind, Becky looked up and smiled when Dan walked toward the desk, two white cartons and a brown paper sack in his hands.

"Let's eat! I'm starved." Dan motioned her over, and offered her one of the egg rolls. The chopsticks caught her eye.

He pointed to them. "We have to use these."

Becky frowned at him. "You're kidding, aren't you?"

"I'm not."

"You said forks," she reminded him.

Dan shrugged innocently. "I lied," he replied. "Come on. Let's try them."

He chuckled at her mock fury, realizing how much fun it was to spend an evening relaxing, enjoying life at a leisurely pace. Doing simple, ordinary things.

Glancing at Becky as she wielded the chopsticks made him realize that he wanted to share those everyday experiences with her. Maybe it was only a dream. If she learned the truth about him, she'd probably bolt. But right now, they had time and opportunity. He ignored the warning bells going off in his head and showed her the correct way to hold the chopsticks.

"There, see?" Becky said after a couple of minutes. "How am I doing?"

"Fine, just fine." Warmed by her lovely smile, Dan grasped a piece of chicken, smiling himself. Even the food tasted unusually good. Becky seemed as excited, as uncomplicated, as a kid. Were simple pleasures really the best? he mused. He'd always suspected it.... With his thoughts engrossing him, he clumsily dropped a water chestnut.

"I can't seem to do this tonight," he muttered.

She laughed. "You're the one who showed me."

Dan shrugged. He loved it when she laughed. Her smile was a delight, and he instinctively knew there'd been precious little happiness in her life recently. He was about to change all that. If he could. And if she let him.

Becky picked up a mushroom. "I see you're better with computers than Chinese cutlery."

Dan snorted. "Apparently. And here I thought I was such an expert."

They continued eating, the air between them alive with tension. When at last they both lowered their chopsticks, claiming they were full, they caught each other's gazes.

Neither moved for a moment. Then his heart kicked into overdrive as he watched her pick up her napkin, stand up and lean toward him to carefully wipe his chin. Unconsciously, she licked her lips, and his eyes followed the path of her tongue. He wanted Becky Thorpe. He wanted to kiss her senseless, tasting all the flavors and textures that were uniquely hers. He wanted to slowly open those little pearl buttons on her blouse and feel her smooth skin. But he didn't think he could stop there....

When desire was this strong, fears were forgotten. Dan grasped her wrist with his left hand and gently pulled her over and onto his lap. His eyes darkened with desire.

Wrapping his arm around her waist, he traced the outline of her lips with his finger. No words were needed as he felt his way along her throat, felt her pulse quicken. And then their eyes said the rest—just before their lips met in a long, demanding kiss. Brushing his mouth against hers, he urged her lips apart. Quickly, his tongue sought entrance into the softness of her mouth. Even as her tongue met his, Dan knew it wouldn't be enough.

"Becky?" The question lingered between them, giving her the opportunity to back out. Instead, she put her arms around him.

Dan swallowed. His heart was pounding, and his hands were shaking as he reached for the top button of her blouse. "All right?" he asked before releasing the button.

Becky felt the cool air on her skin, but it didn't matter. Dan's kisses were all-consuming, creating entirely new sensations. She'd never felt this way, had never felt so beautiful, so desired. Determinedly she pushed aside her fears. She didn't want to think tonight, only feel.

"Just fine," she whispered as she placed her hands on his shoulders to steady herself. She could smell his light woodsy scent. All her senses were on overload as his hands continued on the path he had set. One by one, the buttons gave way. Gently tugging the ends of her blouse out of her skirt, he parted the material.

As his eyes finally saw the lace that covered her breasts, he inhaled sharply. She wore a lace teddy. It was beautiful. *She* was beautiful. Slipping the blouse from her shoulders, he saw the smooth ivory skin and closed his eyes as he inhaled her fragrant scent. And then he was raining tiny kisses on her throat, her shoulders. Tentatively he dipped lower.

This was how it was supposed to feel. She knew, even though she'd never felt it before. She was warm, eager, needful. When Dan hesitated between her breasts, Becky felt herself arch, giving him silent permission to continue. She closed her eyes. She was lost in so many sensations she could no longer think. All she knew was that she didn't want it to stop.

Dan saw as her eyes closed and she threw her head back. He couldn't think of anything but this lovely woman on his lap. Would he be good enough? Would he excite her? He wanted things to be so good between them that, later when she knew the truth, there would be no decision. She wouldn't be *able* to leave!

Becky was urging him on and slowly he pulled the thin straps of the teddy from her shoulders, then gently drew it down, exposing her very skimpy white bra. Only this small bit of lace hid her from his view. He had to see her. The bra straps followed and Dan reached behind her to unfasten the clasp. His movements were smooth, flawless, as if he'd done this a hundred times before. Once she was revealed to him, Dan gasped and Becky lifted her head, watching him as he watched her.

"You're beautiful, Becky," he whispered. "I want to make you feel good."

"You do. Oh, you do!" Becky took a deep breath. "Um, I haven't done much of this before."

Dan studied her eyes for a minute. "You mean lovemaking?"

She nodded, brushing a wisp of his hair away from his face. "I don't make a habit of being alone with a man." She smiled. "Don't worry, though—it isn't my first time."

"Oh." If he'd been thinking straight, he would have pursued that conversation. But of course he wasn't and he didn't.

She held his hands as she guided them to her breasts. "Touch me, Dan, please."

"Oh, Becky," he moaned, as his hands stroked her breasts, between her breasts, softly kissing her as his thumbs rubbed over her nipples. They immediately tightened, and Dan felt himself respond to her.

But he suddenly knew there had to be more than this. More than just two people eagerly seeking relief and little else. He needed to be sure that she was committed to him, that she felt the same certainty he did. He would need that when he told her the truth. He wanted to make their lovemaking memorable. For Becky. For both of them. He wanted it to be a prelude to a life of loving....

"We have to stop," he whispered, drawing away. He couldn't really explain it, but he felt an instinctive need to protect what he recognized as her essential innocence.

"Why?" Becky's arms encircled his neck and she held him close.

"Oh, Becky," he groaned, "do you know what you're doing to me?"

"I hope so." She smiled as he looked up at her.

"It shouldn't be like this, not for us."

"Oh?" She arched an eyebrow. "How should it be?"

"Long and slow, the whole night. And the next night. And the nights after that." Dan took a deep breath as he sat up to slide her bra and teddy back into place. "Be sure, Becky. Because when you come to me again, it's going to be damned impossible to get away."

"I don't want to get away," she whispered.

"Think about it."

Becky nodded as she buttoned her blouse.

"It was a wonderful evening," Dan said as he helped her up, then stood, grasping her small hand in his. "Before you go..."

Once again, his mouth took possession of hers. The kiss was hard and unrelenting. Becky's knees weakened as she leaned into him, and he caught her, aligning their bodies.

Finally Dan groaned and pulled away. "Look what you do to me!" He took her hand in his, guiding it to where she would feel his arousal. "Feel. I want you."

"And I want you." Her words were whispered, breathless.

"Be sure, Becky, be sure," Dan repeated as he draped his arm around her shoulders. "I can't get enough of you."

They kissed again. This time, Dan forced himself away after only moments. "I've never really wanted to play for keeps before." His thumbs stroked her cheeks as he smiled. "Now I do."

Becky nodded.

Dan went on, his voice soft, the sound flowing over her, caressing her, "Because it's never happened before, not like this." He set her away from him before pushing his fingers through his hair. "Becky, there've been other women, but it was never...like it is with us."

She was surprised at his admission, but didn't say so. Instead, she grinned. "I'm glad, Dan."

"I feel *more* with you, *want* more with you. But if you'd rather not pursue this, tell me now, and I'll understand." As she shook her head, he hugged her and whispered in her ear, "I may never let you go, woman. Be very sure you're ready."

"Dan," she began as she placed her hands on either side of his face. "I'm new at this, too. There was only one man before, and it ended . . . badly."

Dan brought her hand to his mouth, kissing each finger in turn. "I'm sorry."

The words were so tender, spoken so sincerely, she felt tears burn behind her eyes. "Oh, Dan."

Dan growled and gave her a final kiss. "Let's go before it's too late."

She let him lead her out of the office.

"Can I give you a ride?"

"No," Becky answered. "I'll take the bus."

"I'd feel better if I drove you."

"All the same," she responded, "I'm perfectly capable of getting home safely."

"At least, let me get you a taxi."

"All right," she conceded.

After helping her into a cab, Dan paid the driver, then stared after the car as it pulled away, wondering if a girl from rural Minnesota could be happy in Los Angeles. He had to face it: California was another world. For one thing, L.A. was full of seekers and drifters, people who'd left their homes, their towns and families, behind. People who were striving for elusive goals—always wanting more. Whereas here, people seemed more content. Everyone had family ties. Parents and grandparents lived in nearby farming communities, like Becky's mother. Could Becky leave everyone, leave everything that was important to her? Could he ask her to do that? He was scared—scared of losing her, scared of making her unhappy, scared of his dishonesty. What was he going to do? Thrusting his hands into his pockets, he let out a string of curses. What on God's green earth was he going to do?

Four

Dan sat at his desk, critically considering his life. It had been five weeks since he'd shared that first hamburger with Becky. Five of the most wonderful weeks he'd ever had. They'd done so many things together.

When they discovered they both enjoyed reading, they'd scoured Minneapolis and St. Paul, seeking out every used-book store. Both of them found several treasures, but Becky'd been thrilled when Dan presented her with a lovely leather-bound copy of her favorite novel, *Jane Eyre*. She thought he was a mind reader until he admitted he'd seen her admire it.

They'd done other things, too. A long walk around the Nicollet Mall. A casual date that found them at the Walker Art Center. A leisurely stroll through a nearby park.

He picked up a paper clip and played with it as he sat daydreaming. They'd also had a not-so-leisurely day at the new Mall of America, systematically approaching the place to cover as much territory as possible in one day. They succeeded in getting sore feet. Dan grinned, remembering the way she'd laughed when he bought her that small stuffed bear.

He would have liked to spoil her, taking her to places she'd never seen. Like the Ordway. Or the Guthrie Theater. But she was adamant about not spending too much money, stating that they both had modest incomes and she really didn't need anything fancy, anyway. He didn't want to raise her suspicions, so he'd gone along with her.

He gazed at the plant she'd given him last week. It was small, but she assured him it would grow rapidly. She'd selected it especially for his office, taking into account that his window faced east.

He picked up a manila folder on his desk, then just as quickly, put it back down. He felt frustrated. He still hadn't told her the truth, and he had absolutely no idea how he was going to. He'd already waited too long.

But he couldn't help it. How was he going to tell her that money wasn't a problem for him? That he had more than he'd ever be able to spend? For that matter, how was he going to tell her *anything?* Who did he think he was, anyway, playing with Becky's future like this? What about *her* needs? What would she think when she learned the truth?

He'd really done it this time. The woman he wanted was within reach, but he was afraid that if she knew the truth, she would slip out of his grasp.

Dan frowned. Becky seemed afraid of something, too. What was she hiding? He'd already talked with her—about everything, including as much about his family as he'd dared, hoping she would share things about herself. And she had. But there was something still hidden away. She'd told him a lot about growing up on a farm and beginning high school. Then she'd skipped several years until she came to work in Roseville. What had happened during that time? He wanted her to tell him, but how could he ask, knowing the secrets he himself harbored?

He'd tried to ask her a few questions about her high-school graduation, but she'd shied away from that topic. Well, he'd grant her the privacy she wanted for now. But he'd find out eventually.

Dan vowed to go slowly, secure in the fact that whatever, whoever, had put the fear in her eyes, it wasn't him. She trusted him. He wasn't worthy of that trust, but it was there.

If Dan was anything, he was analytical, which was the reason he enjoyed computers so much. They were simple and predictable. Every morning, you turned them on and the same menu stared at you from the screen. You typed in some information and the needed response promptly appeared. If only women—or one certain woman—could be like that!

In a few short weeks, he'd fallen in love with Becky. While that was perhaps uncharacteristic of him, it was nonetheless true. He'd actually been attracted to her since his first day at the company. But what he felt now was so much more than that, although the attraction was—admittedly—pretty intense. She made him feel alive, gave him a sense of excitement.

With a sigh, he realized that if his mother had anything to say about it, he would shortly return to California and the life he'd inherited. He remembered how long and hard his father had worked. Every day was the same. After an early breakfast, his dad kissed his mother goodbye and then left for the office. They didn't see him again until eight or nine o'clock that night. Of course, his mother always understood, explaining to Dan when he was a boy that his father was a busy man, that he made important decisions. She assured Dan that both she and his father loved him.

Dan knew that was true, but it was difficult to always be explaining to your friends why your father wasn't at school meetings or important events. Even now, it hurt when he remembered the track award he'd won. His father hadn't been there to see him do it.

It would be the same way for his children. He wouldn't be able to prevent that. His time would be as scheduled as his father's. Which meant that his wife would be alone, trying to fill the hours. And, later, his kids... She'd be raising them virtually by herself. The way his mother had.

Of course, she'd have all the material things she ever needed or wanted. But for Becky, he sensed, that wasn't so terribly important. It was one of the things that drew him to her. She liked to be around the people she cared about—like her mother. She wouldn't be able to stand being so far away from her. And he figured she wouldn't take to the idea of selling the family home and asking her mother to move to California.

He squeezed his eyes shut, trying to stop the beginnings of a headache. He couldn't tell her his secrets yet, he decided. What he'd do was spend as much time with her as he could first. Maybe if she fell in love with him, she'd go to California with him. Maybe if he made her his—in every imaginable way—the choice would be easy. Maybe then, she wouldn't be able to leave him.

"You've been out with Dan Simmons, haven't you?"

Becky took a sip of the black coffee. "Sure." The one-word answer was enough; she didn't see any sense in denying the obvious.

Sarah put her bottle of mineral water down on the table they shared and leaned forward. "Tell me all about it, Becky," she whispered conspiratorially.

"About what?" Playing dumb would give her some added minutes to think, and Becky needed them. She had to be careful about what she said to Sarah. Even though the two were friends, Sarah tended to feed the rumor mill a bit too often.

Sarah rolled her eyes. "Give me a break, Becky. You know what I mean! *What's he like?* I just can't imagine DOS doing anything impulsive."

"DOS?" Becky arched an eyebrow at her friend.

"Yeah, Dan Simmons." Sarah leaned back. "We just found out his middle initial is O. So all together his initials are D.O.S. Pretty appropriate, don't you think? You know, DOS? Disk operating system—computers?"

Becky laughed. "Honestly, Sarah, pretty soon you'll be taking horoscopes seriously."

Sarah shook a finger at her friend. "Don't make fun of it. I'll have you know that according to your horoscope for the next month, your life's headed for a major upheaval."

Becky grinned. "What am I going to do—clean out my closets?"

"Very funny. I wouldn't be so quick to make fun if I were you. You know, everyone around here talks about him."

"I've never heard that much," Becky muttered.

"Of course not," Sarah responded, "you're always busy. But people are definitely interested in finding out more about Dan. He's great at his job, but ever since he was hired, he's pretty much kept to himself. It's almost as if he's . . . hiding something, you know?"

"That's ridiculous," Becky said firmly. "He's just like us—busy with work and struggling to make ends meet."

And yet . . . there were a few things that didn't add up. The expensive books, for instance. But maybe he'd inherited them—that was certainly possible. Becky brightened at the thought. "He isn't hiding anything," she insisted again.

"If you say so," Sarah muttered. "But he's been the main topic of conversation for months."

Becky finished her coffee and picked up her empty cup. "Well, I can tell you this much," she said. "He's fun to be with, smart and a real gentleman."

"So he didn't kiss you on the first date, right?" Sarah drew a deep breath. "Why am I not surprised?"

Becky put her hands in the side pockets of her midnight-blue ankle-length skirt. "I wouldn't say that."

"So he did kiss you? How was it?"

Becky frowned. "Honestly, Sarah, you don't think I'm going to tell you? It'd be all over the office in two minutes."

"Becky, this is Sarah, remember? I already know he's taken you to every bookstore within driving distance." She stood up, too, placing her water bottle in the appropriate recycling bin.

"You know that?" Becky said.

One look at Becky's stunned expression and Sarah began to stammer, "Well, uh, you know, Becky." She hesitated. "The grapevine."

Becky shook her head. "Great. That's just wonderful. I should have known that nothing's sacred around here."

"It's just talk, Becky. Don't let it bother you."

Becky looked at her friend. "You know it bothers me. Why can't people mind their own business?"

Sarah sighed. "Becky, we've had this conversation before. Not everyone keeps to themselves the way you do. And when someone as interesting as Dan Simmons joins the company, there's going to be talk."

"I suppose," Becky agreed. "But I don't have to like it."

"Then just ignore it."

"What else have you heard?"

Sarah hedged. "Nothing much."

"Yeah, right. You're not going to tell me, are you?"

"Becky, I'm shocked! We tell each other everything."

Becky glanced at the clock. "Break's over. We need to be getting back."

Shrugging, Sarah opened the door. "I suppose this means I'm not going to find out more about your budding romance."

"You've got that right," Becky said as they stood in the hallway.

"It's a shame," Sarah teased. "Just when it's really getting interesting, you clam up." Her tone grew more serious. "But people aren't going to stop talking until they satisfy their curiosity. And," she added with a twinkle, "I wouldn't mind learning a little more about DOS myself. In the interests of upgrading my computer skills, of course!"

Becky smiled weakly. "You're incorrigible, Sarah."

Her friend chuckled as she headed down the opposite hallway. "Maybe you're right."

Becky walked back to her office, lost in thought. What Sarah said was true—she *should* ignore the gossip. But she couldn't. She didn't like being the subject of speculation and rumor. And she couldn't help resenting the invasion of her privacy.

Shaking her head, Becky returned to her desk and the stack of reports she'd left only fifteen minutes ago. Two more hours and she could call it a day.

With her oversize Mickey Mouse nightshirt on and her feet in large woolly socks, Becky sank onto her sofa, exhausted. Not that the day had been particularly bad; work was never difficult. But she still felt bothered by the stares she'd endured. The office had never found her behavior all that interesting before! What she'd done—and what seemed to be everyone's business—was go out with Dan Simmons. Ever since he'd arrived on the scene, people had considered him something of an enigma. Now that she thought about it, he *did* seem awfully careful when he revealed anything about himself or his family, even to her. Why?

She scolded herself. Sarah's suspiciousness was beginning to infiltrate her thinking. She was going to have to stop that. He probably just wanted some privacy, that was all. Like her. He went through his day calmly and efficiently, keeping his mind on his work. Since his arrival, the computer system had run perfectly. She admired his dedication to the company.

Becky was not normally a courageous person. This time she'd surprised herself; she'd taken a risk. And it had worked out! All along, Becky had felt that Dan might be interested in her, and so, by some miracle, she'd found the courage to approach him, to respond to his overtures, to go out with him. It was the first time since Michael....

She covered her shapely legs with her old granny-square afghan and snuggled more deeply into the sofa. She closed her eyes, thinking how wonderful it was that Dan was interested in her. He was interested in *her!*

Dan slid his glasses from his face and pinched the bridge of his nose. He'd spent all day staring at a computer terminal and all evening reading at home. He was exhausted and his eyes burned.

Sitting in his favorite chair, he leaned back, stretching his tired muscles. He'd shed his tie right after work; now he unbuttoned a few buttons of his shirt and slipped off his shoes. Staring across the room, he frowned at his computer. The game was going to have to wait. He'd almost finished it, anyway.

Closing his eyes, he indulged in his favorite fantasy. It was about the two of them, Becky and him, lying side by side in his king-size bed. She excited him, unnerved him, urged him to give more, do more. And he did....

Dan imagined tracing the curves of her body, imagined them looking at each other with darkened eyes. Then, in his fantasy, he leaned forward, kissing her eyelids. Finally he whispered, "I love you, Becky," and his lips took possession of hers....

He loved her! It was the kind of love that lasted; he was sure of it. All he had to do was convince Becky she felt the same way.

His phone rang. Rubbing his eyes, he reached for the cordless phone that sat on the table next to him.

"Hello?"

"Dan, dear, I'm so glad I got you at home!"

Dan sighed. "Hello, Mother, what's up?"

She hesitated.

"Mom?" His voice grew anxious and he asked quickly, "Are you all right?"

"Oh, heavens, dear. Yes, of course. Don't worry."

"It's because I love you, Mom."

"I know, dear. I wanted to talk to you before you heard it on the news." She paused for a deep breath.

"Mom, what *is* it?"

"Dan, I'm married." She spoke softly.

Dan wasn't sure he'd heard her properly. No, he couldn't have. He chuckled. "Mom, what did you say?"

Her voice was stronger now. "I said, I'm married."

"I don't believe it!" Dan was out of his chair, grasping for something to make the news a reality. "You're not serious, are you?" He paced the floor. It had to be a joke.

Once the news was out, Audrey seemed to gain momentum. "Of course I'm serious, Daniel Owen Simmons. We flew to Vegas last night and . . . did it. A few of the local reporters have already tried to contact us. We won't be able to keep it quiet for long."

"Vegas?" Dan's voice squeaked as he tried to absorb the news. "Vegas? That's so . . . unlike you, Mother."

"I know, but—"

"Who is he?" Dan interrupted. "Who's the guy?" His foot tapped out a cadence. Had he really been away so long? He'd seen her a few months ago, and she hadn't said a word. Not one word.

"Dan, would you calm down?" his mother replied. "You always get excited when something unexpected happens. I knew you'd take it like this."

Dan clutched the phone. "We're not talking about me, Mother. We're talking about you. Now, I want to know. Who did you marry?"

"George Barrington."

"George Barrington?" Dan echoed. George Barrington had been his father's right-hand man, his associate, for years. On his father's death, George had become acting CEO, with all the responsibilities and privileges the job entailed.

When had the man found time to court his mother, for goodness' sake? Hell, why did his mother want to be courted by this guy in the first place? George Barrington was a *bore*. He was a businessman through and through, a man who couldn't be spontaneous or whimsical if his life depended on it. Dan suspected George had never done anything for mere pleasure. All his actions were tied to the food business, the stock market, the latest developments in the economy. Dan had always thought his father had found a man like himself when he chose George. Predictable, hardworking, methodical.

Well, he'd been wrong. Obviously George did have a few impulsive moments.

"Oh, Dan, dear, don't be so shocked. George is a wonderful man." In disbelief, Dan could almost see his mother smiling as she expounded on the man's attributes. "He's so much fun, Dan."

Dan managed to choke out a reply. "Fun? Old George?"

His mother continued, "He makes me laugh, Dan. I feel wonderful when I'm with him. I feel loved and I—"

"You loved Dad, Mother." Dan didn't know why he felt the need to remind her of this.

"Of course I loved your father. But he's gone, dear. I can't bring him back—and I can't stop living."

She had a point there. Okay, so he was getting used to the idea.

"Where *are* you two living, Mother?"

"In our home, Dan. It was just so much easier that way."

Dad's home—the home his father had designed for his mother. Another adjustment. "I guess congratulations are in order, right?" Dan's mother was silent for a long minute. "Mom?"

Audrey's voice quavered a bit. "Be happy for us, Dan. Please. I know you want to stay in Minneapolis for a while longer. I just wanted you to be aware that news of this might make the national networks."

Dan rolled his eyes. Great! Free publicity about the family again. "Oh, Mom, I am happy for you. You know me. I just have to get used to the idea."

"I know, dear. Oh, wait a minute."

Dan heard some mumbling in the background as the receiver changed hands. "Dan! Are you there?" The booming voice could belong to none other than George Barrington.

"Hello, George," Dan responded.

"When you get some time, come here for a visit, Dan. This is still your home."

Dan nodded wordlessly, but George required no answer to continue. "I hope you decide to return to work soon. We need you at the Simmons Corporation—you know that."

"Yes," Dan answered tightly.

"Selfishly, I have my own reasons for wanting you home," George went on. "Your mother and I are thinking of semiretirement. We'd like to travel, take an extended honeymoon." He paused for a minute. "Son, I love your mother. I hope you and I can be friends."

Dan nodded again. "We are, George. Always have been."

"Yes, yes, I know. But our marriage changes things. I'll make her happy, Dan."

"I know you will." Dan believed it. If George was anything, he was a man of his word.

"Dan, your mother sends her love. We need to be going now—there's a dinner party planned for us at The Place."

"Goodbye, then." Dan remembered the exclusive supper club George mentioned. Everything in their lives was the same—rich, exclusive, reserved—as it had always been. Everything Dan had been born into, everything he wasn't sure he wanted to be.

George hung up, breaking their connection. Dan sat down again. His mother was married. Well, what had he expected, anyway? She was an attractive woman, and in all honesty, he hadn't really expected her to live out the rest of her life alone. But George Barrington? Dan sighed. Here he sat, twenty-five years younger than his new stepfather, wondering how to guarantee a future with a certain woman, while the acting CEO of Simmons Corporation had just done it—and apparently revealed a few surprises about himself along the way. George Barrington, *fun?*

That information was the proverbial last straw. Dan slammed his arm on the arm of his chair. The noise seemed to reverberate through the room, taunting him. It was full speed ahead! If George Barrington could do it, so could he!

He was definitely going by instinct! And he'd have Becky if it was the last thing he ever did.

He glanced at his watch. Ten-thirty. Too late to call tonight.

He'd call her early tomorrow, Saturday, and convince her to spend the weekend with him. The entire weekend. Day and night. He'd make it wonderful, exciting, unforgettable. That way, the secrets he had wouldn't matter. Would they?

Five

The telephone was ringing. Becky opened one eye to stare at her alarm. Six o'clock. Who on earth was calling her at such an ungodly hour on a Saturday morning? She pulled the quilt up around her chin. She'd just ignore it, go back to sleep and wake around eleven, as she always did on Saturdays.

But the phone kept ringing. And ringing. Whoever it was certainly seemed persistent.

Frustrated, she threw back the covers, sighed and reached for the receiver.

"Hello?"

"Good morning!" the bright, wide-awake voice sang over the phone. "Hope I didn't wake you."

Becky sat up. "Wake me? Dan, do you know what time it is?"

The minute of silence seemed extraordinarily long. "Oh, I'm sorry." The apology was soft. "I did wake you."

But to Becky, the delight at hearing his voice made the time unimportant.

He paused, gathering his thoughts. "I thought we might spend the day together. You know, breakfast first, and then maybe the new museum on Larch Street. How about it?"

Becky's heart was racing. An entire day!

"Well?"

Becky swung her feet over the side of her bed, raking her free hand through her hair. "I'd like that."

"How soon can you be ready?" Dan asked. "An hour?"

She cringed when she looked in the mirror. Her hair stood out like a porcupine's quills and her complexion was washed out. She'd have to make some effort to look good in only an hour, but she could do it. "An hour's fine."

"Great. See you then."

Dan hung up the telephone, smiling to himself. Everything was going just fine.

Thoughtfully, he walked into his bathroom, slid the glass door open and started the shower. He stood under the spray, enjoying the water against his skin. While the shower was invigorating, it was a poor substitute for what he *really* wanted to feel.

Becky's skin, naked against his. Cool sheets. Hot responses. His senses were bombarded by his imagination. Tonight he'd know how it all felt with Becky, how it felt to give her pleasure and receive pleasure in return. He wanted to spend each and every night in her bed, making love with her.

And in a few years, he wanted her to have his baby. Feel her body growing with the life they'd created together.

He stepped out of the shower and briskly rubbed the thick towel over his skin. He didn't know if Becky wanted to have children—it wasn't something they'd even discussed—but his instincts told him she did.

Dan smoothed on his shaving cream, wondering for the thousandth time if she'd ever be able to live in a place like L.A. It couldn't be helped. As much as he would prefer to continue his life here in Minnesota, it wasn't possible. He had responsibilities, to his mother, to the company, to the employees and stockholders. *With privilege comes responsibility.* Those four words of his father's echoed in his mind over and over. Privilege. Responsibility. Would Becky understand?

He just didn't know. By the time she found out, however, she'd be so much in love with him that... Dan frowned at his reflection. He tried not to think of what he was planning. It bothered him; he knew he should've been honest with her right from the start. How could he explain his silence to her? She trusted him, and he'd violated that trust. *Would* she understand?

He wasn't going to tell her today, but he'd tell her soon. Very soon. This weekend was special; nothing was going to intrude on it.

Becky finished dressing ten minutes earlier than she'd expected. Wandering into her living room, she spotted her mother's letter on the end table. It had arrived on Thursday; Marge often wrote to save money on phone calls, and Becky was touched by her thoughtfulness. This latest letter was filled with information about the craft show. Her mother mentioned that she'd finished the quilt—it was gorgeous!—and would Becky be able to come home to see it win a ribbon next weekend? It'd be nice to be with her mom for a few days, and the craft show was always fun. Maybe Dan would like it....

Becky knew she'd come a long way. Before meeting Dan, she'd never dreamed she'd want to invite a man anywhere, let alone her hometown. But it was so easy to be with Dan, and she felt ready to show him her childhood home, to have him meet her mother. She'd invite him today.

The morning and afternoon had been good. After a hearty breakfast of eggs, bacon and pancakes, they'd visited the new museum. Then they'd walked the skyway in Minneapolis, staring out at the city. They had held hands, laughed, joked.

After they'd eaten supper at a popular sandwich shop—Becky's choice—she'd invited him to her apartment. That was a small miracle in itself. She'd always been so guarded about her own place that Dan was humbled by the invitation. It showed she trusted him.

While she hung their jackets in the closet, he noticed all the little things in her home. There were tiny exquisite figurines of angels on a shelf behind the couch. A quilted wall hanging decorated one wall, while cross-stitch pictures hung on the others. Several patchwork pillows lined the couch. A bookcase held an eclectic assortment, from the complete works of Shakespeare to current romance paperbacks. And there were plants everywhere, cascading from shelves, suspended from the ceiling, lined up on the windowsills.

"Make yourself at home. I'll start some coffee."

"Sounds good," he replied, hunkering down to read the names of the CDs near her stereo. Then he examined the titles of her books, and finally he studied the framed photographs on one of the shelves. Family portraits mostly. Dan was moved by the obvious love in all three faces.

After satisfying his curiosity, he sat down on the couch. He wondered if she'd ever invited a man here before. He refused to think about how much she trusted him. When the time came, he'd make everything right.

"Here we are," Becky said cheerfully as she walked in with two steaming mugs. Dan unfolded his long frame from the small sofa and walked toward her. She watched him, a spark of excitement in her eyes.

"I was wondering," she began, handing him his coffee. "My mom just wrote me, asking if I'd be able to make it home next weekend for a local craft show. Would you like to come?"

Surprised, he looked at her. "Are you sure, Becky?"

She nodded. "Yes, if you want to. It may be boring for you, but..."

"I don't think it'd be boring at all. I'd love to come."

"You would?"

"Sure. When do we leave?"

"Does Friday evening sound okay? It only takes a few hours to reach Eaton on the freeway. I usually rent a car."

"I'll drive," he offered as he bent to set his mug on the low table. "I don't want coffee, Becky," Dan said quietly as he put his hands on her shoulders. His touch was light. Becky's breath came out in a short gasp.

"Are we changing the subject?"

"We are."

Her eyes focused on the design knitted into his sweater. All day, she had refused to acknowledge that their attraction to each other was growing. Now, in the quiet of her apartment, it was impossible to ignore. She looked up suddenly to meet his gaze and knew he felt it, too. It was powerful and exciting.

Refusing to analyze the situation, Dan watched her as he pulled her to him. He traced his thumb along her bottom lip. She was so beautiful; he had to have her. Now.

Becky placed her hands on his forearms and studied him in return. His face was handsome yet gentle, sensual yet kind. In a few short months, he had managed to make her forget her past. She felt wonderful, as if, in loving Dan, she'd purged herself of the tragic memories. And she did love him.

His fingers touched her hair. He enjoyed the feel of the silky strands. "Becky," he whispered, "you give me inspiration. I want so much when I'm with you. I feel so much." He lowered his mouth to hers. "Tell me you do, too." His last words were lost to her as their lips touched.

His kiss was sweet, undemanding, coaxing a response from her. And she gave it. When her mouth opened, Dan groaned, allowing his tongue to enter her moistness, searching and steadily increasing its demand. While his mouth worked its magic on hers, Dan drew her nearer.

He measured her response, her willingness to be with him. Suddenly kisses were not enough. With a low growl, he pulled her tightly to him so she could plainly feel his arousal.

"I want you, Becky. Now." He held her still, waiting for her answer.

Becky nodded. She'd never felt like this before. And that made her realize she hadn't loved Michael. She'd never trusted Michael with the implicit trust she experienced with Dan, this knowing he would never hurt her. Tonight, she wanted him. He was the man she loved.

Tonight, she was going to make a new start, become a whole person again.

Dan lightly planted kisses on her face before following the angle of her neck down to the hollow of her throat. "I don't care about anything except us. Right here. Right now." He paused. "Are you ready, Becky?"

"Yes," she whispered. And then she began to softly kiss his neck, her arms winding around his waist.

"I . . . I may be a failure in the sex department."

"No, you won't." Dan placed his hands on her shoulders. "And we're going to make love, not have sex."

The slightly veiled admission of love stopped her. "Dan, what did you say?"

"I said love, Becky. *I love you.*"

He smiled, watching her eyes light up with pleasure and confusion and excitement. "You love me?"

"Yes."

Tears shimmered in her eyes. "Oh, Dan, do you mean it? Do you really mean it?"

He chuckled, touching his finger to her nose. "Don't sound so surprised. You're a very lovable woman."

"I love you, too."

"Becky," he whispered, before wrapping his arms around her. "Just let me hold you for a minute."

She did while they both considered the seriousness of their declarations. She knew there was no turning back. She didn't want to.

Dan felt like singing. She loved him! Everything would work out. Life's problems seemed small compared to what he felt. Nothing would come between them; he was sure of it.

"Take off my sweater," he said.

She obeyed, and when it was off, she gazed at him, letting her hands rest on his shoulders. She stroked his arms. She wanted to stroke the thick hair that curled over his chest.

Dan acknowledged her unspoken desire. "Go ahead, touch me."

And she did. Her long nails grazed his skin as she drew her hands along his chest. The hair felt soft, and his heart quickened at her touch. He stopped her.

"My turn. I want this to last."

Her knees felt weak, her body responding to his hands. He pulled up her blue-and-white sweater and reached underneath. Becky gasped as his fingers touched her smooth skin, moving upward to stop at the soft underside of her lace-covered breasts. Dan bent to kiss her, again seeking entry into her mouth and receiving it. All the while, his hands moved, unfastening the front clasp of her bra. He broke off the kiss to pull her sweater over her head. It joined his on the floor.

He slipped her bra straps down, letting the underwear fall to the floor. Then he looked and his hands cupped her breasts. "You are so beautiful. You were made for me. Look."

Becky didn't look. Her eyes were closed, and as she clung to him for support, Dan's thumbs rubbed her rosy nipples, coaxing them into peaks. It seemed to her that her body was intent on only one purpose. The more he stroked her, the stronger her response. She felt warm and wet. She was helpless as he continued his assault.

He lifted her to him, his mouth closing over first one breast, then the other. "You're so sweet, so delicious."

With one fluid motion, he picked her up and walked behind the screen to her bed, gently placing her there. Wordlessly he unbuttoned her navy slacks. Her slacks, shoes and hosiery were quickly removed.

Becky watched him. She supposed she should be embarrassed, but she didn't stop to think about it. Dan was doing a fine job of making her feel beautiful, desired. Never had anything seemed so right to her.

And then her panties were gone. She lay there for him, as his eyes rested on the soft curls that hid her femininity. Silently he stood, shedding the remainder of his clothing.

He sank down beside her, his arm cradling her against him. His arousal was evident, his breath measured.

What followed next overwhelmed her senses so completely that she couldn't have formed a coherent thought if her life had depended on it. They touched each other, Dan leading the way. No part of her body was left unkissed, untouched, and then his hand came to rest at the juncture of her thighs. She tensed.

"Relax," he whispered.

Becky didn't hear him; his touch brought her to the brink of something she'd never known. Instinctively she grabbed at him, her nails scoring his back, and held him tight. She was lost in a web of overpowering sensations. Just before she reached the peak, he moved on top of her, spreading her legs as he entered her.

Intense desire needed intense release. And Becky found it.

Dan was with her every step of the way. His own release came seconds after hers and he sank deep within her, joining her as they rushed into the world of feelings, responses, sensations. And in that moment, their lives were forever altered.

Dan pulled her closer, delighting in the feel of her soft skin next to his. Dear Lord, what had he done? Amid the contentedness, he felt the prodding of guilt.

How was he going to tell her now? She thought she loved an ordinary working person, like herself. Someone who waited for each paycheck to keep him out of debt. How would she feel when she knew the truth?

Becky snuggled closer, a small smile on her sleeping face. It had been so damned good! Today he'd made her his, they'd proved their love for each other, but once wasn't enough....

There was just too much at stake. He loved her. He'd never been more sure of anything in his life. He sat up, watching her as she slept. So peaceful. So contented. And his. Forever. He'd never let her go. His love would be enough—it had to be!

And he'd make damn sure she didn't leave. How was he going to accomplish that? He had absolutely no idea. But he'd do it. He thought of how they'd spend their life together. She could quit work, follow her dreams. They'd make love every night. Warm and willing, she'd come to him and they would soar. Just like tonight.

Dan aligned his body with hers and bent to kiss her. He smiled as she stirred, her sleepy eyes opening to smile back. "Again?" she whispered.

Dan molded her breasts to his palms as he lost himself in their softness.

"Again," he whispered. Love replaced his troublesome thoughts.

Six

Becky opened her eyes to bright sunlight streaming through the bedroom window. Turning, she looked at the man beside her. The man she loved—the man she'd given herself to last night. It was better than anything she'd experienced or expected. They'd made love three times during the night, a night she wouldn't trade for a bucket of gold.

Smiling, she studied his face, admiring the angular cheekbones, the determined set of his chin. She needed to tell him she loved him, that he'd be her only lover for the rest of their lives.

He stretched his long frame, waking slowly. "Good morning." His voice was husky with sleep.

She'd never spent the entire night with a man before. But everything they'd felt and done together seemed so right. How could it not be?

"I love you," she whispered.

Dan propped himself up on his elbow, the sheet covering the lower portion of his body. He grinned. "And I love you."

Becky took a deep breath and sat up. "I didn't think I'd ever say it, not after Michael, but I do. I do love you."

Dan sat up behind her, his hands resting lightly on her shoulders. With one finger he traced her backbone, sending shivers of delight through her body.

"Do you want to tell me about him now?" he asked.

She rubbed her eyes. "I don't know if it's worth explaining."

Dan leaned forward and pressed a kiss to her bare shoulder. "I want to know everything about you, Becky. If it affected you, I want to know about it."

"It's really quite a short story." She moved to a half-sitting position and rearranged the sheet. "It went something like this," she began. "I was completely infatuated with him in high school. I thought it was love. He convinced me it was, so I...I gave myself to him in the back seat of his car."

Becky squeezed her eyes shut. She still felt humiliated by how gullible she'd been as an adolescent.

Dan smoothed the sheet over her breasts. His touch gave her strength and courage, and she went on, finishing rapidly. "I got pregnant, but the baby died when he was three days old. He was premature and his lungs were underdeveloped. And my mother never lets me forget about the colossal mistake of my life—because she doesn't want to see me hurt again."

Dan stared at her. She knew her eyes were too bright and it must be obvious that the memories still gave her a lot of pain. He kissed the nape of her neck, and his quiet understanding was almost more than she could bear. Struggling to hold back the tears, she shivered.

"I'll take it all away, Becky," he said, then gently kissed her lips. "We'll make new memories, a new baby. Marry me." His statements were punctuated by little kisses across her face.

"Marry you?" she whispered as the tears began to flow.

"Of course. How about it?"

Smiling through the tears that now streamed down her face, she threw her arms around his neck and pulled him closer, laughing and crying at the same time.

Dan chuckled. "I take it that's a yes?"

She nodded, still unable to speak.

"Good." He took a deep breath and eased her back on the mattress. Playfully growling, he cupped her breast in his hand. A perfect fit. "Good. Because I want to spend the rest of my life with you."

And before she could respond, he was kissing her quite thoroughly and provocatively.

They made love again. Dan refused to think about his secrets. Soon. He'd tell her soon.

"I'm hungry," Becky announced much later.

Dan arched his eyebrow, an amused expression on his face. "You are? I wonder why."

Becky shrugged, playfully going along with his teasing. "I don't know."

"Could it be because neither one of us has had any sustenance since last night, and it is now—" he looked at his watch "—nearly noon?"

"Could be."

"Well, then—" he gave her behind a little pat "—man and woman cannot live by love alone."

He stood in one fluid motion, unconcerned with his nakedness.

Stepping into his shorts and pants, he faced her. "Let's get dressed and go out."

"Where?"

"The supermarket of course." He picked up his sweater and pulled it on. "We'll get some groceries and come back here. How would that be?"

She nodded. "I'd like that."

"Then what are we waiting for?"

It was Sunday afternoon so the mammoth supermarket, complete with gourmet-food section, was crowded. Entering the store, Dan felt a familiar twinge of guilt. These were the places that had made his father successful. Simmons products were everywhere.

Becky grabbed a shopping cart and wheeled it into the store. He watched her as she looked over the bargains that greeted them by the entrance. She was sexy without being provocative, attractive without being glamorous.

Suddenly he panicked at the thought of telling her the truth. Would she understand his reasons for not being honest in the first place? Would he lose her? He simply didn't know—and he couldn't take that chance. Somehow he had to guarantee that she would remain his lover. And become his wife.

Becky noticed Dan's silence and chose to ignore it. He was probably only preoccupied with some computer idea; he was forever developing new programs at the office. That was it, she decided. He *couldn't* be regretting the wonderful night or his marriage proposal.

Becky shivered with pure excitement as she thought about it. Their lovemaking had exceeded all the romantic notions and fantasies she'd ever had. Just remembering how his hands had roamed her body made her tingle all over. Shamelessly she admitted it to herself: she wanted to be home—in bed—with the man she loved. The man who loved her.

"What do you feel like?" Dan's question startled her.

"I'm sorry, what?"

Dan grinned. "What do you feel like eating?"

Becky grinned back. "Oh, I don't know. I wasn't thinking about food."

"Were you thinking about the same thing I was?"

His gaze warmed her as he let his eyes drift downward. Her breasts peaked under his gaze, and she blushed. "Maybe," she teased. "But we do need to get some food," she added in a determined voice.

"Well, I feel like a BLT," Dan suggested.

"BLT? Full of cholesterol," she replied.

Dan winked. "I know, but what a way to go."

"Okay," she agreed. "If we have BLTs, then we make sundaes for dessert."

"What about cholesterol?"

Becky shrugged dramatically. "I figure it this way. If we've already eaten the bacon, we might as well really clog up our arteries with ice cream. Besides, I love ice-cream sundaes."

"Okay. Here." Tossing a head of lettuce into the cart, Dan proceeded to pick out the best tomatoes.

A few aisles later, he asked, "What kind of ice cream?"

"Chocolate marshmallow, of course."

"Of course?"

Becky rolled her eyes. "I absolutely adore chocolate marsh—" The phrase was never finished as she squealed in delight. "Oh, we've got to have some."

When Dan turned to see what had caught Becky's attention, he gasped. He'd come face-to-face with his lies. "Topping?" Luckily Becky was so entranced in her selection, she didn't notice the catch in his voice.

"Which one?" She turned on her heel, a smile lighting up her face. "Chocolate fudge or marshmallow cream?"

Dan's heart constricted, and his voice lodged in his throat. The doubts resurfaced as he eyed the bottles in her hands. It was all he could do to pretend normalcy.

He gave a nonchalant shrug. "Whichever you prefer."

She shook her head. "No way. It's unAmerican to be so ambivalent about your ice-cream toppings—especially when it's *Simmons* ice-cream toppings."

Dan cringed.

"What's wrong? I didn't say a bad word or anything, did I?" she teased.

"No, of course not. Pick whichever one you want—I like them all." He had to get out of this aisle, away from the truth. Trying not to think about the fact that, in an hour or so, they'd be back at her apartment and he'd be forced to eat the stuff, he motioned for her to put the topping in the cart.

"I'll take them both," Becky decided. "You know, you just can't get enough of these gooey gourmet sauces."

Dan nodded absently.

Becky prattled on, oblivious to his discomfort. "I wonder what he was like," she murmured. By this time, they were at the checkout counter.

"Who?"

"Owen Simmons."

Dan swallowed hard. "Why would you want to know that?"

Becky shrugged as she put their purchases on the conveyor belt. "No special reason. I just thought that a man who knew how to make desserts like this must have been a lot of fun."

"Oh, right." Fun? Dan couldn't remember ever having "fun" with his father; the man lived and breathed business.

"You should be interested," she commented. Dan looked at her with false calm.

"Why?"

"You have the same last name."

Dan responded lightly. "Sweetheart, there are millions of Simmonses in the world."

"Oh, I know. I guess it's just that influential and powerful people have always intrigued me. I wouldn't like to be in their position, and I think the public is too obsessed with the rich and famous—but they *are* interesting."

They were in the parking lot when he answered, "Oh, really? Well, Ms. Curious, you can forget about them. Right now, you have only one person to think about. And that's me."

He grabbed her by the arm, gently pulling her closer. "Don't you forget it."

His mouth found hers, conquering her token resistance with a hungry kiss. It was the kind of kiss that lovers give each other—and Becky was immediately lost in the taste of him.

When her lips parted, his tongue swiftly took advantage, darting into her mouth. Surely and slowly he remembered the feel of her, the taste. Reluctantly he pulled away, massaging her shoulders as he calmed himself. "This is definitely not the place."

Becky nodded. "Let's go home."

Dan growled playfully, then gave her a little pat before opening the car door. "I'll agree to that."

"Well, to quote the only Simmons *I* care about, 'What are we waiting for?'" Her eyes twinkled mischievously.

"Darned if I know," he replied before tossing the grocery bag into the trunk.

Intent on each other, neither noticed the man in the dark blue suit who sat in a black sedan across the parking lot. The man made a few notes, then picked up his cellular phone.

Dan and Becky drove away. John Riley didn't follow. He had gotten what he'd come for.

Seven

It was the day of the craft fair. The autumn air was crisp, the fall colors at their peak. Dan was pleased to be here with Becky. Looking at her in her blue jeans and pink pullover sweater, he had to admit she was in her element. Her eyes sparkled as she looked over each booth, stopping to share ideas or to lovingly touch the hand-stitching in a quilt.

They had stayed at the farmhouse the night before. True to his expectations, Marge Thorpe was a kind person whose hesitance about him sprung, he knew, from her tendency to be overprotective of her daughter. Knowing Becky's past, Dan understood it.

It was obvious Marge loved her daughter. Memories of Becky decorated the small house. As Marge had given Dan a tour of her home, he'd noticed photographs of Becky everywhere—Becky as a baby, taking her first steps, playing on a swing, graduating from high school.

"I couldn't bear to redecorate," Marge had explained. "She's my only child."

Becky's room still remained as she'd left it. It was all pink and white and feminine. Evidence of the girl becoming a woman was everywhere—a baby doll sleeping in a tiny cradle, a baton leaning in a corner, pink ballet slippers dangling from a wall hook and a carefully preserved pink carnation corsage rested on the bureau.

"I've seen everything by now," Becky's voice was clear, a touch of wistfulness in it as she added, "I always enjoy these exhibits. If I lived closer, I'd show a few of my own projects."

Dan placed his arm around her shoulder. "You'd win every prize."

"Only if you were the judge," she returned. She thought for a minute before asking, "Want to see something else?"

"Sure," he replied. "Wait a second, okay?"

She watched as he selected a cross-stitched bookmark she'd admired. Quickly paying the exhibitor, he turned and gave it to her.

"You didn't have to buy me this," she said while she fingered the narrow ribbon in the design.

"I know."

"You don't need to spend your money on me. You may need it to develop your computer game."

Dan playfully kissed her nose with his finger before grasping her hand in his. "Don't worry about it."

"But—"

"But nothing. Now. What do you want to show me?"

"This way.

"Mom likes you," she said as they leisurely walked the two blocks to the little white church that sat on the corner of Spruce and Main.

"She's a nice woman," Dan commented.

"You know—" Becky hesitated "—ever since Michael, Mom has been so protective of me. But she told me last night that you're good for me. She's right."

"Thank heaven," he said. "Because I'm going to be around for a very long time."

They had reached the church. "I never come home without visiting Daddy," she explained as she led him to a small cemetery behind the church. Most of the graves were unadorned, but her father's simple gray tombstone was neatly trimmed with a small silk-flower arrangement. Surrounding his grave were four others decorated in the same way.

Dan watched as Becky knelt beside her father's. "The other graves are my two aunts and grandparents on Dad's side of the family."

Dan thought of his own father, realizing he'd never visited the cemetery after the funeral. The idea had never even occurred to him. He'd never felt close to his father because Owen had always been too busy for him. Watching Becky now, Dan was struck with a sense of guilt. Had he been too hard on his father?

"I'm sorry, honey," Dan mumbled, pushing his own feelings aside. He'd deal with them later.

"Don't be," she replied. "They lived happy lives. Dad was younger than the rest of them when he died, but he always said his life was full of rewards." She thought for a minute before continuing, "I wish I could have helped him more in the end. His medical bills were outrageous. He gave everything to me."

"All parents do that," Dan stated. He had never wanted for material things, but that was one thing his father had made sure of. No one would ever see a Simmons lacking for anything.

"I know," Becky answered. "Still..." Her voice faded and she bowed her head.

A few moments later, Becky stood, her eyes shiny with unshed tears. She gave Dan a tremulous smile.

"Come here." Dan reached for her and she buried her face in the loose weave of his maroon pullover. Soothingly he rubbed his hands up and down her back.

His loving ministrations released her tears, and he continued to hold her as she softly cried. Dan felt a little like a courageous knight—he was ready to slay dragons for her. If he could help it, nothing would hurt her again.

Finally the tears ended and she looked at him. He handed her his handkerchief, which she readily put to use. "It's just hard, you know?"

"I know," Dan agreed, even though he didn't, not really.

Wiping her nose, she said, "Let's go. I want to show you my high school."

"All right." He found he was eager to leave the cemetery and his uncomfortable feelings about his father. Had he just been too damned hard on the man? He didn't know, but he promised himself to ask his mother a few questions when he next saw her.

Becky gave him his handkerchief, which he stuffed into his pocket as they walked away hand in hand. Becky felt closer to Dan than ever. Being able to share this most private part of her life with him had been good.

Dan, however, felt differently. This weekend had proved what he thought all along. Becky was happy close to her family and the places she loved. Would they ever be able to work out a compromise?

He was certain of only one thing. How truly afraid he was to tell her the truth about himself. . . .

One week after the craft show, Dan was sitting in Becky's apartment. They were sharing ice cream again. Ice cream with a Simmons topping. He managed to eat the stuff, but it seemed to stick in his throat, just like his deception.

He realized he needed her in his life. She'd become indispensable to his well-being, and he'd do anything to keep her with him. Anything. Right now, in fact, he was contemplating making her his legal wife before telling her the truth. Once she realized he'd lied, it would be too late. It seemed the only answer. She was the type of woman who wouldn't divorce him; she believed in love that lasted forever, like her parents'. Marge had spoken of her late husband frequently when they'd visited her. It was clear the couple had enjoyed a very special relationship. Becky wanted the same. Marriage seemed the only solution.

He wasn't proud of the plan. Far from it. But he was desperate.

Dan sighed. His father had drilled into him that most people were selfish and egocentric, interested only in their own gratification and that, if you wanted to make it in this life, you took the offensive, grabbing what you wanted, when you wanted it.

Dan didn't believe all that—never had. He enjoyed people, helping them, treating them fairly. In fact, his father used to say that his son had too many scruples.

He closed his eyes as the last spoonful of ice cream slid down his throat. He always treated people honestly. Always! Yet now, he'd managed to deceive the one person whose departure from his life would destroy him. And she would leave; he was sure of it—if he didn't do something soon.

"Marry me tomorrow." The quiet statement slipped out.

Becky looked up. "What did you say?"

"Well, maybe not tomorrow, but marry me as soon as we can arrange it." His voice was stronger now, full of determination.

"Dan, I...I mean—" Becky stood and walked to the window "—I want to get to know you better."

He set his dish down on the oblong coffee table and walked to her. He grasped her shoulders, then his hands found their way through her hair. His touch delighted her and she shuddered.

"You see?" His voice was a whisper in her ear as his finger lightly traced her spine. "We know everything that's important."

"Dan, I'm just not sure. This is all happening so fast. When I agreed to marry you, I figured we'd have a lot of time to do some planning. I need time to think."

But Dan was making it impossible to think. She closed her eyes as his hands found their way under her blouse, quickly unfastening the front closure of her bra. Pushing the lace away, his hands cupped her breasts, molding them. When his fingers traced over her nipples, teasing them erect, Becky sighed.

He was wonderful. He already knew all the ways to excite her. And she knew what kind of man he was. He was everything to her.

"Yes."

"Yes?" Dan echoed as he turned her toward him, quickly sliding her blouse off her shoulders. Slowly his fingers caught the straps of her bra, and it joined her blouse on the floor.

"Yes." Becky smiled up at him.

"Good." His answer was muffled as his mouth found the peak of one breast. Very soon the entire world reeled out of her sight, replaced by a kaleidoscope of feelings....

Eight

The next morning, Dan could barely contain himself. Becky had agreed to marry him as soon as it could be arranged! It would be wonderful. He'd be a good husband. Just thinking about her, her soft body and her passionate nature, was enough to send shafts of desire racing through him. With her by his side, he knew his life would be complete.

Trouble was he could not help feeling guilty about his decision to wait until after the wedding to tell her about himself. In fact, it almost doubled his deception. But was there any other way? The question rolled ceaselessly around in his mind.

He turned on his computer. Staring into the screen, his mind wandered over every word Becky had ever uttered about the rich and famous.

They'd been cuddling on her sofa the night before when a popular television program about the rich and famous had aired. She'd listened attentively, then said, "I wonder what it's like to own a company. So much money, so many decisions. I could never exist surrounded by that much power. It's too complicated."

He'd pursued the subject. "You've said that before. Why does it bother you so much?"

"I don't know. People like that are always on camera. The entire world is watching them, waiting for some juicy tidbit of information. It makes me angry that the public cares about such superficial things." She took a breath, then went on, "I mean, there are people out there doing really heroic things—like working on cures for cancer—but everyone only wants news about the rich. So, if you're one of them, your life would never be yours. I couldn't stand that."

"I'll bet they're used to it," he had muttered.

Becky had walked over to the television to change the station. "I guess. I couldn't. I can't even handle work sometimes, the way everyone likes to talk. Oh, look, here's my favorite show." She'd apparently forgotten her remarks, but he hadn't. And then when they were making the sundaes, she said, "Owen Simmons. Imagine. A guy who made a fortune on chocolate sauce. But then, the Simmons Corporation makes about a hundred different products, doesn't it? I wonder how wealthy he left his family when he died.... Oh, well. It really doesn't matter. Their life is light-years away from mine. His children probably went to fancy boarding schools and Ivy League colleges."

She turned to Dan and smiled lovingly. "I'm so glad you're like me—just a plain, hardworking person employed by an ordinary company."

He closed his eyes. He couldn't tell her. Not until she was married to him. Then he'd make up for it. Hell, he'd spend the rest of his life making up for it.

If Becky had stopped to analyze her decision to marry him right away, she would have been flabbergasted at her sudden agreement. But she hadn't. Not for one second. She was completely in love. She slipped the bottle of clear nail polish out of her top desk drawer. Not even a run in her new panty hose fazed her today. Dan was wonderful to her, in every imaginable way. She dabbed her hose with the polish as she remembered their lovemaking.

She turned on her computer. Work was the last thing on her mind, but it couldn't wait. She'd have to discipline herself. If she didn't regain some control, she'd be fired before she was even married. And she couldn't afford that. Now that she was getting married, she wanted to save all she could so they could eventually buy their first home. It would be wonderful: saving together, finding just the right house; then moving in and starting a family. Thank goodness they both had decent jobs. She was fortunate to have her savings account. She already had enough money for a nice wedding. Not a big, ostentatious one, but enough for a modest party. And surely Dan could wait a *little* longer to give her some time to send out invitations and hire a hall.... Positioning her hands on the keyboard, she grinned. Life was good.

Audrey Simmons sat in her living room, her expression intent as she listened to the voice on the other end of the telephone line.

"He's involved with a young woman, Audrey." John Riley, an old friend of the family, was saying. Audrey should have felt guilty about having John, one of the best private detectives on the West Coast, follow her son, but she didn't. Not one bit.

Dan was her son, her only child, and she loved him immensely. She wanted nothing more than his happiness.

As difficult as it was, she'd accepted the fact that he needed to experience normal life. Being a Simmons was like being a Kennedy—only on a smaller scale. She'd gotten used to it. But Dan never had. Thinking back to his childhood, Audrey remembered the times he cried when his birthday party turned into a photo session for some newspaper. Or that time she'd taken him to Disneyland and they'd been pursued by a photographer for some tabloid.

So, she'd let him go. But that was three years ago, and now the company needed him. *She* needed him. She wanted her new husband to retire. This time, she didn't want to share her husband with the company. If she could just motivate her son to come home.

"What's she like, John?" Audrey interrupted after a few moments of listening to him recite the woman's name, address and job title.

"She seems nice," John replied. "Good-looking in a sort of cute way. She's unsophisticated, a real down-to-earth kind of woman."

"And her parents?"

John paused for a moment, leafing through some of his papers. "Ah, here it is. There's just her mother left. They were farmers, Audrey. Dairy farmers in southeastern Minnesota, to be exact. Becky is the only child."

Audrey thought for a minute. "Dan and this Becky—are they serious?"

John cleared his throat. "They're clearly in love if their performance in the parking lot is any indication."

Audrey smiled. Young love. She was glad Dan had finally found it. He needed someone, and if this girl made him happy, then so be it.

"Do you think he told her about the company?"

John hesitated for a minute. "I don't think so. They eat out in burger joints and buy food in discount stores. Obviously he's not revealing that he's got money. Seems to be enjoying his anonymity too much to make a change."

"I was afraid of that."

"It's going to be a problem, all right," John agreed.

"Then I'll just have to fix it," Audrey stated in her familiar determined tone. When things were important to her, she possessed tunnel vision. And Dan's happiness was very important indeed.

John chuckled. "I knew you'd say that."

"You know me too well, John."

"Anything you want me to do?"

"No. I think I'll handle it from here," she said. "Thank you. You did a great job."

"Any time, Audrey. Any time."

After the line was disconnected, Audrey's brow knitted in thought. Then she reached for the phone again and dialed the number of the company's aviation service.

Dan knew he had to move fast. Disgusted, he threw the Simmons Corporation business report from Los Angeles onto his desk. Lord, how he wanted more time! But time had just run out. They were expanding so rapidly he was needed. It was too much for George and the two vice presidents to handle. Besides, George wanted to retire, and Dan couldn't blame him.

Dan leaned back in his swivel chair, staring at the buildings that made up the Minneapolis skyline. He'd miss this city. He'd grown to love it; it was clean, fresh, full of vigor.

As his eyes focused on the horizon, his thoughts turned to his father.

"Dad, how come you like to make ice-cream stuff?" he remembered asking him—among a thousand other questions his father never seemed to get tired of answering, Dan realized now.

"Because I knew there'd be boys like you who'd love to eat ice cream, Danny," his father had replied, affectionately pulling the front curl on his son's head.

"You mean you made it because of me?"

"I sure did, son. Because of you and your mother."

Until now, that incident was one of the few good memories he had of his father. He'd done a lot of soul-searching since that day in the cemetery with Becky. In his own way, his father had loved him. That's why he'd been so determined to make his company successful. While Dan would have preferred to have his father at home, he was beginning to understand just what had motivated Owen Simmons—the love of a good woman and the son she gave him.

Now that Dan loved Becky, the past was not as painful. Dan wanted to preserve that company and provide for Becky, too. He knew he was sounding a lot like his father, but he would be careful not to spend his entire life focused on business. He'd have a family, too. He'd run the company differently than his father did. Not better—just differently. He'd delegate authority whenever he could.

He made his decision. He would return to Los Angeles as soon as he made Becky his wife.

Reaching for the phone, he punched in a series of numbers. "American Airlines? Yes, I'd like to know about your departing flights to..."

Becky's eyes were round, the sparkle of excitement in them dazzling. Or was it anger?

"Las Vegas!" she exclaimed. "Are you crazy?"

Dan had expected a number of reactions to the plan. But he hadn't expected this. "No, I'm not."

He looked around her apartment, glancing at the mementos that decorated the room. A tiny, ceramic, black-and-white cow sat on an end table next to a framed photograph of Becky and her parents. He picked it up and studied it.

"I'll go get some coffee," Becky muttered as she headed toward the kitchen. Coffee was the last thing on her mind, but she needed some space.

The photograph reminded him that Becky was the type of woman who'd want a nice wedding. She'd want to share that day with her mother in her hometown. Did he have the right to try to talk her into a fast Las Vegas wedding? And why? Because, dammit, he was too afraid to tell her the truth before he had his ring on her finger. He couldn't lose her, and at the same time, he couldn't deny that time was at a premium. He was, in short, caught between a rock and a hard place.

Becky returned with a small tray of Wedgwood blue mugs and a plate of homemade chocolate-chip cookies, which she set down on the coffee table. He stared at the cookies. They seemed to confirm it all—she was a country girl who wanted a simple life with the man she loved.

Could he make her happy? He had to try. Today he'd tell her everything—just as soon as he made love to her.

His desire had been building all day, and when he reached out and began to stroke her face, her slender neck, her breasts, he knew hers had been building equally....

"Let's have some ice cream to go with those cookies we didn't get around to eating," Becky announced later, swinging her legs off the bed.

Dan groaned. "Please, have a heart!" He was spent from their lovemaking, completely satisfied and more than willing to simply lounge around her apartment.

He smiled as he propped up his head on his elbow.

"Oh, come on," she insisted as she hastily pulled on a pair of pink sweatpants and a pink sweatshirt—minus anything underneath; a fact which Dan didn't fail to notice.

While he was relaxed and tired, she seemed rejuvenated by their intimacy, ready to conquer any obstacle.

"Let's get going," she teased, before playfully throwing his slacks at him. "I want to eat and watch the news."

Dan arched an eyebrow. "In that order?"

Becky smiled. "More or less." She sailed out of the bedroom, headed for the kitchen.

Dan's emotions were a mixture of euphoria and despair. Before his eyes, Becky had been transformed into a loving woman. She was sensual, funny, vibrant. While it was obvious she had a mind of her own, he couldn't help but be proud that he added a new dimension to her life.

Dan stretched before standing up, then pulled on his slacks, leaving the top button open. He made his way into the living room.

She watched as he turned on the television. His muscles flexed with every move, leaving her mouth dry. Yes, she loved him as a person, but she also adored him as a man.

"What are you grinning about?"

Becky shrugged, handed him a dish of ice cream and curled up beside him. "Oh, I don't know," she replied.

"Yes, you do. Now tell me—what is it?" He tapped his foot, then declared, "I'll just have to tickle it out of you."

Promptly he took both their dishes and placed them on the coffee table. Then he proceeded to do just that. Amid her giggles, he slipped his hand under her shirt and covered her breasts, delighting in the way the tips peaked as she responded to him.

"Dan, please," she murmured, breathless.

"Please what?" His hands cupped her breasts. "Touch you?" His thumbs gently teased her. "Kiss you?" The question ended on a sigh, just before his mouth touched hers.

Becky poked him in the ribs. "Oh, stop," she begged as she struggled to sit up. "Here's the news. I'd like to see if they mention the political caucus next week."

"I had no idea you were interested in politics," Dan said.

She shook her finger at him. "There's a lot you don't know about me."

He arched an eyebrow. "Oh?"

She nodded. "That's right."

Dan sighed as he turned up the volume on the television. "I'll have to remember that."

But Becky wasn't listening to him any longer. Her eyes suddenly became glued to the television set, her brows furrowed with concern. "Listen. Look at that plane. It's just like I said before. The rich can't do anything without someone watching their every move."

Dan watched in horror as his mother's plane landed—moments before she emerged from the aircraft with George Barrington at her side. He took a deep breath and swallowed, listening to the drone of the newscaster, "... departing now from the plane are Mr. and Mrs. George Barrington, primary stockholders in the Simmons Corporation, a firm known nationwide for its many products. Rumor has it that Mrs. Barrington has come to Minneapolis on business, but plans to visit her son, who's been living here for the past few years...."

Becky turned slowly and looked at Dan. His eyes told her everything she needed to know. Her face was pale, strained, and as she turned to him, he could see the sparkle of unshed tears in her eyes.

"Now I know what the O. in your name stands for, don't I?" Her question was quiet but forceful. "You're Owen Simmons's son, aren't you?"

What could he say? What words were the right ones? How do you explain the long-term lie you've lived to the woman you love? Why did he mess around with the one person who had become his entire life?

"Answer me, dammit!" She stood, a questioning look in her eyes. She wanted him to deny it, he knew that.

"Yes. I am." There was nothing else he could say.

Becky nodded as she walked to her window and looked out. The silence seemed to echo in the apartment.

"Say something, love, anything," Dan pleaded.

Whirling on her heel to face him, she pointed a finger at him. "Don't you ever, ever, call me 'love' again. All those jokes around the office, nicknaming you DOS. Not once did anyone put you together with one of the biggest companies in the country. Not once!" Becky was almost yelling, on the verge of hysteria.

"Becky, don't—" He stepped toward her, desperately wanting to hold her, comfort her, explain to her.

"Stay away from me, do you understand? I never want you to touch me again!"

"Don't, Becky, please," Dan begged, tears welling up in his own eyes. "I love you." It was the only defense he had.

Becky laughed—a short, bitter laugh. "Love. You don't even know the meaning of the word! What was I, anyway? A little fling with some common Minnesota farm girl before you hightailed it back to Los Angeles and your corporate way of life?"

"No, never."

Becky silenced him by holding up her hand. "Well, excuse me, Daniel *Owen* Simmons," she continued, "I don't buy it, not for one second. You can have any woman you want, so please don't think I'm foolish enough to believe you've fallen head over heels in love with me, all right?''

Dan shrugged helplessly. "It's true."

She pointed a shaking finger at the door. "Get out of here, now! Get out!''

Her voice was a mix of grief, anger and betrayal. He knew there was no point trying to convince her in this state.

"I'll be back," he promised, before scooping up his jacket and heading toward the door.

"Don't bother. You won't be welcome." Becky followed him. "Go back to your mother, your company, the women who run in your own circles. And never come back here. *Never.*''

Her last words were punctuated with the slam of the door. Dan pulled on his jacket and slowly walked out of the building into the rich light of the setting sun. But he didn't notice the beauty of it all. Without her, there was no beauty.

Nine

It had been six weeks. Six long, boring, miserable weeks. Six weeks without Becky.

Dan paced the floor of his plush Los Angeles office. He had done the honorable thing. After handing in his resignation in Minneapolis and making repeated futile attempts to explain things to Becky, he had returned to the company that was waiting for him in California.

Why hadn't he played it straight? Because he'd been afraid he would lose her. But in the end, he had lost her, anyway. What was the use? His fate had been sealed from the moment of his birth. He was one of the privileged, the damned elite, a man without choices. A man whose wealth and status dictated his life.

Dan shut his eyes, pinching the bridge of his nose. He had to deal with his pain, realize he'd never get her back. But all he could think of were dishes of ice cream, slow kisses and long nights in her arms.

Becky felt numb all the time now. She pressed the appropriate key to return her computer to DOS, then mechanically went through the motions of cleaning up her desk, grabbing her coat, slinging her purse over her shoulder. She had ceased to live; she only existed.

She glanced at her calendar unnecessarily. She knew what day it was. It was six weeks and one day since the night she'd sent him away. And even though it had been the right thing to do, she couldn't forget him. Smiling sadly, she realized how important he had become to her.

She had found a man she thought she could live with forever, and it had been wonderful. Short, but wonderful. Ruefully she shook her head. Some judge of character she was! The man had lied about everything, and she'd bought it, hook, line and sinker. What a fool she was!

She slammed her desk drawer shut and walked out of her office. If only she could forget his passion, his warmth, his kisses, things would be a lot easier.

Looking around, she saw that the office was deserted. It was long past closing time. She'd worked late again, as she often did now. She couldn't bear to be at home all alone with her memories.

A rhythmic clicking of high heels startled her. She turned and found herself face-to-face with an attractive older woman. The woman was smiling at her, and even though Becky had never met her, she'd recognize that face anywhere. The news media hadn't done her justice. It was Audrey Simmons Barrington, Dan's mother. Becky's mouth went dry.

"Hello, Becky."

Becky swallowed. "Mrs. Barrington." She clasped her hands together and forced the words out. Why had she come? It was much too late for anything now.

Audrey smiled graciously. "Please, dear, relax. And call me Audrey. Can we go somewhere to talk?"

Becky nodded, leading Audrey back into her office. She indicated a chair on the right side of her desk. "Have a seat, please."

"Thank you." Audrey settled comfortably in the chair, crossing her legs and casually dangling one of the burgundy leather heels she wore. Her suit was off-white, elegant yet understated. The burgundy earrings, bracelet and handbag matched her shoes perfectly. Becky took in her appearance and silently admitted to herself that the woman hardly looked old enough to have a son Dan's age.

"If Dan—"

Becky's words were interrupted. "Before you say anything, Becky, let me say what I came here to say, all right? Then you can argue with me all you want."

"All right." The agreement was easy enough; Dan's mother couldn't possibly say anything that would change her mind.

Audrey took a deep breath, gathering her thoughts before speaking. "Before you get the wrong idea, Dan did not send me here and he'll probably have a fit when he finds out what I'm doing."

Becky looked up, surprised.

Audrey smiled. "Yes, I will tell him, Becky. I believe in complete honesty with my son. And now, I'm going to be honest with you."

The story began. Becky listened attentively while Audrey mapped out a sketchy profile of her life with her husband. They had met early in their college days, each one of them the typical financially strapped student.

Becky couldn't help but be interested when Audrey spoke of her love for her first husband, how he had worked endlessly to build a business that would give his family a comfortable life.

But Dan's father hadn't just been successful. He had been outstanding, building a financial empire in ten short years. Ten years during which Dan had been growing up.

Becky felt like crying when Audrey, tears welling up in her eyes, spoke of the daughter she had lost in infancy.

And then she spoke of Dan. Her dreams for him, her aspirations.

"But there's only one thing I really want for Dan," Audrey continued, "I want him to be happy, married to whomever he chooses, and I will welcome her with open arms. I will finally have the daughter I've wanted so badly."

Becky was speechless.

Audrey paused. "The woman he wants, my dear, is you. Oh—" she waved a hand in the air "—he has spoken so highly of you, your ambition and your goals. He's afraid he wouldn't be able to spend much time with a wife and she'd feel cheated or lonely. I suppose that comes from growing up with a father who was seldom at home. But there is one thing that happens to him when he mentions your name that has convinced me he truly loves you."

Becky blinked. "What's that?"

"It's his eyes. They sparkle when he speaks of you. He's just like his father that way—everything he feels is mirrored in his eyes."

"It wouldn't work," Becky answered miserably.

"What wouldn't work?"

"His life is so different from mine," she stated. "I can't handle it when people talk about me. How would I handle the media?"

Audrey gave an indelicate snort. "That's hardly an excuse. You wouldn't have to. That's why we employ people to deal with it."

"But—"

The older woman held up her hand. "He's spoken so much about you I feel as if I know you. You and Dan have so many things in common—a love of books, music, the simple pleasures in life. You both want a family. You love each other. He can deny all these things, but I know him. But for some reason, he's rationalized too much. He thinks he has to live in California, near the company's headquarters. But that's not true. The company is so large we have offices located throughout the country. He can choose the one he wants to for his headquarters. And that's fine with me. Now that I've met you, I can see why he loves you."

Becky's eyes widened as she listened to Audrey enumerate the obstacles and then overcome them. "Do you really think so? We could live anywhere? You know, my mother has asthma—she has to live where there's fresh air and minimal pollution." Becky thought for a minute. "I couldn't leave her."

Audrey studied her future daughter-in-law. "No, of course you couldn't. But again, that's simply no problem. As I've said to Dan many times, we have that jet, as well as several other means of transportation. The company only limits us if we allow it to. Besides—" she paused "—Dan and I have talked since he's been home. He's finally beginning to understand that his father really loved him. Dan has choices to make, my dear. He loves you, and if he thinks for one minute that you could forgive him, he'll make your marriage work."

"Oh, Mrs.—Audrey, I don't know. Do you really think everything could be worked out?"

"Of course," Audrey said decisively. "All you have to do is go to him. He's tried several times to reach you."

"Yes, I know."

"He respects your wishes," Audrey continued. "He'll leave you alone. So it's up to you."

Becky nodded, already planning a trip to California.

Audrey stood and extended her hand to Becky. "I need to be going, my dear. But, please, think about everything I've said."

"I will," Becky replied, clasping Audrey's hand warmly.

"Good. Then I know I'll see you soon. Let me know when I can begin planning the wedding. I love weddings."

And before Becky could respond, she was gone. Becky grabbed her coat and left the office. Why did she feel as if she'd just had a visit from her fairy godmother?

The day after Audrey's visit, Becky was working, her ticket for California waiting to be picked up at the travel agency. It was nearly impossible to keep her mind on her job when the rest of her life was about to be decided. As soon as she saw Dan, she'd know if they had a chance.

Letting her fingers rest on her keyboard, she stared at the monitor. She read her choices: "Word Processing Program''; ''Spreadsheets''; ''Desktop Publishing''; ''Return to DOS.''

Her eyes focused on the last. ''Return to DOS.'' Even her computer was sending her a message.

It's amazing how fast you can reach the West Coast by air, Becky thought. She had just completed her first plane ride. Quite nicely, too. She left the airport quickly, her stomach in knots over the prospect of seeing Dan again. Making her way into the building that housed the Simmons Corporation she felt as though an army of butterflies had taken up permanent residence in her stomach. Whatever happened, she'd never be the same.

Was it too late? Had she thrown away the best thing that had ever happened to her?

Knees knocking, Becky entered the elevator, punching the button for the corporate floor, where she knew Dan's office had to be. The elevator whizzed to the designated place and opened its doors. Before Becky could change her mind, she pushed open the heavy mahogany door to the office. Once inside, she let her eyes travel over the thick, plush, rose carpeting, the handsome, white-upholstered chairs, the glass coffee table and the original framed work of a well-known artist. The entire room suggested wealth and prosperity.

Feeling out of place in her sensible navy midcalf skirt and white blouse, Becky took a tentative step toward the receptionist. And stopped. Completely. The door on the other side of the receptionist's desk had opened soundlessly. Looking up, Becky met Dan's eyes. And time seemed to stop.

''Becky.'' Dan's voice was a mere whisper as he studied the woman he loved. He blinked. She was still there. How he had missed her!

''Dan.'' Neither of them said anything else. Neither of them moved.

He recovered first. ''Come in.'' Dan quietly ushered her into his office.

Once he closed the door, Dan stared at Becky. They were an arm's length away from each other. Her nicely rehearsed speech of apology was frozen somewhere in her throat. The words he planned to say if she ever came back to him were forgotten.

Becky stared at the man who had become her life. The custom-tailored brown suit fit him perfectly. His pin-striped shirt was neatly pressed. The chocolate-brown tie and brown leather shoes complemented the outfit.

With a push of a button, he informed someone he'd be late getting to his next meeting. Several papers lay on his desk, awaiting his signature. Becky decided she'd never seen him look so authoritative, so completely in command. He had power and he knew how to use it. Could everything be the same between them?

"I've missed you." Her words were soft, faltering.

Dan smiled. Lord, she was here! And she was beautiful. "Becky," he began, "please say you've come back to me. Say you'll marry me." He walked over to her.

He was standing so close Becky could feel his breath on her face. In that moment she knew that somehow they'd be together.

"I want to, Dan, but I'm not sure I can fit into your world." She looked at him.

Dan groaned, reaching her, pulling her close. His mouth covered hers, and they both took what they needed.

After several long kisses, Dan drew back, his eyes shining. He smoothed a lock of her hair. "We'll make our own world if we have to. A world for us." He smiled softly at her. "All right?"

"Yes," Becky whispered, her eyes shining.

She had returned to DOS—the man she loved.

SNOW ANGEL
Isolde Evans

To David, Elona & Jennifer—
remember the Good Times

One

Angie stood alone on top of a serene winter world, a world of glistening frost particles and pine-scented air. She could hardly wait to carve tracks into the fresh, deep layer of powder snow that had fallen during the night.

Ten minutes. She had ten glorious minutes before the ski lift opened to the public and her hectic workday started.

Eager to get going, she dug in her poles and gave herself a push. Thirty yards to the steep part of the run, the part she intended to enjoy with reckless abandon.

"I'll give you a fifty-yard head start."

Dave. Dave Marshall. Coming to a sudden stop, Angie jerked her head around. With a frown, she asked, "Where did *you* come from?"

"You don't sound particularly thrilled to see me," Dave drawled, giving her the same dazzling, cocky smile he used to give the photographers after winning a race.

She shrugged. "Should I be?"

Slowly his smile faded. "Listen, Angie. I'm sorry about your parents...."

"That was eight years ago, Dave. You're a little late with your condolences."

"Yeah, I know. My mother wrote to me in Switzerland and told me about the avalanche. You probably won't believe me, but I made several attempts to write to you."

"Oh?"

"Hell, Angie," he said impatiently, "I never was any good at putting my feelings on paper. I planned on telling you how sorry I was in person."

"Thanks. Thanks a lot." Deciding they had nothing more to say to each other, she sprang into action, settling her weight near the back of her skis so they wouldn't get bogged down in the fluff. Her rhythm evened out. A spray of white followed her every move like a curving veil. She heard only the gentle swishing sound of the skis and the wind in her ears. Dave was a mere blur at the periphery of her vision, but he was there, causing spurts of adrenaline to rush through her veins. Just like old times, she thought with a lump in her throat. A sense of freedom returned, of reliving the days of her carefree youth. Her heart nearly burst with the thrill of competition.

Angie managed to get ahead of Dave. The drop-off was coming up. She knew just how to take it; with any luck he'd forgotten about it. Flying through the air, she let out a high-pitched shriek of pure pleasure, then sank low to cushion the impact of her body hitting the slope.

"Yippie!" he hollered.

Darn. He'd made it. Not only that, he kept inching up, getting ahead, spraying her with snow. "Oh, no, you don't," she grumbled.

The shortcut! She headed for the trees. "Uh-oh." She'd have to slow down. No, maybe not. She set her edges and streaked past a tree. Made it. Another tree coming up, then the bend. Through and out. Her heart beat furiously against her ribs.

"Watch out!"

The warning came too late. With a scream, she rammed into Dave. Landing on her back, she heard the clicking of releasing ski bindings, metal grinding on metal. A sheet of cold covered her face.

Her lungs weren't working. She tried to take in air but couldn't. Near panic, she tried again and succeeded. She'd live. Nothing else hurt—so far. Blinking, she exhaled, then inhaled again.

"Hey, are you okay?" Dave's voice was a raspy whisper, laced with concern. Warm fingers brushed at the snow on her face. When she could see, she found herself within inches of his compelling blue eyes. Was she in heaven? No, not yet, but this was close. *Dave, oh, Dave. How I've missed you.*

She'd been fifteen when he'd left, and secretly in love with him. But Dave had thought of her as a little sister, a ski buddy. Pushing her memories to the far recesses of her mind, she asked, "Who won?"

"I guess it's a draw." A delighted smile flickered across his face, then died. "You've grown up," he said, almost as if he was in awe of her.

Angie saw something surface in Dave's eyes that hadn't been there before. Admiration? No, it was more than that. It was an awareness of her as a woman. Her heart did a strange little flip-flop. Their breaths mingled and became one before floating away. Something melted inside her, telling her she'd never really let go of him. She swallowed, even though her throat felt dry. "Of course I've grown up. I'm twenty-eight years old, Dave." Becoming conscious of his weight on her, Angie wanted to throw her arms around him and hold on.

"A tumble with you packs more of a wallop than I'd imagined," he said on a soft laugh.

She drew a fortifying breath filled with his subtle cologne. "I hope you didn't hurt anything . . . vital."

"I'm about to find out." He scrambled to his feet and shook out his arms and legs. "Nope. Everything seems to be intact. I'll be able to ski again."

Angie suppressed a groan. Skiing was all he'd ever cared about.

Dave took her hand and pulled her to her feet. Brushing the snow off her shoulders, he said, "Sorry I ran into you."

"It was my fault."

With a slight shake of his head, he tapped his index finger against her cold nose. "You were always quick to take the blame when things went wrong. My little ski buddy hasn't changed all that much, after all."

The softness in his tone was nearly her undoing. Where had all her anger gone? For years she'd carried it inside her and nurtured it, hoping for a chance to tell Dave to go to hell, but now...

Trying to pull herself together, she glanced at the trampled snow. "My sunglasses are missing."

He found them, picked them up and wiped the snow from the lenses.

"Don't bother." Anxious to get away from him, she took them and stuffed them into her parka pocket.

"In a hurry?"

"I have a group of beginners waiting for a lesson."

Dave picked up Angie's skis and positioned them so she could step into the bindings, then handed her the poles. As he brushed the snow off his Icelandic wool sweater, her attention was drawn to the impressive width of his shoulders, making her even more aware of his stunning masculinity and doing nothing to calm her nerves.

When she had trouble getting her right boot tip fitted beneath the toe piece of the binding, he immediately bent to scrape a lump of snow off the bottom of her boot. His hair, not quite as blond and not nearly as long as it used to be, appeared to have been styled professionally. Despite the snow crystals clinging to it, it had hardly suffered from the crash.

"Okay now?" he asked.

"Okay." No, she was far from being okay. But then, he didn't have to know that. She pointed her skis down the hill and took off, hoping to flee from the confused thoughts raging in her mind and the unreasonable longing churning in her heart.

When Angie entered her ski shop, which was housed in a converted barn along with the cafeteria, she found it crowded with people needing to be fitted with rental boots and skis. She took off her yellow parka with the ski instructor's emblem sewn to the sleeve and flung it over a wall hook. Removing her headband, she ran a hand through her short dark hair and gave Gina, her part-time help, a smile of apology. "Sorry it took me so long."

"Don't worry about it," the redhead assured her. "Scott's here."

Scott, a student at Weber State College in Ogden, was another part-timer.

Angie breathed a sigh of relief. "Who's next?" She eyed a teenager looking eager to get on the hill.

"Uh, I'm enrolled in the beginners' course," the lanky youth said sheepishly.

"Good for you. Let's start you out on some fairly short skis." Angie grabbed a pair of 175s from the rack. "And don't feel embarrassed. Everyone has to start sometime. By the end of the program you'll be better than a lot of hotshots who never bothered to learn proper technique. How about boots?"

"Yeah, size ten. And thanks for the pep talk."

Angie gave him an encouraging smile and guided him toward the boot rack, where she had him sit on the bench while she opened the buckles of a boot. "By the way, I'm Angie Torlund. I'll be your instructor."

"I'm Curt. We just moved here from Arizona."

"Welcome to Utah." Angie knelt. "Okay, let's see if you can squeeze into this. Make sure your sock doesn't wrinkle. Good, now bang your heel against the floor. Got enough room in the toes?"

"Sure do. Are you the owner of the Torlund Ski School?"

Angie nodded. "My grandparents started the business a long time ago, at another ski area."

Someone sat down next to Curt. Angie looked up. Seeing Dave, her pulses quickened. "What can I do for you, Dave?" she managed levelly.

"How about a cup of coffee?"

"Help yourself," she offered with a nod toward the coffee machine.

She finished up with her young customer and took care of two others. Out of the corner of her eye she watched Dave stroll toward the paneled wall to look at a display of photographs her father had taken of the many racing teams he'd coached. There were even some of her and Dave accepting trophies.

Angie, three years younger than Dave, had been in a lower division, but they'd practiced together all the time. They'd been inseparable until Dave had left the valley to work with a more prestigious ski coach. Angie had never forgiven Dave for breaking her father's heart.

As Dave studied the pictures, Angie studied him. The smooth gloss of youth had given way to a weathered look, a look that made him even more attractive than he'd been at eighteen. Now that the room had emptied, she wanted to ask him how he'd acquired the small scar above his left eyebrow, but instead, she asked, "Need a refill on your coffee?"

"I'm fine, thanks." He came toward her and leaned a hip against the counter. "All this time I pictured you with your hair long, but you've cut it all off."

"Not all of it." Her eyes locked with his, and her knees weakened.

"You've filled out very nicely. Grown a few inches, too."

"I'm five six," she told him, fully aware of his appreciative gaze sliding over her trim figure. She had to get out of here before he noticed the warmth rising to her face. Grabbing her parka, she added, "See you around, Dave."

"Wait. I came to sign up for your group lesson."

"You?" She turned around to stare at him.

"I'd like more insight into the latest teaching techniques."

"You're not planning on becoming a ski instructor, are you?"

"I might give it a try."

"Have you quit racing?"

He nodded. "Busted my knee. But it was time to move on to other things, anyway."

Angie couldn't decide if she should be sympathetic or not. He didn't seem too distressed about the end of his professional racing career. But if he wanted a teaching job here at Paradise Valley, instead of going for a coaching job at a prestigious resort, he had to be in pretty bad shape.

"How much is the lesson?" he asked.

"You don't have to pay me."

"I insist."

She shrugged and pointed at the fee schedule tacked on the wall. "Cash or charge?"

"Cash." He pulled a money clip from his zippered back pocket.

Angie nearly gasped when he tossed a one-hundred-dollar bill on the counter as if it were yesterday's newspaper. At least he wasn't destitute. She gave him back his change, then turned toward a side door. "Gina? I'll be back in an hour, okay?"

"Have a good one."

Angie strode out of the shop ahead of Dave. Having him in her class would be the pits, she decided as she pushed to open the glass-paneled door. She wouldn't be able to concentrate.

"You won't show off in front of my beginners, will you?" she asked him after they'd stepped onto the wooden deck and were headed down the wide ramp.

"I'll make lots of mistakes." He placed his hand over his heart. "Big mistakes."

"Hmm." Giving him a suspicious glance, she nearly bumped into Bob Bates, the silver-haired owner of the resort. "Oops. I didn't see you coming, Bob."

Bob smiled at her, then glanced at Dave. "Dave, I need to talk to you. Would you mind coming up to the house with me?"

Dave rubbed his hand across his square chin. "I was just about to take a lesson from Angie."

"I'll be happy to refund your money," Angie offered quickly.

"A lesson?" Bob asked, looking perplexed.

Dave nodded. "I'd like to familiarize myself with current teaching methods."

"Ah!" Bob nodded thoughtfully. "I suppose there's a big difference between coaching and teaching the basics."

"There sure is," Dave replied.

Bob glanced at Angie. "You'll be teaching another group lesson tomorrow morning, won't you?"

Reluctantly Angie nodded.

"I guess I could take tomorrow's lesson," Dave said. "Would you mind, Angie?"

"Suit yourself." Angie lifted her skis from the rack, making a valiant effort not to stare after the two men. What did Bob Bates want from Dave that couldn't have waited an hour?

Two

Angie spent the rest of the day vacillating between hoping to catch another glimpse of Dave and being glad she hadn't.

At four o'clock, after all the rental skis had been checked in, she closed the shop and headed for the cafeteria, where the ski patrolers and instructors often gathered to unwind before going home.

But this afternoon Angie found herself alone in Gossip Corner, a space separated from the rest of the large room by a colorful fence made of discarded skis. Instead of dropping into one of the old easy chairs flanking the potbellied stove, as she might have done if she'd had someone to talk to, she turned around and headed toward the exit.

Outside, the crisp cold air prompted her to quickly zip up her parka and put on her gloves. The sun had disappeared behind the mountain, and the parking lot, where most of the skiers were loading their cars, was in deep blue shadow.

Angie was the last person to get on the lift before it shut down for the day. She skied halfway down beneath the lift, then took a hidden trail leading to her cabin. The roof of the A-frame was covered in snow, which made the house nearly invisible among the trees. After she'd opened the lower-level entry door, she stowed her gear, then climbed the stairs to the main floor.

Electric baseboard heaters, set on low so the power bill wouldn't break her budget, kept the chill from the house, but she preferred the coziness of a roaring fire. She piled newspaper and kindling in the hearth, then struck a match. When the flames shot up, she added a couple of logs. Satisfied they would take, she moved to the fridge to pour some milk into a large mug, which she put into the microwave to heat. Then she stepped up to one of the two sliding doors leading onto a balcony that wrapped around to the kitchen entrance.

The lights coming from the homes located on the other side of the Paradise Valley golf course gave her a sense of security. Not that she minded living by herself. She'd gotten used to it and even welcomed the absolute quiet of her sanctuary—especially after a hectic day like today. Or did she? If she was honest with herself, she'd admit she wanted company more than anything else tonight. Dave's company, to be precise. It would be so easy to abandon her resolve to loathe him for what he'd done to her father and be friends once again.

She'd just added cocoa mix to the milk when she heard the muffled slam of a car door. Looking out the kitchen window, she saw that a van had pulled into the driveway and that the man walking toward her house was Dave. Her heart took an unexpected leap, and with each thump his feet made on the redwood steps, her excitement increased. When he knocked, she forced herself not to open the door right away, not until at least five seconds had gone by. Then she reached for the doorknob and swung open the door.

"Hi, Angie."

"Hi, Dave." He looked too darn gorgeous in his suede leather jacket, tight-fitting jeans and cowboy boots. Almost lethal. She stepped aside for him to enter. When she got a whiff of his cologne, she unwittingly inhaled a little deeper. Expensive, she mused, and definitely designed to have a powerful effect on women.

"How about having dinner with me?" He shut the door and leaned against it, his head tilted at an expectant angle.

"I don't think so."

"I know you've just gotten home. You must be starved."

"I had a good lunch."

"That was hours ago."

Angie turned and walked toward the fireplace, picked up the poker and rearranged the wood.

He came up beside her. "Heard from your brother lately?"

Angie shook her head. "No. His phone's been disconnected. It worries me."

"I was hoping Tony would get in touch with you so you wouldn't have to hear this from me."

Her eyes narrowed. "Hear what?"

"I saw your brother in Reno a week ago. He sold his share of your business."

Angie stared at Dave in disbelief. "No. That's impossible. You've got to be mistaken." Her voice had risen to a frantic pitch. She didn't want to believe Dave, but his somber expression told her he was telling the truth. She swallowed a lump blocking her throat, but she couldn't get rid of the bitter taste in her mouth. "Why did you wait until now to tell me?"

He gave an apologetic shrug. "I didn't want to spoil your day. I knew this would come as quite a shock."

Groaning, she shoved her fingers through her hair. "Blast! I didn't think he'd find a buyer."

Dave cocked his head. "I wonder why he didn't approach you about buying his share in the ski school."

"He did. I told him I didn't have the money. It was important to me that he hang on to his inheritance."

"Tony was eager to invest in some new invention that's supposed to revolutionize the ski industry."

"He's always got some kind of scheme going. None of them has ever panned out."

"Listen, Angie. I have some good news to help you get over the bad news."

She shook her head in defeat. "After what you've just told me, there can't be any good news."

A faint smile crossed his features. "Oh, but there is. You see, I'm the one who bought your brother's share."

"You?" Angie let out a relieved sigh. "You'll sell it back to me, won't you? I'll pay you extra for your trouble. How much did it cost you?" She held her breath, wondering where she'd get the money. But if necessary, she'd put a mortgage on her house, something she'd managed to avoid doing so far.

Dave cleared his throat. "To be honest with you, I'm not interested in selling it." A smile touched his lips. "You're looking at your new partner, Angie."

"Partner? No, no, no. You don't want to do that. You couldn't make a decent living."

"I've got big plans."

"Really, Dave. The business is too small."

"It won't be for much longer."

"You'll be better off selling—"

"Listen to me, Angie. I've just bought the resort. The agreement was signed this afternoon."

"What?"

"I've bought Paradise Valley."

Angie gulped. "You've bought the resort? All of it?"

"The whole thing," he confirmed, his eyes filled with mirth.

"Well, I'll be . . ."

"Aren't you going to congratulate me?"

"Congratulations. Bob's been trying to find a buyer for years, but I never dreamed it would be you." And she certainly hadn't expected him to have a say in her ski school. She had to talk him into selling Tony's share to her. She owed it to her father to keep Dave Marshall, the man who'd turned his back on a dedicated coach and mentor, out of the family business.

But how? She'd seen the steely determination in his eyes, the same kind of determination he'd always shown just before pushing himself out of a starting gate.

Dave interrupted her musings. "Sure you don't want to come up to my place and have dinner?"

"Some other time. I need time alone to think."

"I understand."

"Where are you staying?"

"I've rented the Lander cabin for the season. I'll be building my own place in the spring. Paradise Valley is going to become Utah's finest family vacation spot. You won't recognize it after all the improvements go in."

Angie's brow creased. "If you're going to be busy expanding and running the resort, why would you want to be involved in my business?"

"I want to attract clientele from out of state. That means I can't afford to have a ski shop that doesn't offer the latest equipment, brand name ski apparel and so on. As your partner, I'll stock the shop, put in a large rental department, hire more instructors and—"

Angie saw red. How dare he! "If there's any hiring of instructors to be done, I'll be the one doing it."

He put his hands on her shoulders. "I didn't mean I was going to do the actual hiring. Look, we can work out the details later, when the time is right."

"And when will that be?"

"I'll have to wait for the lawyers to get on the ball. There'll be a bunch of papers for us to sign." He gave her a bright, confident smile. "Well, if you're not going to have dinner with me, I'll take off. How about skiing with me in the morning?"

Angie was about to fabricate an excuse when it dawned on her that she'd better start being nicer to Dave; she desperately needed to persuade him to sell Tony's share back to her. "I'll meet you at eight-thirty at the lift."

"Thanks." At the door, he turned unexpectedly and kissed her cheek. "Sorry about all the upheaval, Angel."

"Don't call me Angel, Dave," she said while flipping on the floodlight that illuminated the stairs and part of the driveway. "I outgrew that nickname a long time ago."

"What should I call you?" he asked with an amused twinkle in his eyes. *"Ma petite?"*

"Cut it out!" She gathered a bunch of snow from the railing and threw it at him, but he ducked before it could find its intended target.

"You've lost your touch, Angel."

"Get out of here before I throw you off the balcony."

"Yes, ma'am." Laughing, he ran down the stairs.

Tucking her wet hands beneath her upper arms to warm them, Angie watched Dave get into his van and back out of the driveway. Would she be able to tolerate having him around without falling apart and letting him see how much she still cared for him?

Sighing, Angie turned and went inside. She had no choice but to make the best of a rotten situation.

Remembering her mug of hot chocolate gone cold, she put it back into the microwave. While waiting for it to heat, she picked up the kitchen wall phone and dialed Tony's old number on the chance that he might have another number by now.

"The number you have dialed is no longer—"

"Damn you, Tony!" she shouted into the receiver, drowning out the uncaring, automated voice. "How could you betray me like this? How could you do this to the Torlund Ski School? You knew how much work I put into keeping it going the way Dad would have wanted me to. You knew, and still ..."

A sob escaped her. She hung up the phone and touched her forehead to the cool wall. No use crying over spilled milk, she thought, trying to regain her equilibrium. Somehow she'd have to find a way to undo what her brother had done.

Three

When Angie reached the bottom of the big lift on Sunday morning, Jake, the lift operator, stopped shoveling snow onto the ramp. "Morning, Angie. Couldn't ask for a nicer day, could we?"

"It'll be a busy one."

He came closer, the soles of his rubber boots leaving patterns in the snow. Leaning on the handle of his shovel, he asked, "Want to hear some exciting news?"

"Only if it's good news."

"Dave Marshall is back." His weather-beaten face creased into a million wrinkles.

"I know." She tried to change the subject. "Coffee at ten o'clock?"

"Sure. He's turned into a damned fine fellow. Just the kind you've been holding out for."

"You're wrong, Jake. Dave Marshall isn't the hero you think he is."

"You used to have quite a crush on him, as I recall."

"Not me," Angie was quick to say. A surge of heat traveled upward from her midsection. How could Jake have known about her feelings for Dave?

Jake looked at her with a critical squint. "Come on, Angie. That's why you practiced with him all the time."

"I . . . I practiced with him because I wanted to win."

"Then why'd you quit after he left?" he asked softly.

Angie swallowed. "I don't know. Guess I got tired of it."

"Honey, you moped around for weeks, even months, after he left the valley. It took you a long time to get over him, didn't it?"

"It was just puppy love, Jake."

"First love is special. More powerful than anything that comes later in life. Emotions run deep at that age."

"Maybe so, but—"

"Here he comes."

"Hello, hello." Dave, his skis over his shoulder, approached them with a smile as brilliant as the snow. He wore a sleek one-piece racing suit today, its predominant color a touch bluer than his eyes—eyes that seemed to penetrate her very soul. A heady weakness stole over her, making her wonder if Jake's theory about first love was right on target. Finally Dave tore his gaze from hers to acknowledge Jake. "Nice morning, isn't it?"

"Sure is, son. Say, could I get your autograph sometime?"

Dave winked at him. "If you'll turn on the lift and let us go up right now."

"My pleasure." Beaming, Jake rushed toward the control hut.

Angie waited for Dave to step into his skis, then they both skated to the spot where the chair would pick them up.

Having started the motor, Jake came to hold the chair for them. "Sure glad to hear you're buying the place, Dave."

"So word's already gotten around."

"Sure has. Don't take long around here."

The chair came and scooped them up, preventing further conversation. After they'd settled themselves and were headed up the mountain, Dave turned to Angie. "Why didn't Bates ever develop this place more? There's so much potential here."

Angie shrugged. "I suppose Bob realized it would be a giant headache for him." She paused, then added, "He's made his money and probably decided to coast until he could find a buyer."

"He didn't find a buyer—the buyer found him," Dave said on a chuckle.

"Did running into Tony start you thinking about buying Paradise Valley?"

"As a matter of fact, it did. I didn't know it was for sale until your brother mentioned it."

"Then you wouldn't have come back if it hadn't been for your interest in the resort."

"Probably not," he admitted, draping an arm around her shoulder. "But I'm glad I did."

Angie felt like pushing Dave off the lift. Paradise Valley and the friends he'd left behind had meant nothing to him. He'd never bothered to write, not even after her parents were killed. Damn him, anyway.

"How about jumping a few moguls? Viking hasn't been groomed yet."

"All right." Angie gulped back tears of frustration and sadness. Sitting beside Dave in the early-morning sun, suspended in midair and surrounded by serenity should have been heaven on earth. Instead, it was agony. She wished she hadn't agreed to ski with him. Maybe she should try to get out of it. "I'd better set the poles for the girls' racing team this morning."

"When's their first competition?"

"December twentieth at Snowbird. I'm a little worried about it."

"What about the boys?"

"Rusty."

"Would you like me to help you?"

Angie was tempted to tell Dave she didn't need him, but that wouldn't be fair to the kids. Paradise Valley badly needed to win a few events this season to boost team morale, and having an Olympic gold-medal winner for a coach would give everyone the incentive to work harder. "Thanks for offering."

"I may not be qualified to give beginners' lessons, but I sure as hell can coach."

"You lied to me yesterday. You never had any intention of becoming a ski instructor."

Dave gave her shoulder a squeeze. "You can't blame a guy for trying to prolong his time around a beautiful woman, can you?"

She groaned and rolled her eyes heavenward. Even though an echo from the past made her want to lap up his compliment, she forced herself not to let it get the upper hand.

Dave chuckled. "Let's go set the race course."

"Okay." They'd reached the top and skied off the ramp. "The poles are stored in that shed over there." Angie headed toward a small A-frame structure. After coming to a stop in front of it, she unsnapped her bindings and opened the door.

As she handed Dave a bundle of bamboo poles, he asked, "You're not using hinged plastic poles?"

"No."

"That'll be the first thing I'm going to buy."

Frowning, she threw some poles into the snow. "Suit yourself."

"What's the matter?"

"Nothing's the matter. Neither is there anything wrong with these." She wasn't about to admit that new poles simply weren't in this year's budget.

"You'll see a difference, Angie. Plastic poles help a racer hug a gate much more closely."

"I'm not convinced of that."

"You will be once you try them. They're a marvelous invention."

"My father never found fault with these poles." She came back out, put on her skis, grabbed a bunch of poles and said tersely, "Let's go."

"So that's it. Because your father never found fault with these poles, you refuse to, either." He picked up a bundle and came up beside her. "Look, he would have changed over."

"Maybe."

"No, not maybe. Any good coach can see the advantages."

Angie looked at the prospective race course she had mapped out in her head. She wished her father were still around so she could ask him what to do. She felt desperately alone. But she wasn't going to give up. She'd hang on to the Torlund Ski School, her legacy, somehow.

Forcing herself into action, Angie started setting the course while Dave handed her the poles. When they were through, she looked back up the hill, satisfied with her work.

"Good job, Angie."

"Thanks for your help." She glanced at her watch. "It's time for my lesson."

"Go on. I'll be down in a minute."

Nodding, Angie pointed her skis down the hill and headed for a group of adult students waiting near the designated sign stuck in the snow.

"Good morning, folks. I'm Angie. I'll be your instructor for the next six Sundays. How about telling me your first names, so I won't have to say, 'Hey, you, don't stick your behind out like that.'"

Her comment elicited laughter.

Out of the corner of her eye she saw Dave sneak into line. When he introduced himself, Angie quickly scanned her students' faces. It didn't surprise her that no one recognized him. Even if her pupils were familiar with the ski world, they certainly wouldn't expect a famous racer to show up for a beginners' lesson.

"Okay, let's learn how to sidestep." Angie demonstrated how to dig the ski edges into the uphill side of the mountain, poles carefully planted out of the way.

Dave deliberately acted clumsy. He even fell a couple of times.

Angie marveled at his acting ability and could hardly keep a straight face. Finally she gave him a warning glance. "Dave, come on, you can do better than that."

"Yes, ma'am," he said, little devils jumping around in his eyes.

Angie bit her lower lip to keep from grinning. "Now, folks, let's try a snowplow turn. Plant your poles in front of you, like this. Ski tips together, tails out." She went through the procedure and watched the group of eight eager pupils line up.

As they struggled to keep from falling, she called out appropriate instructions. "That's good. A little more bend in those knees. Weight on the outside, shoulder downhill. That's it. Great. Next. Let's keep coming."

When one of the students fell, Angie showed him how to get up with the help of his poles.

Dave came gliding past her, sticking out his rear end and pretending to be on the verge of losing his balance. "How am I doing, teach?"

"Stop that nonsense," she chastised him quietly.

"I'm having too much fun," he hollered as he threw his arms in the air, bent backward and let his ski tips separate.

Angie groaned. He was overdoing it. If he didn't watch out, he'd pull a muscle.

The next time her pupils skied past Angie, Dave came zooming toward her with his arms flailing, his legs wide apart. "Dave, for heaven's— Oh, no!" He made a quick snowplow stop before gliding into her, his skis outside hers. His arms came around her as if he needed her to hold himself up.

A soft oath died in her throat. She realized she wanted to stay where she was and forget the world around her. Had she gone mad? Pushing her hands against his chest, she looked up at him and said, "If you don't mind, I'd like to get on with the lesson."

"I'll let you go if you promise to come to dinner tonight."

"That's blackmail."

"If you don't say yes, I'll kiss you right here in front of the class," he threatened, a crooked grin on his face.

"You wouldn't dare."

"Wouldn't I?"

Afraid of how she might react to his kiss, she gave in. "Okay, okay. I'll have dinner with you."

"That's better." Obviously pleased with himself, Dave let go of her and scooted backward.

Flushed with embarrassment, Angie glanced at her students, who seemed to have found this little sideshow amusing. "All right, folks, I think you're ready to try the small lift. Let's head down this easy slope. If you get going too fast, remember to snowplow. Wait for me by the fence to the right of the lift."

Angie saw to it that everyone made it. After she'd explained how to get on and off, she asked the young man running the lift to slow it down. The students filed into line and got on without difficulty.

Dave rode up with Angie. "I haven't had this much fun in a long time," he admitted. "By the way, you're a great teacher. Don't you ever miss racing?"

"No. I love teaching and coaching more than anything. It's very rewarding."

"I'm happy for you."

"Will *you* miss racing?"

His smile faded. "I'll be busy managing and improving the resort."

"You didn't answer my question, Dave," she reminded him softly.

He inhaled deeply, then let the air out in a whoosh. "Oh, hell, Angie. Nothing can compare with racing." His voice indicated frustration, as well as disillusionment. "It's been my whole life."

"Yes, I know." Angie's heart filled with compassion. Dave had just allowed her a glimpse into his soul. He'd let her see his vulnerable side, no doubt unintentionally. She felt the urge to touch his hand and give it a reassuring squeeze, but he'd think she was pitying him.

The lift stopped. Angie craned her neck. "Uh-oh. Someone fell."

"You didn't expect all your students to make it down the ramp without falling, did you?"

"No, I suppose I expected a few mishaps."

The lift started again.

"Hold my hand when we get off the lift, okay?" he asked when they neared the top.

"Oh, for heaven's sake, Dave."

"Please?"

"All right." Reluctantly she offered him her gloved hand. "Lean forward, Dave," she added loud enough for the other students to hear.

Everyone cheered when they managed to get off the lift without falling. Angie asked her students to line up for a series of turns. To her relief, Dave behaved like a model student, earning compliments from a couple of the women.

At the end of the lesson, Angie reminded her students to come up and practice on their own.

"What's next?" Dave asked her.

Angie used a pole tip to release her bindings. "I'm going to have a cup of coffee with Jake."

"In that case, I'll take a look around and talk to the ski patrollers. Oh, what about the racing team?"

She stepped out of her skis. "If you want to meet me in half an hour at the bottom of the big lift, I'll introduce you to them."

"Will do."

Angie swung her skis over her shoulder and headed for the shop. She'd expected Dave to invite himself along. It bothered her that he hadn't, but it bothered her even more that she felt so disappointed.

Four

When Angie approached the lift, all ten of her girls were crowded around Dave, giggling and looking up at him with teenage adoration. She stopped just outside the circle to watch the girls make absolute fools of themselves. From the look of things, she'd have trouble getting any work out of them today.

"Let me see if I have this right. You're Michelle, you're Kim..." Dave repeated everyone's name without a single mistake.

When he spotted Angie, his smile intensified. "Let me guess. Your name is Angie."

The girls giggled some more.

Angie scooted forward. "Since you've already gotten acquainted, let's head for the top."

The girls began skating to the lift line. When Dave and Angie lined up behind them, Trisha turned and batted her lashes at Dave. "I'll ride up with you, Dave."

"I'm riding up with Angie. We need to discuss your lesson plan."

"How about next time?"

"I'm afraid not. We have a lot of things to discuss."

Trisha sighed. "Oh, well." The girl standing next to her whispered something in her ear. They both laughed.

Angie and Dave boarded last. When they were settled, Dave put his arm around her shoulder and leaned over to kiss her cheek. "This is to show the girls I'm already taken, okay?"

"That's not really necessary, is it?" Goose bumps streaked down her arms. She was tempted to turn her head and offer him her lips, but she had enough sense not to give in to that absurd notion.

Someone whistled. "Is that part of the lesson plan? Do we get to do the same thing?" Trisha called back over her shoulder.

Dave laughed. "No chance. I only kiss women over twenty-one."

"I'll be twenty-one in four more years."

"By then I'll be a family man with a wife and kids."

"What a bummer."

Angie cleared her throat. "Are you really planning on settling down and raising a family?"

"I've been thinking about it." He gave her a smile geared to melt the snow off the mountains. "Paradise Valley is a good place to raise one, don't you think?" Before Angie could comment, he added, "Clean air, country environment, good schools and a job at the resort when they're old enough."

"You've got it all figured out." Angie lifted her ski tips in preparation for getting off the lift. "Who's the lucky lady?"

"I haven't found her yet. But I'm working on it."

"I see." In her teen fantasies Angie had seen herself walking down the aisle with Dave, but to him she'd just been a ski buddy, a little sister. She probably always would be, so there was no point in resurrecting yesterday's dreams. Besides, things had changed, and she'd better not lose sight of her goal. Over dinner tonight she would try to reason with

Dave, make him see that keeping Tony's share would be just a nuisance to him, a headache he didn't need.

Reaching her students, she said, "Okay, girls. Let's have you make a run while Dave and I watch from up here. Wait at the end of the course."

One by one, the girls showed their best form, no doubt trying to impress Dave. Two of them fell briefly but were quick to recover and go on.

"They're not bad," Dave said, his voice filled with admiration. "You've done a great job with them."

"Thanks." Angie glowed from his praise.

"I have a few pointers for them. Minor things. Shall we?"

"Okay. You go through the gates and show them your stuff. It'll really make them want to work hard."

"I hate bamboo poles," he said with a challenging gleam in his eyes. "I can't wait for the plastic poles to get here."

"What if I don't like them?"

"If you really don't like them after giving them an honest try, well . . ."

"Well, what?" she challenged.

"Then I'd say you're being stubborn and unreasonable." He pushed off.

Angie let out a frustrated groan, but her annoyance disappeared completely as she watched Dave shoot through the gates. Taking in the sheer beauty of his fluid, precise movements, she almost forgot to breathe. He was truly a champion. No one would ever suspect he could no longer compete on the professional circuit. But a course set up for novices was a far cry from the grueling challenges facing a professional racer.

Before he had finished the run, she began to follow, skiing to one side of the race course.

"Now that Angie has joined us, let's discuss how we might improve," Dave told the girls. "Michelle, you need to look ahead to the next gate a little sooner, okay? Jennifer, you caught an edge because you didn't shift your weight soon enough in the fifth gate. And get a little closer to the poles, okay? By the way, we'll be getting hinged poles pretty soon. Right, Angie?''

"We'll try them," she reluctantly agreed. "Let's make another run, girls."

On the way to the top, Angie said, "I still can't believe you can afford to buy Paradise Valley."

"I've got some big-time investors interested in my project. I'm only putting up a hundred thousand of my own money."

"Did you make *that* much on the racing circuit?"

"I had some good sponsors, along with an investment counselor who kept me on the straight and narrow. If I spent my allowance before the month was out, I had to live on peanut-butter sandwiches."

"Does an investment counselor have that kind of authority?"

"I gave it to her," he said with a grin. "Her name is Flo Marshall."

Angie laughed. "Your mother? I think I like her."

"Do you remember my parents?"

"Uh . . . just vaguely. I heard they moved out of state."

"They bought a motel in Jackson Hole, Wyoming. They always thought you were a great little racer."

"I hope they'll take notice that I've grown up. Some people seem to have trouble realizing that."

"Meaning me, huh?"

"Yes, you."

He turned to give her a long, contemplative look. "How come you've never married?"

Angie shrugged. "I've been too busy to think about marriage."

"Come on, sweetheart. You're not that busy in the summertime."

"That's what you think. I have a seasonal job with the Internal Revenue Service in Ogden after the resort closes."

"I didn't know that."

"How could you? You've been gone for almost thirteen years."

His brows shot up. "The way you say that bothers me somehow. It's almost as if—" He stopped himself and shook his head. "I'm probably way off base."

"Go on, tell me."

"It's almost as if you're holding some kind of a grudge. As if you're angry at me for leaving when I did."

"Not me. But some people around here wondered why you never bothered to write."

Dave sighed. "I tried to write, but I'm lousy at putting words on paper."

"You could have sent a card."

"I could have, but a card seemed inadequate, especially after your parents' accident. I felt like being with you and putting my arms around you and...oh, hell, Angie. I haven't been much of a friend, have I?"

She turned her head so he couldn't see evidence of the sudden sting of tears in her eyes. She furiously fought them back.

"Listen, Angel," he said quietly. "I'll try to make it up to you. I'll do my best to make life easier for you from now on."

"I like my life just fine the way it is."

"It'll get better. We're going to turn the ski shop into a summer sports shop. We'll sell golf and tennis equipment, bicycles, swimsuits—that sort of thing."

She gave him a surprised glance. "Thanks for telling me."

"We'll make money hand over fist."

"Oh, sure."

"We will. If I didn't believe that, I wouldn't have bought the resort."

"Do you equate making money with success?"

"What kind of a question is that?"

"Just answer me."

"You don't make money on the circuit unless you come in first."

"You're not on the racing circuit anymore, Dave."

He sighed. "I know, but I consider myself in a race for success, and I don't intend to lose."

Angie nodded. She didn't doubt that he would be as successful a businessman as he'd been a racer. But would he thoughtlessly step over people to get to the top? The way he'd done in the past? Would he betray her and her ideals? She would have to wait and see.

An hour later, when Angie told the girls practice was over, she heard groans of disappointment.

"Already?"

"Can't we make one more run?"

"Yes, please."

Angie sighed. "I can't believe I'm hearing this. Usually you can't wait to get your practice over with and go off on your own."

"Today is special because of Dave." Trisha sidestepped closer to him and gave him a smile meant to dazzle. "We like having you for a coach, Dave. You're fabulous."

Dave gave a quick, pleased laugh. "So are you, girls. You're great little racers." He glanced at Angie. "When's the next practice session?"

"Saturday."

"Hmm. Does anyone come up during the week to practice?" He looked from one girl to the next.

"They're in school during the week," Angie reminded him.

"I wish there was night skiing at Paradise Valley," Kim said.

"There will be," Dave told her. "It's in the works."

"It is?" Angie's jaw dropped in total surprise.

"Uh . . . I guess I forgot to mention it."

"How soon will we be able to night ski, Dave?" Michelle asked.

He turned to smile at her. "I can't say for sure, but I hope to have the main runs lit by the first of December."

"You?" Michelle's eyes nearly popped out of her head. "Are *you* putting up the lights?"

"Not personally. I might as well tell you girls—I'm the new owner of Paradise Valley. It'll be in the paper when we advertise our grand-opening celebration."

"Wow! Great!" Excited chatter filled the air.

Angie glanced at her students. "Say goodbye to Dave, girls. You've taken up enough of his time."

Reluctantly they took their leave.

Dave chuckled. "I don't remember your ever being as silly as these teenagers are."

"I wasn't."

"No, you were kind of serious, all right."

"How many more surprises do you have up your sleeve?"

"Surprises? Oh, you're talking about night skiing."

"And a grand opening. If there's anything else, I'll probably find out through the newspaper."

She wanted to grab him by the throat and throttle him, but instead of giving in to the childish impulse, she merely stared at him, hiding her hurt and the deep disappointment that he hadn't seen fit to discuss his immediate plans with her.

"I suppose you have a right to be annoyed. I should have told you about my intentions before I announced them."

"I'll see you around." She pushed her poles into the snow and took off.

"Hey! I'll see you this afternoon at the boys' session, okay?"

Angie didn't bother to answer. She just skied faster.

Five

Angie stepped up to the order window of the cafeteria. "Colleen? I'd like a hamburger and fries. And a carton of milk."

"Coming right up." The older woman took a meat patty from the refrigerator. "Have you heard the news?"

"About Dave Marshall being the new owner?"

Colleen dropped the patty onto the grill. "Isn't it great? I understand he's got big plans for Paradise Valley."

"He does. Holler when my order's ready."

"Give me five minutes."

Angie was on her way down the hall to her ski shop when Dave walked through the outer door.

"Hey, Angie, let me buy you lunch."

"No, I'm going to buy *you* lunch for helping me with the team. Just ask Colleen to put it on my tab."

He came closer and looked at her as if trying to gauge her mood. "Thanks. I will."

Surprised Dave had accepted her offer, she stepped across the threshold of her shop and took a deep breath in hopes of calming her nerves. Jeez. All Dave had to do was *look* at her, for heaven's sake.

Gina lifted her coat from the wall hook. "Do you want me to come in tomorrow?"

"I'll be okay tomorrow."

"You haven't made out the schedule yet."

"I'll get on it right now." She picked up a pencil and took a sheet of paper from the shelf behind the counter.

"The new instructor came in to ask for an advance on his commission. I told him to call you."

Angie frowned. "I hate it when people do that. It screws up my payroll records." Not only that, it threw off her careful planning; she couldn't afford to pay an instructor until he had earned his cut.

Dave came in with a plate in each hand. "Here's your lunch, Angie." He put both plates on the counter. "I couldn't help overhearing your last remark. Aren't your payroll records computerized?"

Angie had been planning to get a computer sometime in the future, but Dave's patronizing tone made her angry. "Why should I use a computer for something I can do faster by hand?"

"How about your inventory?"

"Dave, I don't have a computer." She gave him a mutinous glare. Furthermore, she wouldn't be able to afford a computer anytime soon, now that she had to find the money to buy Tony's share back from Dave.

"In this day and age you can't run a business without a computer system."

Gina headed for the door. "I'll see you on Tuesday, Angie."

"Thanks, Gina."

Dave took his plate over to the bench and sat down. Stretching his booted legs out in front of him, he said, "Once you get used to computers you'll wonder how you ever got along without them. There's no need to be afraid of them."

"I'm not afraid of them, Dave. I sit in front of an IRS computer all day long during tax season."

"Must be a boring job."

She shrugged. "It pays the bills."

"Well, you won't have to work anywhere else once we get going up here. You won't have to drive through the canyon every day."

Thinking of her old Ford Mustang, with its 200,000-plus miles on it, she gave a reluctant nod.

"Hey, how about a little more enthusiasm?" He came up to the counter and stole her last french fry. Instead of eating it, he held it up to her mouth. She pressed her lips together defiantly.

He traced their shape with the tip of the fry. "I'll bet I can get you to open up," he teased, a challenging gleam in his eyes.

"Mm-mm," she hummed, too stubborn to simply move out of his reach. This moment reminded her of old times, of precious, carefree times.

"Come on, Angel."

"I told you not to call—" The french fry slid between her teeth. "Dammit, Dave," she mumbled. "I told you not to call me that."

"It made you open up, didn't it?"

"You're sneaky." She reached across the counter and tried to give him a push. When he captured her hand and stroked her palm with his thumb, a wave of pleasure engulfed her, drowning out his next words, drowning out everything but his exquisite touch. Her gaze stayed riveted to his. "What . . . did you say?"

He leaned forward, and his face came dangerously close to hers. "I don't remember," he said in a tone that sounded almost like a purr.

Her heartbeat drummed in her ears. She nervously licked her lips. Was he going to kiss her? And was she going to hold still and let him do it?

When a man and two boys walked in, she jerked her hand out of Dave's as if she'd been caught doing something illegal. "May I help you?"

"My sons and I would like to take lessons."

"You've come to the right place." Angie put on her professional smile. The man's colorful ski outfit looked brand-new. So did his sons'. "Is this your first visit to Paradise Valley?"

"Yes, ma'am. A colleague of mine recommended your school."

Dave stepped away from the counter. "I'll see you later."

Angie nodded and opened her appointment book. "We'll have an instructor available for a semiprivate lesson in about twenty minutes."

"Dad! That was Dave Marshall," the older boy said.

"Who?"

"The racer. I've got a poster of him hanging in my bedroom."

The man gave his son a condescending smile. "Sure, sure."

"It really was, Dad. Why don't you ask the lady? She was talking to him."

Looking embarrassed, the man started to apologize for his son's rude behavior.

Angie raised a hand. "It *was* Dave Marshall. He's the new owner of Paradise Valley."

"Can we take a lesson from him?" the boy asked.

"He's not an instructor," Angie said, trying not to show her irritation. She wondered how many more people would ask to take lessons from Dave once his presence here became common knowledge.

"We'll have to rent some equipment for today." The man glanced at the rack filled with skis and poles. "Skiing is new for us."

"I'm sure you'll enjoy it." It took Angie about fifteen minutes to get the boys outfitted. When Mark, a physical-education major and one of her best instructors, came in, she introduced him to his new students and sent them on their way.

Scott came in at one o'clock, freeing her for her coaching session with the boys' racing team.

When she got to the lift, she again found Dave surrounded by kids with shining, adoring eyes. Fortunately the boys weren't as silly as the girls; she couldn't have taken another session like that today.

Dave had already set up a tough practice course by relocating the poles from the girls' course. Angie wasn't surprised when he managed to make the boys work harder than they'd ever worked. When they were through, he helped them gather the poles. Angie tried to pitch in, but Dave told her she wasn't needed. Feeling like a fifth wheel, she reluctantly returned to the shop.

Scott was in the back room filing ski edges. The familiar smell of hot wax permeated the air. Angie leaned against the door frame and watched him.

He looked at her quizzically. "How'd the team do?"

"Great."

"Then how come you're frowning?"

"Am I?"

"Uh-huh."

"I don't have any reason to frown. Dave and the kids got along beautifully."

"Making you feel left out?"

She gulped. "No, of course not. I'm grateful for Dave's help."

Scott's warm, hazel eyes locked with hers. "Come on, Angie. We're friends, remember?"

She crossed her arms over her chest. "I guess I do feel a little left out."

"If I were you I wouldn't worry. The newness of having Dave Marshall around is bound to wear off."

"Maybe."

"You seem to be tired tonight. Why don't you let me close the shop for you?"

"Thanks. I'd appreciate it. I'll take care of the cash-register receipts before I go." Scott usually dropped off her deposit at the bank, saving her a trip into town.

When she got home, she immediately ran water into the tub in anticipation of a leisurely bath.

The phone rang just as she was about to take off her clothes. She answered it in her bedroom.

"Hi, Angie. Don't forget dinner tonight," Dave said. "I'll come and get you around six."

"I can walk up the road by myself."

"You might run into the big bad wolf."

"I already have," she said, and quickly hung up.

With a little smile on her face, she took off her socks. Actually, Dave didn't really seem like a big bad wolf anymore. He was obviously trying to make up for the hurt he'd caused her father by helping her with the racing teams. Would Dad have wanted her to work with Dave? Would Dad have forgiven him?

Not sure what he would have done, she finished undressing and immersed herself in the warm, scented water. Heaving a contented sigh, she tried to think of the evening ahead. It was definitely not a date. Dave merely wanted to discuss business with her. The fact that he'd threatened to kiss her in front of her class if she didn't agree to have dinner with him meant nothing. He'd just been teasing his old ski buddy.

But what about the way he'd looked at her this morning and then later when he'd held her hand? Just thinking about it made her tingle all over. "I'm being an idiot," she murmured to herself. She was reading more into his actions than was good for her.

Realizing the water had cooled, Angie decided to turn on the shower and wash her hair. By the time she'd dried it and dressed in jeans and a bulky black sweater, it was five o'clock—time to turn on the TV and catch the news. Throwing one more glance into the bathroom mirror, she stopped to apply lipstick. Maybe it wouldn't hurt to use a little perfume. She reached for the atomizer. The fragrance Gina had given her for Christmas a year ago had hardly been used. She applied some of the light, flowery scent to the side of her neck. For good measure, she lifted her sweater and squirted some between her breasts. If she didn't use the stuff occasionally it would go bad, she told herself.

Downstairs, she turned on the TV and headed for the recliner. It had been her father's favorite chair. She picked up the afghan her mother had crocheted and curled up in it. Sometimes she had trouble remembering her parents' faces, but there were moments when she thought they were still around—Mom cooking in the kitchen, Dad sitting in this very chair reading the paper.

While the commercials were playing, she closed her eyes. What kind of dinner had Dave planned for her? Whatever it was, he'd probably serve it with wine and soft music. He'd sit close to her on the couch and put his arm around her, and he'd try to kiss her. In a low, seductive voice he would tell her how good her perfume smelled and that it was driving him crazy. That *she* was driving him crazy. And she would tell him . . . she would tell him . . .

From faraway, she heard a noise. Someone knocking on her kitchen door. Opening her eyes, Angie glanced at the digital clock on the TV. How had it gotten to be six already? Dave. He'd come for her. Stretching, she called, "Door's open."

"Angie?"

Surprised to hear Bob Bates's voice, she jumped to her feet. "Yes?"

"We're headed up to Dave's place. He asked us to stop by for you."

"Uh . . . you're going to see Dave?"

"We're having dinner at his place, along with a few other people."

"Oh. I didn't know." So she wasn't the only one having dinner with Dave. Why hadn't he told her? Why had he let her think she'd be the only one there, being wined and dined and—

"We'll wait for you in the car."

"I'll be right down." Trying to swallow her disappointment, Angie went to turn off the TV. Just about to push the button, she hesitated and listened. "Channel Six has learned that Dave Marshall, Olympic Gold Medal winner and professional ski racer, has bought Paradise Valley resort. He will be featured on 'Update' between ten-thirty and eleven Saturday night. The Golden Eagles hockey team has won for the third—"

Angie silenced the TV and hurried to get her dress boots from the hall closet.

Since Dave was going to be on TV, she should ask him to say something about the Torlund Ski School, about the role her grandparents and parents had played in the development of the local ski industry. And she hoped he'd remember to mention that her father had been his first coach. That kind of publicity would make an impression on people and do more good than an expensive ad.

After she'd climbed into Bob's four-wheel-drive truck next to Fern, his wife, she said, "I just heard Dave and Paradise Valley mentioned on the evening news."

Bob shifted the truck into gear. "Too bad we missed it. They told me they'd have it on tomorrow night."

"Bob called in the information earlier today," Fern said to fill her in. The woman's white hair was back-combed and flipped up on the right side. She'd worn it that way ever since Angie could remember. "What did they say?"

Angie shrugged. "Not much. Apparently they're going to feature him on 'Update.'"

"Isn't that marvelous?" Fern squeezed Angie's hand. "Dave is going to do wonders for Paradise Valley. In a way I wish we didn't have to leave."

"Just remember your arthritis, hon," Bob reminded her.

Fern sighed and flexed her fingers. "How can I forget?"

They'd reached the cabin Dave had rented. It had been built by the Swiss engineer who'd installed the lift cables and had taken his pay in the form of a building lot. The driveway was plowed and four cars were parked in it. Half a dozen more were parked alongside the narrow road. The porch light illuminated icicles hanging from the patio railing, making them look like golden crystals.

"Looks like Dave decided to have a real party," Angie observed while helping Fern from the truck.

"It was Bob's idea," Fern said. "He rounded up some of the residents along with a few ski patrollers. Valley Catering is going to bring up fried-chicken dinners."

"I see." Angie linked her arm with Fern's. Bob came to support his wife's other side.

The snow crunched beneath their feet. A million stars twinkled in the crisp night sky, making Angie wonder if

Mother Nature had hung them there specially tonight to celebrate Dave's purchase of the resort. Would it be a good thing for Paradise Valley, or would Dave turn out to be one of those callous businessmen who cared only about profits?

When they neared the front door, the muffled sounds of music and laughter could be heard. Instead of knocking, Bob simply opened the door. Angie followed Fern inside the crowded, heated room.

"Bob, Fern, over here," one of the ski patrollers called.

Angie wiped her feet on the braided area rug before she stepped across discarded footwear and advanced toward a massive chair overflowing with coats. She added hers to the pile.

Dave stood near the fireplace, talking to several people. She couldn't help noticing the enticing shape of his backside in his designer jeans. A shiver raced up her spine. Years ago she'd dreamed of making love with him, of offering him her virginity. She mentally shook her head. What a naive little girl she'd been.

Dave turned. His eyes lit up when he saw her, causing her pulse to quicken as if she was about to race in a major downhill event. She couldn't understand herself. She wasn't a dumb teenager anymore and should know better than to let her hormones take over.

"Hi, Angie. Let's get you a drink." He draped his arm around her shoulders and guided her toward the kitchen.

Angie didn't object, but his touch elicited another burst of sensual awareness. She had to stop this juvenile reaction to him, and soon.

Dave pointed at the kitchen counter. "What'll it be?"

"I'll just have a soda." Wine always made her defenses slip. And she didn't like beer.

"Let me get it for you." He filled a glass with ice and poured from a large plastic bottle.

Angie studied Dave's hands. They were long and slender, like those of a concert pianist. What kind of music were they capable of playing on a woman's body? *Stop that.*

How many ski bunnies had he taken to his bed? How many women had whispered his name in the throes of passion? *Dammit—stop that!*

"There you go." He handed her the glass.

"Thanks." Angie made sure she didn't come in contact with him. "Channel Six announced your purchase of Paradise Valley tonight."

"I thought they might. They're sending some people up tomorrow to interview me."

"Would you say something about the Torlund Ski School, about my grandparents starting it after they came from Norway, and my parents—"

"Sure. Why don't you write it all down for me?" He stepped closer to let someone pass by him. A moment later that same someone threw open the refrigerator door, pushing Dave against her.

Angie's drink spilled down the front of her sweater. She gasped. When Dave stepped back, she saw it had also spilled onto his soft, chambray shirt.

"I'm sorry," the fellow said, peeking around the door.

"No harm done," Dave assured him with a congenial smile. He picked up a paper napkin and started dabbing the clear liquid off her chest.

Angie stood perfectly still. She should tell him to stop, that she was capable of taking care of herself, but for some reason she'd lost control of her logical self. She was unable to do anything except feel the immense pleasure of his touch. Her nipples hardened, her breath quickened, and her knees weakened. Oh, Lord! Didn't he realize what he was doing to her? Did he think she was still a little girl? Her well-rounded curves ought to give him a clue.

Their eyes met. His hand stilled and a chagrined expression appeared on his face. "I think I've got you dried off okay," he said, his voice suddenly raspy. "I'll go put on another shirt." He left the kitchen in somewhat of a hurry.

Angie took a deep, steadying breath before she lifted the half-empty glass to her lips and drank what was left. When she put the glass in the sink, she saw that her hands were shaking.

No doubt Dave had noticed her reaction to his touch and had fled from the kitchen to get away from her. How utterly embarrassing! She was tempted to leave now so she wouldn't have to face him again—at least not tonight. But somehow she got through the evening with no further mishap—and no further contact with Dave.

Six

Angie was about to unlock the door to the ski shop on Monday morning when she heard voices coming from the cafeteria, which hadn't yet opened for the day. One of the voices belonged to Dave. Curious, she moved farther down the hall until she had an unobstructed view of the room.

Dave, sharing a booth by a window with two men, glanced in her direction. A preoccupied half smile crossed his face. "Angie, come and join us."

Dave introduced the men as power-company representatives. A blueprint lay spread out on the table. She recognized it as a map of the ski runs with overlapping circles added.

"We were discussing the installation of halogen lights for night skiing," Dave explained as she sat down next to him.

Angie unzipped her parka. "I don't suppose you need my input on anything."

"We've pretty well got things mapped out." Dave put his hand on the back of her neck and squeezed lightly. "All we need now is a cup of coffee. Is there any way we can get some?"

Angie did her best to ignore the sensual tingle that raced across her skin. She was tempted to tell Dave if he wanted coffee he'd have to wait until Colleen opened the kitchen, but she managed to swallow the urge. "I'll go make a pot. I know where all the stuff is." Smiling, she slid out of the booth. If doing favors for Dave helped get her business back, the effort was worth it.

When she brought steaming cups of coffee to the men, Dave invited her to stay.

Angie shook her head. "I can't. It's time to open the shop." She raised a hand. "Nice meeting you, gentlemen."

She was about to enter her shop when the front door opened and a man and a woman with Channel Six emblems on their jackets walked in.

"Hi. Do you know where we can find Dave Marshall?" the woman, a petite brunette, asked.

Angie nodded and pointed at the cafeteria. "He's just finishing up with some men from the power company."

"Thanks." They hurried past her.

Angie pulled her lower lip between her teeth. Darn it. She should have taken the time to write down what she wanted Dave to say about the Torlund Ski School. Maybe if she hurried she could get it done before they started rolling. She stepped behind the counter, grabbed a sheet of paper and a pen and began scribbling furiously.

On their way out the door, the men from the power company thanked her once more for the coffee, upsetting her train of thought. When Colleen said good-morning, Angie just raised a hand in order not to lose her concentration. Five minutes later she put down the pen and quickly read what she'd written to make sure it sounded okay. Satisfied, she headed for the cafeteria and approached Dave.

"What was the most exciting experience you've ever had as far as pleasure skiing is concerned?" the woman was asking him.

"I'd have to say heli skiing in New Zealand." Dave turned his head. "Angie, I'd like you to meet Ross and Vivian.

Folks, this is Angie Torlund. She runs the Torlund Ski School."

After how-do-you-dos had been exchanged, Angie handed Dave the folded paper. "You asked for this."

"I did?" He unfolded it and glanced at it before he nodded and put it in the breast pocket of his shirt.

"What type of improvements are you planning on making?" Ross asked Dave.

"There'll be two more lifts to the top, a new operations building housing the ski shop and the school, a cafeteria, restaurants, shops. The works. We'll have condominiums, nine more holes of golf, a large indoor-outdoor swimming pool, tennis courts and a spa."

"Sounds ambitious."

Angie momentarily held her breath. She was too stunned to move. She'd had no idea he intended to expand the resort that much. It was almost scary.

"I plan on sinking every penny I've saved into this project," Dave told them.

Vivian turned to her colleague. "The sun is in perfect position for some shots of Dave with the ski runs in the background."

"Right. We'll talk more later."

Everyone rose. Not knowing if she should join the trio, Angie hung back. Since Dave didn't turn around and encourage her to come outside, she decided to disappear into her shop. If they wanted her for anything, they'd know where to find her—for the next half hour, anyway. After that she'd be on the hill coaching her Mighty Mites, kids between the ages of five and eight.

"Hi, Angie." A little girl, followed by her mother, came skipping into the shop. "Guess what? I got new ski boots. They used to belong to my brother."

"You're growing too fast, Sarah," Angie said with an affectionate smile. "Pretty soon you'll want to ski with the big kids."

"I know." Sarah hopped onto the bench and took off her furry après-ski boots.

Sarah's mother held up a pair of tiny boots and skis. "Morning, Angie. Would you mind adjusting Sarah's bindings to fit the bigger boots?"

"No problem." Angie took the skis and boots and headed for the workroom. Placing them on the table, she asked, "What's Sarah weigh?"

"Gee. I think...I'm not sure," Sarah's mother said, eyeing the scales. "Sarah, come in here and step on the scales for Angie."

Sarah did as asked. Angie glanced at the digital readout, made a mental note of the five-year-old's weight gain and adjusted her ski bindings accordingly.

When Angie took her class of eight little racers over to the lift, she noticed that the TV people were still filming Dave. Leaning over the side of the chair as it glided above their heads, she could see them but couldn't hear what was being said; the boy riding up with her was telling her about his new puppy.

Oh, well. Chances were Dave had made a plug for the Torlund Ski School by now.

Getting off at the midpoint ramp, Angie led the Mighty Mites toward an easy slalom course she'd set up first thing that morning. "Let's have Matthew go first."

"Okay, here I go," Matthew said, getting into position.

"Ready, set, go." Angie never used a watch to time the kids. She wanted them to have fun, to taste the pure pleasure of tackling the course, of getting better and better at shooting through the gates. She also hoped to teach them that it didn't matter how many times they fell as long as they picked themselves up and went on.

When Sarah, the last child to go through the gates, fell after passing the third gate from the bottom, Angie quickly skied toward her.

Dave seemed to come out of nowhere and reached her first.

"Are you okay?" he asked the little girl.

Sarah nodded. "My ski came off."

"I noticed. We'll have to be sure and check your bindings."

"I just adjusted them this morning," Angie told him, unable to keep the defensive note out of her voice.

"It won't hurt to double-check them."

Instead of answering him, she sidestepped toward Sarah to help her up, but by the time she got there Dave had put her back on her feet and was in the process of fitting her boot to her ski. After he'd brushed the snow off her pink one-piece suit, she smiled at him and said, "There's some more here."

Holding out one arm, she pointed to a light dusting of snow near her wrist.

"All right." Chuckling, Dave brushed the snow away. "Better?"

"Mmm, there's more here." She held out her other arm.

"Sarah, you haven't finished your run yet," Angie reminded her gently. Jeez. Not even five-year-old girls were immune to Dave's charm.

"What's your name?" Sarah asked him.

"Dave. And yours?"

"I'm Sarah. And that's Matthew, and—"

"Sarah, let's not waste any more time," Angie felt obliged to tell her. "We don't have all day."

Sarah heaved a huge sigh. "Okay." Getting ready to finish her run, she turned to Dave and asked, "Are you going to ski with us?"

"No, he's not," Angie said before Dave had a chance to tell Sarah otherwise. "He already knows how to race." The last thing she needed was Dave's interference with her Mighty Mites. For reasons she didn't understand, she wanted to keep them to herself.

"I'll just watch for a while," Dave said. "Show me how good you are."

"Will you watch me, too?" a little boy asked him.

"Me, too!" another one piped up.

Angie groaned inwardly. "I'm sorry, kids, but Dave has more important things to do, I'm sure."

"I can spare half an hour," Dave said.

Angie felt like throwing something—a boulder, preferably—at his head to wipe that innocent grin off his face. He knew darn well she'd been trying to discourage him from hanging around.

"Really, Dave, that's not necessary." Would he ever get the hint? If not, she'd have to come right out and tell him to get lost. She wasn't about to let him win this round.

Remember to be nice to him, an inner voice warned her. *It'll make negotiating that much easier.*

"I know it's not necessary, but I'd enjoy watching these little tigers."

"We're Mighty Mites," six-year-old Kristin informed him.

"Is that so?" Dave grinned at her, then at Angie. "Well, coach? Ready for another run?"

Swallowing her annoyance, Angie gave a curt nod. She avoided riding up on the same chair with Dave, and she avoided talking to him while the kids made another run through the gates. But when he asked her how the kids were doing on their times, she had no choice but to tell him she didn't use a stopwatch.

"I don't understand. Aren't they being groomed to compete?"

"They are."

"But—"

"They'll be ready when the time comes." Angie forced a smile onto her lips. "This isn't the first Mighty Mite team I've coached, Dave. I know what I'm doing."

"I'm sure you do. Oops, somebody fell." He pushed himself off and quickly went to Kristin's rescue.

Watching him help the little girl up, Angie had a sneaking hunch that Kristin had fallen on purpose because she wanted Dave to brush the snow off her parka.

Angie shook her head in exasperation. He'd make a good father, she couldn't help thinking as she watched him give Kristin the same kind of attention he'd given Sarah. How could she not be in love with him?

I'm not in love with him! Not anymore.

Seven

Back at the ski shop, Angie finally remembered to ask Dave how the interview went.

"Great," he told her with a satisfied nod.

"I hope it helped that I wrote things down for you—"

"Oh, damn!" He hit his hand against his forehead. "I forgot all about it. They got me talking about other stuff. Jeez, I'm sorry, Angie."

Angie looked at him for a long, silent moment while she tried to swallow her disappointment. " 'Sorry' doesn't cut it, Dave."

"I know. Look, there'll be other TV interviews. Next time I'll give a long speech about the school."

"Don't patronize me." She tried to step past him, but he held on to her arm and swung her around to face him.

"I wasn't patronizing you." His low, controlled tone made her feel a bit uneasy. "I was trying to make up for my negligence."

She moved her arm to let him know she didn't like being manhandled, but instead of letting go, he put his free hand on her other arm and squeezed. Suddenly the anger evaporated from his face, softening the lines of his mouth. When he drew her closer to him and moved his hands to her back, she clasped her parka to her chest as if it were a shield capable of stopping the onslaught of emotions threatening to overwhelm her. Looking up at him, she felt light-headed. Her lips opened to utter a meaningless protest, yet in her heart she knew she wouldn't stop him if he tried to kiss her. She craved his kiss more than she'd ever craved anything in her life. She'd waited years for this moment.

The gentle touch of his cool lips on hers immediately inflamed her senses, obliterating all rational thought. A tiny moan escaped her, a moan that seemed to reverberate to the edges of the universe. He responded with a sharp intake of breath and a tightening of his embrace. The tip of his tongue advanced just enough to explore the rim of her mouth with velvety, tantalizing strokes that tore the remnants of her inhibitions to shreds. She opened up to him, inviting him to taste to his heart's content while she did the same in return. Lifting her arms, she draped them around his neck and lost herself in the pleasure of the moment. His scent, a combination of fresh air and expensive after-shave, affected her like a heady wine; she couldn't get enough of it.

"Uh . . . excuse me."

Angie heard the distant voice but didn't want to acknowledge it. She wanted no part of the real world and resented the intrusion. When Dave severed the kiss and lifted his head, she gulped back a *no!*

"Mr. Marshall? Sorry I caught you at a bad time."

Dave sighed. "You must be the man from the computer store."

"I am. Where would you like me to set things up?"

Dave partially let go of Angie. Her parka began slipping to the floor, but she caught it just in time. Leaving one arm around her waist, he glanced at her. "It's up to you, Angie. You'll be the one using the system more than anyone else."

Angie stepped away from Dave and shook her head in exasperation. "I told you I get along just fine without a computer." The warmth in her heart turned to frosty disdain. She had looked forward to someday shopping for a system, to going from store to store hunting for a bargain, and Dave had just taken that pleasure away from her. Darn him.

Dave turned to look at the salesman. "I'll have you set up in the cafeteria for demonstration purposes. We'll decide on a permanent location later."

"Okay. I'll start bringing in the equipment."

When he'd gone, Angie stepped behind the counter and gave Dave a hard, reprimanding glare. "I hope you don't expect me to pay for half of that extravagance."

Dave rested his lower arms on the opposite side of the counter. "Don't worry. I'm planning on paying for all of it."

"Fine." The intensity of his blue gaze caused an unwelcome blush to creep into her cheeks. How could she have allowed him to kiss her? How could she have been so incredibly stupid?

"All I ask is that you learn how to use it."

She headed for the bench and pulled her ski boots out from under it. Sitting down, she added, "I'm not the least bit interested in listening to your computer demonstration."

Dave came to stand in front of her with his hands on his hips and his legs spread in a stance of macho superiority. "Look, Angie. It doesn't make sense for you to fight me on this. I'm buying the system to make things easier for you."

"Don't do me any favors." She pulled off an après-ski boot and dropped it onto the floor with an angry thud.

"Why are you being so damned stubborn about this?"

"What gives you the right to make decisions without consulting me?"

"I thought we'd decided a computer system would be beneficial."

"Oh, come off it, Dave. You know very well I didn't give my approval to purchase one."

"You're not purchasing it—I am." He crouched down in front of her and put his hands on her knees. "You're hurting yourself by trying to hang on to the past, sweetheart. Think about it, okay?" He rubbed his hands back and forth on her thighs.

She stiffened. "In the future I expect to have some input on what we buy or don't buy."

"I'll be sure to remember that." He rose and headed for the door. "See you later."

Making a split-second decision, Angie added, "And don't think you can kiss me whenever you feel like it. It's a known fact that business and pleasure don't mix."

He glanced at her through narrowed eyes. "You're absolutely right, Angel—I mean, Angie. I won't kiss you again." With a casual wave, he turned and left.

Angie leaned against the wall and closed her eyes. No more kisses. She had done the right thing by telling Dave that, hadn't she? Of course she had. Getting romantically involved with him would be dangerous. He'd betrayed her father, and she had no guarantee he wouldn't betray *her* someday. Why should he be different from her own brother?

On a sigh, she got up and went to hide in the back room, where she wouldn't have to see that blasted computer guy walk past her shop. However, when two of her instructors walked in to schedule classes for the following week, she had to leave her sanctuary to take care of them.

From the open doorway, Angie noted that Dave and the salesman were now deeply engrossed in looking at the computer system. She was tempted to join them, but if she did,

Dave would think she condoned his behavior and had forgiven him for it.

Half an hour later, Dave walked in with a big grin on his face. "I got a great deal on the system. Now, how about coming up to my cabin for lunch? I have to get rid of some leftover fried chicken."

Stunned that he could act as if nothing out of the ordinary had happened just a short while ago, Angie forced herself to act likewise. "Even though chicken sounds a lot more appetizing than a hamburger or a hot dog, I can't leave the shop unattended."

"Is that what you usually have for lunch?"

She shrugged. "What else is there?"

"Veggies, yogurt, tuna on whole wheat bread—that sort of thing."

"I guess I should fix myself a decent lunch to bring down."

"Are you taking your vitamins?"

She gave a quick laugh. "It's been years since anyone has asked me if I'm taking my vitamins."

"Well, are you?" He looked at her as though her answer really mattered to him.

"No." Warmth spread across her skin—a special warmth that made her think back to the days when her parents were still alive, when she had taken their love and their caring for granted. Would she ever have that again? Would Dave be the one to give it to her? No, she mustn't think along those lines.

"You should."

Before Angie could thank him for his concern, a woman and two men entered the shop. Their obviously expensive designer ski outfits made her wonder if they were lost; Paradise Valley couldn't possibly be on their list of resorts to visit.

"Dave, baby!" The woman rushed toward him with out-stretched arms.

Angie could only stare as Dave's expression changed from disbelief to delight. "Brigita." He embraced the tall, slender young beauty. "What brings you to Paradise Valley?"

"I came to see you," she said in a strong Norwegian accent. After giving him a quick kiss on the lips, she added, "I've missed you like crazy. How is the knee?"

"Good as new. How did you find me?"

"We're staying at Deer Valley for a few days before we move on to Colorado. Last night someone said you bought this ski resort. Is it true?"

"It's true."

"Fantastic!" She whipped her head around, causing her waist-length, blond braid to fly. "Meet my friends, Olaf and Gared."

Dave extended his hand. "Hi, fellows." Looking at Angie, he added, "This is Angie Torlund, our ski-school director."

"God morgen." Angie raised her hand, but stayed behind the counter, fully aware that the woman was giving her a more than casual inspection. Was she in love with Dave? Was she someone Dave had gone to bed with? Angie felt a fierce stab of jealousy. What was the matter with her? She had no claim on Dave. She'd even warned him not to kiss her again.

Brigita smiled at her. "You are Norwegian?"

"My father was. Unfortunately I remember only a few words of the language."

"Ah." With an incline of her head Brigita turned back to Dave. "According to the road signs, your Paradise Valley is located in a village called Eden. You can't get much closer to heaven than that, love."

Dave laughed. "You may be right. Have you had lunch?"

"Not yet."

Olaf said, "Brigita wouldn't let us stop. She was too eager to get here."

The blonde gave Dave a meaningful glance. "It's been a long time, my friend."

Dave raised his brows. "Yes, it has been. How about coming up to my cabin for lunch? I happen to have some leftover chicken dinners on hand."

"Wonderful."

Dave glanced at Angie. "I'd like to have you join us, Angie. Is there anyone who can tend the shop?"

"I'll page Scott. I'm sure he can do it for a while." She couldn't stand the thought of being left behind.

"Fine. We'll wait for you in the parking lot."

"I'll catch up with you."

Luckily Scott walked in a moment later, clumps of snow clinging to his sweater. When she asked him if he'd watch the shop for her, he looked at the clock. "I've got an anatomy class at two-thirty. What's up?"

"Dave invited some out-of-town people to his cabin for lunch. He asked me to join them."

"I saw them head down the ramp. Who's the woman?"

"She's a friend of Dave's."

"I see. Go on, get out of here. But be back by a quarter to two."

"Thanks a million, Scott."

"Want some advice?"

"Advice?"

"Keep cool. If this woman meant anything to Dave, he would have mentioned her by now."

"I don't care how he feels about her."

"Sure. And I'm Santa Claus."

"Oh, hell, Scott." Angie moved toward the door. Forty-five minutes. Would that give her enough time to find out what Brigita was all about? Why she'd come here? Walking down the ramp, Angie saw that Dave had pulled his van into the loading zone.

He rolled down the window. "Hop in! They're going to follow us in their Jeep."

"Okay." Angie scurried around to the passenger door. Seating herself, she said, "So, tell me more about your friend."

"I first met Brigita in Oslo a few years ago. She invited the whole American ski team to her house for her sixteenth birthday party."

"The whole team? How did her parents feel about that?"

"Her parents happened to be out of town, but the cook and the butler acted as chaperons."

"A rich ski bunny. What more could you want?"

He pulled out onto the snow-covered, sanded road. "Brigita is like a little sister to me."

Yeah, sure. Angie produced a watery smile. "Why is she here?"

"She's always looking for new places to ski. She didn't realize we don't have much to offer yet."

"Hmm." Angie looked out the side window. Not much to offer? *She wants you, Dave,* she was tempted to tell him. Instead, she said, "I suppose she and her buddies will want to go back to Deer Valley right after lunch."

"I've invited them to spend the night. I'll take them up to Powder Mountain tomorrow morning and to Snow Basin tomorrow afternoon to let them try something different. They'll enjoy the short lift lines."

"Deer Valley has short lift lines." Surely Dave knew the resort sold only a limited number of lift passes every day, making it a popular place for the wealthy.

"True, but their goal is to try as many different resorts as possible during their six-week tour of North America. Want to come along?"

"I've got a business to tend to. I can't run off and play whenever I feel like it, like some people."

Dave sighed. "I hear you. I'm going to give you a chance to take some time off after they're gone. I'll take care of the shop part of the time."

"Why don't you make it easy on yourself and just sell your share back to me?"

"I can't do that, Angie." Dave shot her an exasperated glance but said nothing more.

After he'd parked the van in his driveway, they both got out and waited for the Jeep to pull in behind them.

"Nice cabin, Dave," Brigita said. "Is it yours?"

"I'm renting it." Walking toward the door alongside her, Dave told her what his plans were.

Olaf and Gared, both lean, blond and blue-eyed like their female companion, smiled at Angie and politely waited for her to follow Dave and Brigita before they brought up the rear.

"If you want to wash up, the bathroom is down the hall, second door to your right," Dave told his guests before he turned to Angie. "Come and help me heat up the chicken."

Angie followed Dave into the narrow kitchen, where he opened the refrigerator, grabbed five boxes of chicken and set them on the counter. "You go on and entertain your friends," she told him. "I'll holler when lunch is ready."

"Thanks. You're a doll." He patted her back, reached past her and got five plates from a cupboard.

"Listen," Angie said, trying to ignore the tingles that rushed across her skin. "Brigita is welcome to stay at my house tonight. I know you're short on sleeping space."

He lifted a bottle of wine from a small rack. "It's sweet of you to offer, but she can sleep in my bed."

Angie's heart dropped through the floor. Now she knew what she hadn't really wanted to know. "Well, I just thought . . . I should have realized. . . ."

"We'll be okay." He uncorked the bottle. "I discovered a closet full of sleeping bags and pillows."

"Whatever." Angie pressed the start button on the microwave.

"We've got a lot of catching up to do," he added as he left the kitchen.

"I'll bet you do," she muttered to herself. Images began to flash across her mind—disturbing images of long limbs intertwined, hands stroking, bodies fusing, soft sighs mingling with deep moans of satisfaction. Her breath caught. *Don't do this to yourself. Dave's love life is none of your business.*

She'd never been up in the loft, but she guessed it had only a cozy double bed in it. Anything wider than that would have been difficult to get up the narrow, winding staircase.

Somewhere in this cabin there was a hot tub; she remembered it being delivered while the cabin was still under construction. No doubt Dave and Brigita would make good use of it.

Dave peeked into the kitchen. "About done?"

Angie handed him two plates. "The last one's warming up."

"Great."

She picked up the two remaining plates. The visitors had taken off their jackets and were sipping wine. After setting the food on the coffee table, she went to get her own plate and glass.

Olaf and Gared scooted apart to make room for her on the couch. Dave and Brigita had taken the love seat, which left her no choice but to sit between the two men.

"We'll drive into town this afternoon and get some party food and drinks," Brigita suggested. Looking at Dave, she added, "Don't worry. I don't get drunk anymore. I've grown up."

"Remember Bad Gastein?" Dave asked on a soft laugh. "That wild party at the Hotel Kaiserhof?"

"I don't remember much about it, but I do remember you carrying me up to my room."

"You were a little hellion in those days."

Batting her lashes, she leaned into him. "I was trying to get you to notice me."

"Oh, I noticed you all right."

Brigita sighed. "Remember Christmas Eve in Zermatt?"

"I'll never forget it as long as I live. I don't know how you talked Santa Claus into letting you borrow his sleigh."

Angie listened as an animated Brigita conjured up one fond memory after another, drawing Dave back into a world filled with excitement. He clearly missed it. She could see it in his wistful expression, hear it in his voice. This peaceful valley offered him none of the glamour and thrills he'd become accustomed to.

When Dave rose to get some more wine, Brigita turned to Angie and said, "Have you been to Europe, Angie?"

She shook her head. "No. But I plan on doing some traveling someday." Fat chance.

"If you come to Oslo, you must look me up."

"Thanks. I'll keep that in mind." Angie didn't think for one minute the invitation was genuine.

"More wine?" Dave asked everyone.

Angie declined, even though her glass was empty. She knew her limit. As soon as she'd finished her meal, she rose and told everyone she had to get back to work. Dave got to his feet, as well. "I'll have to ask one of you guys to move the Jeep so I can use my van."

Brigita touched Dave's arm. "Angie is welcome to take the Jeep. You can drop us off in a while."

Dave glanced at Angie. "Okay with you?"

She shrugged. "Fine. Is the key in it?"

"I have it." Gared handed it to her. "You don't worry about car thieves here?"

"Car thieves? In Paradise?" Angie couldn't help teasing him.

He laughed. "I should not have asked such a dumb question. Maybe I would like to live here."

"The quiet life isn't for everyone," she said meaningfully, watching Dave out of the corner of her eye. "Especially not for people used to lots of action."

"By the time we get back home, I will have seen enough action." He glanced at Brigita before he turned back to Angie. "I hope to find a wife and settle down."

Groaning, Brigita raised her eyes to the ceiling. "Don't be a bore, Gared."

Sitting down again, Dave clamped his fingers around the back of Brigita's neck and shook her gently. "Hey, maybe it's time you thought about settling down yourself, princess."

"Not me." She looked deep into Dave's eyes. "Unless . . . someone offered me paradise."

Angie's heart took a wild leap. How was Dave going to respond to that?

"No one can offer you paradise. You and the man of your choice will have to create it together," he lectured gently.

A lump in her throat, Angie turned and walked out of the cabin. Did Dave really intend to find a wife and settle down in the valley? And if so, would he choose a local or someone more sophisticated? Someone like Brigita?

Driving down the road, Angie hoped no one expected her to come to Dave's cabin tonight and join the party. She had better things to do with her time than to watch Brigita flirt with him.

Angie didn't see Dave or his friends again until they came into her shop at the end of the day. Brigita told her how much they'd enjoyed skiing Paradise Valley's slopes, adding, "You have very good mogul skiing."

Angie nodded. "I guess Dave told you about his plans to put in more lifts."

"Yes, and night skiing. It will be fabulous here once he adds some fine restaurants and good night-time entertainment."

"Uh . . . Paradise Valley is a family resort."

Dave looked at the clock. "I guess we'd better head for town. Angie, plan on being at my place by seven, okay?"

"I'm sorry, Dave, but I've made other plans for the evening. I didn't know I was invited to your party."

"Of course you were invited."

"Thanks, anyway. I'll see you all in the morning."

Telling her good-night, the Norwegians filed out of the shop.

Dave asked, "What are you going to do tonight?"

"I have a date."

His eyes narrowed. "What time will you be home?"

"Late. Unless I decide to sleep over."

"Anyone I know?"

"Does it matter?"

"Uh . . . no. No." Reluctantly he headed for the door. "Well, have fun."

"Thanks. I will." Feeling shaky, Angie looked out the window and made sure Dave's van had left the parking lot before she picked up the phone and dialed. When a male voice answered, she breathed a sigh of relief. "Hi, Phil. How does dinner out and a show sound to you?"

Eight

During a quiet moment, Angie glanced out her shop window at the pristine white mountains bathed in sunshine. It was another crisp, clean day, perfect for skiing. She pictured Dave standing on top of a run, claiming it as his own, his breath visible, his smile competing with the brightness of the sun, his chest heaving with exhilaration....

"Come on, Angel, let's have another race," he'd say with a wink, and she'd laugh and take off, her heart bursting with joy, filled with the knowledge that they belonged to each other, that nothing could come between them ever again. They'd float into shimmering clouds, where Dave would lift her into his arms and carry her toward a bed of white roses. She'd sink into it and reach out to him...but then suddenly he'd turn his head toward something in the distance, something calling out to him. "Sorry, Angel, I have to go now."

Her arms would drop. She wouldn't be able to move. She'd open her mouth to tell him she loved him, but no sound would come out....

"Angie? Hey, Angie."

Angie turned away from the window. The dream faded and reality returned. "Jake. I didn't hear you come in."

"I need to do some measuring on the back wall of your shop."

"In here? How come?"

"Dave wants me to figure out how best to cut an opening through it and build a temporary office in the space behind it."

Angie frowned. "Are you sure? He didn't say anything to me about it."

"Must have slipped his mind." Jake walked toward the wall in question. "We'll have to take down these shelves, I reckon."

"Wait a minute, Jake." Angie came around the counter. "On the other side of that wall is Gossip Corner."

Jake ran his hand over his gray hair without looking her in the eye. "I know. Gossip Corner was nice to have, but things are bound to change some now that Dave owns the place."

"Dad built Gossip Corner. He always said it was one of his better ideas."

"I know, honey." Jake gave her upper arm a pat meant to comfort her. "I'll just go ahead and measure, if you don't mind."

"Be sure that's all you do. I want to talk to Dave before you start tearing into things."

"Is he around? I haven't seen him yet this morning."

"He's up at Powder Mountain with some people from Europe."

Jake turned to look at her with narrowed eyes. "Wish you'd gone with him?"

Angie's heart lurched. Jake was too observant. "Of course not. Somebody's got to stay here and work."

"Things ain't going so good, are they, sweetheart?"

Tears pooled in her eyes, and she swallowed hard to stop them from overflowing. "I wish he hadn't come back."

"You don't mean that."

She turned and went back behind the counter. "And I wish Tony hadn't sold him his part of the business. Dad would turn over in his grave if he knew."

"Now why would you think that?"

Before Angie could say anything more—not that she had an answer for Jake—several customers wanting to rent ski equipment walked in, keeping her busy for the next half hour. Gina and Scott came in just before ten, freeing her to teach.

At first Angie had a hard time keeping her mind on her work, but about ten minutes into the lesson she got involved in her students' efforts and began to enjoy herself. Not until she returned to the barn did she start getting angry again.

Waving to Gina to let her know she was back, she walked past her shop and headed for Gossip Corner. Inside the area, a potbellied stove stood on a brick platform, surrounded by three upholstered chairs, two rocking chairs and an old leather love seat—all donated by staff who enjoyed shooting the breeze after a day of skiing.

She sat down in one of the rocking chairs and glanced at the wall in question. Her father had put up several narrow shelves to display Grandpa Torlund's memorabilia from the Old Country. She closed her eyes, conjuring up the past. She could still hear her father's deep, rumbling laughter, see his hazel eyes sparkle with contentment, sense the camaraderie between him and the skiers. How would he have felt about Dave's buying Paradise Valley and changing everything? Would he have let him do away with Gossip Corner?

"Angie?" Gina's voice interrupted her musings. "We need you in the shop. Some of the college kids came up early."

"Okay." On a heavy sigh, she rose and went back to work.

At one-thirty in the afternoon, just after Gina and Scott had gone to lunch, Dave strolled in, causing her heart to skip a beat. Did he have this effect on everyone or just on her? He wore a white sweater and tight-fitting red ski pants. His face looked slightly flushed, his hair windblown.

"How's it going, Angie?"

"What are *you* doing here?"

"I had Brigita drop me off at the cabin before she and the guys went on to Snow Basin." He made his way over to the bench and sat down. "I started feeling guilty about neglecting my duties."

Angie frowned. "You're limping."

"I guess I overdid it this morning, but it's no big deal. Just a little kink."

"Hmm." Angie pursed her lips. "It probably hurts more than you're willing to admit. Better put an ice pack on it."

He rose and came to stand in front of her. "Thanks for your concern." A softness, an inner glow that spoke of repressed passion, came to his eyes, taking her breath away.

"You're welcome." In an instant she was back in that bed of white roses. This time, however, she wasn't paralyzed. As if they had a will of their own, her hands slid upward to his broad shoulders, then to either side of his neck and around to the nape. She flowed toward him, into him, becoming part of him.

Dave cleared his throat. "A woman who doesn't want to be kissed by her business partner shouldn't be giving off signals that tell him something entirely different," he said, his voice raspy.

Mortified, Angie managed to step away. How could she have let herself forget reality? "You don't know the meaning of the phrase 'business partner,' *partner*."

"I don't?"

"How dare you send Jake in here to tear up my shop without my permission?"

"Hold it." He raised both hands, palms facing her as if to ward off further accusations. "I was going to talk to you about adding a small office—after I got Jake's opinion on the feasibility of it."

"Why didn't you talk to me about it first? On the other side of the wall happens to be Gossip Corner."

"I had a hunch you'd get sentimental about it, but you're not doing yourself any good by trying to keep things the way they were when your father was alive."

"You're missing the point, Dave. This has nothing to do with my father."

"It has everything to do with him." He crossed his arms over his chest in a gesture that smacked of righteous indignation.

She threw up her arms. "Dammit, Dave, how can I get through to you? All I want is to be treated as an equal partner."

"You *are* an equal partner."

"Not in your eyes. You still see me as your little ski buddy."

"The hell I do."

"Fight nice, you guys," a smiling Jake said from the hallway.

Angie groaned. "Why don't you tell Mr. Hotshot Resort Owner it's not very smart to alienate people?"

Jake chuckled. "I'm sure he knows that. Now, you two kiss and make up before everyone standing in line out here starts making bets on the outcome of this fight."

Angie gulped. It *had* gotten strangely quiet in the cafeteria line.

"Well?" Dave, a devilish gleam in his eyes, came toward her with open arms. "We'd better do what Jake says."

"In your dreams." She rushed past him and headed for the relative safety of the back room.

When Dave followed her, she turned away from him and pretended to be studying the calendar.

He came up behind her. With his cheek close to hers, he said, "I apologize. I should have mentioned this project to you first."

"Yes, you should have." Some of her anger left her, but she stubbornly kept her position, wishing he wasn't so near. When his arms came around her midsection and he pulled her against him, giant goose bumps chased each other across her skin. She had to put some distance between them.

Grabbing his wrists, she tried to pry his hands away. When he wouldn't loosen his grip, she said, "Let go of me, Dave. I wouldn't want to be accused of giving you any wrong signals."

"Afraid your lover might object?" His eyes hooded, his expression a mixture of curiosity and regret, he finally let go of her.

Angie took a deep breath. "I'm not going to answer that." Was he bothered by the idea of her having a lover? Did he care—just a little?

"I'd like to meet him. You're welcome to bring him to the cabin tonight. We're having one more get-together before Brigita and her friends take off."

"You're having another party?" she asked, her tone openly disapproving.

"Sure. Why not?"

"How can you stand to party all night and ski all day?"

His smile faded. "We didn't party all night. We were in bed by eleven. That is, Brigita was. The rest of us were stretched out on the floor."

"Give me a break, Dave. I'm not a dumb sixteen-year-old anymore. I can handle the idea that you and Brigita sleep together."

"We don't. We never have. Not that it matters one way or the other what you think."

Angie's face grew hot. Was he telling her the truth? Logic told her he had no reason to lie. She'd behaved like a jealous teenager just now. "I'm sorry, Dave. I guess it's my turn to apologize."

"Apology accepted." His expression softened. "Now, let's start over. Are you going to invite your friend to my party?"

"I won't be able to. Phil's back on the road. He drives a truck between Ogden and California."

Angie doubted Dave would catch on that she was talking about her second cousin, the same cousin who had run into her on the ski hill and caused her to sprain an ankle when she was fourteen. Dave had been there to carry her off the hill. During those moments something profound had happened to her, something so awesome it had made her forget the pain in her foot. Had it been love? Or merely adolescent infatuation?

"I hope you'll come, anyway, to even out the male-female ratio a little," Dave coaxed with a grin. "Brigita has offered to fix a Norwegian dish. She calls it *baccarat*—or something like that."

"*Bacalau?*" Angie's mouth began to water.

"Yeah, that's it."

"Grandma Torlund used to fix that. It's out of this world."

"Got you interested, have I?" he asked on a chuckle.

"What time do you want me to come over?"

"Between six and six-thirty."

"Should I bring anything?"

"Just your swimsuit for the hot tub. Brigita has the menu all worked out."

"I'm surprised she knows how to cook. Didn't she grow up surrounded by servants?"

"She spent most of her childhood in the kitchen, helping the cook and doing her homework. Her parents weren't around much."

"That's sad." Angie's heart went out to the young woman, her earlier jealousy all but forgotten.

"Want me to tend the shop this afternoon?"

"You'd better go home and elevate your leg."

"I told you, it's just a little kink."

"Fine." If he wanted to act macho, she'd let him. "I could use some help this afternoon. It's going to be a madhouse when all the college kids get here."

Dave nodded. "Just tell me what to do."

Angie moved toward the shop. "I'll familiarize you with the cash drawer first."

"That shouldn't take long."

Ignoring his gibe, she stepped behind the counter and pushed a lever on the register. The drawer sprung open. "We keep checks and large bills on the bottom, under here." She lifted the black plastic tray to show him.

"By the way, you'll be getting a new cash register along with the computer. It's part of the system."

"This one works just fine," she objected, her anger rising again. Slamming the drawer shut, she opened the scheduling book. "This is how we keep track of the lessons."

"Hmm. Kind of tedious, isn't it?"

She glared at him. "It's a proven system that's never failed me yet."

Dave scratched his chin. "After you've gone through the training program, you might want to play with other methods."

"What training program?"

"Uh . . . the one we're signed up to take at the computer store. You and me both."

Angie closed the book—very deliberately, very quietly—while taking a deep breath and counting to ten. "How nice of you to tell me."

"Look, Angie. Let's not fight each other. We're both on the same side here, you know. We need to sit down and draw up some kind of plan. We need to figure out how we're going to run our business, what our goals are and so on."

"I'm glad you said 'we'. I was under the impression you wanted to do it all by yourself."

He sighed. "Of course not. It's just...I'm not very good at teamwork, but I'm willing to learn."

"Really?" Angie's voice dripped with sarcasm.

"Really. I've been trained to depend only on myself, not on anyone else, and it's hard to change that."

Angie pulled her lower lip between her teeth. He was right. A racer had only himself to depend on. But still . . .

"By the way, don't you have a cousin named Phil?" He tried to change the subject.

"Uh-huh." She busily turned the pages of her appointment book without looking at him.

"What does he do for a living?"

"He works for UPS."

"Driving a truck between Ogden and California, by any chance?"

She watched as a huge smile spread across his face.

Nine

Angie put Dave to work fitting boots and adjusting ski bindings. Some of the college students wanted to talk, telling him they'd watched him race in the Olympics and that they were thrilled he'd bought Paradise Valley.

At four-thirty, Brigita walked in, looking thoroughly pleased. "Dave, you should have come with us. We had a marvelous time!" she gushed. "I had no idea you have two fantastic resorts nearby."

"In a couple of years we'll have three," he said with a grin, adding, "Are you going to start dinner now?"

"Right away." She turned on her heel and walked out of the shop with a provocative swing to her hips.

Angie, who had watched the interchange between Brigita and Dave with keen interest, pretended to be deeply engrossed in her scheduling book. Was he telling the truth about their not sleeping together? *Forget about them. Just forget about them,* she chided herself.

After Scott and Gina had left for the day, Dave sank onto the bench hugging the wall. "Angie, we need someplace to set up the computer system. I'll also need a desk for myself, a phone and a file cabinet. Where do *you* think we should locate a temporary command center?"

Angie finished counting the rental skis before she turned to him. "You're actually asking for my opinion?"

"I'm asking."

Her heart made an optimistic thump. Because he was trying, she decided to meet him halfway. "I suppose Gossip Corner will have to go."

His brows shot up in surprise. "You mean that?"

"I'll have to round up some boxes."

"I'll help you." He rose and came toward her. "Isn't this better than fighting? We're going to get along just fine, partner."

She raised her chin. "As long as you don't act like a jerk, we will."

"I'll do my best not to act like a jerk if you'll promise not to stand in the way of progress. Deal?" He stuck out his hand.

"Deal." The warmth of his touch sent tingles up her arm, but she tried not to dwell on the emotions rising inside her. Stepping up to the counter, she picked up a bunch of keys. "I'm ready to lock up."

"Can I give you a lift home?"

"Thanks. It'll save me some time."

Walking down the ramp behind Angie, Dave said, "It's been a busy day. Don't you think you'd better hire at least one more instructor right away?"

"I'm going to interview a couple of women tomorrow."

"Good idea." He unlocked the passenger side of the van and helped her get seated. "What kind of women?"

"Well-qualified women. I have their applications on file."

"Next season we should look into recruiting some instructors who've made names for themselves. There's a guy in Jackson Hole who'd be good to have around. People fly in from all over the country just to take lessons from him."

"He'd be too expensive."

"Not necessarily. He works on commission."

"Why would he want to teach here?"

Dave sighed. "Your negative attitude is getting to me. I'm trying to build something here. I don't need to be shot down by you every time I mention making improvements."

"I'm just being realistic."

"No, you're being obstinate." He pulled into her driveway and turned to her. "You haven't been able to let go of the past, have you, Angie?"

She opened the door. "Don't try to analyze me."

He sighed. "I'll wait for you if you like."

"No, you go on. I'll walk up."

"Whatever."

Watching him drive off, Angie contemplated staying home rather than joining him and his friends. But if she did, he'd probably accuse her of sulking. Frowning, she turned around and trudged up the long driveway to her house. The phone rang as she walked in the door.

"Hello?"

"Hi, Sis."

"Tony! I've been trying to reach you. Why in the world did you—"

"Before you light into me, let me just say I did you a favor."

"A favor! Are you out of your mind?"

"It made Dave come back, didn't it?"

Angie gulped. "I . . . I didn't want him to come back."

"Oh, come on, Sis. Who else have you been saving yourself for?"

"You're totally wrong. You're—"

"Let's talk when you've had a chance to think about what I've said. Later, Sis."

"Don't you dare hang up on me," Angie screamed into the dead line. Shaking all over, she flung herself onto the couch and raked her fingers through her hair. How dare he! Didn't he realize what Dave Marshall had done to their father?

A sob escaped her, and she let the tears come. "You're an idiot, Tony," she sobbed into the stillness surrounding her. "A meddling idiot. But I still love you."

When Angie approached Dave's cabin, she wondered why the lights weren't on. Was the electricity out? The door opened before she had a chance to knock. "I'm sorry, Angie," Brigita said in a half whisper. "There has been a change in plans. We won't be having a party, after all."

"Oh?" Angie realized Brigita was wearing a man's shirt and nothing else. Inside the living room, candles burned. Dammit! Why hadn't Dave had the decency to call her?

"But I'll give you some of my *bacalau* to take home." She held out a paper sack. "It's still hot."

"No, thanks. I'm not all that crazy about it." Angie turned and walked back out into the night, hard-pressed to keep her composure. Kicking at clumps of snow, she felt tears pool in her eyes. Why did it have to hurt so much? What Dave and Brigita had going between them shouldn't matter to her. But it did, dammit. It did.

She thought she heard Dave call her name. Impossible. Just wishful thinking. He had other, more important things on his mind.

Angie closed the flaps of the last box filled with mementos that had graced Gossip Corner for the past twenty years. The wall looked empty, dead. She sighed. Was she really trying to hang on to the past? And if so, what was wrong with that?

Stacking the box on top of the others, she considered taking them down the back stairs to the storage room, but she decided to wait and let Dave do it. "He might as well do something," she mumbled to herself. She was the only one in the building, having come down at seven this morning after tossing and turning all night.

But Dave wasn't going to get here anytime soon, not after the exhausting night he must have had.

"Morning, Angie," Dave said from just inside the front door. Pressing her lips together, she pretended not to have heard him, but in the quiet of the morning his voice rang loud and clear.

"Angie?"

"Leave me alone."

He came around the corner. "I know you're upset with me for what happened last night. Please, let me explain."

"Why didn't you just take off with your precious ski bunny? You don't belong here."

"Listen to me."

"You had a lot of nerve coming back after what you did to my father."

"What did I do to your father?"

"As if you didn't know. He was as good a coach as you could ever hope to find but, no, you had to go somewhere else. You broke his heart and you never looked back."

"Now, wait just a—"

"You were a selfish, egotistical son of a—"

"Your father was the one who suggested I find another coach. Maybe it's *your* heart I broke, not your father's."

"Mine? Don't be ridiculous." She tried to laugh, but the sound got stuck in her throat. Realizing Dave had uncovered a truth she herself hadn't been able to acknowledge, she turned on her heel and stalked toward the outer door. She had to get away from Dave. It seemed her life depended on it.

"Angie, wait up!"

"Get lost." She didn't turn around.

Dave caught up with her before she'd reached the door. Grabbing her by the arm, he swung her around to face him. "I came down to apologize for Brigita's rude behavior toward you last night. When I found out you'd been there, I tried to catch you and tell you to come back, but you didn't hear me."

"From the looks of things, you didn't really want me to come back, did you?"

Dave sighed. "The candles were Brigita's idea. So was getting rid of everybody. After you left, I had a serious talk with her. I tried to make her see that she's infatuated with a cardboard image, an image that's lost its shine. I told her I'd never race again, that I'm content living here in Paradise Valley. She knows I want to make a new life for myself, a quiet life very different from the one she's used to."

Angie's heart soared. "And?"

"She shed a few embarrassed tears, but she's a pragmatic person."

"I see."

"Angie, I want you to know I didn't hurt your father by leaving when I did. I swear to you that he talked me into it because he knew it was the only way to go if I wanted to compete in the Olympics."

Angie lowered her lashes. "Maybe . . . maybe so."

He let go of her.

Neither of them moved. Angie waited for something more to happen, something profound. When it didn't, an overwhelming sense of disillusionment settled in her heart. Stepping back, she cleared her throat. "I'm going home for a while. I haven't had breakfast yet."

He didn't try to stop her.

Ten

For the next couple of weeks Angie tried to see as little of Dave as possible, which wasn't hard to do. He was busy preparing for the grand opening, and he was pushing to get the lights put in. Besides that, he had meetings with the Forest Service people and problems with environmentalists, who threatened to protest the construction of the new lifts.

Angie watched what was happening from the sidelines, and she found herself feeling sorry for Dave. He looked stressed, and he seemed to be losing weight.

To help him, she made a genuine effort to like the computer, which they'd installed in the new office Jake had managed to build in only two days. Gradually she'd come to realize that she had indeed been trying to hang on to the past by running the business the way her father had run it. She'd mistakenly thought that in doing so she was keeping his memory alive.

When Dave asked her if she'd make the arrangements for a party to be held on the night of the grand-opening celebration, she readily agreed.

"It's for the residents, the ski patrollers and the instructors and their spouses," he added. They were sitting in a cafeteria booth, having doughnuts and coffee.

"I'll call Valley Catering," Angie said, acutely aware of the strain that had developed in their relationship. "Gina will help me decorate. She's good at that."

Dave nodded and stared out the window. He acted as if he'd forgotten she was there.

Finally, her heart in her throat, Angie said, "Dave, would you like to come up to my house for dinner tonight?"

He slowly turned his gaze toward her, and she saw he looked tired. Defeated. But why should Dave feel defeated?

"Sure, Angie." A small smile flickered across his face. "I could use a decent meal."

"Six o'clock okay?"

"Fine." He sighed, giving her the impression he'd just made a tremendous sacrifice by agreeing to have dinner with her. What was wrong with him, anyway?

When Scott came in, Angie borrowed his Jeep to run down to the general store in Eden for some chicken breasts. Dave had better be impressed with the dinner she was going to serve him. And he'd better start cheering up.

By the time Dave showed up that evening, Angie was a bundle of nerves. She knew she was in love with him, and she'd begun to have fantasies about the future, a future that was the fulfillment of her adolescent dreams. But she couldn't allow those fantasies to take hold of her. Dave was probably already tired of Paradise Valley and all the hard work. Maybe that's why he'd been in such a bad mood lately. Maybe he wanted out.

"How about pouring us some of this wine?" she asked after he'd taken off his parka and draped it over the back of a bar stool.

"Sure." He took the cooled bottle from her.

Angie turned back to the stove, lifted the lid off the frying pan and added more orange juice to the chicken. If only she knew what was going on inside Dave's head. "Have a rough day?"

"Not too bad." He came to stand beside her. "Sure smells good, whatever you're cooking."

"It's chicken in orange-and-raisin sauce. My mother's recipe."

"Do I see onions in there?"

She gave him a worried glance. "Oh, I hope you don't mind. I didn't think to ask...."

"No, no. I love onions." His hand settled on the nape of her neck, and his thumb stroked gently back and forth. Angie's breath caught. Didn't he realize what he was doing to her? Didn't he know how much she wanted him?

"We'll be ready to eat in just a few minutes," she said. "Why don't you go sit down?"

His hand slid across her shoulder, then dropped away. "I guess I could take the wineglasses over to the table."

"Yes, please do." Angie checked on the wild rice. It was done. So were the carrots. After she'd transferred everything into serving bowls, Dave carried them to the dining table. She'd placed long-stemmed candles on it, and she'd used her mother's good china.

He held her chair for her, a gesture that warmed her heart. He'd make a wonderful husband and a great father. Kids adored him.

Smiling, Dave raised his glass and said, "To the future, Angel. To a whopping success."

Crystal met crystal. "To the future, Dave." She took a sip of pale yellow Chablis before she added, "Go ahead, help yourself."

"Thanks, I will." After he'd eaten a bite of the chicken, he told her it was out of this world.

Angie beamed, especially when he took seconds and then thirds. He drank most of the wine, and he seemed to be mellowing out. Angie decided this was as good a time as any to ask him some important questions.

While clearing the table, she casually said, "I suppose you'll be hiring a general manager once you've got the operation running the way you want it."

"Whatever gave you that idea?"

"Oh, I thought you might want to move on, that you'll get bored living here, if you aren't already."

"I won't get bored—at least, I don't think I will."

"We don't have the type of entertainment around here that you're accustomed to."

"That reminds me, I'm thinking of adding a comedy club and bringing in some entertainers from the West Coast," he said nonchalantly.

Angie set the plates she'd been carrying on the kitchen counter and turned around to stare at him. "You can't be serious."

"I am." He ambled toward the fireplace and picked up the poker.

"If you open a nightclub, you'll destroy the family atmosphere of Paradise Valley."

"To be competitive, a ski resort has to offer people what they want."

She moved toward him. "Oh, Dave, Dave. Don't you see what you're doing?"

"What am I doing?" he asked irritably.

"You're doing what I was doing. Your need to re-create the type of ambience you got used to while racing tells me you're trying to hang on to the past. You haven't come to terms with the reality that your racing career is over."

"What are you? A shrink?"

"Even though your racing career is over, your life isn't." Tears of frustration gathered in her eyes. "If you try to turn Paradise Valley into another Aspen or Snowbird, you'll lose your edge. You can't compete with the big resorts. Nor should you try. You want to go on catering to families on a budget."

"You don't understand. I'm worried about making this project work. There's a chance I'll go broke...." He inhaled deeply, then exhaled on a tortured sigh.

"Not if you listen to reason."

He pulled her into an embrace and held her tightly. "Oh, Angel," he whispered into her hair.

The tension drained from her body. It felt so good to be in his arms, so absolutely right. She moistened her lips in anticipation of his kiss....

When nothing happened, Angie wanted to die. What had made her think Dave felt anything for her? Anything other than friendship?

Stepping out of his embrace, she glanced up at him and put on a false smile. "Ready for dessert?"

"If you don't mind, I think I'll go home. I'm awfully tired."

Her heart sank. "Suit yourself."

Dave picked up his jacket. "Thanks for a wonderful meal. I needed that."

"It was my pleasure. Well...I'll see you tomorrow." Angie put on a fake smile and opened the door for him. Passing by her, he hesitated, then moved on.

"Good night, Angie."

"Good night, Dave." She waited until he'd gone down the stairs before she sank onto the nearest bar stool and lowered her head to her arms. "Now what?" she asked herself, but she didn't expect to come up with an answer. She should have known better than to get her hopes up.

Angie was glad the grand-opening celebration went off without a hitch. People had enjoyed their free hot dogs and punch, and now that dusk had settled in, the torch-light parade was about to begin. After that, the lights would be turned on, signaling the beginning of night skiing.

Angie hurried to the back of the first-aid trailer, where most of the ski patrollers and instructors had already assembled. They'd pick up their torches at the top of the run and light them. Where was Dave? He was supposed to lead the parade with her. They'd come down the mountain making figure eights.

When she saw him approach, she breathed a relieved sigh.

"Let's go, everybody. It's time."

Angie put on her skis. As if on cue, a light snow started to fall, adding to the celebration. Only, she didn't feel like celebrating. For her, the past week or so had been pure torture. Dave had seemed to avoid talking to her as much as she'd avoided talking to him.

When she got into the lift line, Dave came up next to her. Surprised he wanted to ride with her, hope filled her heart, but she reminded herself the only reason he was doing so was that they were to lead the parade.

For the first half of the ride, Dave said nothing. Neither did Angie. Finally he said, "Angie, I want to apologize for not treating you as an equal partner. Looking back, I can see I made some mistakes."

"Thank you." She glanced off into the distance. "Are you still planning on building a nightclub?"

"No. That's out. You were right to warn me about going that route."

"That's . . . good." She turned her head to look into his eyes and found they'd changed; the sparkle that had been missing from them lately had come back. Maybe she should ask him again now, while she had the chance. "Dave, I've been meaning to ask you if you'd consider selling Tony's share to me now."

Dave sighed. "Why, Angie? Why is that still so important to you?"

"Because...I want to keep the Torlund Ski School in the family. It's my parents' legacy. Someday I want to be able to turn it over to the grandchildren they never had a chance to meet."

Dave draped his arm around Angie's shoulders. "I'm hoping that those grandchildren you're talking about will be *our* children."

She gasped. "What?"

He tenderly touched his forehead to hers. "I love you, Angel. I couldn't tell you before. I knew if I failed, I'd be taking you down with me. And I loved you too much to do that to you."

She choked back tears of pure joy. "I wouldn't have cared, Dave. I love you, too. I've always loved you."

On a soft sigh, she kissed him, and the frustrations of the past few weeks floated off into the night, a night suddenly transformed into a real winter paradise.

THE FAMILY MAN
Danielle Kelly

*To Mom, my biggest fan, and
to my husband, Don, who
believed in me even when I
didn't. This one's for you.*

One

Lilianne Austin stretched out her arm, reaching for her son's kite, tangled in the branch above the one she was perched on. Her fingers came up a good twelve inches short. The elm limb, although sturdy, groaned as she tried inching closer. A cool Colorado spring breeze flirted with her bangs, tickling her forehead.

"You've almost got it, Mom. Just reach a little higher," her eight-year-old son, Jason, instructed from below.

Easier said than done, Lilianne thought as she eyed the Batman kite Jason had so carefully crafted. The plastic casing covering the framework had a Batman emblem on it with strips of white, yellow and black cloth added to the end to make an impressive tail. "I'm trying, Jason," she said, using her legs to slide forward. The bark scratched her bare thighs, making her skin burn. Reaching forward, she realized in disgust that she wasn't any closer to retrieving the kite. Her five-foot-three frame obviously didn't qualify her for kite rescue.

Why had she insisted on saving the kite, anyway? When her son's redheaded friend, Rusty, had offered to climb the tree in her front yard, why hadn't she let him? And where the hell was a man when you needed one? They were so undependable!

"You might have to climb up onto the next branch, Mrs. Austin," Rusty said, squinting up at her.

Lilianne looked down at the freckle-faced boy, intending to tell him she had no intention of climbing any higher, even if it meant abandoning the kite. The ground, seven feet below, loomed up at her, making her stomach pitch recklessly.

"Oh, God," she moaned as she closed her eyes, her head spinning dizzily. She should have known better than to look down. Old fears resurfaced, paralyzing her.

Squeezing her eyes shut, Lilianne willed away the dreadful memory of falling off a ladder as a child, which had resulted in a broken arm. Clutching the thick tree limb with her legs and palms, she forced herself to breathe deeply and remain calm until she regained her equilibrium. She hiccuped.

"Mom, are you okay?" Jason asked worriedly. "You don't look too good."

"I'll..." she croaked, then hiccuped again. She swallowed to ease the dryness in her throat. "I'll be fine. Just give me a, *hic,* minute." Good Lord, what was she going to do? She couldn't depend on Jason to help her out of her predicament. She had scaled the tree easily enough. How hard could it be to get back down?

Drawing a deep breath, she opened her eyes, staring straight ahead.

"You should have let Rusty or me get the kite down, Mom. We're not afraid to climb trees," Jason said.

Rub it in, why don't you? she thought. So she was afraid. Was that such a crime? The hiccups, her body's natural reaction to fear, came more frequently now, shaking her with their force.

"Are you stuck, Mrs. Austin?" Rusty asked guilelessly.

"Of course she's stuck, stupid!" Jason rolled his eyes. "Can't you see she's afraid?"

"I'm not stupid," Rusty said, hands on hips.

"Are too."

"Am not."

"Jason, *hic*, it's not nice to call other people names," Lilianne managed to reprimand.

"Should we call the fire department, Mrs. Austin?" Rusty asked.

Jason snorted. "Firemen rescue kittens out of trees, not people! Jeez, everybody knows that!"

The situation was so ludicrous Lilianne almost laughed out loud, but the thought of losing her balance made her swallow her hysterical giggles. "Boys, I want you to, *hic*, go next door and..." Her voice trailed off as the familiar rumbling sound of a motorcycle reached her ears. Devin, her late husband's best friend, always did have impeccable timing. Her heart flipped in her chest and her body tingled. The flutters were due to her phobia about heights, she assured herself.

Jason, upon hearing the motorcycle, immediately forgot his stranded mother and ran toward the driveway, shouting with glee. Rusty followed him, infected by his boisterous friend's excitement.

"Uncle Devin!" Jason squealed.

Devin McKay pulled his Harley to a stop and switched off the ignition. He turned just in time to catch a flying Jason in his arms. "Hey, there, Tiger," he said affectionately, ruffling the boy's light blond hair. He gave him a squeeze and let him go. Unbuckling his helmet, he got off the bike. "Hi, Rusty," he said to the other boy.

"Hi, Mr. McKay," Rusty answered shyly.

Her fear momentarily forgotten, Lilianne watched through branches and leaves as Devin shoved his fingers through his mahogany hair. It fell in soft, thick waves away from his face. The red T-shirt he wore stretched tautly across his broad shoulders and clung to his flat stomach. Tight jeans, old and faded to a pale blue, revealed incredibly toned buttocks, lean hips and rock-hard thighs. Pulling a baseball card from his T-shirt pocket, he bent toward Jason. The boy's face lighted up with a huge smile, and he threw his arms around Devin's neck. Lilianne's heart constricted and a wave of love washed over her. Devin was so good with Jason and her twelve-year-old twin daughters, Elizabeth and Emily, treating them like his own.

Devin started toward the house, flanked by the boys. "Where's your mom, Jason?" he asked.

Jason stopped in his tracks, his eyes widening at his forgetfulness. "She's stuck in the tree," he blurted.

"She's what?"

"We got Jason's kite tangled in the tree," Rusty informed him, pointing to the large tree in the front yard. "Mrs. Austin climbed up to get it, but now she's afraid to get back down."

Hearing the conversation clearly, Lilianne groaned. Oh, why did Devin have to be the one to rescue her from her foolishness? But she wasn't too proud to accept his help.

"I want to put this card with my collection," Jason said, raptly eyeing the gift Devin had given him. "Want to come with me, Rusty?"

"Yeah." Rusty followed Jason into the house, the kite and Lilianne once again wiped from their little minds.

A smile of amusement tugged at the corners of Devin's mouth as he stared at the large tree. He started forward, his long legs eating up the distance quickly. In a moment he stood directly below Lilianne.

"Hi, Devin." Lilianne gave him a shaky smile.

"Hello, Lily," Devin said, his voice low and husky, almost intimate. The tone he used was the one that made Lilianne's insides melt like warm butter. "Whachadoin'?" he asked, his dark brown eyes glinting with laughter.

Lilianne tried to appear casual, as if sitting in a tree was something she did every day. "Oh, nothing, *hic,* just hanging around."

Devin grinned. Even in her fear she still managed to be feisty, he thought. And incredibly beautiful. She had pulled her reddish gold hair into a ponytail, but a few playful strands had escaped to frame her delicate face. Her eyes, wide and bright, were green, almost an emerald color. She wore a pink blouse and white shorts. His eyes traveled quickly over the length of her, coming to rest on the hands that clutched the tree limb like a lifeline, her knuckles white. A giant hiccup tore from her throat again and her fingers flexed. He frowned, suddenly realizing the seriousness of the situation.

"Lily, are you okay?" he asked gently.

Closing her eyes as her body spasmed with another hiccup, she drew a breath. "I shouldn't have climbed up so high."

"Are you afraid of heights?"

"I didn't think so, *hic,* until now." Her tongue darted out to lick her dry lips. "Remember when I told you I fell off a ladder when I was a little girl?"

"Yeah, I remember," he said grimly.

She smiled sheepishly, her eyes still closed. "Well, I kind of thought about falling off the ladder while I was up here."

"Oh, sweetheart," he said sympathetically, watching as her body jerked with another hiccup. "Why didn't you wait until I got here so I could get the kite down for you?"

One eye peeped open in irritation and glared at him. "How was I supposed to know you were coming over? I'm not telepathic."

Thank goodness she wasn't, Devin thought, because she'd be appalled at the thoughts running through his mind. The way she was bent over the limb made her blouse gape open in front. He didn't think she realized the first button had come undone, allowing him a view of creamy, sloping breasts covered in champagne lace. Every time she hiccuped, they bounced invitingly. He'd often wondered what those soft breasts would feel like in his hands.

Raising his eyes back to her pale face, he concentrated on the matter at hand. Desire coiled low in his body, and unless he controlled the response immediately, he was going to embarrass himself. "I called a while ago, Lily. Didn't Elizabeth tell you I was leaving the body shop early to stop by?"

"No. She's had the phone permanently attached to her ear for the past two hours, *hic,* talking to her girlfriends. I'm surprised you managed to get through." Lilianne shook her head, resolving to buy her daughters their own phone. That she hadn't received Devin's message didn't surprise her.

"Would you like help down?" he asked.

"It would be nice."

"What's my reward for saving a damsel in distress?" Devin's eyes glittered mischievously. Crossing his arms over his chest, he rocked back on his heels.

Lilianne's eyes narrowed. "What do you mean, *hic,* what's your reward? How about being a Boy Scout and doing your one good deed for the day?"

"I've never claimed to be a Boy Scout." The sexy smile Devin flashed Lily made her toes curl in her sneakers. "But in your case, I suppose I can make an exception." He paused a moment, flicking a piece of imaginary lint from his T-shirt. "That is, if you reward me with a nice, hot meal."

"That's blackmail!"

He shrugged. "The way I see it, it's bargaining. You need help out of the tree and I'm hungry. You know what a lousy cook I am."

She really didn't mind his staying for dinner. In fact, she enjoyed his company immensely. She thought of the lonely evening ahead without his presence and answered, "It's a deal."

Devin grinned and stepped forward. Tall and well built, he was an impressive six foot two. All he had to do was reach out and he could grab Lilianne. He placed a large hand on her waist.

"Reach out and put your hand on my shoulder," he told her.

"I, *hic,* can't!"

"Lily," he said in a soft, soothing voice. "I won't let you fall. I'll catch you."

"I . . . I can't," she stammered. Her eyes beseeched him.

Sighing, he leveled his feet apart on the ground, bracing himself for her weight when it came. "Relax, sweetheart. Close your eyes and take a deep breath."

She did as he ordered, letting the tension ease from her body. Without warning, she was hauled from her perch and slid down toward Devin's strong arms. Panicking, she groped for the limb, her anchor, but only succeeded in scraping her backside on a sharp branch protruding from the tree. A loud rip filled the air and a sharp pain shot through her. Strands of hair tangled in the leaves, pulling from her ponytail. Then she was in the safety of Devin's arms, her whole body trembling from the ordeal.

"You're okay, sweetheart." Devin held her body close. "You're just fine."

Lilianne didn't feel fine. She was shaken to the core. "I'm sorry," she murmured against the hollow of his shoulder, her arms wrapped tightly around his neck. "I didn't mean to, *hic,* struggle against you."

"Are you going to be okay?" **He** carried her toward the house, holding her in his arms as if she weighed no more than a bag of feathers.

She nodded her head. "Yes. My rear end is kind of sore, but you can put me down." She pulled her face away from his shoulder and looked into his chocolate-brown eyes. "Thanks for rescuing me," she said in a soft voice.

"Your welcome," he managed around the thick knot in his throat. He wanted to kiss her so badly he could almost taste her. His eyes fell to her lips, debating. No, he thought. He wouldn't risk their friendship for the sake of a kiss. Because it wouldn't be a chaste kiss. He wanted to taste her lips, wanted to let his tongue explore and tease the depths of her mouth. But a kiss like that would alter their relationship, and he wasn't sure she was ready for that.

"You can put me down," she said again, aware of the sensual spell being woven between the two of them. Her hand suddenly felt warm and tingly where it rested on his chest. She noticed that her other hand stroked the hair curling around the nape of his neck. Abruptly her fingers stopped their foray.

"I want to make sure you aren't hurt." Devin maneuvered the front door open, still keeping her in his arms. Turning sideways, he entered the living room. Finally he set her on her feet.

Lilianne twisted around to check the area on her backside that stung. Seeing the tear in her white shorts, along with a goodly amount of white flesh, her face turned a warm shade of crimson. Her silk panties were torn and she could see a trace of blood.

"Here, let me check that cut for you." Devin touched her arm, intending to turn her around to inspect it.

"No!" She jumped back out of his reach. "I'm fine, really."

"Lilianne, I've got blood on me that's come from you." He stood impatiently, hip cocked to the side. "I want to make sure you don't need stitches."

"I don't."

"How do you know? You can't even see the cut." He took a step toward her.

She took a step back. There was no way she was going to let him investigate the cut on her fanny. It started on her buttock and trailed down the back of her thigh. Even though she couldn't see it well, she could feel the burning, stinging line to know what vicinity it was in.

He sighed. "Lilianne, you're being childish."

"I am not." She stuck out her small chin. "I can take care of my own cuts, thank you very much." With that, she backed out of the room until she couldn't see him any longer. Only then did she turn, keeping her hands covering the gaping hole in her shorts.

Devin grinned. Once he heard her bedroom door close, he followed her down the hallway. He opened her bedroom door without knocking.

Lilianne gasped at the intrusion. She was bent over in front of an oval dressing mirror, trying to examine her wound through the slash in her shorts. She immediately straightened. "What are you doing in here?"

Closing the door, Devin leaned against it. His eyes scanned the room, decorated in soft shades of rose and mint-green. The last time he had seen her room had been about a month before Michael, Lily's husband and his best friend, had died. Then the room had been all beige and blue, far more masculine than feminine. Now, the massive four-poster cherry bed was covered in a rose-colored satin-and-lace bedspread, with frilly pillows tossed against the head-board. A sheer fabric was draped from poster to poster, knotted with silk flowers at the top of each pole.

An antique armoire stood open, and Devin could see Lilianne's clothes and shoes inside. Next to that sat a Victorian dressing table with a hand-stitched cushioned chair. The pastel watercolors on the wall added to the softness of the decor. Lilianne had used her expertise as an interior designer to transform the room into a haven of femininity.

The only trace of Michael that Devin could find was a framed family portrait on Lily's dresser. He thought about the man he'd met when he'd been a freshman in high school, and how they'd become the best of friends. Then Michael had met Lilianne and the three of them had been inseparable. Unfortunately Devin had fallen in love with Lily, even though he always knew she was Michael's girl. Out of respect for Michael and their friendship, he'd kept his feelings for Lily tucked away in his heart all these years.

A tragic car accident had severed Michael from Lily's life nearly three years ago. For the longest time after Michael's death Devin had been torn between his feelings for Lily and his loyalty to the man who had been his best friend. He began to wonder if now was the time to reveal the secret he had kept hidden deep inside him. Was Lily ready for it?

Lilianne's voice finally pierced his reverie. He looked at her, his brows furrowed over his eyes. "What?" he said, knowing she had asked him something, but not at all sure what.

"Devin. You seem a million miles away." She moved away from the mirror, removing her reflection from his view. "I asked you what you were doing in here."

He pushed himself away from the door. "I want to check your cut to make sure you don't need a tetanus shot."

"Shot?" she gulped.

Silently he admitted to being a cad. He knew she hated needles. "Yeah. If it's a deep cut you'll have to get a tetanus shot so you don't get lockjaw."

Her eyes widened and she touched her chin. "Lockjaw?"

"Yeah. But if it's only a scratch we can put an antibiotic on it and you'll be fine. Is it a deep cut?"

Lilianne chewed on her lower lip, absorbing what he'd just told her. What if she needed a tetanus shot? What if she didn't get one and got lockjaw? "I'm, um, not sure."

"And you can't see it properly to be sure," he said reasonably. "Now do I check it out, or do I drag you to the hospital and tell them you need a tetanus shot?"

"You wouldn't!"

His mouth curled into a challenging grin. "Try me."

"You would," she said defeatedly. She resigned herself to his looking at her fanny. Humiliation brought a heated flush to her cheeks.

Devin chucked her lightly under the chin, winking. "It's not like I've never seen a bare butt before, Lily."

She shot him an agitated look. "Yeah, I'm sure you've seen your share."

Flashing his bad-boy grin, he gestured toward the canopied bed. "Get up on the bed and lie down on your stomach."

Grumbling, Lilianne did as he asked, keenly aware of the hole in her shorts and panties showing a patch of inflamed and painful skin. *Quit being a ninny,* she scolded herself. *Think of his examining the cut as a gesture of brotherly concern.* She rolled her eyes. Yeah, right.

Devin sat down on the bed, his hip pressing into her waist as he leaned over and inspected the wound. It wasn't as bad as he'd originally thought. The smeared blood made it seem like a deep gash, but the scratch hadn't penetrated anything more than the surface skin. That diagnosed, he let his eyes linger longer than necessary on the saucy curve of her derriere. His gaze traveled the length of her thighs and firm calves, then back up again. Desire twisted his insides.

"Well?" She lifted herself up on her elbows and looked over her shoulder at him, her ponytail flopping to the side. "What's your diagnosis, Dr. McKay?"

"You're fine," he said, forcing his voice to sound normal. He willed away the heat settling low in his belly. "A little antibiotic cream should take care of it."

Lilianne met his gaze. She saw the desire in his eyes, and a strange, long-forgotten warmth spiraled deep inside her. Shaking off the growing sensation, she slid off the bed, careful not to get any blood on the spread. "I'll go take a shower and make sure it's clean before I put anything on it."

He stood. "Good idea." Devin swallowed his offer to apply the salve for her.

Jason chose that awkward moment to barge into Lilianne's bedroom. "Uncle Devin, are you going to get my kite out of the tree?"

"I—"

Lily cut Devin off. "Jason, what have I told you about knocking before coming into my bedroom?" She and Devin hadn't been doing anything improper, but Jason knew better than to enter her room unannounced.

"I'm sorry, Mom," Jason said, his head hanging. "I didn't think you'd be getting dressed or anything with Uncle Devin in here."

She caught Devin's smile of amusement. "Yeah, well, you know the rules. When the door is closed, you knock."

"Sorry."

"I'll get the kite out of the tree for you, Tiger," Devin said. "Go on downstairs. I'll be right there."

Jason scampered from the room.

Turning toward Lilianne, Devin let loose the chuckle he'd been holding back. "Kids," he said, shaking his head. "What time is dinner?"

"Dinner?" What did dinner have to do with kids?

"Our deal," he reminded her. "I save you from the tree and you save me from starvation."

He was a long way from starvation, she thought, taking in his solid frame. "Dinner is at six."

"Good. Set an extra place for me."

TWO

When Devin came back into the house after untangling the kite from the tree, he found Lilianne in the kitchen peeling potatoes. She had showered and changed into a sundress, which he guessed she'd done for comfort's sake. He leaned against the doorjamb, content to watch her prepare dinner.

She was lovely, he thought. She had let her hair down from the constricting ponytail, and the shimmering red-gold tresses touched her shoulders in soft waves. She was also braless. His eyes zeroed in on that fact. Her breasts sloped gently beneath the cotton of her dress and swayed with each stroke of the potato peeler. The side profile he had of her enabled him to study her small nose and the full, lush lips that looked more delicious than a ripe, sweet strawberry.

Lilianne turned her head, her gaze merging with his.

Devin smiled. "Feel better?" he asked.

She returned the infectious grin. "Yes. The cream took some of the sting out."

His bold gaze traveled down her back to the vicinity of her buttocks. "Reach it okay?"

Her face turned pink. "Just fine." Picking up another potato to peel, she said, "Did you get Jason's kite out of the tree?"

"Yes."

She looked at him, her gaze softening along with her tone. "You're a hero in his eyes, you know."

The compliment warmed him, but it brought another subject to his mind. "Yeah, well, I wish *you* would stop trying to be a hero."

Puzzled, Lilianne stopped what she was doing to look at Devin. "What's that supposed to mean?"

Pushing away from the doorjamb, he came up beside her, gently brushing a wisp of hair from her cheek. "It means you shouldn't have attempted to climb that tree this afternoon."

Lilianne ignored the sensual feelings that his light touch evoked in her. Her feminine responses to him happened more and more often lately and were getting harder to control. "Jason loves that kite, Devin, you know that." She tossed the potato aside and started in on a carrot. "What was I supposed to do? Leave it in the tree?"

Smiling lazily, Devin leaned his hip against the counter beside her. "As you may recall, you weren't too successful in bringing it down."

His teasing tone didn't soften the impact of his words. Lilianne stared at him for a long moment, feeling wounded by his gentle gibe. Without replying, she resumed her task, peeling the carrot in her hand to a thin stick.

Grabbing Lilianne's arm, Devin turned her to him, forcing her full attention. "Dammit, Lily, you could have really hurt yourself!"

"I'm fine," she insisted, shaking off his hand.

"Thanks to me. What would you have done if I hadn't come along?" He gave a small chuckle, but there was little humor in it. "Hell, I bet you'd still be stuck up in that tree!"

"Thanks for the vote of confidence," she murmured as she arranged the potatoes and carrots around a seasoned pot roast.

"It's true!"

She shoved the pot into the oven and set the timer. "You're beginning to sound like Michael."

Devin's jaw hardened at the comparison. "Now, what is *that* supposed to mean?" he demanded as she washed her hands.

Lilianne turned to him, wiping her hands on a dish towel. "Michael always tried to shelter me. He never let me do anything for myself. You're the same way."

Devin crossed to her and gently took her shoulders in his hands. "I'm not trying to shelter you, Lily. You can do whatever you please, and you usually do." He let his palms slide down her bare arms until his fingers met hers. In a warm grasp, he enfolded them in his hands. "I'm concerned for your safety, sweetheart, just as I'm sure Michael was."

She turned her head away from his penetrating gaze, afraid he'd see the pain in her eyes. "No, it was more than that," she said softly.

"Lily—" Devin shut his mouth as Elizabeth and Emily strolled into the kitchen. His expression instantly softened at the younger versions of Lilianne, with their sun-kissed copper hair and emerald-green eyes. But where Lilianne was petite, the girls had inherited their father's height, and were already nearly as tall as their mother. They were beautiful girls, and they held a special spot in his heart. A smile from either of them and he turned to mush.

"Uncle Devin!" they chorused in happy surprise.

Dropping his hands from Lily's, he went to the twins, hugging and kissing them both. "How are my favorite girls?" he asked fondly.

"Fine. Great," they answered at the same time.

Devin smiled down at them, clearly remembering the day they'd been born and how proud he had been, right along with Michael. Now that Michael was gone, he felt like their protector, and he did, indeed, help Lily raise them. Like

Jason, they thought of him as an uncle, and he had worn the title proudly.

Elizabeth went to the refrigerator and peered inside. "Are you staying for dinner, Uncle Devin?" she asked over her shoulder.

His eyes caught Lily's across the kitchen. A devastatingly handsome smile claimed his lips. "Yep. My reward for rescuing your mother from the big tree out front."

Emily looked at him curiously. "What was she doing in the tree?"

Lilianne shot him a warning look, but he ignored it, his grin broadening at her expense. "She got stuck while trying to get Jason's kite down."

"Oh, no!" Elizabeth groaned dramatically, pulling the tab on a Coke. "I'm so embarrassed. I hope no one at school finds out about this."

Lifting the lid on the cookie jar sitting on the counter, Emily retrieved a handful of Oreos. "No kidding. We'll never live it down."

Used to her daughter's theatrics, Lilianne plucked the cookies from Emily's hand and put them back into the jar. "You're going to spoil your appetite."

"I'm hungry," she complained.

"Then eat an apple or a banana."

Elizabeth sidled up to Devin and whispered, "Mom just doesn't want us to eat all her Oreos so they'll be there when she gets her midnight cravings."

Devin arched a brow at Lily.

"Mom, can I get a new dress for the school dance?" Emily asked in her sweetest voice.

"We'll see."

"If Emily gets a new dress, so do I," Elizabeth said, not to be outdone by her sister.

Jason raced into the kitchen with Rusty hot on his heels. Not watching where he was heading, Jason bumped into

Elizabeth, which in turn made Rusty slam into him. Elizabeth jumped back as her Coke sloshed over the rim of the can and onto the front of her Bon Jovi T-shirt.

"Hey, watch it, squirt." Elizabeth glared at Jason as she brushed spots of Coke off Jon Bon Jovi's face.

Jason made a face at his sister. "It wasn't my fault, Rusty rammed into me."

Rusty hung his head sheepishly. "I'm sorry."

Lilianne took pity on Jason's rather quiet and shy friend. "It was just as much Jason's fault."

"Was not!" Jason protested loudly.

"You weren't watching where you were going," Emily said.

Jason's chin drew up. "I was too!"

Lilianne stifled the urge to scream in frustration. "Everybody out of the kitchen until dinner is ready," she said loudly.

The room grew quiet and they all stared at her.

"Out!" she said, pointing to the door.

They filed from the kitchen, each one grumbling their own gripes. Devin remained behind, chuckling.

Lilianne shot him an annoyed glance. "What are you laughing at?"

"You." His laughter died, but his eyes sparked brightly. "I was ready to blow a referee whistle."

"I could use one." Opening the refrigerator door, Lily reached in and grabbed a can of beer, which she handed to Devin, then poured herself a glass of iced tea.

Devin leaned against the counter and pulled the tab on his can. A fine spray erupted from the puncture. He took a long swallow. "Cravings for Oreo cookies in the middle of the night, huh?"

His seductive tone touched her spine, sending chills over the surface of her nerves. "So I like Oreo cookies," she said defensively.

Devin's smile was slow in coming, tempting her with a hint of devilry. He leaned toward her, his eyes falling to her mouth. "Tell me, Lily, do you like to eat the whole cookie or are you one of those people who nibbles the cream center off first?"

Unconsciously Lilianne ran her tongue over her bottom lip. "I like to nibble the . . ." She shook her head, snapping herself out of her hypnotic daze. She frowned. "What does it matter how I like to eat my cookies?"

Shrugging, he took a drink of beer. "How a person eats an Oreo tells you how sensual they are."

She rolled her eyes. "You're joking."

"No, I'm not." He looked totally serious until his mouth spilled into a wicked grin. "I'd be willing to bet you're a real sensual cookie eater."

"Can we please drop the subject of cookies?" Who would have thought discussing Oreos could be so arousing? Face flaming, she turned toward the sink and began rinsing dishes.

Devin chuckled. He swallowed the rest of his beer, then crushed the can in his hand. He came up beside Lilianne, pressing the back of his hand against her hip.

Lilianne's eyes flew to his as a slow, burning heat seared her through her dress.

"I need to throw this way," he said, showing her the reason he'd been trying to nudge her over.

Lilianne stared at the crushed can in Devin's hand. "Oh." She stepped to the side, allowing him room to open the cupboard beneath the sink. He dropped the beer can into the plastic bin for aluminum cans.

"I told Jason I'd toss a football with him and Rusty before dinner," Devin said. "We'll be washed up and ready to eat by six."

"Fine. I've got some things to finish up in the office." She watched him leave, wondering at the fluttering sensation in her stomach.

Lilianne sat in the small office in the back of the house, which was once filled with Michael's legal books, papers and degrees. She had since redecorated the room to reflect the business workings of her interior-design company. Books carrying swatches of material and assorted scraps of wallpaper were lined up on the bookcase she'd had installed. Awards for her interior designs done on model homes hung on the wall, testimony to how hard she'd worked over the past two years. The carpet was a soft cream color, the wallpaper a floral pattern of mauve and blue. The window was framed in a valance, cut short with a ruffled edge.

Lilianne tried concentrating on the order of draperies, blinds and wallpaper laid out on the polished desk before her, but her mind refused to cooperate. All she could think about was Devin who, with his tight jeans and sexy smile, set her heart to racing.

Propping her chin in her hands, she tried deciphering the odd mixture of feelings stirring inside her. She'd always cared for Devin, she reasoned, ever since Michael had first introduced him to her. Lately, though, her feelings were growing into something more than simple friendship. Her reaction to his touch put her feminine senses on alert.

Devin had been Michael's best friend for so long Lilianne couldn't remember a time when Devin hadn't been a part of the family. When Michael died, Devin had been there for her, the twins and Jason, helping them through that difficult time.

Remorse rushed through her. Compounded with the pain of losing Michael was the guilt she felt over the sequence of events that had snowballed the months before his death.

Lilianne could vividly remember the arguments she and Michael had had about his spending so much time at the office and so little time with her and the kids. The conflict and tension between them became unbearable, and pretty soon they were virtual strangers living under the same roof.

Then Jason started school, and she was alone during the day, with nothing to fill those long hours. She wanted to go back to work, but the suggestion had been met with staunch opposition from Michael. He'd always controlled the direction of her life, never allowed her any independence. He refused to let her go back to work.

The arguments became more frequent.

Then came the ultimatum, followed by the car accident that had claimed Michael's life.

And now, three years later, she was beginning to feel things for Michael's best friend that confused her. When Devin touched her she felt a strange melting sensation in the pit of her stomach. Her response to him was increasing in frequency, causing her emotions to tumble.

"How's business?"

Lilianne visibly jumped. She looked up to see Devin standing in the doorway. He leaned negligently against the frame, arms crossed over his chest. His shirt, damp with sweat from playing ball with the boys, was molded to his torso. His thick hair was tousled and his eyes sparkled with mischief.

Pushing away from the door, Devin entered the room. "Sorry, didn't mean to startle you."

Lilianne began stacking the papers on her desk. "It's okay. I was engrossed in the order I need to place for the Hartford Model homes." She stood, knowing she'd be working late into the night writing up the purchase order. It wouldn't be the first time her thoughts had wandered to the man now in her doorway and her work had gone neglected. "I need to set the table for dinner, anyway."

"I'll help." He followed her out of the office to the kitchen.

Lilianne opened the cupboard above the counter and stood on tiptoe, reaching for the dinner plates on the second shelf.

Devin reached above her and grabbed the plates for her. As he did so, he crowded her into the counter, the front of his body rubbing against her back. "I'll set the table," he offered.

With conscious effort, Lilianne regulated her breathing. His touch had sent flames licking up her spine. Lately, whenever she came into contact with him, the effect was like spontaneous combustion. If only he knew what he did to her senses.

"So how's business?" he asked again, ambling to the oak table set up in the next room. He placed a plate in front of each chair.

Lilianne stepped to the refrigerator and pulled out a fruit salad she had prepared earlier. She closed the door with her hip. "Great. I should be starting the Hartford model homes next week."

He looked up, seeing her above the half wall separating the kitchen from the dining room. "That's a pretty big account, isn't it?"

Lilianne smiled as she put the bowl in the middle of the table. "For me it is. I'm almost finished with the Meadowbrook Development Project. Will you go to the grand opening with me?"

"You bet. I wouldn't miss it." Opening the silverware drawer, Devin pulled out five knives and forks. "Quite the businesswoman, aren't you?" he teased.

"Thanks to you," she said sincerely. She couldn't thank him enough. He had urged her to follow her dream and launch her own business with part of Michael's insurance money. He had been her main support the whole time.

He shrugged off her appreciation. "No thanks needed. You're the one with the eye for color and design, not me." He placed a knife and fork at each setting. "I barely know the difference between polka dots and stripes."

She laughed, grabbing a few pot holders from a drawer. Turning on the light in the oven, she peered through the window, satisfied that the pot roast had browned nicely. Opening the door, she tested the vegetables with a fork. Assured that the meal was done, she picked up the pot holders she'd left on the counter. Just as she bent over to retrieve the roast, Devin came up behind her and snatched the pot holders from her hands.

"Here, let me do that," he said, gently nudging her aside.

Lilianne's mouth opened to refuse his offer, but he already had the roast in his hands and was strolling to the table with it.

Lilianne called the kids to dinner. The girls talked about the school dance coming up, and Jason went on about a camping trip planned for a group of his friends at the end of the month. All three vied for Devin's attention. Unable to get a word in edgewise, Lilianne sat back, enjoying the lively conversation. Every so often Devin would look up at her and give her one of his special winks and a smile.

At a lull in the conversation, Lilianne jumped in while she had the chance. "I received a call from school today," she said casually, noting how all three kids stopped eating to stare at her with nervous expressions.

"Uh, whose school?" Elizabeth asked tentatively.

"Yours."

Jason resumed shoveling carrots into his mouth while Elizabeth's and Emily's eyes widened.

"What did they want?" Emily asked. "I swear we haven't done anything wrong." She cast a glance at her sister. "At least *I* haven't."

Elizabeth glared at her sister. "I've been good." Smiling like an angel with a crooked halo, she switched her gaze to Lilianne. "Well, what did they want?"

Lilianne took a sip of iced tea, then wiped her mouth with her napkin, deliberately taking her time.

"Mother!" the twins said in unison.

She had to smile. "Mrs. Bailey called to ask me if I'd chaperon the school dance. They're short two volunteers."

"What did you tell her?" Elizabeth demanded.

"I told her yes, of course." Lilianne cut a slice of roast. "I don't have plans for that weekend, and Jason will be camping with his friends."

"You can't be a chaperon," Elizabeth said, horror in her voice.

"This is worse than enduring Mr. Horner's frogs in science class," Emily groaned, covering her face with her hands.

"A fate worse than death?" Devin supplied, amusement pulling at his lips.

"Nothing is worse than having your parent be a chaperon at a dance," Elizabeth informed Devin. Then she looked at her mom. "No offense, Mom, but it just isn't cool."

Devin chuckled.

Reaching across the table, Lilianne patted Elizabeth's hand consolingly. "No offense taken, honey. But since I'm on the PTA, Mrs. Bailey reminded me that I haven't chaperoned yet this year."

"Why couldn't you have told her you'd be sick or something that weekend?" Elizabeth said, pouting.

Tipping back his chair, Devin's chuckle turned to all-out laughter.

Lilianne lifted a brow at him. "Find this amusing, do you, Devin?"

He clutched his stomach. "Very."

"Well, that's nice, because I volunteered you for the other chaperon."

His laughter ceased. The two front legs of his chair hit the floor with a jarring thud. "You did what?"

"Radical!" Emily said.

"Cool!" Elizabeth added.

Jason ignored them all and helped himself to a second serving of fruit salad.

Lilianne flashed Devin a cunning smile. She hadn't really volunteered him for the other chaperon, but his amusement at her expense had annoyed her. She'd call Mrs. Bailey and remedy the situation. Lilianne was sure Mrs. Bailey wouldn't mind having an extra chaperon.

"Lilianne," Devin said, his expression serious. "I can't chaperon a school dance."

"Sure you can. It's quite simple. No parental skills required." She buttered the corner of her roll and took a bite, hiding her smile.

"Please say you'll go, Uncle Devin," Elizabeth pleaded, giving him her best doe-eyed look.

"It'll be so cool if you go with Mom, please?" Emily added. "No boy is going to ask us to dance if Mom is hanging around. If you go, you can keep her busy." She grinned up at Devin, obviously pleased with her reasoning.

The look Devin shot Lilianne clearly stated he'd get even with her. Then a wicked gleam entered his eyes. Leaning forward, he rested his elbows on the table. "Keep your mom busy, huh? Now that's kind of appealing."

Had his voice turned low and husky, or had she only imagined it had? She met his steady gaze, saw the sexy, uninhibited curve of his lips, and her insides began to unravel and melt.

"It'll be so *cool* if you go with Mom." Emily gazed up at Devin with adoration.

"I'll go," he said slowly and deliberately, "as long as your mother promises me a dance."

Lilianne's fork stopped in midair. The thought of her body flush against his sent her hormones in a frenzy. Of course, he hadn't specified a slow dance. She looked up at him. "It's a deal."

It was Emily's turn to do the dishes, Elizabeth's to clear the table and Jason's to empty the trash. They went about their chores without complaint while Lilianne and Devin went outside to the backyard.

Devin watched Lilianne fill a plastic container with water and start watering the plants hanging from the patio beams. He sat down in a glider chair and laced his fingers over his stomach. The sun was retiring for the evening, spreading glorious streaks of purple, orange and red across the Colorado sky.

"Did you get an invitation to Amy and Richard's wedding?" Lilianne asked. Her back faced Devin as she tended to a creeping Charlie.

The engaged couple were mutual friends of theirs. "Yes." Devin stretched out his long legs and reclined in the chair, feeling full and lazy after her delicious meal. He could get used to this, he thought.

She looked over her shoulder at him. "Are you going with anyone?" she asked.

Devin had had his share of women, but he never dated anyone long enough to get serious. His relationships usually fizzled out before the commitment stage, which suited him just fine. He liked female companionship, but there was only one lifetime mate he wanted, and she treated him like a brother. He sighed.

"Haven't really thought about a date," he answered. He hadn't even sent back the RSVP card yet. "How about you?"

"No date." She picked a dead flower off her fuchsia plant and tossed it into the small bucket beside her. "I'm going solo."

He should have known. His eyes slid down her back, immediately picking up on the fact that she wasn't wearing a slip. The dying sun silhouetted her long legs and outlined her hips. "Why don't you date, Lily?" he asked without thinking.

She turned around to face him. "I date," she said, a curious expression on her face.

He thought about these so-called dates. One had been a banker who had been as stuffy as the starched shirt and tie he'd been wearing. Another had been a teacher at a nearby college, whose conversations droned on like lectures and bored her to death, Lilianne had told him. "You've dated some real winners, Lily," he said sardonically. "You've only dated about four times in the three years that Michael's been gone. And I know you've even refused a couple at that."

She bent to refill her container. "I don't want to get tied down," she answered. That was true. She didn't ever want to live under someone's thumb again.

"I'm not talking about marriage, Lily," he said. "I'm talking about male companionship. You're a desirable woman with a woman's needs."

"Leave it to you, Mr. McKay, to be blunt and straight-forward," she said with a wry grin.

He sat up, resting his elbows on his knees. "It's the truth. And I know plenty of men who'd love to ask you out, but you refuse more than you accept. You're very attractive and sexy."

"I'd hardly call stretch marks on my stomach sexy," she said.

"You have terrific legs and a nice, uh, backside." He grinned wolfishly. "Take it from me. I saw part of it earlier."

Her face turned pink. "You didn't see anything."

"I saw enough."

She shook her head at him. "What's the big deal about me dating, anyway? I've got a career and family to worry about."

Yeah, he thought, what was the big deal? Did he really want to see her date and get serious with someone when he wanted her for himself? What he really wanted was for her to date him. Did he even have a chance when she considered him nothing more than a friend?

"I didn't mean to nag you," he said, connecting with her green eyes. "Since neither one of us has a date for the wedding, why don't we go together?"

She removed a weed from the planter running alongside the house. "That would be fine."

He smiled, pleased. "Great. The wedding is at five, so I'll pick you up around four."

She looked up, a soft smile curving her mouth. "It's a date."

He only wished it were.

Three

Although the wedding wasn't officially a date, it felt like one. Lilianne took the opportunity to wear her best dress and purchase a new bottle of exotic, expensive perfume. Applying her cosmetics with a steady hand, she took extra pains to highlight her green eyes. She had her hair styled and curled, and it fell in soft red-gold waves to her shoulders. By the time she finished, she felt like a million bucks.

Her dress, a teal-colored silk, slithered over her body to her knees. A matching sash wrapped around her hips, bisecting the dress into two tantalizing pieces. The neckline cut into a V to her breasts, showing a modest amount of cleavage. She completed the outfit with high-heeled black pumps.

Lilianne heard Devin's Bronco pull into the drive. After checking her appearance in the mirror one last time, she grabbed her clutch purse and headed to the living room. Emily had just let Devin in.

"Wow!" Jason said in surprise. "You look great, Mom."

"Thank you, sweetie," she said, bending down to drop a quick kiss on his head. His honest praise warmed her. She looked up, meeting Devin's appreciative gaze. Smiling softly, she waited for his reaction.

"You do look nice, Lily," Devin said evenly.

"Thanks." Lilianne's bubble burst. That wasn't exactly the response she had anticipated. Maybe she had dressed too conservatively for his taste. "You look nice, too." Lilianne admired the three-piece pin-striped suit that fit his frame to perfection. The suit jacket clung to his wide shoulders, tapering to his lean hips. He looked resplendent, very different from his usual rough-and-ready appearance. His hair had been artfully blow-dried, his face freshly shaven. Citrusy after-shave curled around her senses, smelling clean and crisp.

"You look very handsome, Uncle Devin," Elizabeth said shyly.

"Thank you." Devin gave Elizabeth one of his heart-stopping grins. Slipping his hand into his trouser pocket, he jingled his keys and turned to Lily. "Ready to go?"

She nodded, then addressed the kids. "Take care of your brother, girls. Mrs. Collins next door knows you're here by yourselves, so if you need anything you can call her."

"We'll be fine, Mom," Emily said.

Lilianne smoothed back Emily's silky hair, smiling gently. "I know. I worry too much." The few times she had gone out, she had left Jason in the twins' care, and they'd taken their responsibility seriously.

Devin and Lilianne had decided to go in her white volvo, and he ushered her toward it now, his hand at her waist. He could feel the subtle, sexy sway of her hips. He opened the passenger-side door and waited for her to slide in. As she did, her dress rode up to her thighs, giving him a brief glimpse of sheer stockinged leg before she pulled the silk back down. Desire thrummed through his veins. Damn! She had his body responding to hers like a schoolboy's.

As Devin backed the Volvo down the driveway past his Bronco, he said, "I'm still trying to find the spare time to paint that thing." He figured he'd try for a neutral conversation to keep things on an even keel. "I've been so busy at the body shop with repairs and restorations I don't have the time or room to paint it."

Lilianne glanced over at the primered Bronco. "Oh, I don't know. I think that dull, flat gray color is very becoming."

He chuckled. "Yeah, I'm kind of getting used to it myself. I'd hate to spoil the effect with a smooth glossy coating of black paint."

"So business is good?" she asked, looking over at him.

He nodded. "I've had to hire two more guys to do the bodywork. Pretty soon I'm going to have to find a bigger garage to accommodate all the work."

Devin smiled, remembering the five years he'd spent struggling since first opening his body shop. Slowly but surely business was prospering. He was finally making a name for himself. Word of mouth traveled fast. That and the fact he did beautiful, impeccable work, guaranteeing all bodywork and paint jobs. He rarely had a dissatisfied customer.

Devin turned onto the freeway, picking up speed. "I've got more backup work than I can handle. Cars that need bodywork, company trucks that need new logos on them, people with boats who want them painted and sealed. Just today I received a call from the school district. They want me to strip and repaint their school buses." The pride in his voice was unmistakable.

Devin went on about his body shop, appropriately named McKay's Body Works, but Lilianne wasn't paying any attention. Her gaze was riveted to his profile. She studied his brows, his chiseled cheekbones and square, strong jaw. His nose had a slight bump in it, caused when she, Devin and Michael had gone hiking in the mountains while they were in high school. Not paying attention to where he was going, Devin had walked into a low tree branch and broken his nose. The permanent bump was a souvenir of that lazy spring day.

The memories of the three of them together made Lily smile. They'd forged a special bond that had lasted through the years. Now it was just her and Devin. She couldn't help but wonder if somehow she was being unfaithful to Michael's memory for her growing attraction to his best friend.

Pushing the confusing thought aside, she continued to study Devin's profile. Her gaze fell to his lips, opening and closing in a steady stream of words. They were nice lips, full and sensual. Those lips had kissed her cheek many times in a brotherly sort of way. She wondered what they'd feel like moving over her lips, her neck, her breasts. A tiny moan escaped her throat.

"Are you okay?" Devin asked, staring at her intently.

Lilianne's face heated and she looked away, mortified that such a thought would enter her mind at a time like this. "I . . . I'm fine," she said.

"You were looking at me strangely," he said.

"I was just thinking." She kept her face averted, staring out the window until she felt the blush fade. She wished it was dark out, but it was only four-thirty.

"About what?" Draping his wrist over the steering wheel, Devin placed his other hand on the middle console. He glanced over at her.

I was thinking about your incredible lips on mine. "Uhh . . . nothing," she said lamely.

"You were thinking about nothing?" he persisted, a hint of a smile curling his lips.

"Yes," she said indignantly, green eyes flashing. "I was thinking of nothing."

He chuckled, infuriating her further. "You're blushing, Lily." His tone dropped, low and intimate, as if privy to her innermost thoughts.

She fanned herself with her hand. "It's warm in the car," she grumbled as an excuse, even as the Volvo's air conditioner blasted her with near-freezing air.

"Sure." Devin graciously let the subject drop.

The wedding ceremony was simple and gracious. By the time they got to the reception, which was being held at a country club a few miles away from the church, darkness had fallen. Inside the banquet room the tables were draped in white linen, and chandeliers sparkled from above. A band tuned up their instruments as the guests milled around, waiting for the bride and groom to arrive.

Lily knew most of the same people Devin did. They were standing in a circle of friends when a male voice sounded from behind her.

"Hey, McKay!"

They both turned. A sandy-haired man approached, and Devin stuck out his hand. "Hi, Steve. How's the paint job holding up?"

"Beautifully."

Lilianne studied Steve. He wasn't anyone she knew. Polished and classically handsome, he looked like a business executive. The fingers wrapped around the champagne glass he held were perfectly manicured.

"Steve, this a friend of mine, Lilianne Austin," Devin said politely. "Lilianne, this is Steve Hayes. He's a customer of mine. I've painted his Corvette and I just got through painting his speedboat."

Lilianne didn't miss the way the man's eyes slid over her in open appraisal. "It's nice to meet you, Mr. Hayes."

He laughed. "Call me Steve." He looked back at Devin. "A friend, you say?"

Devin hesitated for a brief second. He wished he had the right to claim her as more. To confirm her as a friend put her on the open market for Steve to pursue. And Devin had no doubt Steve would. The other man had a gleam in his eyes that implied definite male interest. Devin gritted his teeth and forced the words out of his mouth. "Yes. Lilianne and I have been friends for years."

Devin's irritation increased when Steve joined them at their table for dinner. Lilianne sat between the two, her attention constantly diverted by Steve, who poured on the charm, flattering her with compliments, until Devin thought he was going to lose his meal.

Devin swallowed a bite of his chicken with wine-and-mushroom sauce, seething at Steve's cool, suave manners. Mrs. Weatherbee, an elderly grandmotherly woman, sat next to Devin, talking about how her cat was always choking on fur balls. Devin couldn't ignore her, so he listened to her inane chitchat while trying to keep an ear on Lilianne and Steve's conversation. He smothered the anger that threatened to explode and tried replacing it with a calm he didn't feel. He hadn't planned on sharing Lilianne tonight. Especially with a womanizer like Steve!

The band began playing, and Devin took the opportunity to excuse himself from Mrs. Weatherbee and ask Lilianne to dance. He wasn't taking no for an answer.

"Save a dance for me," Steve said as Lilianne walked away with Devin.

Lilianne looked over her shoulder, smiling sweetly in answer.

"Not likely, chump," Devin muttered under his breath.

They danced two fast songs and when a slow song began to play, Devin didn't hesitate to gather Lilianne in his arms. He didn't ask her if she wanted to dance to the slow tune. He didn't give her a chance.

Devin gazed into Lilianne's flushed face, enjoying the way her green eyes sparkled. Her hair, which tumbled in artful disarray around her face, made his fingers itch to slide through the tresses, feel their silky softness. Pulling her closer, he felt sparks of desire course through his body. The feel of her lush curves, her soft breasts pressed to his hard chest, made his heart pound wildly. Daringly, Devin's hand roamed down her back and paused just above her buttocks, rubbing, pressing the sensitive hollow of her spine.

The exotic smell of Lilianne's perfume intoxicated Devin. It wrapped around him, causing his blood to thicken. Catching her heavy-lidded gaze, he held it, then slowly lowered his eyes to her lips. He nearly groaned when her tongue darted out and moistened her bottom lip. Tracking his way back to her eyes, he silently pleaded for permission to taste the sweetness of her mouth.

Lips parting on a breathy sigh, she gave it to him.

"You are so beautiful," he whispered, his head lowering in slow increments.

The sensual bubble cocooning them popped when Steve cut in. He did it so quickly and so skillfully Devin didn't get a chance to protest. Before Devin could comprehend what had happened, Lilianne was out of his arms and in Steve's. Devin stood there, dumbfounded, as Steve whirled Lilianne away. Steve grinned triumphantly over Lilianne's shoulder at Devin.

Fuming, Devin went to the bar and ordered a drink. He watched Steve say something to Lilianne, and Lilianne tilt her head back and laugh. He curbed the urge to punch Steve in his handsome face. He also restrained himself from marching over and snatching Steve's hand away from the curve of Lilianne's hip. How could she let him manhandle her like that? A wave of jealousy gripped his insides in an iron fist. He tossed back a shot of whiskey, wincing as it burned a path to his stomach.

Lilianne forced a smile for Steve, tamping down the warm feelings still swirling inside her from Devin's touch. Why had Devin given her up so easily to Steve? For a moment she thought she had captivated him, that he'd been about to kiss her. She had obviously mistaken the admiration in his eyes for real desire. She shook her head, feeling like a fool for entertaining the notion that there was more to their relationship than friendship. Sighing, she turned her attention to her new dance partner, who was holding her annoyingly close.

"Would you like to go out sometime?" Steve asked her just as she reined in her thoughts of Devin.

She smiled at him, trying to find an easy way to let him down. "I don't have much time to date," she said kindly. "My business and children keep me far too busy."

"Surely you can take time out to have a little fun?" His eyes sparkled devilishly at the word fun.

"I really don't have time." Searching the banquet room, Lilianne found Devin brooding over at the bar. She wondered what had put him in such a sour mood. She watched as an attractive brunette approached him. They talked for a few minutes, then Devin's eyes found Lilianne's. Grasping the brunette's elbow, he led her to the dance floor, pulling her close.

Lilianne's back stiffened as Devin charmed the woman into peals of laughter.

"Is there something going on between you and Devin?" Steve asked, following her gaze.

Lilianne's head snapped back to Steve. "Of course not." She didn't know if she was trying to convince him or herself.

"They why not go out with me?"

Yeah, why not? After all, it wasn't as though Devin was pining for her. Just last week he had urged her to date. But even though Steve was a good-looking guy with a witty sense of humor, she couldn't envision dating him. "I'm sorry. Now isn't a very good time for me."

Steve gave her a light squeeze. "Fine. I understand. Maybe some other time."

Lilianne remained in Steve's company for the remainder of the evening. His persistence left her with little choice. She saw Devin often, always with the brunette. A streak of pain lanced through her when Devin bent his head to speak intimately with the woman and she twined her hands through the hair at the back of his neck. Lilianne didn't fully understand her reaction, especially since she'd never felt such jealousy before. She had to keep reminding herself that Devin was just a friend, a big brother in a sense, nothing more.

Devin finally approached her around midnight. He swaggered up to the table where she sat talking to Steve, and his expression was thunderous. "Are you ready to go, Lily?" he asked in an icy tone.

What had she done to earn his contempt? she wondered. He had been the one who had given her up so freely to Steve to spend his evening with a racy brunette who couldn't control her wandering hands. If Steve's presence bothered him it was his own damn fault.

Lilianne stood up and Steve followed suit. "Steve has offered to take me home," she said.

Devin's mood turned blacker. "If you've forgotten, we drove your car."

"You have to drive it to my place to pick up your Bronco, anyway," she said reasonably.

"Lily..." There was no way Devin was going to let that octopus be alone with her. He didn't want him putting the moves on an innocent widow like Lily.

Grabbing her arm, he excused her from Steve's presence. When they were out of earshot, Devin started in on her. "That's incredibly rude, you know." He pushed back his jacket and placed his hands on his hips. "You came to this wedding with me and I expect you to leave with me."

Lilianne couldn't help noticing how sexy he looked. His hair was attractively tousled from being finger-combed by the brunette, and his eyes, a dark, sensual brown fringed with thick lashes, sparked with anger. His stance, arrogant, cocky and possessive, thrilled her.

"You're right," she conceded. "That was rude of me. I'm sorry."

Devin frowned. He had expected an argument, not this easy submission. Damn it, he *wanted* an argument to blow off some of this steam!

"I'll just tell Steve good-night and then I'll be ready to go."

Devin watched her walk back to Steve, aggravation and frustration curling his toes. When Steve smiled at her and ran his hand intimately down her arm, he thought he'd explode. He spun around and strode to the door before the wedding reception turned into a brawl.

Devin remained quiet and withdrawn as they started toward home, still smoldering over Lily's apparent interest in Steve. At least he'd been successful in getting her to go home with him, rather than have her accept a ride in the close confines of Steve's Corvette. No telling how Steve might have taken advantage of her.

Drawing a deep breath, Devin rolled his shoulders, trying to release the tension coiling his body as tight as a spring. He kept his eyes trained on the road, hating the awkward silence stretching between them.

"Are you upset with me?" Lilianne asked softly when they turned into her street. She tilted her head, her hair spilling over her shoulder in a riot of curls.

Devin knew he had no valid reason to be. He relaxed his clenched jaw. Glancing her way, he saw her worried expression and offered her a halfhearted smile. "No."

"Then what's wrong?" she asked. "You've been acting weird all evening."

"Yeah, I know. I'm sorry." What excuse could he give? He couldn't very well tell her he was as jealous as hell and didn't want any man other than himself around her, let alone touching her, especially after giving her a lecture on dating the week before. "I've been under a lot of stress at the shop lately," he lied. Feeling like a jerk for treating her so badly, he wanted to make amends. "So what's new with Steve?" he asked conversationally, forcing his tone to be light.

"He asked me out on a date," she said nonchalantly.

Devin's blood turned to ice in his veins. "Lily, are you crazy?" His fingers clutched the steering wheel. He pulled the Volvo into her driveway and brought it to an abrupt halt. He jammed the car into park and turned toward her, his expression grim.

Crossing her arms over her chest, Lilianne met Devin's burning stare. "You don't like him very much, do you?" she asked tightly, wondering if Devin was jealous.

"I like him as a customer and acquaintance just fine," he stated brusquely. Turning off the engine, he handed her the key, nearly imprinting it in her palm. "But I don't want you to go out with him."

Even though she had no intention of dating Steve, Lilianne bristled. "I don't think I need your permission to go out with Steve."

He tried to remain calm. "Lily, he's not your type."

Ah, now she understood. Devin was playing big brother, trying to protect his little sister's virtue. It was the last thing she wanted from him. "What do you know about my type?"

"Steve Hayes is a womanizer. You'll end up getting hurt, Lily. The man has more moves than a football player. He uses women."

Cocking a brow, Lilianne smiled ever so slightly. "Need I remind you it was your idea for me to start dating again?"

Steve Hayes had not been what he'd had in mind. "No, you don't need to remind me," he mimicked. "But why in hell couldn't you pick someone who treats women with respect?"

She smiled. Maybe he really *was* jealous! "You're jealous," she said.

"I am not," he grumbled. "I'm just concerned about who you date."

Opening the car door, she looked over at him. The interior light made the crease of concern between his brows more prominent. She'd made him suffer long enough, she thought. "Concern yourself no more. I told him no." She slipped out of the car, closing the door on his astonished expression.

Devin watched Lilianne walk around the front of the car, his fingers itching to wrap around her neck. She'd put him through hell! Getting out of the car, he escorted her to the front porch, his temper cooling on the short walk. He took the key from her hand and opened the door.

Lilianne pivoted toward Devin, smiling. The porch light cast a halo around her red-gold hair, making her look bewitching. Her eyes glimmered like green pools. "Thanks for going to the wedding with me, Devin. It was better than going alone." Placing her hand on his chest, she stood on tip toe to give him a chaste kiss on the cheek.

At the last second Devin turned his head and her lips landed on his mouth. Devin didn't want the sort of good-night kiss they usually shared. Her lips lingered on his a few seconds, as if savoring the feel of him, the taste, then she abruptly pulled away.

Lilianne retreated a step, shocked by the spark of desire the simple kiss had set off in her. Her lips tingled and her stomach fluttered. Had he moved his head intentionally? The innocent look in his eyes confused her.

"Good night, Lily," Devin said, as if nothing out of the ordinary had happened, though she couldn't help note the husky timbre of his voice.

"Good night, Devin." Closing the door behind her, she leaned against it for support, legs quaking. She wondered if she had imagined the intensity of the kiss. She wondered if Devin's heart was beating as erratically as hers.

Devin got into his Bronco and gunned the engine, grinning for the first time since the wedding. The kiss had rattled her. He also knew if he had chosen to pursue the kiss she would have let him. Knowing that was enough to send his spirits soaring.

Four

Devin could smell the sweet fragrance of chocolate the moment he removed his helmet. After hooking it on the back of his motorcycle, he followed the aroma all the way to Lily's front door.

"It's me," he called, opening the screen door and letting himself in.

"I'm in the kitchen, Devin," Lilianne said.

He strolled into the kitchen, instantly assaulted by the delicious baking odors. A couple of dozen cupcakes, sitting on cooling racks, lined the counter in a neat row. A big bowl of frosting sat next to them, a spatula sticking out of the gooey concoction. The sink, piled high with dirty dishes coated in flour and chocolate, attested to all the work.

Swiping one of the warm cupcakes off the rack, he peeled back the paper wrapper and sunk his teeth into it. The cupcake tasted moist and rich, satisfying his grumbling stomach.

"Hey," Lilianne said, wiping her cheek with the back of her hand, leaving behind a streak of chocolate. "Those aren't for you to eat."

He swallowed his mouthful of cupcake, raising his brows in mock surprise. "No?"

She scooped chocolate batter into a paper cupcake liner. "No. They're for the PTA bake sale at Jason's school. I've been working all morning trying to get them done."

"You look like it."

She wrinkled her nose at him. "Gee, thanks. I know I look a wreck, but I wasn't exactly expecting company. Seeing as you drop by anytime you feel like it, you'll have to suffer with a less than perfect me."

He'd suffer those consequences anytime, he thought. She looked just as tempting as her cupcakes. Her hair had been pulled back into a ponytail, leaving red-gold wisps framing her face. Since the oven had been on, the kitchen was warm, and she had on a halter top to keep her cool, leaving her smooth back naked and exposed. The creamy expanse of skin tempted the tips of his fingers.

Finishing his cupcake, Devin let his gaze wander over her white shorts and down her shapely legs to her pink-painted toenails. Oh yeah, he'd suffer seeing her like this anytime.

Lilianne turned toward Devin, giving him the full impact of her curvaceous body. "So, what do you think?"

Devin jerked his gaze to hers, the last of the cupcake catching in his throat like a sticky web. "Of what?" he asked.

She sighed impatiently, as if dealing with a small child. "The cupcakes. What else?"

She'd be shocked to her toes if she really knew what else. He cleared his throat. "It was great."

She cast a tired look at the cooling cupcakes. "I still have to frost them." She glanced at the clock over the sink. "Carolyn's coming to pick them up in less than two hours. I'll never get them done in time."

The timer on the oven went off, indicating the next batch of cupcakes was ready. Lilianne pulled them out.

"Can I help?" he asked, watching her scurry around the kitchen.

Lilianne looked over her shoulder at him, weighing the sincerity of his offer. What man liked to spend his spare time in the kitchen? Holding one end of the hot cupcake tin with a pot holder, she flipped the tin to dump out the cupcakes. The hot pan hit her hand, singeing the inside of her wrist. She immediately dropped it. "Damn!"

A red, angry blister immediately surfaced. Her eyes watered from the pain. Looking up, she found Devin beside her, reaching for her hand.

"Let me see," he said, turning her arm over to inspect the burn.

She sucked in a breath. His touch singed worse than the metal had. "I'm okay."

Pulling her to the sink, he turned on the tap, then thrust her wrist beneath the cold flow. He held her arm, making sure she didn't move.

"Devin, it's not that bad. I'm fine." The feel of the cool water sluicing over her wrist and Devin's thumb stroking the pulse point just below the burn had a slow heat simmering in the pit of her belly. She wanted to jerk her hand from him, but knew how foolish she'd look if she did.

"Do you have first-aid spray for burns?" Stopping the water, Devin examined the blister, then turned on the water once more.

"It's in the medicine cabinet in the bathroom." She looked up at him, trying to regulate her breathing when his gaze dropped to her mouth. "I'm fine, Devin. Really."

He let go of her arm, ignoring her words. "Don't move. I'll be right back."

Lilianne drew a deep breath when Devin disappeared from the kitchen. What in the world was wrong with her? His touch nearly made her knees give way. Looking over at the cupcakes cluttering the counter, she groaned. She'd never have them all frosted and ready to go in time.

"You okay?" Devin asked, returning from his errand, his brow etched in concern.

She realized he'd heard her groan. "I'm fine. I'm just thinking about all these cupcakes I have to frost."

"I'll help you." Shutting off the water, Devin dabbed the moisture from the burn with the kitchen towel. He aimed the first-aid spray and fired. A fine mist settled over the blister. "There, that should help take away the sting." He grinned at her. "Hey, is this the same stuff you used on your fanny?"

Grinning back, she said, "No, I used an ointment." She grew serious. "You really don't have to, you know."

He placed a gauze bandage over the blister and ran a piece of surgical tape over it to hold it in place. "Don't have to what?"

"Help me with the cupcakes." Lilianne shifted on her feet, wishing his fingers weren't everywhere, touching her arm, her wrist, her palm, her fingers.

"I want to," he said. "I love making cupcakes."

She'd bet he'd never made a cupcake in his life. Her suspicions were confirmed after he attempted to frost the first one. A blob of chocolate frosting, two inches high, sat on top of his cupcake. He'd gotten half that much on the paper liner, making it impossible to pick up the cupcake without getting her fingers sticky with frosting.

Lilianne plucked the next cupcake from his fingers. "Here, I'll frost them. You put the sprinkles on them." She handed him a plastic shaker filled with colorful, edible confetti.

Smearing frosting on her cupcake, she quickly finished it, handing it over to Devin in a two-man assembly line. She stopped briefly only to take the last tray of cupcakes out of the oven.

"Michael hardly ever stepped into the kitchen, let alone offered to help," Lilianne said as she passed Devin another cupcake, then licked a speck of frosting off her thumb.

"I'm not Michael," Devin said, a bit of irritation in his voice.

"Yeah, well, most men believe a woman's place is in the kitchen. You know, barefoot and pregnant."

Looking over at Lilianne, Devin wiggled his eyebrows at her. "I agree with the pregnant part. Especially what comes beforehand."

She shot him a sharp look.

Devin placed a confettied cupcake in a box Lilianne had put out for finished cupcakes. "There's nothing wrong with a man wanting his wife to be pregnant. I think it's kind of sexy."

Frowning, she scooped out a knifeful of frosting from the bowl. "Michael would have kept me permanently pregnant if I'd let him."

Devin's look turned lecherous. "A randy old fellow, eh?"

She shook her head, not smiling at his teasing tone. "No, it wasn't that. He just believed a woman's place was in the home, cooking, cleaning and raising kids."

Between sprinkling cupcakes, Devin dipped his finger into the frosting, licking off the rich confection. "Still, there's nothing wrong with a man wanting to come home to an orderly house and a hot meal," he argued.

She looked up at him, her eyes intense. "You don't believe a woman can handle a career and a family?"

"I didn't say that." Devin stared at her, seeing the stubborn tilt to her chin and the fire in her eyes. "Why are you getting so defensive all of a sudden?"

She looked away, grabbing the last of the cupcakes. "Let's just drop it, okay?"

His confetti shaker hit the counter hard, and Lilianne jumped, her gaze jerking back to his. "No, it's not okay," he said heatedly. He propped his hands on his waist. "Don't place all men in the same category, Lily. I realize Michael had certain beliefs where women were concerned." He swiped a hand through the air. "Hell, look at his mother. She doted on her husband and children. Michael was brought up in a household where his mother treated the men like kings and she was expected to be submissive. Did he expect you to be the same way?"

"Just drop it, Devin," she said through her teeth.

"Dammit, answer me!"

"Yes!" she shouted in frustration. "He expected me to be the perfect housewife, hostess and mother. When Jason started school and I told him I wanted to go back to work, he wouldn't let me."

"Wouldn't let you?" he asked quietly.

Lilianne started to clean up the mess in front of her, anything to keep her hands busy. "He said no wife of his was going to work, so I stayed home, just like he wanted." Her words poured out of her seemingly of their own will, having been bottled up for so long. "I cooked and cleaned and took care of the children until I couldn't handle it any longer. Then Jason went to school and I thought I'd go mad staying home all day." She looked up at Devin, the sponge in her hand stilling on the countertop. "I felt like I was losing my identity, Devin. My children were my life, but I needed to do something constructive with my days. I *wanted* to work."

"Did he finally agree?"

She laughed, choking on her bitterness. "Of course not. When I told him I was going to work with or without his permission he issued me an ultimatum—I could choose either career or marriage. Not both. I asked for a divorce, but he died before I filed the papers." Guilt replaced her anger. She resumed cleaning the counter, tossing the cooling racks into the sink, wiping up crumbs. Devin touched her arm and she looked up at him.

"I never knew, Lily. I'm sorry."

She shrugged, a sadness entering her eyes. "The year before he died we fought constantly. He didn't want me to work, but he spent more and more time at the office and away from home." She stared at the wall behind Devin, focusing on the floral wallpaper. "We were growing apart. It was getting to the point that we couldn't even have a civil conversation without bickering about something." She looked up at him. "All I wanted was a job, something constructive to do with my time. Was that so bad?"

"No, but for years you'd stayed home without wanting to work. Did you ever think that the suggestion might have come as a shock to Michael?"

"Yes. I gave him time to get used to the idea, but he became distant and cold. Whenever I tried to talk to him about it we'd end up arguing." She rubbed her forehead wearily with her fingers. "He was so against me working he pushed me over the edge with an ultimatum. He made me choose between him and my independence, Devin. It wasn't fair."

"No, it wasn't fair," he agreed softly. "He must have felt like he was losing control of the situation to take a risk like that. You and the kids were everything to him. He loved you, Lily—you know that."

"And I loved him. That never changed," she said adamantly. "We just became two separate people with different ideals. Just because I wanted to work didn't mean I didn't want to be a wife and mother, too. He wouldn't allow me to do both."

His fingers brushed her cheek. "I always thought you had too much fire for your own good." His gaze slowly dropped to her lips.

Lilianne's breath shortened and her fingers curled into a tight fist. She told herself to step away, but her body wouldn't obey the command. The pad of his thumb caressed her jaw, filling her with a hot, desperate need.

His eyes turned dark and sultry, his voice husky. "Let me taste that fire, Lily." With a single step he closed the gap between them.

Lilianne didn't move, couldn't move. Devin's large hands framed her face with a tenderness that touched her heart. He pulled her mouth up to his at the same time he lowered his head. Bursts of pleasure seared her when his lips melded with hers. Closing her eyes, she parted her lips, allowing his tongue to slide into her mouth. He kissed her like she'd never been kissed before, his lips and tongue a masterful blend of giving and taking.

Devin took his sweet time to sample every taste, every texture of her mouth. His tongue flicked over hers, and she returned the caress, sending a shaft of fire straight to his loins. Instantly, his body craved far more than this kiss could give.

Lilianne's head swam in a fog of desire. Devin angled her head, deepening the kiss even further. Moaning, she swayed into him, pressing her breasts intimately to his chest.

The doorbell sounded in the background. Devin heard it and silently cursed the intruder. Pulling away, he looked down at Lilianne's flushed face. Her breath came out in short pants and her eyes were glazed with passion. He swore again.

Devin shook her lightly, trying to snap her out of her daze. "Someone is at the door, Lily."

"Cupcakes," she mumbled, touching her wet lips.

There was a loud knock on the screen door. Devin glanced over his shoulder, then back at Lily. "Now isn't the time to worry about cupcakes."

"Yoo-hoo, anybody home?" a female voice called.

"Carolyn is here for the cupcakes," Lilianne said tonelessly. "I still have to put them in the box." Stepping away from Devin's touch, she began placing the remaining cupcakes in the small flat box. She looked at Devin, to find him regarding her strangely. "Would you please answer the door?"

Devin looked as though he wanted to say something, but didn't. Wheeling about, he walked out of the kitchen to the front door.

Closing her eyes, a shudder rippled through Lilianne's body. Who would have thought a man's kiss could make her tremble to the depths of her soul? She'd wanted to tear off his shirt and touch the hard planes of his body, explore the toned muscles that made up the man. Her body's instantaneous response to him was almost shameful—and delicious, she admitted. Like nothing she'd ever felt before. How could she face him without thinking about the heat of his tongue stroking her mouth, the way her breasts had been pressed against his hard chest?

"Hello, Lilianne," Carolyn said as she breezed into the kitchen, Devin tailing her. "I'm sorry I stopped by so early, but you were on my way to Marilyn's. I thought you might have the cupcakes done by now."

If Carolyn had stopped by any later she would have found her and Devin in an even more heated embrace, Lilianne was sure. If it weren't for Carolyn's timely interruption she'd have probably been begging Devin to take her to bed. God, she must be one frustrated woman!

"They're done. I just need to put them in the box for you." Lilianne could feel Devin's eyes on her back, possibly tracing the notches in her bare spine. Her hand became nerveless, and the last cupcake slipped from her clumsy fingers. She tried to save it from death on the floor and caught it, upside down, in the palm of her hand, a glob of frosting squishing between her fingers.

"Damn," she swore, staring at the cupcake and the mess in her hand.

"Oh, my," Carolyn said, placing her hand over her mouth.

Devin chuckled.

Lilianne glared at him, knowing his amusement was at her expense.

"If you don't mind, I'll just take these cupcakes and get going. Thanks for your help and support, Lilianne." Carolyn picked up the box and backed out of the kitchen.

Devin's chuckle deepened.

"What's so funny?" She started toward him, stalking him into the corner of the counter.

"You." Devin's mouth straightened, but laughter still lurked in the depths of his eyes. "You're so cute when you're mad."

"You think so?"

"Absolutely."

Slowly, she began peeling back the liner from the cupcake. The sticky frosting held it fast to her palm, enabling her to complete the task with one hand. Keeping her eyes on Devin's face, she closed her palm around the cake, squishing it and the frosting in her hand and between her fingers. Her lips curled into a playful smile.

Devin saw the wicked gleam in her eyes and knew she wasn't about to let him pass unscathed. "I wouldn't do what you're thinking if I were you."

She did, and it felt *so* good. Her hand shot out and rubbed the sticky, gooey cake over his jaw and cheek. He tried to back off, but the counter wouldn't give. She pressed forward, trying to avoid his hands, managing to cover his cheeks, chin, nose and mouth in chocolate before he manacled her wrists. She threw her head back and laughed, feeling young and silly and not caring. He'd deserved it, the scoundrel.

Devin smiled down at Lily, a flash of white teeth back-dropped against a chocolate-coated face. "Ahh, Lily, you shouldn't have done that."

She hooted with laughter, tears of mirth coming to her eyes. "Why not? I feel a whole lot better."

Pulling at her wrists, he brought her in close. "Because you're going to have to suffer the consequences."

Lilianne had mixed feelings about those consequences, even before he started lowering his head. One part of her wanted to lean into his strength and open up to him. Her heart, however, rang out a warning bell. This wasn't a game any longer. Something deep within her told her to be cautious, to tread lightly before she fell hard for Devin—if it wasn't already too late.

"C'mere, Lily," he said, his voice low and sexy.

She didn't move. A giggle caught in her throat when she looked at his face. A piece of cake hung from the tip of his nose.

The fingers encircling her wrists slid to her hand and he interlocked her sticky fingers with his. He coaxed her closer and she obeyed.

Lilianne gasped when he kissed her, his kiss a concoction of chocolate and male essence. He kissed her slowly, deeply, until her knees began to buckle and he had to let go of her hands and cup her buttocks to steady her. At the same time she wrapped her arms around his neck. The kiss went on forever, it seemed, until the slamming of the front screen door jarred her back to reality. They jumped apart, looking guilty and covered in chocolate cupcake.

Jason came barging into the kitchen. "Mom, can I—" He stopped, staring at her peculiarly. Then he switched his gaze to Devin and frowned. "What happened to you guys? Looks like you got slimed with chocolate."

Lilianne smiled, feeling the stickiness on her face, which had come from Devin's kiss. She looked down at her hands, then Devin's coated with mashed cupcake. Devin stared at her, lifting a brow as if to say, "How do you plan to get out of this one?"

Lilianne smiled at Jason. "We, uh, were just eating a cupcake."

"You guys sure are messy. You can hardly see Uncle Devin's face. You'd be dragging me up to the tub if I ate a cupcake like that."

"It was so good, we got a little carried away," Lilianne said.

Jason shrugged, as if how they ate a cupcake was of no consequence to him. "Can I have a dollar? The ice cream man's here."

"I think I have an extra dollar, Tiger," Devin said. He went to pull out his wallet, then remembered the cake on his hands. He turned and washed them in the sink.

Lilianne stared, horrified to see bits of chocolate cake ringing the back of his neck where her hands had been. Jason appeared not to notice and simply waited patiently for Devin to give him a dollar. He skipped happily from the room.

"You, ah, have cake on the back of your neck," she said.

"Wouldn't surprise me." A smile twitched the corner of his mouth. "You have it all over your face."

"I guess I'd better go clean up." Chin high, she sashayed out of the kitchen.

Devin chuckled at the two large, chocolate handprints on her buttocks.

He washed his hands and face and dried them with a paper towel. While he waited for Lily to return, he started cleaning up the kitchen, wondering if she felt the intense feelings he did. He'd loved her for so long he didn't know if he could handle it if she didn't love him in return. Then again, he didn't want to lose her friendship. If he treaded carefully, he figured he could have both.

Ten minutes later the kitchen was spotless and Lilianne hadn't returned. He went in search of her and found her in her office, standing by the bookcase flipping through a wallpaper-pattern book. She looked clean, but she hadn't changed her shorts. He doubted she even knew she had two handprints on her fanny. He also knew she'd be horrified to find out she did.

"The kitchen is clean," he said, moving into the room.

Lilianne looked over her shoulder in surprise. She should have known better than to hope he'd left. He wasn't an easy man to dismiss. That he'd cleaned the kitchen surprised her even more. "Thanks. You didn't have to do that."

He shrugged off her appreciation. "I don't mind."

Lilianne replaced the book in its slot, feeling uneasy now that they were alone again. She didn't care for the serious-ness settling over Devin, the way his eyes watched her every move.

"Lily, I think we need to talk." Devin thrust his hands into the pockets of his shorts.

"About what?" she asked lightly, her smile falsely bright.

"You know about what," he said.

She moved behind her desk, using it as a means to sepa-rate the two of them. "So we shared a kiss. What's the big deal?" She began cleaning off her desk, putting the letter opener in the drawer, rearranging her stapler and tape dis-penser.

"It was more than a kiss, Lily, and you know it." He walked around the barrier of the desk until he stood next to her. She looked up at him and he thought he detected fear in her eyes. Of him? He didn't touch her as he went on. "My feelings for you are changing, Lily. I've always cared for you, even loved you, and I can't fight the feeling any longer."

Her hand trembled as she tucked a stray strand of hair behind her ear. He loved her? His confession shocked her. "I never knew," she whispered.

"Of course you never knew. I made damn sure of it. Michael was my best friend, Lily. I could never betray him that way." He shoved his fingers through his hair, his eyes searching hers. "Ever since his death I've agonized over my feelings for you. I don't want to trample on his memory and I don't want to replace him. But I can't stop the way I feel about you."

His eyes, so dark and sensual, made her heart beat frantically in her chest. He made her feel things she'd never experienced before—fluttering in her stomach, a warmth between her thighs. She swallowed to ease the dryness in her throat. "I care for you, too, but what's happening between us scares me."

"Why?"

How could she tell him the truth, that the thought of commitment to a man frightened her? "You're such a wonderful friend I don't want to risk losing you if things don't work out with us. You're too important to the children."

Propping his hip on the corner of her desk, Devin swung his leg back and forth. "First and foremost, I'll always be your friend. We already know we're compatible. We get along great, but I want to take our relationship one step further so we can explore these feelings we have for one another."

Her eyes widened, an innocence touching her eyes. "You mean you want to become lovers?"

"Possibly." He smiled. "But for now I'll be happy knowing you'll see me exclusively."

Confused by her conflicting feelings, she chewed on her thumbnail. "I don't want to get tied down to another man."

"I'm not asking you to marry me." Not yet, anyway, Devin thought. Picking up a stray paper clip, he rolled it between his fingers. He'd gotten a brief taste of her attitude toward marriage earlier, and it hadn't been a pleasant one. She associated marriage and commitment with being ruled by a man, something she was fiercely against.

"I need space and my independence," Lilianne stated pointedly.

"I can respect that," he said easily.

She looked at him warily and started to lower herself to her chair. Halfway there, Devin grabbed her arm.

"You have two chocolate handprints on your fanny," he said, grinning.

"Oh."

Devin pulled her into the harbor of his thighs. She came without resisting, a positive sign. Setting his large hands on her hips, his fingers flexed into her soft flesh. "We'll take things slowly, Lily, and if you aren't comfortable with the direction they're heading, we'll go back to being just friends."

Resting her hands on his broad shoulders, she looked down at him. "Is that possible?"

He bestowed her with a dazzling smile. "Anything is possible."

"Okay, we'll try it your way."

Five

"Promise us you'll pretend like you don't know us at the dance, Mom," Elizabeth said from the back seat of the Volvo.

Lilianne looked over her shoulder at her daughters, catching Devin's smile of amusement on the way. "I plan on hugging and kissing both of you at least once an hour."

"Mom!" Emily said, horrified.

Devin looked in the rearview mirror, catching Emily's reflection. "She'll do no such thing. I'm going to keep her busy, remember?"

"Thank goodness you came along, Uncle Devin," Elizabeth said in relief.

Looking at Devin, Lilianne smiled. Things hadn't changed much between them since their discussion, except Devin now felt he had the liberty to kiss her or touch her when he wanted to. He did both often, not that she was complaining. It had been a long time since a man had showered her with such attention and affection, and she was enjoying it. The kids loved him being around and never questioned the frequency of his visits.

Devin drove the Volvo into the school parking lot, taking a slot in the front row. Before he could put the car into park the girls were scrambling out.

"From here on, you don't know us, Mother," Elizabeth said sternly.

Lilianne crossed her fingers over her heart as a promise, a gesture her children took seriously. "I promise I won't say a word to you all night long unless you approach me first."

"Deal."

Lilianne watched Elizabeth and Emily walk away. They'd both worn stylish dresses, the new ones she'd bought for them a week before. Their hair shone gold in the evening dusk and hung past their shoulder blades in the back. Elizabeth had left hers straight, while Emily's bounced with soft waves, an effect achieved with Lilianne's hot curlers.

Devin locked the car and grabbed Lilianne's hand, weaving their fingers together. She looked at him, her eyes shimmering. "They're growing up so fast," she said quietly. "Two more years and they'll be in high school. And then they'll be dating!"

Devin squeezed her hand as they followed at a discreet distance behind the twins. "Don't worry. I'll screen their dates."

She grinned, imagining Devin giving one of the girl's dates a stern lecture. "I wish Michael could be here to see them. He'd be so proud."

"Do you miss him, Lily?"

She looked down at her high heels crunching into the graveled parking lot. That was a hard question to answer. She had grieved when Michael died, because he'd been her husband and the father of her children. Sometimes she missed him when she woke up alone at night, but lately she'd begun to wonder if it was actually Michael himself she missed or if it was the warmth of a man cuddled up to her in the night. A man to chase away her fears and reassure her she was doing a good job with the children.

"I miss him at times like this," she admitted. "I know he would have enjoyed seeing the children grow up." She

looked at Devin. His mahogany hair was attractively tousled and his eyes sparkled. He'd worn a pair of new jeans
that outlined the leanness of his waist and the hardness of
his thighs. The respectable blue-and-red-striped shirt he
wore clung to his shoulders and chest. "How about you? Do
you miss him?" she asked.

Hand in hand, they walked up the stairs to the auditorium. "Yes." Michael had been snatched from their lives so
abruptly, in such a devastating way, Devin still felt the loss
of his death. "I miss the easy friendship we shared. He was
like a brother to me."

Lilianne paused at the door and turned to him. "Do you
think he approves of us being together?" she asked softly.

Devin understood Lily's need for reassurance. How often had he spent a sleepless night staring at the ceiling,
wondering the same thing? "I don't know for certain, but I
think Michael would be happy knowing you found someone who loves you and the children. He often told me he
trusted me with his life. I'm sure he'd trust me with his
family."

She smiled at him, that soft, sweet smile that made him
want to give her the moon. "Thank you," she said.

He squeezed her hand, knowing somehow he'd relieved
both their minds of a heavy burden. He opened the metal
door to the auditorium and music blared out at them. He
looked over at Lilianne as two boys squeezed past him to get
in. "I can't believe you talked me into this."

She tugged his hand. "Come on, it'll be fun."

Time passed quickly. Lilianne and Devin monitored the
dance from a distance. For the most part the kids were
good. Occasionally Devin would see a girl and a boy sneak
off to neck. He'd give them five minutes, then drag them
back to the dance. They grumbled, but obeyed.

Devin danced with Lilianne and the other women chaperons, having as good a time as the kids. The loud music

nearly made him deaf and made normal conversation with Lilianne impossible.

"I need some fresh air," Lilianne said, breathing hard after dancing a fast dance with Devin. "I'm going to step outside for a bit."

Before Devin could reply, one of Elizabeth's friends grabbed his hand and tugged him toward the hardwood dance floor. Grinning, he waved at Lilianne.

Outside, a light breeze stirred, enough to cool her off. The sky was clear and bright stars shone like diamonds against black velvet. After a few minutes she went back inside. The lights had been turned low and a slow ballad played over the loudspeakers. She stood at the doorway, letting her eyes adjust to the dimness.

"Wanna neck?" a deep voice asked from behind her.

A shiver raced down Lilianne's spine, and the peaks of her breasts hardened. She spun around and found herself in Devin's arms. "Absolutely not!" she protested, a smile on her lips.

He pulled her deeper into the shadows, his eyes gleaming wickedly. His body picked up the slow, sensual beat of the music, rubbing against hers. "The girls said to keep you busy. What better way to keep you busy than by giving you long, slow kisses?"

Lilianne's breathing shortened and her stomach dropped a couple of inches. "I don't think this is what they had in mind." Resting her palms on his muscled chest, she tried leaning back. He only held her tighter. "Need I remind you we're the chaperons here? What kind of example would we be setting by necking?"

"Let me show you." Two steps back and he had her pinned against the cool brick wall. His mouth found hers easily, parting her lips so his tongue could explore the heated depths within. Her hands crept around his neck, her fingers running through his thick hair.

Lilianne heard boys' voices, but nothing could penetrate the fog of desire clouding her mind while Devin kissed her. He had incredible lips, and the things he did with his tongue were absolutely sinful. He knew when to soften a kiss and he detected the precise moment she wanted more, and complied. His body moved to the beat of the music, his hips gyrating into hers in a slow rhythm that made her tremble.

The voices became louder, then stopped. Devin came up for air and turned his head, spotting two young boys staring at them. Silently he cursed his lack of control.

"Hey, Mrs. Austin is kissing one of the other chaperons," one of the boys squealed, hurrying off to the crowd of kids in the middle of the dance floor. The other boy quickly followed, but not before he looked over his shoulder and grinned at Devin.

In less than a minute the whole auditorium knew that Mrs. Austin, Elizabeth and Emily's mother, had been necking with Mr. McKay. Although most of the kids snickered when Lilianne and Devin emerged from the shadows, Elizabeth and Emily looked mortified to the very tips of their low-heeled pumps.

"At least I kept my promise not to talk to them," Lilianne said, blushing from all the eyes trained on her.

"I don't think it matters much anymore." Devin kept a smile pasted on his face and tried acting like nothing out of the ordinary had happened. He was going to strangle the kid with the big mouth.

The DJ put on another song and announced a ladies' choice. The girls grabbed partners, and the incident was soon forgotten.

Elizabeth and Emily sulked on the way home from the dance.

"Mother, how *could* you?" Elizabeth said.

"I've never been more embarrassed in my whole life," Emily added.

"I think you guys will survive," Devin said sternly.

Lilianne stared at Devin, not knowing whether to be shocked or pleased at his authoritative tone. She had to take into account the twins' feelings about the whole situation. Sure, they'd been embarrassed, but did it bother them knowing that their mother was entering into a deeper relationship with their uncle Devin? Did they even realize the implication of Devin's kissing her?

"Girls, I'm sorry if we embarrassed you." Lilianne twisted in her seat so she could see them better.

"If you want to kiss Uncle Devin, fine. But don't do it where you're going to get caught," Elizabeth said, crossing her arms over her chest.

"Especially by one of our friends," Emily added.

Lilianne cleared her throat, feeling awkward with the next question. She forced it out. "Does it bother you if, ah, Uncle Devin and I kiss?"

The twins looked at each other, as if silently consulting over Lilianne's question. Then they looked back at her. Emily shrugged. "No. Are you going to marry Uncle Devin?"

Lilianne ignored Devin's sharp glance. "No, sweetheart. Uncle Devin and I are just good friends."

Devin wanted to dispute that, but now was not the time.

"Oh," Emily said quietly. "We wouldn't mind if you did. It would be great to have Uncle Devin as a dad."

Don't dig me in any deeper, Emily, Lilianne thought silently. "I'm glad you feel that way. Uncle Devin will always be around for you, honey. You know that, don't you?"

"Yeah."

Lilianne turned quickly in her seat to stare out the windshield before any more uncomfortable questions could be fired her way.

Devin as her husband? Although the thought made her insides warm like sitting before a cozy fire, it frightened the hell out of her. The kids needed a father, not a part-time uncle, but what did she need? Being a woman, she wouldn't mind sleeping next to him at night, making love, then snuggling, but what would happen in the light of day? She imagined herself pregnant again and blanched. If she had another baby she'd be expected to stay home, take care of it, be a housewife. The career she'd built for herself would once again become a distant dream.

She didn't need a man, she reasoned. They were nice for companionship and warming your bed, but she wouldn't allow herself to get dependent on one ever again. Once had been enough.

Devin curled his fingers around the steering wheel, resisting the urge to reach over and grab Lilianne's hands, which were twisting together in her lap. She bit her bottom lip, looking deep in thought. He knew the direction her mind was racing, not hard to figure since he'd seen her reaction to Emily's question of marriage.

Normally Devin considered himself a patient man. He'd shown three long years of restraint in confessing his feelings to Lilianne, but now that she knew how he felt about her, he wanted more. He wanted to share her life, laugh with her, argue with her so he could see her fire, and he wanted to make love to her, feel his baby grow in her belly.

Turning into Lilianne's street, Devin knew he wouldn't be satisfied with kisses and stolen moments forever. After a long day at work he wanted to come home to a wife and family, sit at the dinner table and share the day's events. He could do that now, but it wasn't the same. He'd be spending his nights alone in his own bed while Lilianne slept in hers.

* * *

Three days later, on the evening of the Meadowbrook Development Project opening Devin arrived half an hour early to pick up Lilianne.

Jason answered the door, excited to see him. Devin ruffled his hair as he walked into the house. "Hey, Tiger, where's your mom?"

Jason wrinkled his nose at him. "In her bedroom getting ready."

Devin tweaked his nose. "You all packed and ready to go to Rusty's?"

Giggling, Jason rubbed his nose. "Yep. Rusty's mom bought him the Teenage Mutant Ninja Turtle video, and we're going to watch it tonight."

"Are Elizabeth and Emily here?" Devin asked, looking around the living room, listening for girlish laughter. Nothing.

Jason shook his head. "Nope. They're at a slumber party at Kathleen Dorman's house."

Devin smiled. Great, just as planned. "Why don't you go get your bag and I'll see if your mom's ready." Walking down the hall to Lilianne's bedroom, Devin knocked on the closed door.

"Come in, honey," Lilianne called.

Devin liked the sound of that endearment. He grinned as he stepped into her bedroom. "Honey?" he teased.

Lilianne looked up as she smoothed her dress over her hips. "Oh, hi, Devin," she said, her voice breathless. "I thought you were Jason."

Devin's mouth went dry at the sight of her. She looked gorgeous and radiant in a deep blue dress that clung to her generous curves. The sleeves were short and pulled down off her arms so her shoulders were bare. Lace bordered the plunging neckline. Sheer black stockings tinted her legs and black leather pumps encased her feet. Her hair had been arranged into an old-fashioned topknot. The effect softened her features and made her look young and romantic. Shimmering silver-and-blue earrings dangled from her ears, nearly touching her shoulders.

The dress, alluring and tempting, brought forth forbidden images of stripping it away to discover what lay beneath. Devin's dark eyes scanned the length of her as his imagination went into overdrive, picturing skimpy, lace panties and creamy, silken flesh.

Lilianne twirled for Devin's inspection. "What do you think?" she asked, anticipation making her eyes sparkle.

"I think you look stunning and too damned seductive. What do you say we drop Jason off, then come back home and forget the opening?"

"Devin!"

"Hey," he said, shrugging, "it was just an idea. Can't blame a man for trying."

No, she couldn't, because she felt the same way. For the past couple of weeks all she could think of was him and the depth of their affection for one another. The next step in their relationship would push her over the edge, and she wasn't sure if she was ready to fall. She picked up a crystal atomizer Michael had given her one year for her birthday and noticed how her hand shook. Before she could push the sprayer, Devin took it from her.

"Nervous?" he murmured, looking into her eyes.

She nodded. "A little. Meadowbrook is my first big account. There should be a pretty big turnout."

Lifting the atomizer, Devin sprayed a fine layer of perfume on her neck. Holding her gaze, his finger lightly touched the still-wet spot, then slid down the graceful slope of her throat to the cleavage spilling from the dress. Her breathing deepened. His eyes dropped to her lips, and they automatically parted. One large hand curved over the roundness of her breast while the other slipped to her waist to pull her in close. Her eyes fluttered shut as he slowly lowered his head.

"Mom, are you ready to go yet?" Jason asked impatiently through the closed door.

Lilianne jumped back out of Devin's embrace, appalled that she'd come so close to letting him seduce her with her son in the house.

Devin wanted to howl in frustration. Instead, he cursed vividly, making Lilianne's eyes widen. "We'll be right there, Jason," he growled.

"Okay, but hurry," Jason said.

"You're pushing it, kid," Devin said under his breath. He combed his fingers through his hair. "There are too many damned interruptions."

Lilianne had a hand over her frantically beating heart. She used it to straighten out the bodice of her dress. "You don't get much peace and quiet with kids around."

"We'll see about that," Devin murmured under his breath as Lilianne walked to the bed to retrieve her purse.

The reception for Meadowbrook was in full swing when Devin and Lilianne arrived. There were groups of men in business suits and women in cocktail dresses discussing the merits of Lilianne's interior decorating.

Devin looked around the large reception area. It was a tasteful blend of sophistication and warmth. Lithograph pictures hung on the walls, and silk plants sat on marble pillars.

Lilianne gave Devin a brief tour. He noted how each of the offices had been individually decorated. By the time he'd seen the whole complex he was suitably impressed.

"You did this by yourself?" Devin asked. He grabbed two glasses of champagne off a passing tray and handed one to Lilianne.

Nodding, Lilianne took a sip of the bubbly liquid. "Yes. It took months, but I'm quite pleased with it."

"You should be. You've done an incredible job."

Lilianne's chest swelled with pride. Devin's praise warmed her. She'd completed plenty of small projects, but this accomplishment ranked her as a true professional. She'd already begun receiving referral calls just on the basis of someone seeing the redecoration of this office.

"I'm very proud of you," Devin said, his voice low and intimate around the crowd of people. "I never doubted you could do it."

She smiled at him, feeling a ray of sunshine from the inside out. "Thank you, Devin."

"There you are, Lilianne," a deep voice boomed through the reception area. A small, round man emerged from the throng of people, trailed by his wife, a tall blonde with endlessly long legs.

"Edward." Lilianne stepped forward and accepted the kiss Edward planted on her cheek. She nodded politely to Marcella, whom she'd met before.

Lilianne introduced Edward Livingston, her client, to Devin, and they shook hands.

"Lilianne's quite a gal," Edward said, slapping Devin jovially on the back. Devin was barely able to keep the contents of his glass from sloshing onto the new carpet. "She sat for hours with me discussing just the right colors and details for each office. She was worth every penny I paid her."

"I think her rates just went up." Devin winked at Lilianne.

They spent another two hours being introduced to clients and friends of Edward's. Lilianne smiled and accepted everyone's gracious comments on her work. By the time the night ended, she was exhausted, but pleased with herself.

As soon as she and Devin walked into the house, Lilianne slipped off her high heels. They'd left a lamp on low in the living room, and she tossed her purse onto the couch and turned to Devin. She felt heady with success…and love, she realized, looking into his eyes.

"Thank you for going with me."

"You bet." Shrugging out of his suit coat, Devin draped it over the recliner. He pulled at his tie, loosening it enough to take it off.

All of a sudden, nerves began to flutter in Lilianne's stomach. In the shadows of the lone light Devin looked virile and masculine. She watched as he released the first two buttons of his shirt, revealing the strong column of his throat and tufts of dark curling hair covering his chest.

He came to her and cupped her cheek in his palm, caressing her lips with the pad of his thumb. His eyes grew so dark they looked nearly black. "I don't want to go home tonight and I don't want to settle for a few kisses. I want you, Lily. I want you so badly I can't think straight anymore."

Lily closed her eyes against the feelings raging inside her. If she said yes to Devin she would forever alter their relationship. If she said no, she knew she would always regret it. She loved him, and the strong feelings coming from her heart and soul told her this was right. Taking his hand, she silently led him down the hallway to her bedroom. She turned the bedside lamp on low, then faced him.

Devin finished unbuttoning his shirt and shrugged out of it, all the while watching Lilianne. She crossed the room and stood before her vanity mirror. Her hands shook as she removed her earrings and laid them carefully on the table.

Devin came up behind her, running his hands up and down her arms. He caught her gaze in the mirror. "How long has it been?" he asked gently, already knowing the answer.

"Since Michael died," she said quietly.

His fingers traced the neckline of the dress until he came to the zipper in the back. "Three years is a long time."

Her eyes glazed over with desire. "I never realized how long until now."

Smiling tenderly, Devin unzipped her dress, tracing her spine with his finger all the way down to her buttocks. Palms flattened, he smoothed his hands back up to her shoulders, never breaking eye contact in the mirror. His fingers curled around the edge of the dress and slowly pulled the sleeves down her arms and over her hips, letting the material fall into a silky pool at her feet.

Lilianne hugged her arms over her breasts, thankful the light was dim so he couldn't see the stretch marks on her stomach. Once he peeled her panty hose off, however, there would be nothing left to conceal them.

"Lily, drop your arms," he said huskily. "I want to see you."

She swallowed her pride. "Devin, I don't pretend to have an incredibly toned, young body. I carried twins and it shows."

He skimmed his hands up her ribs, leaving quivering flesh in their wake. "Do you honestly think I care about that?"

"I'm sure you're used to thin, perfectly shaped women. I'm far from it."

"I don't want anyone but you, Lily." He pulled her arms back to her sides, his expression growing hungry at the sight of her full breasts. "I think you're incredibly beautiful." Watching her expression in the mirror, he took the soft mounds in his hands, bringing the nipples to life.

Moaning, Lilianne leaned into his chest. Bursts of pleasure started in her breasts and traveled down between her thighs. Her heart pounded in her ears and every nerve ending in her body tingled.

Kneeling in front of her, Devin removed her hose and panties, kissing her flesh as he bared it. He paid special attention to her stretch marks, running his tongue over them until her fingers wove into his hair to tug him back up.

He pulled out the pins holding the mass of hair on her head, letting the tresses tumble around her shoulders. Burying his hand in the silky tresses, he brought her mouth to his and kissed her slowly, deeply, swirling his tongue against hers.

Lilianne's heart swelled with love for Devin. Her body responded to his like a match to kindling, spreading wildfire throughout her body. Arching her back, she brought her breasts against his chest and rubbed, gasping at the feel of his coarse body hair tickling her sensitive nipples.

Devin was hard and aching. He didn't think he could wait much longer to be inside the warmth and softness of Lilianne's body. Taking her hand, he tugged her toward the bed. He tossed the frilly pillows to the floor, heedless of where they landed. Yanking the satin bedspread and blanket to the foot of the bed, he pushed Lilianne on top of the cool sheet. It took him less than a minute to shuck his shoes, socks, pants and underwear. He came down on top of her, his hard manhood cradled in the cove of her thighs. Running his hand up her thigh, he closed his mouth over hers, kissing her with raw passion. In the next instant he was slowly sliding into her.

Lilianne gasped, lifting her hips for Devin's penetration. He felt so good and so right, his body perfectly aligned with hers. Opening her eyes, she stared into his face, watching the myriad expressions as he thrust deep inside her. Love and adoration shone from his eyes, and pure pleasure curled his mouth.

Soon Lilianne was lost in exquisite ecstasy. With every rhythmic movement of Devin's body a pressure built deep inside her until it finally surfaced. Her nerves exploded into a million shattering pieces, and she cried out, vaguely aware of Devin calling her name, of his body jerking hard into hers.

He collapsed on top of her, and she reveled in the feeling of his weight and warmth. Her hands stroked his back, holding him close.

He lifted his head and stared down at Lilianne's flushed face. He'd never seen a more beautiful woman. Lowering his head, he kissed her slowly and deeply. When he looked at her again her eyes were glazed, her lips swollen and wet.

"I love you," he said, his voice husky.

She smiled, dragging her hands up the slope of his back. "I love you, too."

He shook his head, knowing she'd misunderstood him. "No, I mean I'm in love with you."

She cocked her head to the side. "Isn't that the same thing?"

"Maybe it is to you. I'm not talking about a friendship kind of love, Lily. I love you with everything I am. Like a husband loves a wife."

Lilianne's body stiffened and her hands stilled in his hair at the nape of his neck. Old doubts resurfaced, shadowing her eyes. Her feelings of love for Devin certainly went deeper than friendship, but that didn't mean she wanted to marry him. Suddenly she felt crushed and suffocated. Pushing at Devin's shoulders, she gave him a frantic look, and he rolled off of her.

I'm going too fast, Devin thought, cursing himself for his impatience. He gathered Lilianne to him, holding her close, but saying nothing more. What could he say? He'd poured his heart out to her, and although he knew Lilianne loved him as he loved her, she'd never admit it. She didn't want to be tied permanently to any man. It was as simple and as difficult as that. He didn't know if he could settle for less than marriage to her.

As the night evolved into morning, Devin made love to Lilianne twice more, one time fierce and hard, the other gentle and sweet. His heart became torn between having

Lily, yet knowing she'd never commit herself to marriage, no matter how strong and deep her feelings for him ran.

By morning, he'd made up his mind. He couldn't spend the rest of his life sneaking in and out of Lilianne's bed. He couldn't keep his true feelings about her from the kids, feeling guilty every time they caught them in a heated embrace. He wanted to be a real father to the children, giving them guidance and love without feeling as if he was intruding on Michael's memory.

He was going to take a gamble of a lifetime; all or nothing.

Six

Lilianne awoke feeling lazy and content. Her legs were entwined with Devin's and her head rested in the cradle of his arm and shoulder. Her body ached from the vigorous activities of the previous night, something she wasn't accustomed to. But, she reflected with a smile, she could easily *get* accustomed.

Lifting her head, she peered down into his face, finding his eyes open and looking at her. Smiling, she touched the dark stubble on his jaw. "Good morning," she murmured.

"Good morning, Lily."

He looked awfully serious and deep in thought for first thing in the morning. The pad of her finger ran over the furrows between his eyes, trying to smooth them out. Finally he smiled, then pulled her down for a quick kiss.

Lilianne clutched the sheet to her breasts, feeling self-conscious in the light of day. She ran a hand over her hair, knowing it was a mass of wild tangles. She never looked her best first thing in the morning.

"You look beautiful, Lily," Devin said, as if sensing her discomfort.

"You're a liar, but thank you, anyway. I always look terrible first thing in the morning."

"You look like a woman who's been well and truly loved."

Tumbling onto her back, she stretched lazily. "Ummm, I feel like it. I suppose we should rouse ourselves before the kids get home." She looked at him and grinned. "You know our luck with getting caught."

He came up on his elbow and trailed his hand from her neck to her breast, nudging the sheet aside. Cupping the silky flesh in his hands, he stroked his thumb over her nipple, watching as it responded. "I don't mind getting caught."

She grasped his wrist as his hand slid over her belly. "I'm not ready to explain our new relationship to the kids yet."

He withdrew his hand and his lashes lowered, veiling his mounting frustration. "I guess we'd better get up then." Sliding off the bed, he went into the bathroom, closing the door behind him.

As Lilianne dressed in a baggy T-shirt and an old pair of jeans, she wondered at Devin's cool attitude. This wasn't the man who'd made mad, passionate love to her the night before. He'd withdrawn from her, and it bothered her. Did he regret making love to her? Was she not what he'd expected? Shaking her head of the thoughts, she went to her vanity mirror.

One look confirmed her earlier suspicions. She was truly disheveled. Brushing out the tangles in her hair, she pulled it back into a ponytail. She went into the kids' bathroom and washed her face and brushed her teeth. Staring at her reflection, she noted a certain glow on her cheeks, a sparkle in her eyes. With a lightness to her step she went to the kitchen and started breakfast.

Devin emerged from the bathroom, the smell of sizzling bacon greeting him. He pulled on his underwear, then his pants and shirt. Looking at the bed, he took in the rumpled sheets, remembering Lily's uninhibited response to him the night before. She was everything he wanted in a woman and more. She had a gentle and kind nature, made him laugh, was sensible and hardworking, and passionate enough to keep him well satisfied.

Devin walked barefoot into the kitchen, heading straight for the coffeepot. Bringing down a mug from the cupboard, he filled it with the rich, aromatic brew. He leaned his hip against the counter and watched Lilianne scramble eggs and flip pancakes. He marveled at her ease in the kitchen, then remembered she'd had years of practice.

"How many pancakes do you want?" she asked, bestowing him with a dazzling smile.

Breakfast was the last thing on his mind. His stomach twisted with anxiety, knowing he'd be confronting Lilianne with marriage in a short while. "Two," he answered, taking a sip of coffee.

"You're not very hungry for a man who worked awfully hard last night," she teased.

"It's not food I'm hungry for," he said, straight-faced. He was hungry for much more. Permanency, intimacy, family. He wanted to set down roots and start a new life with Lily by his side, making him complete.

Lilianne flipped two pancakes onto a plate, along with some scrambled eggs and bacon. She handed it to him. "Butter and syrup are on the table."

"Thanks," he murmured. His stomach growled as the delicious smells assaulted his nostrils. Okay, so he was a little hungry for food.

Devin ate everything on his plate and even finished the leftover scrambled eggs and bacon. Taking his plate to the sink, he rinsed it off, then grabbed the coffeepot and filled both their mugs. When he again sat down next to Lilianne, he gazed thoughtfully into the black depths of his mug, garnering the courage to broach the subject of marriage.

"Are you all right?" Lilianne asked, frowning at him. She reached out and touched his arm, drawing his gaze to hers.

Devin drew in a deep breath. "Lilianne, about last night . . ."

Lilianne jerked back her hand as if she'd been burned. "Do you regret what happened?"

He smiled gently. "No, not at all. Just the opposite, in fact. I want what we shared last night every night."

Lilianne visibly relaxed. She ate the last bite of bacon and placed her fork on her plate. "Last night was wonderful, Devin, but when the kids are home I don't think it would be a good idea if you stayed the night."

"That's just the point. I want to spend every night with you."

Her coffee mug halted midway to her mouth. "You mean you want to live with us?"

"In a way." He watched confusion settle over her features. "Do you love me, Lily?"

Her delicate shoulders slumped and her eyes softened perceptibly. "You know I do."

"Enough to marry me?"

Lilianne sucked in a breath. "Devin, I do love you, very much, but I'm not looking for marriage. I told you that."

"Yeah, I know what you told me. Unfortunately I want more. I don't want a bunch of one-nighters, and I don't want to sneak around the children."

"But that's all I can give you, Devin. I can't give you more."

The dark centers of his eyes turned stormy. "Can't or won't, Lily?"

"Both. I love my life the way it is. I come and go when I please. I depend on no one but myself."

"I don't want to take anything from you. I'm proud of you and your business. I'd never demand that you put one before the other."

Her lashes lowered, veiling the skepticism in them. "Why can't we just keep things the way they are?"

Abruptly he stood. Bracing his palms on the table, he leaned toward her. "Because, dammit, I want to sleep with you every night without having to worry about sneaking out before the kids wake up. I want to eat breakfast with the family, and I want to share dinner and discuss the kids' day at school and your day designing. I want to be a real father to the children and, most especially, I want to have a baby with you."

Lilianne gasped, her hand fluttering to the neck of her T-shirt. "I'm too old to have another baby, Devin."

Straightening, he jammed his hands on his hips. "Hell, Lily, you're only thirty-six, hardly near the age of menopause."

"I don't want another baby," she said adamantly, feeling at a disadvantage because she had to look up at him. "I don't want the responsibility of having to stay home all day and take care of a baby while you're out working and the other kids are in school. I'd go crazy!"

"No one says you have to stay home and be strictly a mother. Wasn't it you who mentioned having a family and a career? You can do both and still be happy."

"No, Devin." She sighed, brushing the wispy bangs from her forehead. "I don't want to lose you, Devin, but I can't give you what you're asking."

He stared at her, a muscle in his jaw twitching. "You don't want to need me, Lily, but you do. There's nothing wrong or weak about that."

The authority in his words angered and provoked her. Jumping out of her seat, she jabbed her finger his way, coming precariously close to poking him in the chest. "I don't need you or any other man."

He locked his gaze with hers. "Then I guess it's best if I step out of your life," he said quietly.

Oh, God, what had she done? Lilianne panicked, thinking about how much she loved him and needed him, despite her angry words. "You promised me if things didn't work out between us we could still be friends."

He shook his head, his eyes full of regret. "I can't do it, Lily. I can't pretend we didn't share something rare and special. I love you so much it'll hurt too much to be near you, knowing I can never truly have you."

Lilianne cursed the tears burning in her eyes. Her heart felt like it was being ripped from her chest. "What about the kids?" she asked in a last-ditch effort.

"I'll still come by and see them." He rubbed the back of his neck and stared at the tiled floor. "I love all three of them like they were my own. There is no reason our differences should affect them."

"Don't do this to us, Devin." Lilianne realized she was pleading.

Devin's heart twisted, making the pain course throughout his entire body, but he didn't back down. "I have to. If I don't, I'll only come to resent the situation. I'm greedy, Lily. I want everything or nothing at all. If you ever change your mind, just let me know."

Lilianne lifted her chin high as he walked out of the dining room. She refused to beg anymore. She heard the front door open and close. "Damn you, Devin McKay, for making me care so much. I never wanted to love someone so much it felt like I was dying when they walked away," she whispered. "What am I going to do without you?"

"Happy birthday to you, happy birthday to you, happy birthday, dear Elizabeth and Emily, happy birthday to you!"

Devin clapped and cheered as, together, the twins blew out the thirteen candles on their birthday cake. He nudged Jason in the ribs, who sat next to him. "How about getting us each a big piece of cake?"

"Okay." Jason scrambled off his folding chair. "I better get there quick before Mom gives the corner pieces away."

As Jason raced for the cake, Devin glanced around Lilianne's backyard. Birthday streamers fluttered in the breeze and helium balloons tied to the porch posts strained against their bondage of ribbons. A table with condiments for the hot dogs and hamburgers sat beside the barbecue, covered with plastic now since most of the kids had eaten. The twins were in a circle with their friends, talking and giggling. His gaze finally settled on Lilianne, and his heart lurched, then began a fierce, painful throbbing.

She was wearing a pink blouse tucked into white jeans, and her hair fell in a riot of red-gold waves to her shoulders. She smiled perfunctorily at the children as she served them slices of cake, but she lacked her normal enthusiasm and cheer. It hurt to think he was responsible for this change in her.

Jason brought him a piece of cake, saving him from encountering Lily and seeing close up the dullness of her normally sparkling eyes.

"How come you hardly ever come over anymore?" Jason asked him. The boy shoveled a piece of cake into his mouth, waiting for Devin's answer.

Devin smiled, stiff and forced. "I come over, Tiger. I see you all the time."

Jason didn't look convinced. "You never come over when Mom's around, and you don't stay for dinner like you used to."

Devin's cake landed like lead in his stomach. "I've been busy at the shop."

Jason sighed, picking at his frosting. "Mom's been so grouchy lately. She's always yelling at us, and then she'll burst into tears and hug us and tell us she's sorry." He looked up at Devin, confusion making his brow pucker. "What's wrong with her?"

Devin pushed aside the guilt pulling at his conscience. "She's probably working too hard and she's tired."

Jason shook his head, a little man of wisdom. "I don't think so. Every time I walk into her office when she's supposed to be working she's just staring off into space."

Devin's gaze sought out Lily. He found her smiling at one of the twins' friends, but the smile didn't change the sadness lingering in her expression. His gut twisted when he thought about how much he missed her.

"You never talk to her anymore," Jason said quietly, swinging his legs back and forth under the chair. His expression guileless, he glanced up at Devin. "She always used to laugh and smile when you were around. How come that changed? Did you guys have a fight?"

Devin couldn't lie to Jason. "Yes, we had a...a disagreement, but it doesn't change the way I feel about you or your sisters."

Hanging his head, Jason resumed eating his cake. "I wish you and Mom would make up."

So did he. Devin had never spent a more miserable month in his life. He was beginning to regret his rash decision to stop seeing Lily, but then he realized it was more painful seeing her, knowing she'd never truly be his, rather than not seeing her at all. He thought of her so much he found himself daydreaming while at work. At night he couldn't sleep because he remembered too well the feel of her satin skin beneath his, the way her body responded to his touch. He missed holding her, kissing her, teasing her, talking to her. Even arguing with her.

He was a fool for thinking if he bowed out of her life and gave her room she'd change her mind about marriage. Her stubborn pride would never allow it.

Devin watched Lilianne take the remaining cake into the house. Turning to Jason, he asked, "Are you through with your cake?"

"Yeah," Jason said, handing Devin his plate. He eyed the piñata hanging from a porch beam. Elizabeth had grabbed a broom handle and was getting ready to take her turn trying to break it open. Jumping down from his chair, Jason ran to the end of the piñata line.

Devin chuckled, the sound gratifying to his own ears. When was the last time he'd laughed? He couldn't remember exactly, but he was certain it had been with Lily. He looked toward the house, knowing Lily was inside somewhere. He decided he wanted to see her, talk to her.

As Lilianne cleared the counter of party paraphernalia, then wrapped tinfoil around the leftover cake, she tried not to think of Devin sitting outside, so close, yet so far away. When she'd opened the door to him this afternoon and he'd politely said hello, then walked past her to accept the twins' hugs, her heart had shriveled.

Now her heart felt like a wound, raw and tender. She'd cried and grieved for Devin so much she didn't think she had any emotion left in her. His absence from her life hurt worse than anything she could have imagined, and that scared her witless. That meant dependency, something she refused to accept.

"How are you, Lily?"

Lilianne jumped at the rough yet gentle male voice behind her. The box of foil fell from her nerveless fingers to the floor. She pasted on a smile as she turned. "Just fine," she said brightly, sounding phony to her own ears. "And you?"

"Miserable. Lonely as hell. I miss you." Devin stooped and picked up the tinfoil, placing it on the counter. He met her eyes, so green and full of heartache. His insides tightened, holding back the urge to fold her in his embrace and shower his love on her.

Lilianne's eyes teared, hot and burning. "Don't, Devin. You're the one who asked for this, not me."

He stood, unbending, his expression hardening just a bit. "There is a solution to the problem."

Oh, yes, if only he knew how often she'd considered it! Lilianne turned from him before he could read the truth in her face. Sometimes, when the hurt got so bad and she wanted more than anything to be held in his arms, her cherished independence didn't count for much. Still, she couldn't bring herself to say the words "I need you," to end all the agony and torture ripping her soul to shreds.

"I never meant to hurt you, Lily," Devin said quietly, shoving his fingers into the pockets of his jeans. "I guess my pride is just as stubborn as yours."

I need you! she cried from the bottom of her soul, but the words wouldn't come. Instead, she turned back around and said in an even voice, "Thank you for coming today, despite everything."

He nodded curtly. "I would never miss the twins' birthday, Lily."

A young girl came into the kitchen, her face radiating her excitement. "Mrs. Austin, Elizabeth and Emily are getting ready to open their presents."

Lilianne managed a pleasant smile. "I'll be right there, Cindy."

Devin waited until the girl had left the kitchen. He looked at Lilianne, wishing he wasn't so greedy and could settle for less. "If you ever need me for anything, Lily, you have my number."

"Things aren't the same now," she said, suddenly angry.

Regret filled Devin's dark eyes. "I know, but right now that's all I can give you."

Lilianne watched Devin walk out of the kitchen. *That's all I can give you.* Now that she was on the receiving end of those words, she realized how horribly selfish they sounded.

"Mrs. Austin, Mrs. Austin!"

Lilianne lifted her head from the invoice she was writing

out and frowned at the distant voice calling her name. It sounded like Rusty.

"Mrs. Austin!"

Lilianne rose from her chair and walked out of the office toward the front hallway. Rusty flew through the screen door, his face beet-red and his chest heaving. Tears were streaming down his cheeks and his eyes were wide in fear.

She immediately rushed to him, thinking Jason had yet again provoked the boy—her son had become so rebellious lately. "What's wrong, Rusty?"

"It's Jason," he said between gulps of air. "We were riding our bikes and . . . and he . . ." He started to cry even harder.

Suddenly Lilianne could hear sirens in the distance. Fear ripped through her.

"Jason got hit by a car!" Rusty got out at last.

Lilianne's stomach heaved. She raced out of the house, running as fast as she could to the end of the street where an ambulance and two police cars had come to a stop. She pushed her way through all the gawking neighbors and kids. A scream lodged in her throat when she saw Jason lying unconscious on the pavement, two paramedics working over him. His arm was twisted at an odd angle, and blood ran from his nose. His bike lay in a mangled mess a few feet away.

Lilianne told the paramedics who she was, keeping her hysterics at bay. Her head swirled and adrenaline pumped through her as she accompanied Jason to the hospital, riding in the back of the ambulance by his side. He hadn't regained consciousness. The paramedics couldn't accurately assess any internal damage, leaving Lilianne to wonder if her son would even live.

At the hospital a crew immediately wheeled Jason into the emergency room. The nurses instructed Lilianne to wait in the lounge. The doctor would speak with her shortly, they said.

Lilianne paced the room, heedless of the curious stares cast her way. Horrible, unthinkable thoughts ran through her mind, expanding her chest in anxiety. She had to call someone to let them know what had happened. She dashed to a phone.

Strangely, the first number Lilianne dialed wasn't her parents or her brother's. The deep, smooth voice answering her call automatically soothed her frayed nerves.

"McKay's Body Works." Devin's voice was unenthusiastic after a long day spent priming and painting cars.

Lilianne closed her eyes, feeling a warmth instantly begin to curl through her body. How could she have gone so long without him?

"Hello?"

"Devin," Lilianne began, hiccuping. "I need you."

"Lily?"

The dam of emotions broke, bringing on a torrent of tears. Lilianne couldn't stop the deep sobs ripping from her throat. She'd been so calm and collected through the ordeal thus far, and now she needed someone to lean on, someone to share the pain.

"Lily, what's wrong?" Panic laced Devin's voice.

Lilianne corralled her emotions, dashing the tears off her face with the palm of her hand. "Jason's been hit by a car."

Devin sucked in a breath, then went on urgently. "Where are you?"

"St. Mary's Hospital."

"I'll be right there."

Lilianne continued to hold on to the receiver long after the line went dead, as if she could somehow absorb his strength that way. Then she called her parents and her brother, asking him if he'd pick up the girls from the house and keep them for the night.

Devin arrived twenty minutes later. As soon as he walked into the waiting room, Lilianne rushed into his open arms. Her eyes were puffy from crying and her body trembled with fear. Rocking her gently in his embrace, Devin stroked her hair, whispering, "Shh, sweetheart. Everything will be fine."

Lilianne burrowed closer into the warmth and support of his muscular chest. Her hiccups slowly receded as she breathed in the masculine scent of him.

"How is he?" Devin's hand caressed her back, relaxing her tense muscles.

Pulling away, Lilianne stared up at Devin. "I don't know. They immediately took him in and I haven't seen him since. The nurses won't tell me a thing."

He smiled grimly. "I know. The waiting is the hardest part. I'll be here with you."

Gratitude deepened the green of her eyes. "Thank you."

At last a doctor stepped into the waiting room, his eyes scanning the occupants.

Lilianne was sitting next to Devin on a green plaid couch, her head resting on his shoulder, her hand sheltered warmly in his. They stood as the doctor approached them.

"Mrs. Austin?"

"Yes," Lilianne answered worriedly. "How is Jason?" Behind her, Devin's hands rested on her shoulders, his fingers flexing.

The doctor reached out and touched her hand. "He broke his arm in three places and he has two cracked ribs. He also has a slight concussion."

Lilianne gasped, tears welling up in her eyes. She reached for Devin's hand on her shoulder and squeezed tight. She forced out the words lodged in her throat. "Is he going to be all right?"

"I think so. He didn't sustain any serious damage."

Lilianne closed her eyes and sent up a silent prayer of thanks. She felt Devin's body relax behind her.

The doctor went on, "However, we want to keep him here for a couple of days. Considering the speed the car was reportedly going when your son got hit, Jason is a very lucky young man. Things could have been much worse. He's a strong and healthy boy. He'll pull through just fine."

"Can we see him?" she asked anxiously.

"Of course. Come this way."

Lilianne and Devin followed the doctor down the hall to Jason's room. He left them there, asking that they stay only a few minutes.

Jason lay on the bed, his wheat-colored hair tousled around his face. A nasty-looking bruise discolored one cheek, and his left arm was plastered in a cast all the way from his fingers to his shoulder. He looked terribly pale and vulnerable.

Devin joined her at the side of Jason's bed, offering silent support.

Leaning over, she kissed her son's forehead. "I love you," she whispered.

Jason's eyes fluttered halfway open. "Mom?" he asked, his voice faint and raspy.

She smiled for his benefit, even as fresh tears filled her eyes. Tenderly she brushed a stray lock of hair from his brow. "Yes, sweetheart, it's me."

He swallowed, the effort making him wince in pain. "I'm sorry. I didn't see the car."

"Oh, honey." She touched his cheek, sniffling back a new wave of emotions. "I'm just glad you're okay." A tear slipped down her cheek before she could catch it.

"Don't cry and get all mushy, Mom."

A watery laugh escaped her. "It's what moms do best."

Jason caught sight of Devin and one side of his mouth hiked up in a groggy smile. "Uncle Devin," he rasped.

Devin moved closer and picked up Jason's unharmed hand. "Shh, Tiger. You need to rest and get better so we can take you home."

Jason's little fingers flexed around Devin's hand. "Take care of Mom for me," he said sleepily, his lashes lowering heavily over his eyes.

"I will," Devin promised, his heart expanding at the boy's concern for his mother, especially at a time like this.

Lilianne gave Jason another kiss and promised to be back soon, but the boy seemed to have fallen asleep. She wanted to linger, just to make sure he was truly okay, but Devin gently ushered her from the room, reminding her of the doctor's request to stay only a few minutes.

Devin drove her home. Emotionally exhausted, Lilianne closed her eyes, letting her head loll against the cool window. When Devin pulled into her driveway and cut the engine, he realized she was asleep. Leaving her for a moment, he unlocked the front door, turned on some lights, then came back for her. Lilianne's eyes blinked open when Devin scooped her up into his strong arms. Too tired to protest, she let him carry her into the house to her bedroom. No words were spoken as he placed her on the bed, took off her shoes and smoothed back the hair from her face.

"Sleep well," he said, smiling gently. "I'll call you in the morning."

Panic flowed through Lilianne's veins. She thought of Devin walking out of her life again, of all the pain and loneliness she felt without him. She didn't know if she could endure it anymore. Pride and independence weren't worth much if you weren't happy.

As Devin turned to leave, Lilianne grabbed his arm, halting him. He looked at her, but remained silent.

Lilianne swallowed the huge lump clogging her throat. "Don't leave me, Devin." Her voice cracked and tears misted her eyes. "I need you."

His dark eyes flickered with emotion, but he still didn't say a word. His body coiled up tight, hoping, waiting.

Sliding to the edge of the bed, she drew him near. He came unresistingly. "Almost losing Jason made me realize how precious life is. I don't want to waste it being lonely. My life is empty without you."

Devin pulled Lilianne up, wrapping her in his arms. He buried his face in the curve of her neck, breathing in her scent. "God, I've waited so long to hear you say that." Pulling back, he slid his hand along her jaw, using his thumb to tilt her chin up. He gazed into her eyes. "Staying away from you has been the hardest thing I've ever done. I've missed you so much, Lily. Your warmth, your smile, even your anger."

"Then marry me," she breathed. Her heart opened and rejoiced, knowing she'd made the right decision.

His smile held tenderness and promise. "Ahh, Lily, love, you just try and stop me." Then he kissed her softly on the lips.

Epilogue

Lilianne sucked in her breath as the little life in her belly did a somersault. "Did you feel that, Devin?" she asked, glancing over her shoulder at her husband. Devin sat behind her on the floor, his thighs on either side of her, his hand splayed on her round belly.

"He's got quite a kick," he said, grinning.

"I want to feel!" Jason jumped up from his position in front of the TV to kneel beside Lilianne and Devin. Placing his hands on her stomach, he waited impatiently for the baby to move. Finally it happened again, and Jason looked up, his eyes wide. Delighted laughter spilled from his lips.

"What's going on?" Elizabeth asked, walking into the room, followed by Emily.

"Want to feel the baby move?" Devin asked, slipping his palms lower to make room for two more hands.

"Yeah!" Emily and Elizabeth said simultaneously, rushing to Lilianne's side. They both found a spot on her stomach and waited expectantly.

Just as Lilianne was going to announce that the baby had probably fallen asleep, a foot or elbow—she couldn't tell which—was dragged across the largest part of her distended belly.

"Wow!" Elizabeth said.

"Radical!" Emily said.

Jason giggled.

Lilianne leaned into Devin, thinking she'd never felt so blissfuly happy and secure. She looked at the hands touching her belly, all the life and love each touch radiated to the baby within. Smiling, Lilianne realized how truly blessed she was. She had three beautiful children, another on the way, a thriving career—and the love of a man who made her life whole and complete.

What more could a woman ask for?

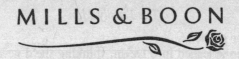

MILLS & BOON

April's Romances

Each month you **can choose** from a wide variety of romance with Mills & Boon. **Below are** the new titles to look out for in April.

HOT BLOOD	Charlotte Lamb
PRISONER OF PASSION	Lynne Graham
A WIFE IN WAITING	Jessica Steele
A WOMAN TO REMEMBER	Miranda Lee
SPRING BRIDE	Sandra Marton
DESPERATELY SEEKING ANNIE	Patricia Knoll
THE BACHELOR CHASE	Emma Richmond
TAMING A TYCOON	Leigh Michaels
PASSION WITH INTENT	Natalie Fox
RUTHLESS!	Lee Wilkinson
MY HERO	Debbie Macomber
UNDERCOVER LOVER	Heather Allison
REBEL BRIDE	Sally Carr
SECRET COURTSHIP	Grace Green
PERFECT STRANGERS	Laura Martin
HEART'S REFUGE	Quinn Wilder

LEGACY of LOVE

April's titles

DARING DECEPTION
Brenda Hiatt
Regency

Gavin Alexander, sixth Earl of Seabrooke, needed an heiress—fast! His newly acquired title came with a mountain of debts, and he was fast losing face with polite society. So when Thomas Chesterton offered his sister—and her fortune—to him, in repayment of a gaming debt, Seabrooke thought his problems were over. But his betrothed, Miss Frederica Chesterton, was not one to go meekly to her fate!

In desperation, Frederica infiltrated Lord Seabrooke's household, posing as an assistant housekeeper. While there, she unearthed two disturbing discoveries—Lord Seabrooke was guarding a secret, and Frederica was close to losing her heart in spite of it!

THE OUTRAGEOUS DOWAGER
Sarah Westleigh
Regency 1814

Lady Alexia Hamilton, Dowager Countess of Amber, had been given little choice in her first marriage, though she had come to love her kind, elderly husband. But, having lived the past few years immured in the country, Lexie intended to enjoy her return to London, a city en fête. A fact which got her into trouble, from which she was rescued by the Marquess of Stormaston. Storm was entranced by Lexie, and determined to make her his mistress—but Lexie wanted marriage! Who would win this amusing battle of wills?

LEGACY of LOVE

April's titles

THE BANDIT'S BRIDE
Ana Seymour
Mexico 1915

Snatched by Pancho Villa's notorious outlaws, Meg
Atherton's only thought was escape. Shrewd Meg was
sure she would have found a way but for Timothy Carson,
Villa's American bandido, whose mysterious charm held
her captive as surely as any bonds.

Carson didn't enjoy kidnapping helpless females. But he
soon realised that Meg was far from helpless, and his
increasing desire for the flame-haired beauty had no place
in an outlaw camp. He was definitely for sending her
home. But marriage-minded Villa had other plans…

SILVER AND STEEL
Susan Amarillas
Montana 1879

Alex Moreau commanded respect both in the wilds of
Montana and in Washington's political arenas. But when
Mary Clancy came to town Alex's ordered life was turned
upside down. For here was a woman whose passion stirred
his blood. And whose heart and soul echoed his own
desire.

Mary was determined to save her fledgling town, even if it
meant running a railroad through Alex's beloved Crow
territory. But she soon realised that Alex's charm was a
further obstacle to surmount. And when he pulled her into
his tempting arms Mary knew she was in danger of losing
her battle…

Temptation

THREE GROOMS:
Case, Carter and Mike

TWO WORDS:
"We Don't!"

**ONE
MINI-SERIES:**

GROOMS ON THE RUN

Starting in March 1996, Mills & Boon Temptation brings you this exciting new mini-series.

Each book (and there'll be one a month for three months) features a sexy hero who's ready to say "I do!" but ends up saying, "I don't!"

Look out for these special Temptations:

In March, I WON'T! by Gina Wilkins
In April, JILT TRIP by Heather MacAllister
In May, NOT THIS GUY! by Glenda Sanders

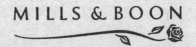

MILLS & BOON

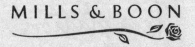

MILLS & BOON

MEDICAL ROMANCE
LOVE ON CALL

The books for enjoyment in April are:

Temptation

Coming up in
BACHELOR ARMS...

When Blythe Fielding planned her wedding and asked her two best friends, Caitlin and Lily, to be bridesmaids, none of them had a clue a new romance was around the corner for each of them—even the bride!

These entertaining, dramatic stories of friendship, mystery and love by **JoAnn Ross** continue to follow the exploits of the residents of Bachelor Arms. If you loved the male Bachelor Arms titles you'll love this set featuring the female residents of this lively apartment block.

Look out for:

THREE GROOMS AND A WEDDING (April 1996)
LOVERS AND STRANGERS (May 1996)

MILLS & BOON

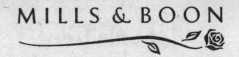

May's Romances

Each month you can choose from a wide variety of romance with Mills & Boon. Below are the new titles to look out for in May.

LAST STOP MARRIAGE	Emma Darcy
RELATIVE SINS	Anne Mather
HUSBAND MATERIAL	Emma Goldrick
A FAULKNER POSSESSION	Margaret Way
UNTAMED LOVER	Sharon Kendrick
A SIMPLE TEXAS WEDDING	Ruth Jean Dale
THE COLORADO COUNTESS	Stephanie Howard
A NIGHT TO REMEMBER	Anne Weale
TO TAME A PROUD HEART	Cathy Williams
SEDUCED BY THE ENEMY	Kathryn Ross
PERFECT CHANCE	Amanda Carpenter
CONFLICT OF HEARTS	Liz Fielding
A PAST TO DENY	Kate Proctor
NO OBJECTIONS	Kate Denton
HEADING FOR TROUBLE!	Linda Miles
WHITE MIDNIGHT	Kathleen O'Brien

LEGACY *of* LOVE

May's titles

FAREWELL THE HEART
Meg Alexander
Regency 1815

Accompanying her newly married sister, Elizabeth, to England, Miss Harriet Woodthorpe had no idea what awaited them, but it rapidly became clear that the family thought the Duke's heir, George, had married beneath him. Harriet bristled—more so when their neighbour, Lord Ashby, unaccountably began to take liberties with her person!

If Hugh thought that she would countenance his lecherous ways, he was wrong—but a worse thought intruded. Was Hugh—the man she now loved—responsible for the peculiar accidents that had befallen Elizabeth since she began increasing?

A BIDDABLE GIRL?
Paula Marshall
Regency 1818

Miss Cassandra Merton was seriously worried about her future. The death of Earl Devereux meant she might no longer have a roof over her head, for who was to say what the new Earl, Jack, banished twelve years ago in disgrace, would do?

To her shock, he proposed marriage—the only way to gain his estates according to his father's will. He clearly thought this dowdy mouse would make a biddable wife, whom he could ignore at will—but, once married, Cass would show him how mistaken he was!

LEGACY *of* LOVE

May's titles

ANGEL
Ruth Langan
Montana 1867

Did Christmas angels ever wear dusters and wide-brimmed hats? In Montana they must, for Quin McAllister seemed just that when he stepped out of the wilderness, right into Cassie Montgomery's life. Yet she knew that the happiness couldn't last, for Quin was a man who needed to roam free…

Gambler Quin McAllister was half in love with Cassie long before he ever met her, thanks to her husband's letters. But he was lost when he finally saw her in the flesh. For here was a woman worth risking everything he had on a chance to win all he'd ever desired.

LORD LIAR
Laurie Grant
Sherborne 1088

Ranulf of Kingsclere had always been Aldyth's hero, even in childhood. Yet what cruel twist of fate had turned the perfect Norman knight into an arrogant stranger, a man impossible to love?

Aldyth of Sherborne! The one woman whose soul mirrored his own. But Ranulf's oath-sworn loyalties forced him to lock his love deep inside his heart. For he was the keeper of dangerous secrets that would rock the very throne of England…!

Spoil yourself in May
with these four novels from

THE LAST HERO by Alyssa Dean

Rebels & Rogues

For Commander Wade Brillings, duty came first. So when he suspected that beautiful Cassandra Lloyd was part of a smuggling ring, he had to stick close to her. *Really close*. Experience told Wade to keep his hands off her, but his heart said something else…

THE TEMPTING by Lisa Harris

Secret Fantasies

Do you have a secret fantasy? Carol Glendower does. She wants her husband back—alive and well. A mysterious turn of events means Carol now has a chance to find Evan again. Are her dreams taunting her? Or is there a chance that this could be for real?

NOT THIS GUY! by Glenda Sanders

Grooms on the Run

Single-mum Angelina Winters couldn't believe her luck when she met charming Mike Calder. For a while, she thought she and Mike had a good thing going, but then she saw his list of what he wanted in a woman and realized she scored a perfect zero!

LOVERS AND STRANGERS by Candace Schuler

Bachelor Arms

Cynical reporter Jack Shannon hoped that by moving back to Bachelor Arms, he could lay old ghosts to rest. Sexy Faith McCray had a few ghosts of her own. She wanted to give Jack all the love he'd ever need—but was he brave enough to accept it?